Death to the Centurion

By Mark Misercola

Twilight Times Books
Kingsport, Tennessee

Death to the Centurion

This is a work of fiction. All concepts, characters and events portrayed in this book are used fictitiously and any resemblance to real people or events is purely coincidental.

Copyright © 2001 by Mark Misercola.

All rights reserved. No part of this book may be reproduced, stored in a retrieval system or transmitted in any form by any means electronic, mechanical, photocopying, recording or otherwise, except brief extracts for the purpose of review, without the permission of the publisher and the copyright owner.

Twilight Times Books
POB 3340
Kingsport TN 37664
http://twilighttimesbooks.com/

First paperback printing, June 2004

Library of Congress Cataloging-in-Publication Data

Misercola, Mark.
  Death to the centurion / by Mark Misercola.
    p. cm.
  ISBN 1-931201-26-9 (pbk. : alk. paper)
  1. Comic books, strips, etc.--Authorship--Fiction. 2. Heroes in mass media--Fiction. 3. New York (N.Y.)--Fiction. 4. Serial murders--Fiction. I. Title.
  PS3613.I84D43 2004
  813'.6--dc22
                      2004002846

Cover art by John Heebink

Printed in the United States of America.

*To my son, James, and to Larry Seigel,
my two favorite superheroes.*

"Whom the gods wish to destroy, they first call promising." Cyril Connolly

Chapter One

New York City

It is only now, years after all the grisly details have come to light, that I can finally convey this story in its entirety. Here I was, Richard Stewart MacAllister, at twenty-three years of age, Excelsior's newly minted senior writer, already working late on the first day of my job.

Granted, a retirement party isn't exactly hard work, particularly when you're single and always on the hunt for a free meal. But it was just too good an opportunity to pass up—the retirement party to end all retirement parties—in the Grand Ballroom of the Waldorf Astoria for none other than Matt Payne, the legendary artist who created the Mighty Centurion and single-handedly gave birth to the comic book industry.

After fifty years, Payne was finally calling it quits with Excelsior Comics, which as of nine o'clock that morning, just so happened to be my new employer. And I couldn't have been more excited to be on board. Comic books were in my blood. How I got there is a long story. Like most of the kids I grew up with, I devoured just about everything I could get my hands on—from Captain Marvel to Wonder Woman and everything in between.

Then, after graduating from college, I stumbled into the business by accident. I developed a superhero of my own that captured the industry's attention, and parleyed it into what I thought was going to be a cushy job for the company I'd idolized as a kid. So there I was, living out a childhood fantasy in a business of childhood fantasies. Little did I know this really marked the beginning of one of the most bizarre chapters in my life. And you should know from the start that while I had a front-row seat for most of this adventure, I was not privy to all of the back-room conversations, hidden agendas, and underhanded schemes that led to many of the tragic events that occurred while I was at Excelsior. But in comic book companies there are no secrets—at least not for very long. People talk, the walls talk, and sometimes even the characters themselves have a few things to say, too. In piecing together this account, I have endeavored to draw upon the experiences of all three, while bringing something of myself to the story, too.

It all began that warm spring evening as Matt Payne was closing the book on his amazing career. Fifty years in a business that relentlessly demands new ideas and fresh approaches was much too long for a temperamental prima donna like Payne. I don't know how he did it. But this much is certain: The end hadn't been easy, even for a tough old bird like Payne. On a night that should have been filled with joy and celebration, he felt worn out and tired—tired of dealing with the mental midgets and pencil-pushing bureaucrats who had slowly reduced his mighty Roman Sentinel of Light to little more than a caped clown. He was plenty angry, too, over the path he was now being forced to take, and it consumed him at almost every turn.

Others, like Sterling Sanborn III, the renowned British publishing magnate who had recently become Excelsior's new owner—and the man most directly responsible for Payne's involuntary departure—saw things a little differently.

"In my esteeee-mation, there is no single person, no one indeeeee-vidual, who has done more for this business than Matth-ewwwww Payne," Sanborn proudly proclaimed from a podium at the head table, in such perfectly British English that everyone in the packed room—myself included—paid more attention to the way he was saying than what he actually said.

"Matt Payne gave the world the Centurionnnnnnnn. But he also gave us the ideals that the Centurionnnn represents…honest-eeeeee…integrit-eeeeeeee…and, of course," Sanborn bubbled, "jus-tissss."

Polite applause spread across the room. Payne slowly fingered his cigar and nodded appreciatively. Coming from a snake like Sanborn, the accolades meant nothing to him. Absolutely nothing. Payne didn't care that Sanborn had saved Excelsior from bankruptcy. He would have rather seen the company go belly up than become part of Sanborn's evil empire.

By the same token, Sanborn considered Payne little more than a has-been; a rusty relic from another era who couldn't turn out a best seller if his life depended on it. So, all things considered, it would be fair to say that both men hated each other.

"The man is an asshole," Payne whispered to his devoted wife Alix, a silver haired Gena Davis look-a-like, who sat stoically next to her husband of thirty-six years. "A supreme asshole."

Sanborn cleared his throat, inhaled with the force of a giant wind tunnel, and paused. Such fine words wasted on an insignificant asshole, he thought.

"So tonight," he continued without missing a beat, "we are here to honor a giant of a man who has given generations of children all over the world-d-d-d-d an adventure they'll never forget."

To look at his frumpy, pear-shaped frame, you'd never know that Sanborn presided over a media empire that specialized in sleaze and slander. He owned dozens of racy tabloid newspapers and magazines; scores of second-rate radio and television stations; and a host of publishing houses from Toronto to Sydney that made Harold Robbins seem like Shakespeare. On paper, of course, he was worth more than eleven billion dollars. But it was all *funny money*; his empire was leveraged to the max with every conceivable financing scheme known to man. Even that didn't stop him from dressing the part of the self-made, rags-to-riches British press lord. He looked like a cross between Alfred Hitchcock and an overstuffed walrus, a moniker so appropriate that it became his unofficial calling card. But his appearance was merely a ruse—a carefully crafted public persona that was designed to keep his foes off balance. Tonight was no exception. None of us knew it then, but Payne's retirement party really wasn't for Payne's benefit at all. Heaven forbid! It was meticulously choreographed—right down to the 60-piece orchestra and sparkling crystal—to impress one Jack Morgante, a buttoned-down, no-nonsense senior vice president from Pinnacle Studios in Hollywood, who had just flown into New York to wrap up negotiations on a Centurion movie.

Why Hollywood wanted to do a film on a long-time loser like the Centurion was beyond Sanborn. But with American action hero films cleaning up at the box office, Pinnacle was anxious to nail down a bankable comic character of its own and Morgante was just the man to pull off the deal. He was Pinnacle's "A" Team, the go-to-guy who specialized in finishing off difficult deals.

So far, however, Sanborn had presented a formidable challenge. He was a ferocious negotiator, particularly when the odds were stacked in his favor. He preyed on companies in dire straits—companies like Excelsior—with one foot in the grave. He cared nothing about the people who worked at these firms and made no pretenses about it. People, he often said, were "our greatest renewable resources." What he really wanted (and got) was unlimited access to the company's multi-billion dollar employee pension fund, which he needed to continue financing the operations of his cash-hungry, debt-ridden empire. But even that wasn't enough. A movie deal would mean millions more in royalties and licensing fees. Not to mention a passport into Tinsel Town, where Sanborn could finally go head-to-head on the big screen with his arch-rival, Sydney Lockwood, the Australian entertainment and media mogul, whom he hated even more than Payne.

Sanborn peered down at the carefully crafted notes his assistant had prepared for the evening.

INSERT NAME HERE, it read, *WE WILL ALL MISS YOU!*

Sanborn cleared his throat. "Ahhh-hemmmm, Matth-ewwww Payne, we will all miss you!"

More applause filled the ballroom.

"The Centurrrrionnnn is the legacy that you leave to the world, and I can assure you that he will be in good hands—"

Again, right on cue, he was interrupted by applause.

"Please, please, pleassssse." Sanborn raised his stubby right hand until the room was silent. "Matt, yours is a talent that cannot easily be duplicatated-d-d-d, nor can it be magically reincarnated like the Centurrion-n-n-n—"

This time, the room erupted in laughter, and the Walrus, fully in command of the situation, planted his hands on his belly and roared like Fezziwig on Christmas Eve.

"But Matt, before you go, we would like to present you and your lovely wife, Ali-i-ixandra, with a small token of our appreciation for all the sacrifices you've made for Excelsior Comics over the past fifty years."

Sanborn reached deep into his suit pocket, retrieved an envelope containing a pair of tickets, and held them up over the top of the podium for everyone to see.

"We're sending both of you on a cruise!" Sanborn grinned. "An around-the-world cruise!!"

With that, a chorus of "ooohs" and "aaahhs" gushed forth. Robin Leach couldn't have played it any better.

Alix grabbed her husband by the shoulders and planted a big kiss on his lips. "Finally," she said to him, "I was beginning to think the only way I'd ever get to see the world was on a senior citizen's tour."

When the applause ended, Sanborn moved in for the kill. "Matt, you've spent fifty years here at Excelsior saving the world from evil and I don't think you've ever taken a vacation. Now a grateful world is finally yours.

"Ladies and gentlemen," Sanborn said. "It is a great honor for me to present to you the man of the hour—Excelsior's real-life super hero—Mat-t-t-t-t Payne!!"

The ovation was deafening. Everybody in the room stood and cheered, and the old ballroom soon looked like a political convention on fire. First, the orchestra snapped to attention and promptly launched into a mind-blowing rendition of the Centurion fanfare, the same blaring theme that had opened the old black-and-white Centurion television serials years ago. Then a giant caricature of the Roman Sentinel of Light rose from beneath the stage as thousands of red, white and blue balloons cascaded down from the ceiling onto the floor.

Payne took a long drag on his cigar and slowly rose to his feet.

"Now dear," Alix grabbed him by the hand, "be gracious."

Payne winked—a devilish "wait-'till-you-get-a-load-of-me" wink if ever there was one—and scrambled up to the podium next to Sanborn.

"Matttt," Sanborn grinned and wrapped his pudgy arms around him. "On behalf of all your colleagues—on behalf of all your friends at Excelsior Comics—I want to say congratulations and bon voyage!"

Flash bulbs and strobe lights sparkled around the stage, as the Walrus waddled back to his chair next to Morgante.

All in all, it was quite a spectacle, particularly for someone like me, having just bolted from cross-town rival Renegade Comics—Sydney Lockwood's Renegade—where such excess would have qualified as a capital offense.

"I've dreamed about meeting this guy and working with him since I was a kid," I said. The guy sitting next to me, Mike Billington, one of the best story line artists in the business, didn't answer.

"But wouldn't you know it," I continued, "the day I come in he ups and retires before I even get a chance to introduce myself."

Stone silence. Billington was a man of few words and many rules. And Rule Number One was explicitly clear in these kinds of situations. *Never say anything worthwhile to anyone who has been with the company less than a week.* It wasn't anything personal against me. Having survived two tours of duty in Vietnam, and the equivalent of two more in the jungles of Excelsior, Billington knew that trusting a rookie could get you killed.

"Puh-lease!!!" Payne pleaded from the podium as the applause continued. "If you don't let me speak, I may never leave!"

Finally, after several minutes, the cheers fell silent. Payne closed his eyes and soaked up every inch of the room.

"Friends! Romans! Countrymen!" he crowed. "Behold my retirement!"

The room erupted once more. It was vintage Payne, the egomaniac everyone loved, poking fun at himself and his beloved Centurion all at the same time.

"Years ago, we had something special here," he continued. "We built this company one page at a time, one character at a time, and one comic book at a time. We did it with imagination and guts. It was all wonderful stuff, too. Our books had great stories. They had character. Good triumphed over evil. You knew the difference between right and wrong. All for a nickel. Now everything's different! Today, we're big business. We're driven by demographics, psycho-graphics and polls. Instead of values, we give kids these slick graphic novels at seven or eight bucks a pop and what do they get? Super heroes that look like hoods. Heroines that dress like cheap whores. And villains that give new meaning to terms like 'sick' and 'demented'."

Billington winced. His own comic character—an Arnold Schwarzenegger look-a-like with a passion for laser warfare and voluptuous love slaves called "The Silencer"—was exactly what Payne was referring to.

"In our day," Payne resumed, "superheroes didn't have nervous breakdowns. They didn't have identity crises. They didn't get their faces bashed in or their capes ripped apart. And God knows, they certainly didn't question their own sexuality. Hell, we wouldn't have been caught dead using that word in a comic book to begin with!"

The room suddenly fell silent. Dead silent. And Sanborn's stomach started to churn. *What the Christ is he trying to prove?*

"Nowadays," Payne continued, "everything is team work. We've got a team that thinks up ideas. We've got a team that massages the ideas. And then there's another team that screws up all the good ideas. We even have a retirement team. Yeah, that's right. We've got a team that looks at your age and your salary, and when they add up to a certain number, they say 'that's all folks.' And you know what? It really stinks!"

By now you could hear a pin drop in the ballroom.

"We are very fortunate because our crack retirement team is here with us tonight, and I want to introduce you to the geniuses who decided that it was time for me to float away on an iceberg. First, I'd like you to meet Malcolm Evans. Comptroller Malcolm Evans at the very end of the dais. Malcolm and I go back six, maybe seven weeks now. He is the guardian of our budgets."

Evans, a very methodical and proper British fellow Sanborn had imported from his London office to reign in costs at Excelsior, looked as if he was about to wet his pants.

"One day, about three weeks ago, Malcolm comes into my office all excited," Payne gushed. "He tells me, 'WEEEE must shave an eighth of an inch off the page.' I said, 'Excuse me?' Malcolm slaps a comic book on my drawing table and says, 'WEEEE must shave an eighth of an inch off the page.' Why, I ask, would WEEE want to shave an eighth of an inch off the page? Well, it turns out that Malcolm, here, had gotten out his little solar-powered calculator and figured out all by himself that if WEEE cut the page size WEEE could save about three-hundred thousand dollars on an average press run.

"'OK, Malcolm, budddy,' I says, 'I'll cut the page size. I'll redo all the illustrations, but I'll cut it. And I did! You know what? WEEE would have saved three-hundred thousand dollars on the issue, except for one little thing. The front cover had already been printed in the larger format. So WEEEE had to run all the covers over again, and instead of saving three-hundred thousand dollars, WEEE spent an extra half-million bucks."

Sanborn, hearing this for the first time, nearly popped a fuse.

"But, hey, what's a half-million bucks among friends, huh Malcolm, old pal?"

Evans buried his face in his napkin and started to cry.

"Now," Payne resumed, "let me introduce you to another esteemed member of our retirement team—Marty. Marty Robinson."

Payne waved to Robinson, who was also sitting at the head table next to his wife. Robinson, being the schmuck that he was, waved right back.

"Marty, God bless his soul, he's Mister Family Values. His job is to make sure that all of us creative types are setting the proper moral tone in our work."

Robinson, a neurotic workaholic with a terrible stutter that Payne loved to mimic, sat there nodding his head in righteous agreement, oblivious to the fact that he was being roasted over the coals.

"Three weeks ago, my assistant and I were working on this scene where the Centurion saves a cow from a raging inferno. Now this wasn't just an ordinary cow. It was a SACRED COW with very special super powers. And it belonged to the big cheese—Jupiter, the chairman of the board of all Roman gods. So we took special care to ensure that this was a cow befitting a god. It was big. I mean REALLY BIG! And you know how it goes with sacred cows—nothing can touch them. When the fire starts, it's a job that only the Centurion can handle. So that's what we decided to put on the front cover—the Centurion saving this sacred cow.

"No sooner do the boards go into Marty for approval than he comes rushing out of his office so upset he can hardly talk. Finally I says, 'Marty, is something WRONG?' Marty points to the cover, going 'L-L-L-Look at this!' So I look at it and I ask, 'What's wrong?' Marty goes, 'the-the-the-the the udder. L-l-l-ook at the udder!!' I look at it again. It's an udder, all right. Marty says, 'it's too-too-too b-b-big.'"

A few hoots and howls broke out from the crowd. And Payne paused for a moment, a very long, dramatic pause, and just stared at us in silence.

"Then Marty says, 'G-g-g-get r-r-r-rid of it.' I looked at the illustration again, and it suddenly hits me. 'My God, Marty, you're right. I don't know what could have come over me. In this day and age, when we've got front covers featuring mutilations, human sacrifices and bondage, not to mention half-naked women, the last thing a kid needs to see is a cow's udder!'"

Robinson, still oblivious to the chorus of laughter that was spreading throughout the room, continued to grin. He actually believed that he had made the world a little less filthy than the day before.

"Marty," Payne looked directly at Robinson's table, "I can't thank you enough. I've been drawing cows for years now, and when I think of all the young minds I've corrupted along the way, it just tears me apart inside."

Payne paused for a moment, pretending to fight back tears. "Marty, you made me see the light. As long as I live, I'll never, EVER, mess with a sacred cow again. I want you to know just how much this means to me. You've got to be the luckiest guy on the face of this earth. You've got a great family—a beautiful wife and kids—"

Robinson's wife, a tall brunette, waved to the crowd.

"And you've got two Cracker Jack secretaries, who were so nice to me whenever you'd send them over to shred my illustrations that I just can't let this occasion pass without introducing them.

"First, there's Barbra Gordon. She's been with Marty for fifteen years—at five different companies. And she's one of the best kept secrets in the business. Barbra, would you please stand up and take a bow—"

The spotlight technician in the balcony frantically crisscrossed the room looking for Gordon.

"She's over at table twenty-two," Payne pointed. "Way back there in the corner."

Gordon finally appeared in her seat, about as far away from Robinson's table as you could get, all dolled up like a cheap stripper in an extremely low-cut, crushed velvet gown that revealed most of her forty-inch D bust. The applause suddenly stopped, and this time Robinson went numb. At first, Gordon refused to stand.

"Now don't be shy, Barbra," Payne said. "Stand up so everyone here can see you."

Gordon slowly rose to her feet and waved.

"Ladies and gentlemen, Barbra Gordon. Let's give her a hand."

We all hesitated at first, but eventually everyone obliged. Yet Payne wouldn't let it go.

"Barbra, why don't you take a bow? You deserve it."

Gordon shook her head from side to side.

"C'monnnnn," Payne egged her on, with the help of a few slightly inebriated friends at the back of the room who started chanting her name as if they were at a hockey game.

"BAR-BRA, BAR-BRA, BAR-BRA…"

Gordon finally caved in and leaned forward at a ninety-degree angle, providing everyone with a panoramic view of some of the most magnificent cleavage east of the Hudson.

"Now," Payne continued, "sitting right across the table from Barbra is the equally lovely Lisa Ivendetti, who also works for Marty. Lisa has one of the toughest jobs in the business. Every night, when we go home, she meets with Marty in his office to personally review all the changes that he's made in our work and to sort of, you know, give it her own verbal stamp of approval. Lisa, why don't you stand and be recognized!"

The spotlight inched over a notch to Ms. Ivendetti, a nineteen-year-old vixen from Yonkers who aspired to a career in the adult film industry. Unlike Gordon, Lisa wasn't shy in front of a crowd. She jumped up from her seat like an eager young gymnast, extended her arms above her head, so that it was impossible to miss her ultra-tight black blouse, matching leather mini-skirt and fish-net stockings.

"Marty," Payne snickered, "I think I'm going to miss you twice as much as everybody else, old pal."

Robinson, now white as a ghost, wasn't smiling anymore.

"Of course, there's one more member of Excelsior's retirement team that I simply can't ignore," Payne said. "You all know him. He's the jerk who gave me these tickets."

Every eye in the room immediately zeroed in on Sanborn, who at that moment was on the verge of exploding with rage.

"Ladies and gentlemen, I can't think of anyone who did more to force me out the door than Sterling Sanborn the Third," Payne continued, the venom pumping through his veins at warp speed. "And I would like to propose a toast to him now—"

Sanborn buried his head in his hands. There wasn't much he could do, not now, not with Morgante sitting there next to him, taking it all in. So we stood and raised our glasses in his honor.

"To Sterling Sanborn the Third. LORD Sterling Sanborn the Third. Without his insight, without his wisdom and intelligence, none of this tonight would be necessary."

Payne then promptly hoisted a glass of champagne and swallowed it whole. And before anyone could sit down, he let it all hang out—the bitterness, the resentment, and the fury that had been bottled up inside him since the day Sanborn first arrived at Excelsior.

"This used to be such a fun business," Payne said. "Now all that's changed, thanks to our exalted imperial leader here. But one thing hasn't changed—people still want stories that are driven by emotion and intellect.

"The next time you go out and kill or maim one of the good guys, the next time you beat one into a pulp—all for the sake of higher sales—think about who you're really hurting. Somebody out there, somebody maybe just seven or eight years old—your son, your daughter or maybe your grandkid—is watching you rub out a character they believe in. Someone they care for."

Payne looked out across the room, fighting back tears. And we all stared back in a stunned silence.

"I say screw the accountants! Screw the lawyers, screw the pencil-pushers!! And screw the bastards who think they know how to run this business by the bottom line!! Don't let them take the fun out of the comics. If you give kids a good product—a good story with heart—the bottom line will take care of itself."

Payne shook his head in disgust.

"For Chrissakes people wake up! Don't let Sanborn do to you what he's doing to me. Don't let him ruin your characters like he's ruining the Centurion and everything else here!"

Then he turned and spoke directly to the Walrus. "Now for you, Lord Sanborn Almighty, I have a special going-away gift of my own. A few of my friends have decided to join me in retirement."

As Payne stepped away from the podium, suits and gowns at three tables near the front of the ballroom stood and walked toward the dais—artists, writers, illustrators, pencilers and story liners—some of the most talented and experienced people in the business.

"I don't believe it," Billington whispered, "half the creative staff is walking out with him."

One-by-one, they paraded by the head table in a stony, bone-chilling silence, stopping directly in front of Sanborn. Then, with the precision of a military drill team, they all raised their right arms and collectively popped Sanborn the bird.

It didn't last long—maybe fifteen seconds tops—but for Sanborn it must have seemed like an eternity.

"Let's get the hell out of this Mickey Mouse organization," Payne said.

And with that, the entire ensemble turned and marched out of the ballroom single-file, leaving Excelsior a crippled company of comic book orphans; a factory of make-believe characters with no one to bring them to life.

Those of us who remained just stood there, gazing up at the stage.

Finally, Sanborn lumbered up to the podium, grabbed the microphone, and for the first time in his life, the Walrus who spoke like Churchill didn't know what to say. He would have still been there had it not been for the quick action of Leo Corbett, his Brooks Brothers aide, who instinctively knew how to enflame a really bad situation without even trying. Corbett ran up to the podium, placed his hand over the microphone and frantically whispered into Sanborn's ear.

"He took the tickets," Corbett said, completely unaware that Sanborn had been using a lapel mike that was still live.

"Whatttt?" the Walrus bellowed. "The son-of-a-bitch took the fucking tickets too?"

Sanborn's shouts echoed throughout the ballroom, into the kitchen, up through the balcony and clear through to the lobby. When he realized what was happening, he grabbed Corbett by the shoulders and flew into an even wilder frenzy.

"Jez-us Christ! This thing is still on, you idiot!"

Sanborn ripped the microphone from his tie and tossed it to the ground, as Corbett dove for cover.

Then Sanborn latched onto the podium with both hands, as if he was about to heave it across the stage, and yelled at the very top of his lungs: "Everybody just go home—now!" Then, with all the grace of a stampeding heard of buffalo, he charged off the stage until he finally disappeared through a rear doorway.

And just like that it was over. Confusion reigned everywhere. Two tornadoes had passed in the night, leveling just about everything in their path. But for me, the real storm was just beginning.

Chapter Two

Excelsior Comics
Midtown Manhattan

The next morning, I arrived at Excelsior's art deco headquarters in midtown Manhattan bright and early—why I don't know. The entire building was practically deserted. The only other person on the third floor at seven a.m. was Mitch Gerber, Payne's long-time understudy. He was standing in front of the bulletin board near the men's room where I spotted him reading THE announcement—the one he had been both dreading and looking forward to for thirty-five years.

Matthew Payne, a senior illustrator in Graphics, has retired from the company after fifty years. Mr. Payne is sixty-seven years old.

"Je-zus Christ," he mumbled to himself. "Two lines? That's all they gave him? He creates the Centurion, THE Centurion—single-handedly puts comic books on the map—and all he gets is two stinkin' lines."

Not much of a send-off," I said.

Gerber cautiously eyeballed me, took one last drag on his cigarette and dropped what was left of it on the floor.

"Personnel," he sighed, "assholes. "

It was no secret that Gerber had fantasized about this moment practically from the day he started—thirty-five years ago. The promise that he would someday assume the duties of a living legend was the only thing that had kept him going, so much so that along the way he became blinded to the obvious—the Centurion was no longer a major drawing card for the company. But that didn't matter. *No one, Gerber said to himself, knows the Centurion like me. No one is as dedicated to upholding the legend of the Centurion like I am. And no one can emulate Payne's style like I can.* With Payne's departure, he was certain his promotion would come to pass. That was until he read THE announcement. It wasn't at all what he had envisioned. Over the years, he had written it himself a thousand times over:

"Matthew Payne, the creator of the Centurion, and the father of the comic book industry, is gone. In this moment of great crisis, there is only one man alive with the skills and the talent to answer the Centurion's call—Mitch Gerber. As you know, Mr. Gerber has been the real creative genius behind the character for many, many years. He has sustained the Centurion through good times and bad. The world will

be a safer place now that the Centurion is in his capable hands. We wish him God's speed."

Two lines. Gerber scratched his head. *Two lines and not a word about succession.* "This whole place is really going to hell," he said to me, as if I was responsible for the current situation. And then he slowly walked away.

Five floors above, in the more elaborate confines of Investor Relations, Northrop Matthews Jr., a New England blue blood whose very name indicated that nature had erred once before, casually flipped through the morning's edition of *The Wall Street Journal* over a Starbucks coffee and a croissant. As director of Investor Relations for Trieste Communications, Sanborn's holding company and Excelsior's new parent, Matthews was required (among other important things) to know the business of business. So every day, without fail, he'd march into work with his *Wall Street Journal*—the daily diary of business—tucked conspicuously under his arm. And as soon as he was safely secluded in his office, he'd toss the first two sections of the paper into the trash and dive headfirst into the stock tables to check his own personal portfolio. It was a ritual that Matthews lived for.

That, more than anything else, may explain why my first impression of him wasn't profound. Matthews had a refined but ruthless air about him, the kind of self-centered person who'd sell his mother for a price (or at least give it careful consideration). Which is probably why he and Sanborn worked so well together. Both worshipped at the same altar—*the Interdenominational Church of Increasing Shareholder Value*—and there was nothing they wouldn't do for the benefit of the stock price.

One important difference distinguished the two. Sanborn loved the entertainment business—the hype, the hypocrisy and the fame. Matthews, on the other hand, despised it, particularly the ludicrously demeaning little comic books that Excelsior churned out. He put up with it all only because he saw entertainment as his ticket to greater glory; a springboard to more money, more prestige, and more excitement in a field that he really longed to conquer—accounting.

Matthews' only downfall was his stomach. It was as jumpy as Mount Etna; which is a distinct disadvantage in Investor Relations. Pressure went with the territory. One slip of the tongue, a false rumor, or an inadvertent typo on an earnings release could permanently torpedo a company's stock price. Twenty years of just such anxiety had, in fact, taken its toll. His hair was thinner, his nerves were shot, and he had become a slave to a raging ulcer that could erupt anywhere, at any time, particularly whenever the going got tough. It wasn't the best of combinations for someone whose fortunes depended so heavily on the daily gyrations of the stock market and Sterling Sanborn III. Yet if nothing else, he remained a man of great will. And he coped with it in the only manner he knew how—by toughing it out with lots of coffee, plenty of artery clogging pastries, three packs of Marlboros a day, a generous supply of Pepto Bismol, and a conveniently positioned barf bag for any and all emergencies.

Today, so far at least, he had no reason to use it. Market futures were up. Interest rates were heading lower, which was always a good sign for entertainment stocks. And the infantile analysts who followed the company continued to eat up every positive word he'd utter about Trieste without so much as even questioning its validity. He'd even found a way to weasel out of Payne's retirement party the night before to witness a rare overtime win by the Knicks at the Garden. All things considered, it was the perfect environment for Trieste's stock to thrive. And what was good for Trieste was good for Matthews, since most of his personal holdings were tied up in the company's stock, which, as I later learned, was Wall Street's answer to Chernobyl. Everything Trieste owned was dicey. But Matthews would have it no other way. "Only big bets lead to big rewards," he'd often say. And Matthews was betting big time.

Using his index finger as a guide, he made his way down a long gray column of type. "Top Air, no. Top Services, Trans Lux, Trans King, Trans Shipping ... no, no, no." And then finally, there it was, the very center of his universe. "Yessssss, Trieste Communications."

Last bid, 101 1/8, a new high—the third this month. He read it out loud. "Last bid, one hundred one and an eighth."

It was music to his ears, a daily reaffirmation of his superb Wall Street management skills. There was more where that came from, too. He quickly pushed aside the *Journal* and swiveled his chair toward the Quotron computer terminal on his credenza. Then with one finger of each hand he slowly pecked away at the keyboard, expecting to see more of the same positive numbers coming in overnight from the overseas markets.

"*C-u-r -r-e-n-t Q-u-o-t-e-s*

"*L-o-n-d-o-n*

"*T-C-O-M*"

Up flashed the response. "*Last bid, London, 79 1/8, down 22.*"

Matthew did a double take. *Down 22? Has to be the computer, he told himself. Trieste doesn't move like that, even when the foreign markets are under pressure.*

He keyed in the stock symbol again. But the answer came back the same: "*Last bid, London, 79 1/8, down 22.*"

Matthews quickly typed in a new order, this time on the Tokyo stock exchange.

"T-o-k-y-o/T-C-O-M"

The screen went blank, but only for a second, and when it recovered the news from Japan was even worse.

"Last bid, Tokyo, 66, down 35 1/8."

Matthews stared at the screen, completely dumbfounded. It was not a new sensation. Here he was, responsible for safeguarding billions of dollars of shareholder investments, and he had no idea why the company's stock price had dropped so precipitously overnight. There were no earnings surprises on the horizon, and sales were in line with expectations. Granted, Trieste's debt level was extraordinarily high, but Wall Street was well aware of it. So there was nothing new from a financial performance perspective that should have triggered a sell-off. Or at least he thought so. Before he could clear the screen a tiny note popped up at the bottom of his computer screen.

"NEWS, TCOM, 7:01 AM."

Matthews moved his cursor over the headline and promptly called up the story.

"C'mon, c'mon, I haven't got all day." Then, as he retrieved a cigarette from his pocket, a headline appeared at the top of the page.

"CENTURION CREATOR CREATES MIGHTY FURY."

Matthews' throat tightened.

"AP, NEW YORK—MATTHEW PAYNE, THE LEGENDARY CREATOR OF THE CENTURION, BOLTED FROM HIS LAVISH RETIREMENT PARTY HERE LATE LAST NIGHT, TAKING MORE THAN HALF OF THE COMPANY'S STAFF WITH HIM.

"AS HUNDREDS OF GUESTS LOOKED ON, PAYNE UNLEASHED A BITTER ATTACK ON EXCELSIOR'S OWNER, BRITISH PRESS LORD STERLING SANBORN III, AND HIS SENIOR AIDES."

Matthews yanked off his glasses and rubbed his eyes in disgust. *What's the big deal, he wondered? Artists leave all the time. What's this got to do with the stock?* And then he got his answer.

"THE DEVELOPMENT TRIGGERED A MASSIVE SELLING SPREE AS INVESTORS IN LONDON AND TOKYO DROVE DOWN TRIESTE'S STOCK PRICE BY 30 PERCENT OVERNIGHT.

"EARLY TODAY, THREE MAJOR BROKERAGE HOUSES LOWERED THEIR EARNINGS ESTIMATES FOR THE COMPANY, AND ANALYSTS EXPECT

SELLING TO CONTINUE WHEN TRADING RESUMES LATER TODAY IN NEW YORK."

A cold chill ran up his spine. He had seen panic selling like this before. And he knew if he didn't act fast the company would almost certainly lose millions in market capitalization. Worse yet, his own personal fortune would be wiped out.

So Matthews did what any real man with guts would have done under the circumstances. He threw up. Then, when it was over, he sat in his chair, wiped the sweat from his brow, picked up the phone and frantically called the one person he knew who could enlighten him in the midst of his fog.

"Hullllll-o?"

"Quick is Jimmy there?" Matthews asked.

"Jimmy?" the husky voice on the other end of the line said.

"You heard me, put Jimmy on!" Matthews snapped. "It's urgent."

"Whoooooom shall I say is calling?"

"Cut the crap, Sal. You know full well who this is."

Sal grinned. He loved pissing people off, particularly impatient twerps like Matthews. "Hang on, sport," he said. "Hey, Jim-meeeeee, it's Warren Buffet on da line from Omaha."

Five minutes later, Matthews could hear heavy breathing on the other end.

"Jimmy, is that you?"

"Northrop?" It was a heavy-slung Brooklyn Nawthwopppp. "This had betta be good to interrupt me dis early."

"It is," Matthews said, "we got a slight problem here."

"Your pwoblems started da day you went to work at that cwappy outfit, pal," replied Jimmy Montana, the sole proprietor of the Comic Cave; a 360-pound gorilla who held the singular distinction of being New York's largest comic book dealer, no matter which way you looked at him.

Matthews took a deep breath. "We had a little situation last night—"

"Liddle?" Montana jumped in. "You call Matt Payne and half da staff walkin' out liddle?"

"Then you know what happened?"

"Do I know? Do I know? Of course, I know," Montana said. "Da whole freakin' world knows. Didn't you read da Journal dis mornin'?"

Matthews paused. "Ummm, I'm just going through it now—"

"Try page one, genius," Montana said. "Or try da Times, da Post, da Daily News, or CNN. Payne had every freakin' reporter in town dere last night. Waddya expect?"

"But it shouldn't affect the stock price like this," Matthews said.

"Who you kiddin' Nawthwopppp? Dat stock price is gonna drop like a lead balloon as soon as da opening bell sounds on Wall Street."

"But there's no reason for it, Jimmy. The Centurion's impact on revenues is negligible."

Montana shook his head. "Look, Mista Wall Street, here's how it works. Collectors can smell a dive a mile away. Payne's old books and all da old books from dose artists who walked out wit' him are gonna skyrocket in value."

"You shittin' me?" Matthews asked.

"Payne knew exactly what he was doing when he walked out da door."

"He did?"

"Whaddya think we're doin' right now, sport?" Montana said. "Every freakin' Centurion in da house with Payne's signature on it is getting marked up thirty percent when we open."

"Thirty percent?" Matthews couldn't believe it.

"Dat's right, laughing boy. And lemme tell ya sometin' else. Dere's some pretty bad stuff in dere too." Montana held up the latest issue and scratched his head.

"Foist-class shit if you ask me, Nawthwopppp."

"But that's the last issue you'll ever see from Payne or any of those other clowns," Matthews said. "You know we'll find new artists and writers and all the regular titles will live on."

"It don't matta, buddy boy," Montana said. "You could have Jesus Christ himself drawing the new books. Nobody's gonna buy 'em ... even if you drop da prices. It's da artists dat makes 'em valuable. Now ya got titles with no names behind dem. It's da kiss of death, I'm tellin' you. Dey're all gonna sit dere on da shelves and collect dust. Eventually, da dealers won't carry 'em either."

Matthews felt like puking again. "Well, what the Christ are we gonna do, Jimmy? You can't live off the old issues forever."

Montana laughed. "When was the last time you walked into a comic book store, genius? Excelsior ain't da only game in town. We carry one hundred sixty-three freakin' titles from twenty-two companies around da world. If yours don't sell, I'll dump 'em all and use da space for titles that are gonna move."

Matthews buried his head in his hands. "All right, Jimmy, enough. Help me out here. There's a lot at stake. Tell me what you think we oughta do—PLEASE."

Montana bit off the end of a new cigar, scratched his forty-eight inch belly, and spit the tip onto the floor.

"Listen carefully, genius. You gotta do some-ding big. REALLY BIG! You gotta make people forget about Payne and everybody else that waltzed out da door wit him. You gotta give 'em a reason to buy da new books. A big name artist, a big, gory story line, a little sex, a little violence—whatever. Dat way, da new ones will sell and dey'll have value as potential collector's items someday. Got it?"

Matthews took it all in. "Do something big ... new artist ... lotsa sex ... violence. Got it. What else? I'm listening."

"Dere's one more ding," Montana said. "Whatever you do, you better do it fast."

CLICK.

Upstairs, nine flights above, in the ornate wood-paneled office of the publisher, the telephone conversation between Sanborn and Pinnacle's Jack Morgante wasn't going much better either.

"Jackkkkk, Jackkkkk, Jackkkkk, it was all just a little missssss-understanding. A slight tiff among the famil-eeeee, nothing more than—"

"Save your breath, Sterling. People in Hollywood read the papers too," Morgante continued. "They're not going to touch a property that's damaged goods."

Sanborn knew all about the headlines. His antique Victorian desk, which was usually a picture of perfection and neatness, was covered with discouraging headlines.

"*COMIC LEGEND DRAWS PICTURE OF DISARRAY AT EXCELSIOR,*" screamed the lead story on the front page of The Wall Street Journal.

"*CENTURION CREATOR REFUSES TO FADE AWAY,*" proclaimed *The New York Times*.

And from the *New York Post*, Sydney Lockwood's flagship tabloid, came the unkindest cut of all: "*SANBORN'S ROYAL PAYNE!*"

"Jackkkkk, what's a few headlines?" Sanborn joked. "You know the meeeeeedia. It makes good copy, that's all. People here have short memorieeeees. They'll forget all this by tomorrow. You'll seeeeee."

Morgante grabbed the phone cord, dragged it over the side of his hotel bed, over the glimmering naked body of someone whose name he didn't even know, and walked quietly into an adjoining bathroom where he wouldn't be heard.

"Sterling, you know as well as I do what drives the movie business—drawing power," Morgante whispered. "Pinnacle is interested in the Centurion because he tests well with baby boomers who have lots of discretionary income to spend at the box office. But after last night, who's going to pay to see him now? Who's going to buy all the merchandising—the dolls, the videos, the games—if the character's tarnished?"

"Oh, but we can fix that," Sanborn insisted. "We'll get out a few new issues, really jazz the old chap up, and it will be all right in no time."

"I don't know," Morgante said. "Payne is really synonymous with the Centurion. We were counting on him to help generate pre-launch publicity. You know—*Good Morning America, Today, Entertainment Tonight, Letterman, Oprah*. I don't think you can get him back in the fold—not after last night. Even if you do, there's no way we're going to put him in front of the cameras if he's that volatile."

Sanborn swallowed hard. "Jack, we'll get a new artist on the character right away. Someone with a little pizzazzzz, someone with a little creativit-eeeeeee, someone who'll make everyone forget about Payne and we'll get this image thing all straightened out."

"I'd like to believe that, Sterling," Morgante said, "really, I would. But superhero movies are expensive. You're talkin' millions for special effects alone. Millions more for talent. You need a big name star to play the character and a big name writer to do the screenplay. Before we commit a dime, you've got to do something dramatic to get people back into the fold."

"I promise you, Jack, we'll do that," Sanborn said. "By God, we willlll. But you've got to give me a little time. Maybe a few—"

Morgante heard a muffled cry from naked and nameless in the bedroom. "Ohhhh, Jack-ieeee? Jack-ieeee? Where's mommy's little baby gone?"

Sanborn heard her voice, too, and smiled. He knew from his own Hollywood sources that Morgante had a weakness for well-developed women, particularly drop-dead blondes with excellent oral presentation skills and unending stamina. So when Morgante returned to his room after Payne's retirement dinner he found a very special dish waiting for him, complete with the bed turned down.

"By the way, Jack, did you enjoy the room service last night?" Sanborn asked.

"Why, uh yes, now that you mention it," Morgante said sheepishly.

Sanborn sensed the tide was starting to turn. "Wellll, we always like to take care of our business associates, Jack."

"Sterling, I'll tell you what," Morgante said. "I'm leaving this afternoon for L.A. and I'll tell my people that it was all a smoke screen to buy some time and draw attention to the character, O.K.?"

"Splendid idea," Sanborn replied. "Splendid!!"

"But don't take too much time straightening this out. Hollywood moves quickly. Pinnacle needs this project soon. If there isn't some good news pronto, the studio may tell me to start shopping over at Renegade."

Sanborn cringed. Nothing could be more revolting. "God forbid, I'm sure it won't come down to that, Jackkkkkkk."

"This is a good time for super hero movies," Morgante said. "The trend lines are strong. Lots more coming down the pipeline, but you really gotta jump on it when it's hot… "

He stopped abruptly as naked and nameless began caressing the back of his neck.

"Otherwise, you'll miss… "

Naked and nameless took the receiver from his hand and placed it back in the cradle.

CLICK.

Chapter Three

Excelsior Headquarters
Midtown Manhattan

Sanborn hung up the phone feeling positively elated. A glimmer of hope—however slight—remained for his precious movie deal. But the euphoria was only momentary. Time was short and his problems were mounting by the minute. He gazed across his desk—like a giant bull walrus surveying his rock—and fumed at all the headlines.

"*Sanborn's Royal Payne!* How humiliating," he yelled at the top of his lungs. "How incredibly humiliating! All we had to do was sign the damn contract! Now months of negotiations could be down the drain, and years of equity in the character are gone."

Sanborn scooped up the Post—Sydney Lockwood's *Post*—and flung it across the room. "You're going to have to do better than this to steam-roll this project, Sydney. Do you understand?"

From behind the door came an unexpected reply. "Mister Sanborn?" It was a very nasal "Misstuuuuur Sanborn?"

Esther Gott, his prim and proper secretary, peered in through the opening like a well-fortified battleship.

Sanborn sneered. Nothing infuriated him more than to be interrupted in the middle of a snit. "What is it now, Miss Gott?"

"Would you like me to call Mister MacAllister and Mister Billington in for a conference, sir?"

"Who?" Sanborn asked.

"The creative people you had asked to see."

"I did?" Sanborn replied.

"That you did, sir."

"Now why in the world would I want to see them, Miss Gott?"

"I believe," she said, "it concerns the Centurion, Mister Sanbornnnn, from last night."

Sanborn's eyes became as large as saucers. "Oh yessssss. By all means! Get them up here right away, Miss Gott! And be quick about it!"

Gott jumped and headed back for the door. "By the way, I have a Mister Matthews waiting on the phone for you, sirrrr."

"Who?" the Walrus asked.

"Mister Matthews ... Northrop Matthews from Investor Relations, sir."

"Well then, Miss Gott, seeing as I am not a mind reader, would you please enlighten me as to what in the hell Northrop Matth-ewssss from Investor Relations wants?"

"I believe it has something to do with the stock price, sirrr. I think he said it's ... oh, how did he phrase it?" Gott peered down at her note pad. "I think he said the stock price is 'tanking.' Yes, that's what he said. Tank—"

The Walrus's eyes suddenly bulged from their sockets, and his face turned as red as a beet.

"Goddam-m-m-mit, Miss Gott! Don't just stand there. Put him through, I say. Put him through this instant!"

"Yes, sirrr," she snapped. Gott quickly marched back to her desk and picked up the phone.

"Mister Matthews, I'll switch you into Mister Sanborn now."

A few minutes later, Billington and I found ourselves sitting outside Sanborn's office wondering why we were there.

The setting couldn't have been creepier. It was nothing like what you'd expect to see in a chairman's office. Everything was old and dusty—strictly funereal—like the Harvard Club in New York on a Saturday night. The radiators hissed like snakes. The dark hardwood floors creaked and life-sized portraits of old comic book characters, some of which I had never seen before, lined the walls like giant baseball cards.

"Gentlemennnn, would either of you prefer coffee or tea while you are waiting?" Esther Gott asked.

Before I could answer, Billington grabbed my arm.

"You know, it's awfully early Miss Gott, and I think my friend and I could use something strong to wake us up."

"Very well," she replied. "How do you take your coffee?"

"Black would be fine—" I started to say.

But Billington jumped in again. "Better make it two blacks with lots of cream and sugar. We're watching our caffeine intake, you know."

Gott glared at Billington. Creative types. They're all alike.

"As you wish," she said. "I'll be back shortly. Make yourselves comfortable."

As soon as she had disappeared into the adjoining hallway, Billington scrambled over to Gott's desk and sat quietly in her chair.

"We don't have much time," he whispered. "Just do as I say and no one will get hurt."

"Hurt?" I asked.

"Stand by the door and keep an eye out for her."

"Are you out of your mind?" I asked.

"Go to it, now," he said, with the air of a commanding general.

Once I was in position, Billington grabbed the phone on Gott's desk and simultaneously depressed the "mute" and "speaker phone" buttons.

"What are you doing?" I asked.

"Intelligence gathering," Billington replied.

When he released both buttons, Sanborn's tinny-sounding voice—as panicky as I've ever heard him—poured forth from the speaker.

"How could it have dropped so much?"

"The financial markets hate uncertainty, Sterling," Matthews calmly responded. "And Payne's departure makes it look like the situation here is, shall we say, unstable."

"How bad is the damage?"

"I would say we're going to be down at least twenty percent—maybe more—at the opening in New York."

"Damn it-all," Sanborn replied, his jowls as flush as the red carpeting on the floor.

"Umm, Sterling, there's, ah, more to it than just the stock price."

"Bite your tongue, Matthews. What in the world could possibly be more important than the stock price?"

"Word on the street is filtering out about last night. Prices are going up on all of Payne's existing work—his old issues—and on all the other titles that walked, too. Unless we do something to counter it, something really high profile, new issue sales are gonna die before they hit the stands. We won't be able to give them away. "

"Izzzzatt so?" Sanborn inquired.

"There's more. It's a vicious cycle, Sterling. If the kids turn their noses up the collectors won't buy, and eventually the dealers will refuse to carry the titles."

"Hmmmmmm, now this is distressing," Sanborn said.

"It gets worse. If the analysts pick up on it, the blood bath is only going to intensify, Sterling."

The line fell silent for several seconds, as Sanborn closed his eyes and brought all of his business prowess to bear on the immediate problem at hand. He was at his very best in times of crisis, if for no other reason than he had manufactured so many of them himself.

"Alllll right, Matth-ewssss," he finally said. "What do you intend to do about this mess?"

Matthews nearly swallowed his tongue. "What am I, uh, going to do—"

"Come now, Matth-ewwss," the Walrus barked. "This is why we pay you so much; to think great thoughts and solve great problems like this one. Certainly you must have a solution, otherwise you would not have called me. So out with it, my boy."

Matthews did all he could to keep from heaving all over the phone. But somehow, he managed to pull himself together just long enough to remember what Montana had told him.

"Well, I-I-I-I d-d-d-do have one idea, sir. It's a long shot. But we've got to move on it fast."

The Walrus quietly pulled a tiny micro-cassette recorder from his desk and started taping the conversation. "Go ahead, Mister Matth-ewsss, I'm all ears."

"First thing we have to do is replace Payne. But you've got to get somebody good—a name player—with a strong following who will take all the attention off the Payne mess. Do you have someone we can tap, Sterling?"

Sanborn looked down at his calendar and saw my name.

"As a matter of fact," Sanborn started, "I already have someone in mind—"

"Good, but you've got to make the announcement today," Matthews said. "Call a press conference this afternoon—and we'll patch the analysts in on a conference call. We'll tell them we're re-evaluating the Centurion and have some very big news."

"Yes, yes, very good, Mis-terrrr Matth-ewwwss," Sanborn said. "Then what?"

There was another long pause. Matthews didn't know what to say next, because he couldn't remember anything else that Montana had told him.

"Ummm, I'm not exactly sure, Sterling."

"What do you mean, you're 'not exactly sure'?" Sanborn asked.

This time, Matthews panicked. We could hear him pacing back and forth in his office like a caged lion. Then he ran his hands through his hair and began stuttering uncontrollably.

"I-I-I-"

As he circled around his desk, he somehow managed to wrap the telephone cord around his coffee mug. A few seconds later, the cup flipped into the air like a pinwheel, blanketing his sleeve and shirt with scalding hot coffee.

"Oh shit!" he blurted out at the top of his lungs. "I'd like to kill the son-of-a-bitch that cooked this up—"

I beg your pardon?" Sanborn asked.

"You heard me," Matthews continued. "Everyday it's the same thing with this guy. I'd like to bury the rotten bastard once and for all—"

Sanborn was intrigued. "What did you say, Matth-ewwwss?"

Matthews didn't answer. When he realized exactly what he had said and to whom he had said it, he draped his hand over his mouth and froze.

"Sterling," he finally spoke up. "I'm sorry. I, uh, don't know what came over me—"

"No, no, no," Sanborn replied. "Say what you said before again."

Matthews paused to collect himself. "Sterling, I'm sorry, I don't know what else to say. It was nothing personal and—"

"No, no, no," the Walrus chimed in. "Tell me the part about killing the Centurion."

"Killing the Centurion?" Matthews had no idea what Sanborn was talking about.

"Yes, that's what you're proposing, isn't it?" Sanborn said. "Kill the character off once and for all."

"I am?" he asked.

"It makes perfect sense," Sanborn said. "Nobody buys the title anymore. We really ought to kill him off. Nobody would miss him."

"It would?" Matthews asked in disbelief.

"Of course it would! No one ever kills off a super hero, especially not an American icon. That's part of the problem. We have all these titles hanging around that nobody reads! But just think of the sensation it would create if we did away with the Centurion once and for all. It would deflect all the attention away from the stock. It would create a media frenz-eeee. The headline writers will go wild. I can see it now: 'Death to the Centurion!' America's Sentinel of Light Bites the Big One!'

"People will go crazy when we take it away from them," Sanborn continued. "The clamor for a Centurion movie will be treeeee-mendoussss!"

I don't remember what Sanborn said next, most likely because I spotted Esther Gott heading back down the hall with our coffee.

"Mike! Mike! She's coming. Cut it off!"

Billington quickly hit the conference button and placed the receiver back in its cradle.

When Gott walked through the door both of us were sitting perfectly still, like porcelain dolls, across from her desk.

"Your coffeeeee, Mister MacAllister."

I smiled—a flustered smile, to be sure—and took the cup from the tray. "Thank you so much, Miss Gott."

"Your coffeeee, Misturrr Billingtunn. Cream and sugar."

Billington frowned. "Oh, no thank you, Miss Gott. I only drink mine black. Very black."

Gott glared at him again and returned to her desk, muttering silently to herself.

"You play it on the edge, don't you?" I whispered into Billington's ear.

He scratched his sandy beard, a long and contemplative scratch. Then he looked me straight in the eyes.

"You wanna end up like your legendary has-been did?"

"Of course not," I said.

"If you wanna survive here you gotta keep one step ahead of the enemy, otherwise he'll step all over you."

"Gentlemennn!" Both of us jumped. Esther Gott, looking like she was about to announce a royal audience with the king and queen, stood before us. "Mister Sanbornnnn will see you now."

"We have been summoned," Billington said.

"Now what?" I asked.

Billington smirked. "Play dumb. He'll never know the difference."

So off we went, like condemned men being led to the guillotine, knowing fully well that Sanborn's Centurion problem was about to become our problem. As we approached his office, the giant oak doors suddenly swung open. Sanborn, grinning from ear to ear like the ghost of Christmas Present, greeted us with open arms.

"Gentlemen! Gentlemen!! Come in, come in, I say. I've been looking forward to this meeting all morning."

Sanborn slammed the door in Gott's face, wrapped his arms around our shoulders, and escorted both of us across the room to a giant bay window with a fifty-yard-line view of Central Park.

"Quite a panorama, wouldn't you say gentlemen?" he asked. "I tell people on a clear day I can see the muggers at work!!" Sanborn started to laugh uncontrollably—a lusty, bellowing laugh that quickly turned into a coughing fit.

"It cost me one point three billion dollars to get that view," he said, when he finally recovered. "Hard to believe a comic book company could be worth that kind of money. But it was a steal, gentlemen, because this is one of the most desirable locations in all of Manhattan. In fact, the building is worth more than the firm. But when I get done, that's all going to change. Excelsior Comics is going to be worth ten times what I paid for it. Ten times I tell you!"

Billington's eyes rolled toward the ceiling. *The ego has landed.*

"Ah, but I'm forgetting my manners," Sanborn continued. "Mister Mac-Alleeeesterrrrr, this is your first week on the job, is it not?"

"Second day," I said.

"Well, my boy, let me be among the first to welcome you to Excelsior Comicsssss."

"Thank you, Mister—" I reached out to shake his hand but Sanborn cut me off.

"You know, it isn't often we get someone of your cal-eeeee-ber to jump ship from Renegade. It was quite a coup. I trust you're becoming accl-eeeeemated to our cozy little surroundings?"

I glanced at Billington, who nodded, ever so slightly.

"Oh, you could say that, sir. I feel like I've been here a lot longer than just two days."

"And you can thank your lucky stars that you're not working for Dead-Wood anymore, Mister Mac-Alllleeester. Because if you had stayed, twenty years from now you'd still be working on that same stupid character you were doing—the one with the funny tights ..."

"The Intruder," I quickly interjected.

"Yes, that's it," Sanborn said. "The Inhaler."

"He's their second-biggest selling issue," I said.

Sanborn shrugged. "Two, three, whatever. It doesn't matter. Dead-Wood squanders good talent on dopey titles, Mister Mac-Alleeesterrr. Of course, he's got the money to do it. We don't have that luxury here. When we hire good talent, we find challenging assignments for them."

Billington held back a laugh. *We work them to death is more like it*, he thought.

Sanborn pulled a freshly wrapped Cuban cigar from his breast pocket and waddled over to his desk. "We think you are capable of bigger things, Mister Mac-Alleeesterrr. Much bigger. Why settle for anything less than the greatest comic book hero of all time?"

I could see the windup coming.

"What kind of opportunity do you have in mind, Mister Sanborn?" I asked.

"Wellll, it's an op-p-p-p-portunity of shall I dare say mighty proportions," the

Walrus said. "The kind that only comes about once in a lifetime. A chance to alter the course of history; to reshape the future of the comic book industry forever—"

Billington couldn't stand it anymore. "You want us to fix the Centurion mess, don't you?" he asked.

Sanborn's face turned three shades of purple, and then he exploded like a rocket on liftoff.

"FIX IT????!!" he yelled. "I don't want YOU to do anything of the kind, Mister Billeeengton. I want Mister Mac-Alleesterrrrr to fix it! YOU, Mister Billeengton, have your own titles to worry about and I can't take you off them. But you know how things work around here so I want you to help Mister Mac-Alleeesterrr in your spare time. And gentlemen, let me be clear. I want more than just a fix. I want you to do something so spectacular—so TOTALLY unexpected—that everyone forgets the Centurion ever existed!!"

"That's not gonna be easy," I said. "There's a lot of tradition behind the Centurion—"

The Walrus frowned. "The hell with tradition! The Centurion is old, he's tired, he's all washed up! Look at this garbage—"

Sanborn opened his desk drawer, grabbed a handful of recent Centurion issues—all new and unsold—and threw them across his blotter with such force that his jowls shook from side to side.

"Kids don't buy tradition! They want violence! They want blood! They want sex! Lots of steamy flesh, the miserable little beggars. They want the kind of vile crap that you create, Misterrrr Billeengton."

Billington bristled. "So you want us to make the Centurion more like the Silencer?"

"No, no, no," Sanborn said, shaking his head. "That's not enough, Misterrr Billeengton. I want you to silence the Centurion."

Both of us tried to act surprised.

"You can't be serious," Billington said.

"Oh, but I am serious, Misterrr Billeeengton. Dead serious."

"Then why don't you simply drop the title? It's no big deal."

"Ah, maybe not to you, Mister Billeeeengton. But it is a BIG DEAL to me. I want it to be the most spectacularrrrr, the most violenttttttt, the most blood-curdling death in the history of comic books. Think about it! No one has ever done anything like it before. It will become the biggest, grizzliest funeral of all time. It will be so big that we'll have to run second and third printings. Maybe more! Then the stock price will double, and those fucking idiots from Holl-eeee-wood will come begging for a film contract—"

Sanborn, realizing that he had said too much, stopped abruptly in mid-sentence.

"And then," Billington interjected," everyone would stop buying Matt Payne's old books and start buying new issues again before we all go out of business."

Sanborn wheeled his leather chair around, and sat with his back to us staring out the window at the cold gray morning.

"You know, Misterrr Billeeengton, we could all stand to forget about Matt Payne for a while. A long, longgggg while. That miserable son-of-a-bitch will never set foot in this building a-gain. And with any luck, maybe his cruise ship will wind up on the bottom of the Atlantic and we'll never see or hear from him either."

And then, just as it appeared as if he would work himself into a frenzy, Sanborn swung back around and smiled.

"Gentlemen, if you pull this off you'll both be bigger than Matt Payne ever was," the Walrus said. "This will be the greatest thing to hit the comic book industry in years. Fans will worship you like gods!"

"Excuse me," I said, always the good Boy Scout. "But if we do this, do you have any idea how we're going to pull it all off?"

"Why, Misterrrr Mac-Alleeeesterrr," Sanborn said, flashing a wolfish grin. "You'rethe expert here. That's why we brought you on board—to shake this place up and take us where we've never been before. It's the perfect challenge! And I have the utmost confidence that you'll be more than up to the job. You'll have access to the very best and brightest talent we have. In addition to Misterrr Billeeeengton here, I've arranged for Vicky Connors and Julie McKinney to do all the art work! From this moment on, you're heading up the Centurion task force. And together, I'm sure you'll all rise to the occasion."

I wasn't so optimistic. To me, killing the Centurion seemed almost blasphemous; like burning the American flag or blowing up your first car. "Are you absolutely certain you want to do this?"

"Oh, quite sure, Misterrr Mac-Alleeester, quite sure. The time is long overdue. And speed is essential. Do you understand?"

We both nodded, as if we had any choice in the matter.

"Very good, gentlemen! We'll announce all this at a press conference later today," Sanborn said. "Whatever you're working on now, get it done fast. And one more thing. I don't want any of the specifics leaking out about this until we're ready to publish. Do I make myself clear, Misterrrr Mac-Alleeeester?"

"Understood," I said reluctantly.

Then he turned to Billington. "And what about you?"

"I don't know a thing, chief," Billington said.

"Yes, how true," Sanborn sighed. "Now I want to see storyboard sketches in ten days, not a moment later."

Ten days? I nearly went white. Ten days to kill off the world's greatest superhero and have it all sketched out? It was hardly enough time to flesh out a story line, let alone develop storyboards. Sanborn knew it too, but he didn't care.

"That's not nearly enough time to put this all together," I protested.

"Misterrrr Mac-Alleeesterrr," he said, opening the door to his office. "Time is a luxury we don't have."

As we walked out into the waiting room, Esther Gott was talking to two maintenance men about the illustrations on the wall.

"Which one of dese frames comes down, lady?" one of the workers asked.

Gott pointed directly at the Centurion's picture.

"It's that one," she said, "Take that horrid thing down immediately."

"Any special place you want it?"

Gott looked at the piece and frowned. "Burn it," she said. "The sooner we get rid of it the better."

Chapter Four

Jersey City, N.J.

Long after Sanborn's press conference had ended, and long after Billington and I had gone back to work, another element of this story began to unfold across the Hudson River at the Scout Television Network in Jersey City. Anchorman Phil Plunkett, a newscaster I'd never even heard of, had one burning question on his mind.

"How do I look?" he asked, for the third time. "How do I look?"

"Great, Phil, positively great," said a positively bored assistant producer near the anchor desk.

"What about my tie?" he asked. "Is it straight? Are you sure it's straight?"

"Straight as an arrow, Phil. Real straight."

Plunkett adjusted his tie, shuffled the news script in front of him, and waited for last-minute instructions from the production booth.

"Phil?" intoned a voice that he despised from an overhead speaker. "Why don't we just forget about your tie and try smiling into the camera."

"Right," Plunkett replied. He immediately swiveled his anchor chair ninety degrees, like an official anchorman should, so that he was looking directly into the lens of Camera Two. Then, without any prompting, he flashed his million dollar anchorman smile for the camera lens.

"Very good, Phil," the producer said. "Let's see if we can hold that pretty smile right into the promo."

Plunkett froze in position. Head, shoulders, anchor desk, logo, and smile. It was exactly what he was supposed to do and he wasn't happy about it. *A baboon could do this, he thought. That's all they really need, a baboon to sit here and smile through all the murders, the muggings, the drownings, and the political scandals day after day, newscast after newscast. God forbid, they should ever want someone to report the news. Or maybe even tell the truth once in a while.*

Of course, had he really wanted to report the truth Plunkett could have kept his dignity and stayed in newspapers. But his $22,000 a year salary wasn't enough for his wife, Maxine—the former Maxine Driftwood of the Scarsdale Driftwoods—who had always dreamed of living in a mansion in Greenwich, Connecticut, and driving a BMW—and she never let him forget it. So when the big TV offer finally came through, he took the job just to shut her up. But fame and fortune came with a price. Having covered the entertainment industry for years, he knew that the only way to succeed as a television anchorman was to leave his brain at home. And that's exactly what he did. At the time, it didn't seem like such a big sacrifice. But now that he and Maxine had finalized their divorce he was having second thoughts. What Plunkett really craved—more than anything else—was to sink his teeth into a good story before he became as loony as the people he worked with.

"Ten seconds to promo," the producer announced. "Ready on Camera Seven. Cue in on my signal."

Plunkett silently counted down the seconds on his own.

"Four, three, two, one ... intro."

"This is a Channel Seven Eyewitness News Brief. Now live from our Scout Studios is Phil Plunkett ..."

"Cut intro," the producer barked. "Camera Seven, feed it NOW."

The red light atop Camera Seven sprang to life and Plunkett's image appeared on more than a dozen tiny television screens throughout the studio. Staring directly into the camera like a man on a mission, he took a deep breath and let it rip: "Coming up tonight on Eyewitness News at eleven: Denver Dad Dies in Daring Daylight Drive ... Race Relations Remain Rocky in Riverside ... and Comic Company Cracks Centurion Case!"

As soon as he finished, the screen faded to black. "Cut to commercial," the producer ordered.

Within seconds, the big studio lights and the camera feeds went limp. After a minute or two, a pair of burly technicians jumped up onto the stage and began re-arranging the set for the late newscast. But Plunkett stayed locked in position, smiling broadly into the camera, re-reading the last few lines of his script on the TelePrompTer.

COMIC COMPANY CRACKS CENTURION CASE. *Hmmmm.*

"Uhmm, Phil," the producer finally said, "we're done, Phil. You can go back to the newsroom like a good boy until ten fifty-five."

Plunkett, lost in thought, folded his desk script neatly between his hands and quickly grabbed the first assistant producer he could find.

"Connie, what's this here about the Centurion?"

She looked at the script and then checked it against a story list on her clipboard.

"Comic company, comic company, comic—oh, yes, here it is Phil," she said. "Some dopey story about the appointment of a new guy to do the Centurion. It's summer, things are slow, I guess."

Plunkett scanned the story carefully.

"Matt Payne bolts from sight ... owner appoints replacement ... for a live report from the scene ..."

Can this be true? Plunkett scratched his head. *Could this really be who I think it is?*

He had to be certain. So when no one was looking he opened the top drawer of his anchor desk and fumbled through a jumble of paper clips and empty aspirin bottles, until he found what he was looking for—one of his son's Centurion comic books. Excelsior Comics Number 652, to be exact.

THE ADVENTURES OF THE CENTURION. TRACKING BIG FOOT! BY MATT PAYNE.

My God, it is him, Plunkett thought—*Matt Payne, the man who had drawn each and every one of the three-hundred and thirty-two Centurion comic books that he had read from his son's collection, was gone. Unbelievable!*

Plunkett immediately grabbed the red phone at his anchor desk, and started dialing.

"Hello?"

"Maxine? Is that you?" he asked.

"You were expecting Barbara Walters maybe?"

"Is Larry around?"

"Phil, we've been through this a hundred times. You can't have him until Friday night. It's only Tuesday, and I don't want to hear any more of this—"

"Oh, for Chrissakes, Max," Plunkett interrupted. "All I want to do is say hello to the boy. Do you think you can arrange it without consulting a lawyer?"

There was silence on the other end.

"What do you wanna talk to him about?"

Plunkett sighed. "We've been through all this before, Maxine. I don't have to tell you a goddamned thing."

"Oh yes you do," she snapped, "if you want to talk to him."

"Maxine, if you must know I'm calling to tell him that I haven't paid your Saks charge yet this month. In fact, I have one day left before they cancel your card. And I'd like to get his opinion on how difficult it would be for you to renew that precious line of credit without me."

There was a long pause on the other end of the line. "Larrrrrry, your father's on the phone."

"Thank you," Plunkett said.

"Just remember," she said, popping her bubble gum. "You don't get him before Friday."

Maxine handed the receiver to the boy, a blond-haired twelve-year-old who was as sharp and precocious as they come at that age.

"Hi, Dad, what's up?" he asked.

"Ummm, your comic books," Plunkett started, "I'm calling about your—"

"Dad," the boy interrupted, "don't tell me you left another one in the men's room."

"No, no, no, son," he replied. "It's nothing like that at all. I was just calling because we got this news report here about Excelsior Comics. It says they've got a new guy doing the Centurion. You know anything about it?"

"Are you kidding?" Larry asked. "Everybody's talking about it. You should have seen the comic book store after school today. It was mobbed."

"Big stuff, huh?" Plunkett asked.

"All the prices on the old issues were marked up—two and three times the original price. Jimmy and Nathan even bought a couple of issues and they hate the Centurion."

"Why are the prices going up?" Plunkett asked.

"Geez, Dad. Don't you know anything? The betting line is Matt Payne's replacement is gonna bomb. So all his old issues have doubled and tripled in value."

"Pretty big news, huh?" Plunkett asked.

"You don't know the half of it."

Plunkett scribbled down what he could on a notepad. "Care to tell me about it, son?"

Larry hesitated. He was smart enough to know when he was being pumped for a story.

"What's it worth to you?" the boy replied.

"What do you mean 'what's it worth to you?' I'm your father!"

"It's still gonna cost you," Larry said.

Plunkett frowned. "Name your price."

"First I want you and Mom to get back together again."

Plunkett flinched. "Give me something reasonable, son."

Larry thought for a moment. "I want all my old issues back."

Plunkett cleared his throat. "Uhmmm, can I have until this weekend to finish up the ones I'm reading now?"

"Yeah," the boy said, "but I want every single one back—in plastic sleeves with no creases—or no deal."

Five minutes later, Plunkett hung up the phone like an excited school kid and immediately called the production booth.

"This is Phil, put Manny on the line," he said.

"Hang on."

It was not a particularly good time to talk, it just never was for someone who was perennially constipated like Manny Schaffi, but he picked up the phone anyway. "Phil, what is it now?"

"Did you know we've got a really big story buried in the lineup tonight?" Plunkett said.

Schaffi scanned his clipboard for a clue. "Oh? And what story might that be, Phil?"

"The comic book story. The one about the Centurion. We just promoed it on the news break."

Schaffi found the story in a stack of papers on his desk and quickly eyeballed it.

"I see it, Phil," he said. "It's no big deal. The only reason we're carrying it at all is because it's the Centurion."

"That's why it's so big," Plunkett said. "This Payne guy is special. It's like replacing Picasso or Mozart—"

"C'mon, Phil, it's only a comic book. It's not like this guy painted the Mona Lisa."

"Get real, Manny. Everybody knows who Matt Payne is and he just walked off the job. The price on his work is skyrocketing. The company he worked for could be in big trouble. I think we oughta at least—"

"Phil, Phill, Philll," the producer interrupted, "you scare me when you think. We don't pay you the big bucks to think. We pay you to read the news. That's all, Phil."

"But I'm telling you, Manny, this is big. Really big."

Schaffi took a deep breath. "So, ummm, what would you have us do with this earth-shattering development, Phil?"

"There's only one thing we can do," Plunkett said. "We gotta lead off the eleven o'clock newscast with it. You just can't bury a big story like this."

"Lemme get this straight, Phil. We've got fatalities from a head-on collision, we've got a tense racial situation in the city that could blow up at any time—all with great visuals—and you think a story about a comic book is more important? Is that right?"

"You've got it," Plunkett said firmly. "Besides, we do all those other stories every night of the week. Same thing, night after night. This is different. And I guarantee you nobody else has the whole story."

"Phil," Schaffi interrupted, "when was the last time you took a vacation?"

"Damn it, Manny. I'm not jerkin' you around. This is important."

Just then, an aide tapped Schaffi on the shoulder and pointed to his watch. "Staff meeting," he whispered, "NOW."

"Phil," he said. "I want you to listen to me. Go back to your dressing room, relax, smoke a couple of cigarettes, maybe get a quick massage, put some fresh makeup on, come back in an hour and read the news just like we've prepared it. Okay?"

Plunkett didn't respond.

"Phil? Do you hear me, Phil?"

"Yeah, I hear you," he said. "Just forget I even called."

Plunkett slammed down the phone, scooped up the newscast in his hand, and stormed off the set, angry with himself for having even tried.

Chapter Five

Brooklyn, N.Y.

Sometimes news travels in mysterious ways.

In his rush to tell the world about me, Sanborn conveniently neglected to tell the rest of the company.

"Let them watch it on TV like everyone else," he told Matthews. "It's cheaper."

Maybe so, but not everyone at Excelsior was glued to their television sets that evening. Mitch Gerber hadn't seen a television newscast in years. As it so happened, Gerber found himself sitting later that evening in his dentist's chair—about as far removed from Phil Plunkett and the Scout network as he could get—waiting pensively for the calming effects of the nitrous oxide that he was inhaling to kick in.

"Breathe through your nose, Mitch," the dentist said, "and pretty soon you won't feel a thing."

Gerber took a deep breath. Nitrous—"sweet air" as he liked to call it—was better than downing a pint of Jack Daniels and a six-pack of beer. It was the perfect prescription for his overly sensitive gums, and just about everything else that was troubling him.

Slowly, he began to forget about the day that had just passed, about his disappointment over Payne's retirement memo, and all the other things that had gone wrong in his life—a child lost at birth, a failed marriage, and the nervous twitch in his right hand—his drawing hand—that prevented him from being a truly extraordinary illustrator.

None of that mattered now. Everything around him was becoming a blur. His skin tingled. And he began to feel like he could do anything, even manage the Centurion. He would do a fabulous job, too. Sales would boom. Comic book fans everywhere would know that he was the artist who restored the Centurion to glory. And then the fame and fortune that had been denied him for so long would finally be his.

Of course, Gerber had had these same nitrous-induced delusions before; each and every time he went to the dentist for a cleaning. But what he hadn't experienced—and what he wasn't at all prepared for—was the mysterious voice that suddenly reached out to him from nowhere.

"*Thou have been chosen as the keeper of the Centurion, my son!*"

Gerber's heart rate kicked into overdrive and he started to shake. "What the Christ—"

"*Thou have been chosen as the keeper of the Centurion!*" This time the voice was much louder.

Gerber looked straight through the eyes of his dentist, who was working on his mouth like a jackhammer, and saw the face of a god—a Roman god.

"Who-who-who are you?" he asked.

"*Do not fear me. I am Apollo, god of the sun, keeper of the flame of the Roman Sentinel of Light.*"

Gerber recognized the words instantly—every schoolboy who'd ever read the story of the Centurion knew them by heart. And like Moses at the Mount, he was not afraid. Just accepting.

"I am your humble servant," Gerber replied.

His dentist laughed and adjusted the halogen lamp dangling overhead. But to Gerber's fuzzy brain, it only illuminated Apollo's figure even more.

"*Use your powers wisely to protect mankind from the evil that lurks in the dark side of humanity. Always protect the Centurion from danger. Let nothing stand in your way.*"

"I will honor your command," Gerber silently obeyed. "I will do my duty. I will fight evil. I will uphold the great tradition of the Centurion. I swear it with my very life…"

Like Gerber, Julie McKinney wasn't in much of a position to pay attention to the news that night either. With final projects just days away, she found herself that night cramming over a warm beer at the Alibi, a seedy watering hole just a few blocks from school where she could study in peace, without being interrupted by the usual barrage of annoying after-hours phone calls from Excelsior. She'd been working like a dog on her master's degree and now the end was finally in sight. Two years before that, Julie had walked away from BBDO, one of the city's busiest advertising agencies, where she was little more than an overworked face in a crowd. What she really wanted was a top spot in a smaller shop, where her work would be appreciated. So she chucked Madison Avenue for graduate school and a fresh start. Her internship at Excelsior was strictly a means to an end. She needed the hard-driving experience like a hole in her head and couldn't wait for it all to be over. But she also needed the credits to complete her studies and the money—what little the job paid—for tuition.

"You sure I can't get you anything to eat, Miss?" the bartender asked.

Before she could answer, a voice from the television set above the bar caught her ear.

"...and finally, we'll take you live to Excelsior Comics for the latest developments in the adventures of the Centurion! These stories coming up next on Eyewitness News at eleven!"

Julie's eyes widened. "I'll be damned," she said to a friend, "I bet they named somebody to replace Matt Payne. The poor slob."

Billington offered to break the news about Centurion task force to Vicki Connors, since he knew her better than I did. But at that moment, she was in the middle of a personal crisis of her own making. The setting couldn't have been more conspicuous: A crowded sushi restaurant in SoHo where she was sitting nose-to-nose at a tiny table across from her soon-to-be ex-boyfriend, a pony-tailed television producer from Queens who liked to tell everyone that he chummed around with New York's Hollywood elite—the DeNiro's, the Scorceses, and the Alec Baldwins—even though none of them knew him by name.

"It's not that I don't love you," Andy Giancomo said, sheepishly. "I just think it would be good for both of us if we saw some new talent."

"Is that what this is all about?" she asked. "Is this just a talent search for one of those bimbo talk shows you produce?"

"Vicki, Vicki, Vicki, baby," he said, wary of all the eyes around them. "Calm down. There's no reason to get hostile here."

Connors grabbed the napkin from her lap and wrapped it tightly around her fist.

"Hostile?" she fumed. "You don't know the meaning of the word hostile, pal."

Though he outweighed her by some sixty pounds, Giancomo knew he was no match for Vicki when she lost her temper.

"All right, all right," he said, as heads turned all around them. "We've had some good times, you and me. Really, we have. It's just with you working so damn much we hardly ever get to see each other anymore—"

"Don't give me that crap," Connors interrupted. "I don't work any more or less than you do. The only difference is I'm good and I get paid for what I do."

Giancomo winced. He wanted out of the relationship and at this point was willing to try anything to get out of the situation—even the truth. "OK, Vicki, you want it straight? I'll give it to you straight. You don't love me and you never have. You love your characters. End of story. Now that may be fine for you, but it's not for me. I don't like playing second fiddle to Neanderthals with names like Caldor the Jungle King and the Assailant. It would be one thing if they were real. But how can I compete against make-believe super men?"

Silence.

Giancomo couldn't believe it. *Maybe it's getting through to her, he thought. Maybe, she'll finally understand.*

Then again, maybe not.

"Let's get one thing straight," Connors said with a look of pure fury in her eyes, "don't blame your insecurity on my work. My characters are my business. You don't like them because they're everything you're not, you spineless worm!"

"Vicki," he pleaded, "you're not making this any easier—"

Connors grabbed a hand roll from her plate with her chopsticks.

"You want it easy? I'll make it easy." And then, with every eye in the restaurant locked onto their table, Connors promptly shoved the roll—chopsticks and all—into his mouth.

"I want you to remember something," she said, while Giancomo gagged. "In this life, there's only one thing more final than breaking up with me. Death."

It wasn't until much later that evening, long after she had polished off half a bottle of wine and a box of Godiva Chocolates in her Manhattan apartment, that Connors stopped thinking about Andy Giancomo long enough to listen to the backlog of messages on her answering machine.

BEEP!

"Vicki, it's Mike Billington, about three-thirty. When you get in, give me a call. I've got something really important to discuss with you. Bye."

BEEP!

Connors looked at her watch. Ten fifty-nine. Too late to try him now. So as the answering machine played on, she picked up the remote from the night stand in her bedroom and pointed it at the television.

BEEP!

"Vicki, it's Mike again. It's around eight-thirty. Listen, it's really important that we talk tonight. I'll be up late—past midnight—so give me a call at home—259-2801."

BEEP!

That's odd. Billington rarely calls at home, she thought, much less twice on the same night.

She started dialing Billington's number, but stopped short at the sound of Phil Plunkett's voice.

"This just in to Eyewitness News," he boomed. "Hang on to your hats, boys and girls, the mighty Centurion may have a new lease on life tonight.

"Less than twenty-four hours after legendary comic book artist Matt Payne bolted from sight, Excelsior Comics' new owner, Sterling Sanborn the Third, has launched a desperate bid to rekindle the aging Sentinel of Light and save his struggling company from an early grave.

"Sanborn is replacing Payne with Rick MacAllister, a young upstart who's jumped ship from Renegade Comics to head a special team that has been charged with breathing new life into the character."

Back at the studio, pandemonium suddenly erupted in the production booth.

"What the hell is this?" Schaffi yelled. "This isn't supposed to lead off the newscast!"

Plunkett couldn't hear the uproar from the anchor desk, and even if he did, he had no intention of stopping. He leaned over on his elbow, nuzzled up closer to the camera lens, and with a look that he reserved for only the most serious stories, said:

"We now take you live to Maria Vasquez-Mitchell for all the latest at Excelsior's headquarters in midtown Manhattan. Maria...."

Connors dropped the phone and watched intently at the image on her screen. She knew the setting well. The gothic brass-framed doors at the entrance of Excelsior's headquarters on Fifty-Ninth Street provided a convenient backdrop for Maria Vasquez-Mitchell, Scout's politically-correct, drop-dead gorgeous news ace, who stood ready to break yet another bombshell from Eyewitness News. With the camera tightening in on her face, she took a deep breath, pursed her highly-glossed lips behind her microphone, and promptly froze.

Special team? What special team, she wondered? I don't know anything about a special team.

For the first time in her career, she didn't know what to say.

"Maria?" Plunkett asked from the studio. "Maria, can you hear me?"

"Uh, yes, Phil," she finally said. "I hear you."

"Then go ahead, tell us everything you know about this fast breaking story."

Maria Vasquez-Mitchell swallowed hard and did the only thing she could under the circumstances—she began reading from her notepad.

"Um, as you said Phil, we're here live at, um, Excelsior Comics where earlier today it was announced that Rick MacAllister, the man who made the Intruder famous at Renegade Comics, has been tapped to replace Matt Payne, the creator of the Centurion. Here's how it happened."

Videotape of the press conference flashed up on the screen, and Maria Vasquez-Mitchell quickly bolted into the station's remote truck.

"Give me that goddamned phone," she said to her producer. "Manny? Manny? What the hell's going on? I don't know anything about any special team. They didn't say a word about it at the press conference."

"We're trying to get to the bottom of this too, kid," Schaffi replied. "Just hold tight."

Back in the studio, Sanborn's image appeared on the monitor.

"It gives me great pleasurrrre to announce today that a fresh new talent has been seee-lected to take over the Centurion," the Walrus gushed. "I give you Rick Mac-Alleeeester."

The camera pulled back and there I was stepping up to the podium, adjusting the microphone, having not the faintest idea of what to say. But before I could even utter a word, Sanborn pushed me aside and grabbed the mike from my hands.

"Ummm, Mister Mac-Alleeester will have total creative control of the Centurionnnn," Sanborn said. "The Sentinel of Light is entirely in his capable hands."

And with that, the tape stopped dead in its tracks thanks to a very confused and inexperienced technician in the production booth who inadvertently flipped the wrong switch, sending the live feed—with full sound—back to Maria Vasquez-Mitchell, who was still sitting in the remote truck, talking to Schaffi on the phone.

"Who the fuck does he think he is, Manny? Phil muscles in on my story and now I'm supposed to send it back to him for more analysis? Where does he get the balls to—"

"Maria listen to me carefully," Schaffi interrupted. "At this very moment we're live, and everything you're saying is being broadcast to seven million homes across New York, New Jersey and Connecticut."

She looked up at the camera like a deer caught in the headlights. "Oh shit."

Thinking quickly, Maria Vasquez-Mitchell dropped the phone, grabbed her microphone and smiled.

"Sanborn refused to comment about the company's stock price, which fluctuated wildly in heavy trading today on Wall Street. But he did issue a short statement after the press conference promising, quote "more new surprises," end quote, for Centurion fans in the months ahead. If today is any indication, the latest chapter in the exciting adventures of the Centurion are going to continue at Excelsior Comics for some time. Now we go back to our studios to Phil Plunkett for analysis. Phil...."

Plunkett's beaming face immediately reappeared on screen.

"Thanks, Maria. Sterling Sanborn the Third has a lot riding on this effort. With sales plunging and comic book dealers across the country marking up prices of old issues, the very future of his shaky entertainment empire may be at stake here. So Sanborn is pulling out all the stops to revitalize the Centurion and pump up flagging sales. That's where Rick MacAllister comes in. Eyewitness News has learned exclusively that MacAllister will be heading up a team of specialists—some of the best talent in the business—to revitalize the Centurion."

Plunkett's face disappeared and was replaced by a picture of Billington superimposed over the front cover of a Silencer comic book.

"Where did that graphic come from?" Schaffi asked.

"Beats me," a puzzled assistant shrugged, "But there are two more like it in the graphics bank, and he's controlling the cues from a remote at the anchor desk."

Schaffi lunged for the control panel, frantically flipping switches in an effort to override Plunkett's commands.

"This is news?" he screamed. "What's next—Homer Simpson gets a tummy tuck?"

Schaffi started to bolt for the studio door, but an assistant held him back. It was no use. Plunkett had literally hijacked the news studio and was taking everyone along for the ride.

"The Centurion team," he continued, "includes Michael Billington, the creative genius behind guerrilla warfare king, 'The Silencer,' and one of the industry's most renowned illustrators, Vicki Connors...."

Back in her Manhattan apartment, Connors gazed at her television set in horror.

"No way!" she shouted. "NO WAY you're going to get me to work on that piece of crap!"

Plunkett paused. "Also joining the task force is Julie McKinney, a student from the Pratt Institute in Brooklyn."

Across town at the Alibi, Julie McKinney nearly choked on a chicken wing. "Hey, kid," the bartender asked, "isn't that you on TV?"

McKinney swallowed hard.

"ONCE AGAIN," Plunkett intoned, "stunning news for comic book fans! Excelsior Comics has named a replacement for Matt Payne. He's Rick MacAllister, one of the industry's hottest storytellers. Can he breathe life back into the world's greatest super hero and save Excelsior Comics from a fate worse than death? Stay tuned. You can bet we're going to keep following this big story."

At that exact moment, a cold wind swept across Avenue J in Brooklyn, and a groggy Mitch Gerber felt a sudden chill.

"Mitch? Mitch?" his dentist asked. "Are you okay?"

Gerber felt like he'd been run over by a truck. He didn't even know where he was.

"Mitch, the nitrous mix was a little too rich," the dentist said. "You started to hallucinate. You're coming out of it now. We've upped the oxygen. Just lie still and relax for a few minutes until your head clears."

Gerber took a deep breath. The euphoria he had experienced before was gone, but not the voices. What he heard was Plunkett's voice coming from a small black and white TV in the dentist's reception area. But in his current state, he couldn't distinguish fact from fantasy. And he assumed the broadcast was a special message just for him.

"Recapping tonight's Eyewitness News, Excelsior Comics has appointed Rick MacAllister—one of the hottest story tellers in the business—to revive the Centurion!"

Over and over again, the words continued to repeat themselves, like a record spinning out of control.

"He's Rick MacAllister—one of the hottest story tellers in the business...."

"He's Rick MacAllister...."

"Rick...."

Then suddenly it all stopped, and Gerber closed his eyes. In the dark recesses of his mind, the vision that had appeared to him before returned in vivid detail. And Apollo spoke to him once again.

"*PROTECT THE SENTINTEL OF LIGHT, MY SON. FIGHT THE EVIL THAT LURKS DEEP WITHIN THE DARK SIDE OF MANKIND. AND NEVER LET ANYTHING STAND IN YOUR WAY.*"

When Gerber opened his eyes he was fully in control of his emotions. "Nothing," he whispered to himself, "will ever stop me."

Like I said, news travels in mysterious ways. And sometimes it doesn't travel well at all.

Chapter Six

Excelsior Headquarters

The very next morning the tide had turned. The reviews were in from Sanborn's press conference, and they were all glowing.

"Excelsior Draws A New Line for the Centurion," proclaimed the Daily News.

The Wall Street Journal, as always, took an introspectively upbeat view, asking in a front page, dual-bylined essay, *"Will a New Centurion Fly?"*

The New York Times, taking its usual tone of understated intellectual pomposity, reported on page D-6: *"Excelsior Sends Dream Team to Rescue Centurion."*

Lockwood's Post, as usual, refused to yield an inch, and bluntly screamed forth: *"Sanborn's Payne Killer!"*

Of course, there was no mention anywhere that this would be the Centurion's swan song. That would come later—MUCH LATER. For the moment, Sanborn was content to let everyone believe that my job was simply to remake the character, not kill him. And why not? Everyone seemed to buy it. Even the financial markets were suckered in. Many of the same analysts who had urged investors to sell Trieste's stock just a day earlier reversed course—proving once more that the herd mentality was alive and well on Wall Street—and issued "buy" recommendations en masse. From there, the stampede was on. Bargain hunters embarked on a feeding frenzy that pushed Trieste's stock price back up twenty-seven points.

Sanborn was ecstatic.

"Excel-l-l-lent, Mister Matt-hewss! Excellent!" he gushed, while leafing through the newspapers on his desk. "Hollywood wants quick action, and by God, they shall have it!"

Matthews smiled, a gutsy, self-confident smile befitting a man who now believed he had singled-handedly rescued the company from the brink of financial ruin.

"All in a day's work," he said. "Think nothing of it."

"Now this is what I want you to do," Sanborn said. "I want you to overnight a copy of all these newspapers to Jack Morgante at Pin-n-n-nacle Productions in Holl-e-e-e-wood. And I want you to send him a little note with it."

Matthews whipped out a pad and pen and started scribbling.

"I want it to say, 'Dear Jack…I thought you might be interested in seeing….'" Matthews rushed to keep up with him. *"Dear Jack…. "*

Sanborn hesitated. "No, scratch that. Make it, 'My dearest Jack'…." Matthews wrote even faster. *"My dearest Jack…."*

"No, no, no," Sanborn interjected. "How's this? 'Jack, BABY.'" Matthews shrugged.

"Yes, that's it," Sanborn continued. "That's how they all talk in Holl-e-e-e-wood. Start it, 'Jack, BABY. The adventure is just beeeee-ginning. Stay tuned for the next thrilling epeee-sode of the Centurion.' Got it?"

"Stay tuned for the next thrilling episode of the Centurion," Matthews repeated. "I got it. Do you want to sign it?"

"No, no, no," the Walrus responded. "Sign it, 'Love, Amanda, Room 159.' " Matthews was puzzled. "Amanda? Are you sure?"

"Actually, no, now that I think of it," Sanborn said. "I can't remember if it was Amanda or Jennifer that we set him up with. Go down to the third floor and find out which one of them slept with Morgante. Then tell her to sign the letter."

"Will do," Matthews replied.

"Very good," Sanborn said, wringing his hands. "Now, speaking of thrilling epee-e-e-sodes, where's the stock price at?"

"It's up three more points. That makes thirty points altogether since the big run up at the opening bell," Matthews said.

"Wonderfullllll, Mister Matt-hewssss. Wonderful."

But there was one fly in the ointment. "Something really unusual happened on the overseas exchanges last night that you should look at, Sterling."

Matthews handed Sanborn two stock charts tracking Trieste's overnight performance in London and Tokyo. In both cases, the patterns were identical. The stock dropped quickly at the opening bell, and then staged a dramatic turnaround in mid-session that continued right up through closing.

Sanborn studied the charts, then rose from his chair and waltzed toward a giant aquarium at the center of the room.

"Hmmm," Sanborn rubbed his chin, "now what do you make of this development Mister Matt-hewssss?"

"The only thing I can think of is the Scout Network report last night sir," Matthews said. "It had a lot more information in it than the papers did—"

Sanborn tossed some frozen shrimp into the water. "Yessss, yesss, yesssssss, I saw the Scout report. Hard to believe one of Lock-jaw's stations uncovered so much."

"When that report reached London and Tokyo on Scout's Global Entertainment Network, our stock price started shooting up," Matthews said.

Sanborn stared silently into the fish tank, watching with absolute delight as a school of piranhas tore the tiny shrimp apart.

"Are you telling me, Mister Matt-hewssss, that our stock price went up because of a positive news report from one of Deadddd-Wood's television stations?"

"It would appear so, Sterling."

The Walrus quickly gazed at the charts and then erupted into an earth-shattering belly laugh that literally rattled the glass aquarium.

"HAWWWWWWW, HAWWWWWW, HAWWWWW!! I love it! I love it! God how I love it so! I bet old Sydney's having a royal shit fit over the whole thing right now!"

When he finally calmed down, Sanborn studied the charts more closely. "But how could this be?" he asked.

"Scout broadcasts twenty-four hours a day around the world," Matthews explained. "So they reach all the overseas markets while they're trading."

The Walrus persisted. "Which means getting some very well-placed news in the right hands at Scout here in New York could have a decidedly positive impact on our after-hours trading overseas."

A silent alarm went off in Matthews' head. "Well, yes, that's true. But I don't think we want to go there, Sterling. The Securities and Exchange Commission takes a very dim view of companies that purposely leak insider information ..."

Sanborn's complexion changed quickly.

"Yes, yes, yes, you are so right, Matt-hewsss," he said, tapping on the side of the aquarium. "And that's why I'm asking. If I didn't know better I'd say we have a leaky roof of our own to contend with right here in this building."

Matthews gazed up at the ceiling.

"The damn place is so old it leaks like a sieve."

"No, no, no," Sanborn said. "We have a spy in our midst."

"A spy?" Matthews asked.

Sanborn edged closer to Matthews and whispered into his ear. "How else would you explain the Scout report? Only four people knew about the task force yesterday. You and me. And MacAllister and Bille-e-e-ngton. Now who do you suppose spilled the beans?"

Matthews shrugged.

"You didn't say anything, did you?" Sanborn asked.

Matthews shook his head from side to side. "Of course not, Sterling. My lips are sealed."

"Well, I certainly didn't say anything," Sanborn added. "So who does that leave us with?"

Before Matthews could answer, Sanborn held his finger up to his lips. "Shhh! The walls have ears. We could have a very serious security breach on our hands here. And we have to get to the bottom of it before Lock-jaw figures out what we're up to. He's a crafty old cuss. He'll put that army of artists at Renegade on our tails and try to outdo us before we've even started."

"I agree," Matthews nodded. "We can't let this continue."

"Ex-x-x-x-xactly," Sanborn replied, "which is why I want you to find out who our spy is."

"Me?" Matthews asked.

"You're pretty sneaky, Matthews. You're perfect for the job."

A knock at the door from Esther Gott put a quick halt to the conversation.

"Mister Sanbornnnnn?"

"What is it now, Miss Gottttt?"

"There's a camera crew from CNBC in the lobby, sir. They want to talk to you about the Centurion. Do you wish to see them?"

"Do they have an appointment?" the Walrus asked.

"No, sir," Gott replied. "They just showed up unannounced."

"Then tell them to go away. I've done all my talking for now—"

"Wait a minute," Matthews interrupted. "Did you say CNBC?"

Gott looked at her notes. "CNBC. That's what Security said."

"So???" Sanborn asked.

"So this might just be the answer to our prayers, Sterling," Matthews said. "CNBC is the dominant cable business news network. If you want to reassure investors about the company and DENY the allegations in the Scout report you go on CNBC."

"You mean Tom Broke-jaw?" Sanborn asked.

"No," Matthews said. "Maria Bartiromo, Wall Street's money honey. Get to her and you've got every analyst and broker in New York in the palm of your hands. If the story airs tonight on the East Coast, it will also reach all the brokers and money managers in Los Angeles before they go home."

Los Angeles! Sanborn's face lit up with excitement. "And we don't have to worry about insider information?"

"Not if you don't tell them anything they don't already know," Matthews replied.

That iced it. "Excellent, Mister Matt-hewssss! Excellent! We'll tell them exactly what they want to hear, Miss Gotttt. Have the camera crew wait in the lobb-e-e-e-e. I'll join them there in ten minutes."

But before Gott could leave, the heavy oak doors behind her swung open with a thud, and in marched Vicki Connors looking for a fight.

"Sterling, how dare you! How could you saddle me with a dog like the Centurion?"

Sanborn calmly and deliberately leaned back in his chair, fingered his suspenders, and pursed his lips.

"Why, Missssss Connorsssss," he began, in his very best BBC voice, "do come in and make yourself at home."

Connors leaned over his desk and looked Sanborn straight in the eye.

"Cut the crap, Sterling. You're not dealing with one of your usual low-level artistic flunkies here. I told you once before—I'm not lifting so much as a pencil for that Neanderthal flea bag. Got it?"

Sanborn paused and took a deep breath. He had been expecting a confrontation for some time. Just not at the moment.

"Miss Connorsssss, such emotion! I'm not asking you to marry the Centurionnnnn. I just want you to spend a little time with your colleagues and get rid of the old chap."

"Sterling," she charged, "I know how you operate and it's not going to work. All you want is my name on your precious Centurion, so my fans will buy the title."

"You're being far too kind to yourself, Miss Connorsss. Far too kind."

"The hell I am, Sterling. Like I'm not wise to that little stunt you pulled on the news last night? If you didn't want me so badly, you wouldn't have gone to such lengths to tie my name to the project without even telling me first."

Sanborn frowned. "Your name was never even mentioned at the press conference."

Connors promptly flipped Sanborn the bird. "When has that ever stopped you, Sterling? Let's get one thing straight. I don't work on characters that have been comatose for twenty-five years. My characters have life. They move. They're now. They're happening. They're cool. The Centurion isn't going anywhere regardless of what you and the rest of your Keystone Cops do."

She was dead serious. But it didn't matter to Sanborn. All he cared about was Connors' name. It was golden—the hottest name in the business, and he wanted it on the front cover of the Centurion's final book next to mine so it would sell big time. But his patience with her was wearing thin.

"Now see here, Miss Connorsss. I've had just about e-e-e-nough—"

"No, you see here, Sterling. I don't need you, I don't need this flea-trap operation you call a comic book company. And I sure as hell don't need the Centurion. If you don't like it maybe I should take a stroll over to Renegade."

Matthews sat there like a star-struck teenager. *What power. What forcefulness.* He eyed her left hand. *And no wedding ring!* The perfect woman for a man of his caliber and growing stature. But he knew if he didn't act quickly, she would walk right out the door and out of his life forever.

"Ah, excuse me," he interjected, like a politician who believed his own press clippings, "maybe I can help here."

He turned to Connors and said firmly, "We certainly appreciate your situation, Miss Connors. And we recognize that the Centurion is not the kind of character who's going to enhance your magnificent career—anymore than you've already done. At the same time, I don't think it's any secret that we need to make some dramatic changes around here to turn this company around. We need someone like you, someone with your great talent and stature to help pull this off. So we're asking that you put aside your own titles for a short time, for the good of the company, and help us bring this historic concept to life."

Connors, unconvinced, started to her shake head. But Matthews wasn't to be denied.

"Miss Connors, I know this is a terrible inconvenience. But I'm sure we can work up a suitable contractual arrangement with performance incentives that would alleviate your concerns and allow you to do a great job."

"Performance enhancements?" Connors asked suspiciously. "What kind of performance enhancements?"

Matthews smiled. "Perhaps stock options might be of interest to you?"

The Walrus nearly swallowed his tongue. But before he could object, Matthews calmly raised his hand.

"We don't want to take you away from your regular titles forever—just long enough to get this project off the ground, and um, flying, if you know what I mean."

Connors was flabbergasted. The last thing she expected was a contract and options.

"Are you serious?"

Matthews nodded. "Oh, very serious, Miss Connors. Very serious."

"And stock options? You'd really grant stock options?"

Matthews smiled once again. "Gobs of them, Miss Connors."

"All right," she replied, "but the contract must be absolutely clear. I want off this project in three weeks. Not a day more."

Matthews turned his head at Sanborn and winked. "How's that by you, BABE?"

The Walrus didn't pick up on the cue and bristled.

"Make it four weeks and you've got a deal," he said, reluctantly.

"Three-and-a-half weeks and that's final," Connors shot back.

Sanborn ran his fingers across his forehead and all around his very flushed face. "Ohhh, very well, Miss Connors. Three-and-a-half weeks it is."

Matthews clasped his hands together. "Fine. We have an agreement. I'll have Legal draw up the papers this afternoon."

And just like that it was over. Matthews had rolled the dice for the second time in two days and had come up a winner. Connors' name would be on the front cover of the Centurion's final adventure right next to mine. Sanborn would have his best seller. And Matthews would get a chance to know the company's superstar artist a little better.

"Now, Miss Connors," Matthews said, "if you don't mind, I think you'll find the rest of the task force waiting for you downstairs."

Connors nodded, turned and walked silently toward the door.

"I want the contract this afternoon," she said tersely.

"Oh, you'll have it, I promise," Matthews said. "I'll deliver it personally." *Honey, I'd drink your bath water this afternoon,* he fantasized, *if you asked me to...*

Connors glared at him and marched out the door.

"YOU IDIOT!" Sanborn screamed, as soon as they were alone. "WHY DID YOU OFFER HER A CONTRACT WITH STOCK OPTIONS??"

"Sterling, Sterling, Sterling," he said, calmly. "Think about it. We've just put a gun to her head. If she doesn't get this thing finished in three-and-a-half weeks—if she doesn't do a spectacular job—she'll get blamed. We won't. If she walks, we go public with the story and nobody in the business will look at her, let alone hire her. We can't lose with a contract. She can."

Sanborn waddled over to his aquarium and stared silently at the piranhas circling near the top of the tank. "The sharks would circle around her quickly if she fails," he said.

"That they would," Matthews added, sensing the kind of power he could exert over her in the coming weeks. "That they would."

"You know, Matt-hewsssss, I'm beginning to like the way you think," Sanborn said, flashing that devilish smile once more. "It's time we expanded your scope of responsibiliteeeees. What exactly is it that you do here again?"

Matthews was taken back. "Sterling, I head up Investor Relations."

"Investor Relations is boring," Sanborn snorted. "You talk to the same mindless imbeciles on Wall Street every single day. One day you tell the analysts bad news and the stock goes down, then you call them back the very next day and say, 'the news isn't really all that bad,' and it goes up. They're like little puppies. They beg. You give. They beg some more. You do pre-disclosures, and they just lap it up. I would e-e-e-e-magine after a while it gets very tiring."

Indeed it had. "Now that you mention it, Sterling, the job has grown a little tedious—"

"I knew it!" Sanborn gushed. "I'm going to give you the most critical job in the whole company next to mine, Matt-hewssss. I want you to take personal charge of the Centurion operation."

Matthews' heart slumped. It wasn't at all what he wanted. "But Sterling, I've never been involved in the creative side of the business. I don't know a thing about making a comic book character."

"Welllll," Sanborn mused, "that's never stopped us around here before. I need someone devious that I can count on to keep on top of that task force. I want to know what they're doing all the time. Make sure they stay on schedule. I want to see progress! Bring me page proofs! Bring me illustrations! Bring me sketches every single day if you have to! And when you find out who our leak is I want to know imme-e-e-ediately Mister Matt-hewssss. Do I make myself clear?"

Matthews started to squirm—the mere thought of having to baby-sit subordinates was revolting—and Sanborn sensed his unease. So he threw Matthews a bone.

"One more thing," he said. "Don't let Miss Connorssssss out of your sight. Watch her like a hawk all the time! She's the key to this operation. If she bolts to Renegade, we're sunk. Do you understand me?"

Connors? Matthews started to feel better. More than better. He felt practically giddy. "Don't worry about a thing, Sterling. It will all go according to plan. I won't let her or the others out of my sight."

Sanborn crushed a few pieces of dried shrimp in his hand and dropped them into the tank, quickly prompting another feeding frenzy and grinned.

"I'm counting on it, Misterrrrr Matt-hews," he said, grinning, "I'm counting on it."

Chapter Seven

Excelsior Headquarters

The Centurion task force was less than a day old, but to me it already seemed like a year.

For starters, Sanborn put us in this dungeon of a conference room, deep in the bowels of the old Excelsior Building, that hadn't been used in years. We inherited four swivel chairs, one ratty LazyBoy recliner, a few creaky drawing tables, plenty of sweaty steam pipes, a family of ravenous mice, and a mountain of musty old comic books that hadn't been touched in years.

"Not exactly the Four Seasons," Billington joked when I turned on the lights.

If that wasn't bad enough, it became painfully apparent from the start that the chemistry among our little group was less than compatible. Combustible might be more like it. Instead of killing off the Centurion, we were on the verge of killing each other. By noon, we had already discussed and rejected more than a dozen possible scenarios.

"How about this," Billington offered. "A band of mutant guerrillas from Mars surround the Centurion and shoot him up with Xenon gas, the only substance that can harm him. The Centurion fights valiantly, but he takes a terrific pounding. He gets all beat up and his costume gets torn to shreds. In the end, they're too much for him. The guerillas capture him and put him in this chamber of horrors—just the kind of thing he's gotten out of before. But this time, they release the Xenon gas and he starts to suffocate. Slowly his super powers disappear and he dies. Just to make sure he's dead, the guerillas pile on him and pull him apart—total dismemberment—and they put his head on display as a trophy."

Vicki Connors raised her eyebrow and pretended to gag. "Mutant guerillas?"

Billington quickly sketched a mutant guerilla—one-hundred percent certifiably ugly—on his pad and held it up for everyone to see. "Cute, huh?"

Connors gagged. "You can't be serious. No one's going to buy that crap."

"How can you say that?" Billington snarled. "It's heart-pounding, it's gory, it's dramatic and blood-curdling. What more could you want in a story like this?"

"How about a little originality?" Connors replied. "This is the same sappy formula you use in every one of your stories. It's about as fresh as an old cigar."

Before anyone could utter another word, a shadowy figure appeared from behind the door.

"My, my, my, is this creative tension or is this creative tension?"

Matthews—our newly minted boss—waltzed into the room like a fast-moving thundercloud.

This wasn't the same Norbert Matthews we had overheard talking to Sanborn twenty-four hours ago. He was a changed man; all-new, all-knowing, all confident, all devious, and all full of himself.

"Now what do we have here boys and girls?" Matthews leaned over carefully and examined the pile of rejected sketches on the floor.

"We're not ready to discuss specifics yet," I said. "We're still working out the details—"

Matthews stood up and raised his right hand. "I know, I know. You're still in the conceptual stages. How droll. You said the same thing an hour ago. I hope I'm not detecting a pattern here, Mister MacAllister. For your sake, as well as mine. If you know what I mean."

Matthews held one of the discarded sketches up to the light. "Now this—THIS—might have some possibilities. Think of how horrified all those little twelve-year-olds will be when the world's mightiest superhero turns into Monkey Chow!"

Matthews laughed, a sinister, evil Vincent Price laugh that made even Connors shiver.

"What a terrible thing to say," snapped Julie McKinney. "You sound as if you take pleasure in scaring little kids."

Matthews casually adjusted his cuff links and collar. "We're going to have to do much more than scare the little buggers, Miss McKinney. We want them to be so sickened by the specter of the Centurion biting the dust that they'll all run home and tell their mommies and daddies what's happened to their beloved hero—"

"That way," Billington interrupted, "the baby boomers will run out and buy the last issue in droves, Trieste's stock price will continue to rise, and you and Sanborn will be even richer than you are now."

Matthews crushed the illustration into a tiny ball and tossed it into the trash.

"I can assure you Mister Billington that if you make the Centurion's death as bloody and horrific as we've asked you to, there will be no shortage of buyers," he sneered. "First the children, then the parents, then the comic book collectors, the media, and eventually, when sales match expectations, more investors than ever before will climb on board. So the sooner you do your job, the sooner this company's health will be restored. And then we'll be able to keep you and all your dysfunctional little colleagues here gainfully employed."

Then he slowly turned and cast a loving smile in Connors' direction.

"I'm so sorry to have to put you through all this, my dear. I had hoped this would be a pleasurable experience for everyone concerned."

Connors eyed him suspiciously from her chair. She detested Matthews almost from the moment she had met him. And she didn't like it that he was coming onto her like a lovesick elephant.

"I'd just as soon gag on my own vomit than have a 'pleasurable experience' with you. Got it?"

Matthews was floored. No woman had ever stood up to him so forcibly. No one had ever resisted his charms in such a direct manner. From anybody else, he would have been mortified. But coming from her, he found it positively, undeniably exhilarating. That is, until Connors crossed the line.

"In case you forgot, I have a contract," she said, handing it to him. "And it's signed. One way or the other, thanks to you, I walk away from this Mickey Mouse project in three-and-a-half weeks."

I stifled a laugh. But McKinney and Billington caught a serious case of the giggles. And that did it. It was more than Matthews' newly inflated ego could stand. Suddenly, the blue blood in him started boiling and his starry-eyed gaze turned serious. Dead serious.

Demean me, walk all over me, he thought. *But don't ever question my judgment in front of the hired help, bitch.*

Matthews grabbed the contract from her hand. "We will honor your contract, Miss Connors. But so shall you. For if this effort fails to ignite sales your name will be plastered all over the front cover of one of the most colossal marketing blunders of our time. I will see to it PERSONALLY."

With that, Matthews straightened his yellow power tie and marched quickly out of the room.

I didn't quite understand what he meant at first, but Connors got the message loud and clear. She had more to lose than any of us. Without her reputation, she was nothing, even to a potential employer. And it was clear that if the Centurion's demise bombed, Sanborn would hang her. In signing the contract, she had handed him the rope to do it.

Vicki's face turned beet red and her eyes welled up with tears. "Oh my God. How could I have been so naïve? They're going to blame this all on me. The world will think I blew this assignment. My name, my credibility—I'll be ruined."

"Vicki, get a grip on yourself," I said. "Nobody is going to get ruined. We're in this together, and we'll get through it together."

"You don't get it do you? she said, as the tears streamed down her face. "Sanborn plays for keeps. It's worse than being fired. He destroys reputations. He takes away your drawing power and squeezes you right out of the business. If we fail, he'll crucify me. Then eventually he'll come gunning for all of you."

I looked at Billington, as stoic as ever standing by his drawing table. He didn't say a word.

"I have to go," Connors said. With that, she gathered her purse and a few sketches and practically flew out of the room.

I didn't try to stop her. But to this day, I wish I had.

Scout Network Studio
Jersey City, New Jersey

For the first time in fifteen years—from the moment he had entered the world of broadcasting—Phil Plunkett's life wasn't going exactly according to script. His comic book "exclusive" had the whole industry buzzing. Competing networks were crediting Scout with the scoop. CNN and ABC had even called to interview him about the story. But not everyone at Scout was impressed. Tapes of the newscast were being replayed all over the studio. Reporters and technicians howled at the way he had hijacked the production booth. One radio disc jockey at a local Scout affiliate even replayed audio portions of the report on his morning show as a gag. All of which made Scout's top brass in New York very angry.

"Phil, in all the years I've been in this business, I've never seen anything like the stunt you pulled last night," charged Will Booth, Channel Seven's reigning and all-powerful station manager. "What made you think you could take it upon yourself to change the newscast like that without telling anyone first?"

Plunkett didn't answer. For too long he had played dumb, selling his soul for the sake of a paycheck. But no more. His moment of liberation had arrived. And he had decided he would do what any self-respecting journalist with a scoop would do in this situation—rub everyone's noses in it.

"Do you know what kind of chaos we'd have here if everybody just decided to rewrite the newscast whenever they felt like it, Phil?" Booth asked.

Plunkett shrugged. "Dan Rather does it."

"Goddammit, Phil!" Booth yelled. "You're not Dan Rather. You want people to like you, don't you?"

Plunkett nodded. "Sure, I do."

"You want people to watch you, don't you, Phil?"

"Of course."

"You want people to believe what you're saying, don't you, Phil?"

Plunkett nodded again.

"You don't want some strange idiot walking up to you on a street corner, clubbing you over the head, and asking you for some goddamned frequency, do you Phil?"

"No, no, I guess not."

"Then take my word for it, Phil, you don't want to act like Dan Rather. It's just common sense."

Booth ran his fingers through his silver hair—what little was left of it after thirty-three years in this god-forsaken, deadline-driven, image-obsessed business—and popped a videotape into the VCR behind his desk.

"Every time I look at this tape I get a little angrier, Phil. You ignored every single plea from the production booth to stop. And you blind-sided the remote crew with an intro that they had no idea was coming."

Booth fast-forwarded the tape to the exact spot where Maria Vasquez-Mitchell had started her live report the night before.

"Look at this," he pointed to the monitor. "You got Maria so flustered she couldn't even roll her 'R's.'"

Plunkett forced back a laugh.

"Here we are trying to up our audience demographics in the Hispanic market and what happens? We've got an Hispanic reporter live on air who can't even roll her 'Rs'."

Booth rolled the tape forward again. "But it gets even better. You stacked the graphics bank with pictures no one knew anything about, and you rigged it up so you could work it all by yourself from the studio. If that wasn't bad enough, you drove Manny so wild that he nearly had a heart attack at the end of the broadcast."

Plunkett wasn't surprised—Schaffi was a heart attack waiting to happen.

"Phil, what do you have to say for yourself?"

Plunkett leaned back in his chair and propped his feet up on Booth's desk. "Give it to me straight," he said. "Did I look good or what?"

Booth buried his head in his hands and rubbed his eyes in frustration. "You know, Phil, you deserve to be thrown outta here on your ass."

Then he exhaled and stared at Plunkett as though disaster was imminent.

"And if it was up to me, Phil, you'd be filing for unemployment right now. But it's not. Damn, if you're not the luckiest son-of-a-bitch alive today."

Plunkett sat up straight. "What do you mean?"

"The overnight Nielsens came in and last night's show was the highest-rated newscast we've had in three years."

"You're kidding?" Plunkett asked.

"No, I'm not," Booth deadpanned. "Not only did people watch, they've been lighting up the switchboard like a Christmas tree ever since."

Plunkett jumped from his chair and shook his fist. "Yessssss!" he shouted at the top of his lungs. "I knew I was onto something."

"Apparently Sydney thought so too," Booth said, with a truly pained look on his face.

Sydney? Plunkett couldn't believe it. "Sydney Lockwood saw the report?"

"He picked it up off the network satellite feed in Australia." Booth picked up a fax from his desk marked "Urgent/Confidential" and began reading it out loud.

"'Phil's onto something over at Excelsior. No telling what Sanborn's got up his sleeve. Pass along my compliments—he did a hell of a job. Tell him to continue running with the story. We'll all be watching. Sydney Lockwood.'"

Booth shook his head. "It came in this morning from Brisbane."

Plunkett was ecstatic. At last! Recognition for something other than a nice smile.

"Uh, there's one more thing, Phil," Booth said sheepishly. "It pains me to do this, but Lockwood also asked me to present you with this cash award for $2,500 for breaking the story."

He flung the check across his desk in Plunkett's direction.

"Go after the story, like the man says, Phil, but so help me, if you ever pull another stunt like this, I'll have you doing the weather outside. Understand?"

Plunkett cocked his eyebrow, his left "now-isn't-this-a-surprising-development" eyebrow, leaned over Booth's desk and winked. "You betcha."

"All right, that's enough," Booth said. "Take your check and get the hell outta my sight."

Plunkett quickly headed for the door. "By the way, Will," he said, "how's Manny doing?"

Booth downed what little was left of the cold coffee in his mug. "He's in good condition. But they want to keep him in the hospital for observation until the end of the week. Just in case."

"Gee, I'll have to pay him a visit," Plunkett said, waving the check in his hand. "I can't wait to tell him the good news."

Chapter Eight

Excelsior Headquarters

Back in New York, a pony-tailed television cameraman adjusted a microphone clip on Sanborn's tie.

"This will only take a minute," he said. "Then you can sit down."

"Take your time, my good man, take your time," the Walrus said. "Nothing is too good for our friends in the me-e-e-e-dia."

Matthews waited anxiously in the distance for the arrival of Maria Bartiromo, Wall Street's reigning media queen.

"Remember, Sterling," he whispered just before the camera crew ushered him into an obscure corner, "steer the conversation toward all the positive things we're doing to improve Excelsior's performance. That's what the analysts will be looking for. And if she asks, deny everything in the Scout report."

Sanborn nodded. He knew exactly what to do. A few moments later a ravishingly beautiful woman with chestnut brown hair and fiery red lips walked up to Sanborn and introduced herself.

"Mister Sanborn," she said, all sugar and smiles, "my name is Maria Bar—"

"No need for introductions, my dear," the Walrus interjected. "I'm one of your biggest fansssss."

"Well, aren't you sweet, Mister Sanborn," she said. "Now this won't take long at all. As soon as the cameraman gives us the cue, we'll start taping. You just relax."

"Very good," Sanborn said. "I am in your capable hands."

Matthews, watching quietly out of camera range, couldn't wait for the interview to begin for he knew the exposure would almost certainly cause Trieste's stock to jump.

Once the lights were in place, and Sanborn and the Queen were seated, the interview shifted into high gear.

"We're here today in New York with Sterling Sanborn the Third, Chairman of Excelsior Comics, which publishes such well-known comic book characters as the Centurion, Commando and Caldor the Jungle King," the Queen proclaimed into her microphone.

"Mister Sanborn, why don't you say hello to our viewers."

Sanborn stared at the camera somewhat puzzled. "You want me to say hello, my dear?" he asked.

The Queen giggled. "Now don't be shy, Mister Sanborn, the camera won't bite you."

Sanborn stared directly into the camera lens, like a fish peering out of an aquarium, and reluctantly obeyed. "Ah-hem. Hel-l-l-l-o and welcome to Excelsior Comics."

"Very nice, Mister Sanborn," she smiled. "Yesterday, right here in this lobby, you announced a replacement for Matt Payne, the man who created the Centurion. Tell me, how do you replace a living legend?"

Sanborn cleared his throat. "Welllll, there aren't a whole lot of living legends walking around out there looking for work. But we really didn't focus so much on that aspect of the search. We wanted someone who would preserve the great tradition of the Centurion-n-n, someone who would do what was best not only for the long-term health of the character, but for the compane-e-e-e-e—"

Before he could finish, the Queen retrieved a large tubular canister from behind her chair. "Mister Sanborn, this contains a very special drawing of the Centurion. Actually, it's a poster. Would you mind holding it up so that everyone at home can see it?"

The Walrus eyed the tube as if it had some exotic disease. *This is really peculiar,* he thought.

"Mister Sanborn?"

"Uh, whatever you'd like, my dear," he said.

Sanborn slowly rose from his chair, held the rolled poster up to his chin, and then let it unfurl over his pear-shaped belly. It was a standard issue Centurion poster, complete with Matt Payne's autograph scrawled across the bottom.

"The Centurion's been around for a long time, almost fifty years now, isn't that right Mister Sanborn?"

"Yes, that's correct, my dear. But—"

The Queen cut him off again. "Would you mind telling our viewers what goes into the making of a Centurion comic book?"

This time Sanborn frowned. He had no idea. But he tried once again to steer the conversation toward the company's performance.

"Ummm, it's a very detailed pro-cessss," he said. "Much more intricate than you can possibly eeeee-magine. But, you know, we're looking for some very big things from our new Centurion team. And I can promise you and everybody who's watching today that that this makeover will have a tre-e-e-emendously beneficial impact on the company's performance. And furthermore—"

"Excuse me, Mister Sanborn," the Queen interjected. "I have a letter here that we recently received from eleven-year-old Larry Siegel from Elkins, West Virginia. He writes, 'I love the Centurion. He's my favorite super hero and I've written several adventures about him for my English class. I think they'd make great comics. In fact, they're probably a lot better than some of the new ones you've been coming out with.'"

The Queen batted her thick eyelashes and paused. "Isn't that cute?"

Sanborn forced a smile. "How quaint."

"Well, Mister Sanborn," the Queen said, "how about it? What do you have to say to young Larry and all our viewers? Do you ever use story ideas from your readers?"

Sanborn honestly didn't know. And at this point, his patience was all but gone.

"Ummm, excuse me, my dear," he said, putting his hand over her microphone, "isn't CNBC interested in more important things than this?"

"Why, Mister Sanborn," she replied, "I don't know. I'm not with CNBC. You'll have to ask them yourself."

Sanborn's eyes shifted quickly from side to side. "You're not from CNBC—CEEEEE-NBC?"

"Oh, no, Mister Sanborn," the Queen smiled. "I'm with the Cable Broadcasting Network for Children—CBNC."

"But you're Maria Bartiromo," Sanborn said.

She shook her head and laughed. "No, no, no Mister Sanborn, people mistake me for her all the time. I'm Maria BARBIE. And this is a feature for our Saturday Morning Children's Hour. You know, 'Kiddie World,' where we go 'round and 'round and 'round the world."

Sanborn's face turned bright red. His blood started to boil. And worst of all, he had forgotten once again that he was wearing a live mike on his lapel.

"Do you mean to tell me I'm being interviewed for a goddamned kidde-e-e-e-e-e show?"

Barbie gasped. "Why, yes, Mister Sanborn," she said. "We told the security guard where we were from and he said he checked it out with you."

"Well, obviously he didn't check bloody-y-y-y well enough!"

Then, in full view of the camera, Sanborn flung the Centurion poster across the lobby and ripped the microphone off his tie.

"Mister Sanborn!" Barbie couldn't believe it. "You wouldn't want to disappoint the children now, would you?"

"To hell with the bloody little beggars," he yelled. "If they were buying the Centurion in the first place, I wouldn't be going through all this bullshit right now! Good day, Miss Barb-e-e-e-e-e-e!"

With that, Sanborn stormed off the makeshift set and scurried into the elevator. Matthews buried his head in his hands, and grew sick to his stomach just thinking about the damage this would inflict on Trieste's stock.

After Connors left, Julie, Billington and I continued working well into the night. Billington was convinced we were onto something big, so we stayed at it. The next thing I knew, it was nearly midnight and I was running out of gas.

"A tired soldier's a dead soldier," Billington said. "The war can wait. Time to call it a day."

He picked up his trench coat and headed out the door, clutching a wrinkled issue of *Soldiers of Fortune* in his hand.

I should have followed right behind him, but I didn't. I slumped back in my chair—alone with my thoughts—and stared aimlessly at the storyboards he and Julie had been working on. It was an awful, ghastly scene. Here was the mighty Centurion, once the very picture of strength and virtue—the character I used to imitate as a kid—being beaten to a pulp.

"You know you really shouldn't take this so personally."

I jumped. I thought I was alone. But when I turned around I saw Julie's smiling face staring back at me.

"It's not like the Centurion is real or anything. It's just ink and paper."

"I know. But when I see this, I just get this awful feeling deep inside."

"Maybe you're working too hard," she said.

"Is there any other way to work around here?" I asked.

"We say the same thing at school before finals," Julie replied. "But we never let that get in the way of a good time."

"So what do you do?" I asked.

"Hit the Alibi."

"I know the place," I said. "How do you think I survived four years of graphic design at Pratt?"

Julie smiled, an impetuous sort of smile. "I was supposed to meet some friends there tonight. But they canceled. Wanna go?"

I hesitated. There was so much to do and I couldn't work over the weekend because I was flying back to Buffalo in the morning for my mother's surprise birthday party. But something inside me said go.

"What the hell, why not?"

So I grabbed my coat from the chair, shut off the lights and locked the door. All the regular staff artists and writers had gone home hours ago, and the cleaning crew didn't work on Friday nights. So I assumed we were the last to leave the building. We weren't.

As soon as the elevator doors closed behind us, Mitch Gerber appeared from the shadows and quietly made his way down the narrow, marble-lined hallway that led to our conference room. In all the years he'd been at Excelsior, Gerber had never done anything like this before. But these were desperate times. It was bad enough that I had the job he wanted. Now the rumors that he had been hearing all day—horrible rumors about the Centurion's fate—were making things even worse. He had to find out what was really going on.

Getting inside the conference room was no problem. Gerber was small enough to slip through an old air vent just above the floor line in a dark corner of the hall. Once he was in, he carefully popped the metal grate back into place. And when he was sure that no one had followed him, he pulled a penlight from his pocket and began poking around.

Gerber moved quickly from table to table, until he stumbled into a large easel at the front of the room with some of our early sketches. When he regained his footing, he flashed his light on the pad and couldn't believe what he saw—his beloved Centurion, the very light of his life, being extinguished right before his very eyes.

Gerber fell to the floor in anguish right next to our reject pile. Of course, he didn't know it was trash. But when he recovered, he saw it all—a veritable gallery of death—including one headline that confirmed his worst fears: "The Final Chapter: Death to the Centurion."

"My God!" he gasped. How can they do this? *How can they just throw away fifty years of tradition? What kind of sick people are they?*

"Nooooooo!" he finally screamed, forgetting where he was. "I won't let them do this to you, my son."

Gerber furiously ripped apart several sketches and flung them to the floor. He was about to go for more, but stopped suddenly when he heard a noise outside the old conference room.

He listened for a moment or two, but all he could hear was the sound of his own heart pounding. He inched his way toward the door, like a church mouse. But there was nothing. No sounds. No shadows dancing in the light under the door. Just dead silence. When he was certain he was alone, Gerber slipped back through the air vent and into the hallway. He reappeared a short time later—shaking like a leaf—outside his own office several floors above. But when he turned on the lights, his heart nearly stopped.

"The late hours making you a little jumpy Mister Gerber?"

Sitting in his chair with his feet perched comfortably on his desk was Matthews.

"I admire your dedication, Mr. Gerber. But do you always do your homework on the lower level of the building?"

Gerber went as white as a ghost.

"Come, come, come, Mister Gerber, relax," Matthews said. "I know how you creative types are. Great ideas don't happen behind a desk. They come to you on the subways, in the shower, and sometimes even in very dark places. Isn't that right, Mitch?"

Gerber nodded. "Yeah, something like that."

"Exactly!" Matthews sat up straight in Gerber's chair and folded his arms across his chest. "Everyone needs their own little fortress of solitude to get their creative juices flowing. I can see where you might find the dungeon an ideal incubator for good ideas."

Gerber thought for second about where he had been and what he had just seen.

"You ain't gonna find any good ideas down there," he said.

"My sentiments exactly, Mitch. And that's why I'm here. I'm having a little problem downstairs with the creative team that Mister MacAllister is heading."

Gerber slowly shook his head in disgust.

"Ahhh, do I detect some professional jealously here, Mitch?"

"Jealously? I ain't got nothing to be jealous of."

Matthews grinned. "You think you could do a better job?"

"Hell," Gerber replied, "a blind man could do a better job. I was drawing the Centurion before any of 'em was even born—"

"You know," Matthews interrupted, "that's exactly what MacAllister said, too."

Gerber looked up. "He said what?"

"You heard me. I was right there when he said it. Sterling Sanborn said to him, 'Why should I pick you over Mitch Gerber to handle the Centurion? He really knows the character better than anyone else.'"

"What did MacAllister say?"

"He looks Sanborn straight in the eyes and goes, 'Gerber's too old. He's not with it. He ought to be put out to pasture.'"

Gerber's jaw tightened like a vice. "Why that little creep."

"Oh, there's more, Mitch," Matthews continued. "I could tell you stories you wouldn't believe."

Gerber pulled up a chair and sat down. "Try me."

Matthews looked quickly from side to side and then whispered into his ear.

"Confidentially, just between you and me, I think he's out to destroy the company," Matthews said.

"How so?" Gerber asked.

"Well, I don't have proof but I'd bet my life he's secretly plotting to kill off the Centurion."

Gerber tried to act surprised. "You mean he's not supposed to kill him?"

"Oh, no, absolutely not. Sanborn ordered the task force to remake the character. Polish him up, return him to the glory years of the past. Those where his exact words."

"Then why would he want to kill him?" Gerber asked.

Matthews lit a cigarette and inhaled. "You figure it out, Mitch. Lockwood's been trying to bury us for years. But he can't do it from the outside. So he sends in one of his top guns—MacAllister—to spy on us and bring us down from within.

"MacAllister weasels his way into a plum job—the job that you rightfully deserve. He starts leaking highly sensitive information about us to Lockwood's TV stations. Then once he's won over Sanborn's confidence and has free reign, he sets his sights on the mother load—the Centurion. If he brings down the Centurion, all our other characters will fall like dominos."

"Jez-us Christ," Gerber said.

"It's flawless," Matthews continued. "Except for one thing."

"What's that?" Gerber asked.

"You and I are onto him. We're going to stop him before he can do any more damage."

"We oughta call the cops right now," Gerber said.

Matthews frowned. "That's not exactly what I had in mind."

"Maybe the FBI," Gerber continued.

"Can't do that either," Matthews said.

"Why not?"

"We don't have any evidence, Mitch. The first thing they're going to ask us is 'where's the evidence?' We need something to hang him with."

"What kind of evidence?" Gerber asked.

"I need something concrete I can take to Sanborn that would prove MacAllister is plotting to kill the Centurion and take us all down."

Gerber scratched his head. "You mean like illustrations?"

Matthews rubbed his hands together and grinned. "Exactly. But I can't get to them. I'm not welcome in that conference room anymore. And to be honest, I'm not quite as adept as you are at covert surveillance."

Gerber thought for a second. "I can get you illustrations. Lots of them from down there."

"Excellent!" Matthews forced back a grin. It was exactly what he wanted to hear. *He could keep tabs on us without getting his hands dirty.*

"You know the old saying, Mitch. One man's trash is another man's treasure. Maybe yours."

"Will it help get rid of MacAllister?" Gerber asked.

"Not only that, Mitch, it might even save your precious Centurion from an early grave."

Gerber's hand stopped shaking. "You'll have something on your desk in the morning. Leave it to me."

"Very good, Mitch. I won't forget this."

Matthews rose from the chair, straightened his gold cuff links, and walked to the door. "You know, it's such a shame that the younger artists are so disrespectful these days. Somebody really ought to teach them a lesson."

Chapter Nine

Puerto Vallarta, Mexico

Early the next morning, Matt Payne was standing atop the observation deck of the luxury cruise liner 'Royal Oaks,' off the coast of Puerto Vallarta, Mexico, smoking a Cuban cigar in stony silence. He had never seen a sunrise as spectacular as the one that greeted him early that day. And God, how he hated it—not just the nauseatingly unrelenting sun, but the fresh air, the glistening water, and most of all the phony American tourists who would soon be racing from one end of the boat to another, drenched in sun tan oil, searching for the perfect tan. This was light years away from where he really wanted to be—back at his old drawing table slugging it out against impossible deadlines.

Of course, Payne knew he'd hate the cruise even before he stepped on board. But he would rather have choked to death than give up the tickets from his retirement party in New York. Besides, Alix deserved a vacation. In all the years he had worked at Excelsior, the most extravagant trip they had ever taken together was to Myrtle Beach. And even that was just for a few days. This time he'd endure it all just for her.

"Matt," Alix called out from the deck below. "What are you doing up here all by yourself?"

He held both arms out to the sea, as if he were about to part the water.

"My dear," he shouted back to her, "I'm marveling at the breath-taking pace of life here in Mexico. I don't know how much more excitement I can handle today."

Alix ran up the stairs, still the picture of health and vitality after all these years, and looked him straight in the eyes.

"Matt Payne! You're beginning to sound like a constipated old fart."

Payne fingered his cigar and grunted. "I AM a constipated old fart. The food on this tub is killing me."

"Well, here's your chance to get away from it all," she said. "The first shuttle for town is leaving in ten minutes. It's not too late to sign up. Come with me."

"And miss another once-in-a-lifetime opportunity at intellectual enlightenment with the natives?" he said. "You go dear. Enjoy yourself."

Alix scowled. "We've been away for two days and all you've done is lumber around this ship like a wounded sea elephant."

Two days, Payne thought to himself, *it feels more like two years.*

"If you're going to feel sorry for yourself, you're going to do it alone because I'm taking that tour," she said.

"Very well, my dear. Whatever makes you happy."

"Here," she said, handing him a large envelope, "maybe this will make you feel better. It came when we docked—express from New York. See, they haven't forgotten about you completely."

Payne's face lit up. *At last, signs of intelligent life.*

"And one more thing, mister." Alix snatched the cigar from his mouth, and tossed it overboard.

"Hey! Why'd ya do that?"

Alix put her hands on her hips. "What did Doctor Mattimore say about being careful in a tropical climate with your asthma?"

Payne shook his head from side to side. "Yeah, well, what the hell does he know anyway?"

Then she planted a kiss on his cheek and marched down the stairwell to the main level.

"Don't drink anything that doesn't come in a can!" he yelled to her.

Then, when he was sure she couldn't see him, Payne galloped down the stairwell on the opposite side of the observation deck and rushed back to their cabin. Once inside, he ripped open the envelope and pulled out a large sheet of drawing paper, which was folded neatly into napkin-sized squares, and a single, badly typed letter.

Payne opened the letter and slowly read it aloud.

"The Sentinel of Light faces his darkest hour. Death knocks at the door. But do not fear. Justice will prevail. We will carry on the fight in your absence. We will not abandon the Centurion, nor will we rest until our hero is saved."

Great. Just what I need, he thought. *Even here the crackpots still manage to find me.*

Payne unfolded one of the illustrations and gasped. "My God—" There, staring back at him in a lifeless pose, was a sketch of the Centurion impaled on a flagpole beneath Old Glory. Payne recognized the style instantly—it was Billington's handiwork. That much he was certain. And it nearly brought him to tears.

"Oh, Lord, those rotten bastards! You miserable, rotten bast—"

Before he could finish the sentence Payne dropped the illustration and gasped for air. He tried desperately to inhale but nothing was reaching his lungs. All he could feel was pain—intense, heart-pounding pain.

He sat up on the edge of the bed, hoping to catch his breath. But it was no use. It was as severe an asthma attack as he had ever experienced, and the only thing that could save him was his inhaler. But where did he put it? He frantically scanned the room. Was it in the desk? The chair? The bookshelf? *Think, man. Think quickly.* Then he remembered. It was in the top drawer of the dresser.

Payne staggered across the room, the attack intensifying with every step. By the time he reached the dresser, his face was blue. *Can't breathe. Need air. Please, God, let me breathe.* He lunged for the inhaler, but it was too late. He felt a cold, suffocating chill racing through his lungs, and then he collapsed, face first on the dresser.

Chapter 10

Buffalo, N.Y.

By the time I had boarded a flight for Buffalo that very same morning, two things had happened.

First, Sanborn's televised tirade on the Children's Network had quickly become a media sensation. What should have been nothing more than a harmless appearance on a Saturday morning kid's show was getting top billing on every network news broadcast around the world. Everyone who saw the report condemned him. Politicians, business leaders, schoolteachers, mothers and anyone else who could get access to a television camera and a microphone all weighed in against him. Had it not been for the fact that the financial markets were closed for the weekend, Trieste's stock would have almost certainly taken a nosedive right then and there.

Second, I didn't want to admit it, but I had a great time with Julie at the Alibi—a really GREAT time. We talked all night—right up until they closed the joint—about the Centurion, Sanborn and life in general. I kept thinking it was probably the beer. But there was more to it than that. When she voluntarily gave me her phone number and a kiss good night, I found myself not wanting to leave.

Canceling my trip home wasn't an option. Ma would have killed me if I had missed her eightieth birthday party. The entire family was coming in from all over the country to celebrate. My older brother, Scott, his wife and three kids were there from California. My younger sister, Colleen, and her brood—four boys, her husband and an Irish Wolfhound named Sam—had made the trek from Vermont. There would also be an assortment of aunts, uncles and cousins on hand—relatives I'd only see at weddings and funerals.

As for Mom, time had done little to slow her down.

"Richard Stewart Mac-Allister!" she said, shortly after I had walked through the door. "Just because you've flown in all the way from New York doesn't mean that you've got a license to turn this place into a pigpen."

"Ma," I smiled, "now why, after all these years, would I think that?"

"Oh, don't I know you, Richard," she said, scowling at my luggage on the floor. "In all the years you lived here, you never picked up a thing. Heaven knows I tried to change you. You're just like your father, you are. I can only imagine what your apartment must look like."

"If you ever come to New York to visit," I said, "you might just be surprised."

"Oh, no. You can keep New York. I had enough lunacy in my life raising you and your brother and sister. I don't need to go all the way to New York to go crazy again."

"It's good to see you too, Ma," I said, hugging her.

"Just the same, Richard, get your bag upstairs before the rest of the family shows up for the party. Understand?"

"Aye, aye, captain," I said with a formal salute.

"And while you're here," she continued, "do something about that bedroom of yours. You moved out and I inherited your junk. All those silly comic books. If you don't do something with them I'm going to throw them away."

Comic books? "All my old comic books are here?"

"That and God only knows what," she said. "You should have seen what I found in your brother's room when he left."

"Gee, Ma, those comic books might be worth a fortune."

Ma frowned. "Only if you find somebody dumb enough to buy them from you, Richard."

So much for the homecoming. But I didn't mind. Next to the turmoil at Excelsior, this was heaven. So I picked up my bag and marched upstairs. How quiet the house seemed. I peered into Scott's old room, half expecting to see him lumbering about in his shorts. The bathroom door was open—something I never saw as long as Colleen lived here. My room was exactly as I had remembered it; sports pennants and posters still adorned the walls; my maple-colored bed was there—sagging as it always had in the middle; an old black and white picture of my father, who had died in an explosion at the steel plant when I was just a kid, sat on top of the dresser. And hanging on the closet door was a giant poster of the Centurion leaping into the air. The old guy looked pretty good, too. But when I reached inside for a hanger I jumped.

"BOOO!"

"Uncle Ricky! Uncle Ricky! Did I scare you?"

Staring back up at me with the biggest toothless grin I've ever seen, was Scott's oldest son, my nine-year-old nephew, Stewart.

"How long have you been in there?" I asked, my heart racing.

"A long time, maybe ten minutes," the boy giggled. "But Grandma told me it was okay. She let me stay overnight so I could surprise you. Were you really surprised?"

"More than that," I said, as I hoisted him off the ground with a big hug. "What have you been doing in here while you were waiting?"

Stewart handed me a comic book and a flashlight. "I was reading your old comic books, Uncle Rick."

I recognized it instantly. It was Excelsior Comics Number One, a reprint of the very first Centurion issue.

"My God, I haven't seen this in ages," I said. "I betcha it's worth some money."

Stewart shook his head. "Twenty-five bucks tops."

"But it's the first issue—"

"It's an anniversary reprint, Uncle Rick," he said. "It doesn't appreciate like the original."

"How do you know?" I asked.

"I looked it up in my price guide. A real number one goes for about $150,000."

"When did you become such an expert on comic books?"

Stewart popped his bubble gum and sat down on the edge of the bed. "I've got over three hundred comic books at home."

"Three hundred?" I asked. "Where did you get all the money?"

"Mom gave it to me. She says it's worth it if I stay out of her hair."

"You ever read the Centurion?" I asked.

Stewart rolled his eyes. "Nobody reads the Centurion anymore, Uncle Rick. He's not cool."

"Says who?" I asked.

"Welllll, none of my friends read him."

"What do they read?"

"Commando, Punisher and T-MEN—they're awesome."

"They're nothing compared to the Centurion," I told him.

"What makes him so special, Uncle Rick?"

"This is where it all started," I said, flipping through the book. "If it hadn't been for the Centurion there wouldn't be any Commando or Punisher or T-MEN."

Stewart scratched his head. "Go wan…"

"No, you go wan," I said. "Listen to this."

I stretched out across the bed, propped my head up on a pillow, and started reading out loud.

"*'An American excavation team is sifting through the rubble of an ancient Roman aqueduct when the earth begins to rumble.'*

"*'The team, led by the world-renowned archaeologist, Dr. Clayton Moore, is doomed. The force of the earth's motion brings the ancient stone walls of Rome tumbling down around them.'*

Stewart nuzzled up next to me to get a better view. "Are they buried alive?"

"Yep," I said. "They're trapped."

"Are they all gonna die, Uncle Rick?"

"What do you care? I thought you didn't think this was cool?"

Stewart rubbed his nose, just like his father, and sat completely still. So I turned the page and continued reading.

"'The tunnel leading out of the room is cut off by falling rock. Dr. Moore and three of his associates are hopelessly trapped and only a few minutes remain before their air supply is exhausted. But wait!' "

Stewart jumped.

"'One young man manages to escape. Peter Adams, a graduate student, vaults into an underground passageway, narrowly averting death.'"

Stewart's eyes were now glued to the page, exactly the way mine were when I had read the Centurion for the first time.

"'Dazed and injured, Adams wanders aimlessly around the underground passageway, desperately looking for a way out. Professor Moore! Professor Moore! Are you there, Peter asks? No answer. Finally, Adams stumbles over a giant rock and falls through a gaping hole in the ground.

"'When Adams regains consciousness he can't believe his eyes. He has emerged in an ancient underground burial vault.' "

Stewart reached over and grabbed the comic book from my hands. His eyes were as big as silver dollars.

"Are there people buried in there?" he asked.

"Yep, but not ordinary people."

"What kind of people, Uncle Rick?"

"Read it for yourself," I said.

Stewart did exactly that, picking up where I had left off.

"'While searching through the treasures, a ray of light breaks through a hole in the top of the cave and temporarily blinds Adams. He stumbles into a statue—a golden statue—of the ancient Roman god of the sun, Apollo.'"

"'Immediately, the room is filled with intense light radiating from the broken statue. The floor rumbles and the vault shakes with even more intensity than before. Suddenly, from out of nowhere, a bolt of lightning smashes into the wall behind him...and the statue of Apollo springs to life.'"

As he continued reading, my mind began to wander and my eyelids grew heavy. At some point, I must have dozed off and started dreaming. I found myself a young boy at church with my family on Easter Sunday a long time ago. In my hands was

Excelsior Comics Number One—the very same book that Stewart had discovered in the closet—and I was reading each page as if my very life depended on it.

"*Do not be afraid, my son. This is the tomb of the Centurion, the Roman guardian of justice, and these are the graves of the men who have become the Sentinel of Light throughout the ages. Thou are the first mortal to set foot in the tomb of the Centurion in a thousand years. The power of the Centurion is yours. Use its force wisely to protect all men from the evil that lurks deep within their hearts.*

"*Your life now has new purpose. You must always use your powers to fight evil. Never let anything stop you, my son ... never.*"

The entire story of the Centurion's life from death to rebirth replayed itself in my mind, a thrilling adventure ride that got better with every page. But then, suddenly, the thrill came to an abrupt halt. Everything around me seemed to dissolve—the comic book, the church, my mother, my brother and my sister. In their place stood an animated Centurion just like the one in my poster, decked out in full battle garb, drawing his sword from his side.

I reached out for him, but his hand suddenly pulled back and he recoiled in pain—unbearable pain.

The next thing I remember was awakening with a start.

"Uncle Rick, Uncle Rick! Wake up! Grandma says if we don't come downstairs and help her set the table we're not going to get any birthday cake."

Slowly, I sat up and got my bearings. I felt as if I had been sleeping for days.

"How long was I out?"

"Two hours." Stewart answered.

"Did you finish the Centurion?" I asked.

"A long time ago."

"The whole thing?"

"Uh-huh."

"Well, what do you think?" I asked.

Stewart handed the comic book to me and shrugged.

"What's that supposed to mean?"

"Too bad they don't make 'em like that anymore."

Stewart ran toward the door and stopped. "Grandma says you better not bring your comic books downstairs or you'll never see them again."

I got up to follow him, but something made me stop. Had the Centurion remained true to his original form—strong, vigilant and forceful—he would sell today.

Then it hit me. It could happen all over again. Here was a superhero who could recreate himself every generation. It was life from death; the heart and soul of the Centurion's story was a literary device as old as man. Payne himself had cast the die more than half a century ago. There was no reason why the Centurion couldn't come back from the dead once again—but this time like he was in his original, classic form. It would definitely sell.

The more I thought about it, the more sense it made. But I had to work fast while the idea was still fresh. So I fumbled through my wallet for Julie's phone number in New York and quickly starting dialing.

"Hello?"

"Julie?"

"Rick? Aren't you at your mother's?"

"Yep."

"Well, I was hoping you'd call but I didn't think it would be this soon."

"I just got this great brain storm and I couldn't wait to tell you about it."

"It must have been all the beer you drank last night," she giggled.

"No, it wasn't the beer, but something just as good," I said. "I think I've found a way to do more than just kill off the Centurion."

"You want to kill him off twice?"

"Not exactly," I replied. "But what would you think about killing him off and bringing him back to life?"

"Like resurrecting him from the dead?" Julie asked.

"Yeah, but not like he is now. We bring him back like he was in the beginning—the way Payne created him."

"You mean like the guy hanging on the wall at Excelsior with the heavy duty jaw?"

"That's it," I said. "It still works. It's the way the Centurion ought to be."

"What about Sanborn?" Julie asked.

"If we position it right, he's going to love it. Killing him off will create the big bang he wants. Then we'll make an even bigger splash when the old guy comes back to life."

"Have you figured out how we're going to resurrect him and make it believable?"

"Don't have to," I said. "It's been done before. Get this—in the very first issue he comes back from the dead. I've got it all here right in front of me. All we'll have to do is work out a new story line for the sequel."

"But we don't have much time, Rick."

"Do you think you can get Vicki and Mike together at the office when I get back in tomorrow night?" I asked.

"When's your flight?"

"I get into New York at six-thirty. I can take a taxi from the airport right to the office."

"I'll meet you there," Julie said. "And I'll call the others"

"I'll see you when I get in."

"Have a safe flight and give Ma a hug for me," Julie said.

"Thanks."

CLICK.

I hung up the phone, pulled out a pad and paper and immediately started writing. I felt like a kid again.

Chapter 11

Rye, N.Y.

Maxine Plunkett warmed her hands by the glow of the fireplace and admired her new twenty-four carat diamond engagement ring. Maxine wasn't the type to waste time. Once her divorce from Phil Plunkett had been finalized, she moved quickly to line up a successor. But this time she used her head, not her heart, and her husband-to-be was loaded.

"Tell me, Maxxi." A tall burly figure held her in his arms and gently kissed her on the lips. "Why do you love me so much?"

"Off hand, I can think of a few billion reasons, sweetie," she said with an adoring smile.

"A toast then," he said, raising his champagne glass. "To us."

"A toast," she said. "To you and me and our beautiful new home in Greenwich."

Rule Number 68: When you win big, live it up because the next battle could be your last. Mike Billington had just won his biggest battle ever—Maxine Plunkett had agreed over dinner to become Mrs. Michael Billington, wife of the lone surviving heir to Warren Billington's family fortune—and he was ready to celebrate. Who would have guessed it?

"I can't wait to tell everybody," he said.

"What about Larry?" Her son was her only real concern.

"Larry's a smart kid," Billington said, pouring more champagne. "He probably already suspects something's up. It's better we're up front with him from the start."

Maxine gave him a big hug. "I know, darling. I know. Let's just get this over with. It's not easy being the mother of James Bond Jr. For all I know he could be listening outside the door right now."

Billington's heart suddenly skipped a beat. *Outside the door?*

He quickly lunged for the swinging doors that separated the living room from the kitchen. But Larry wasn't on the other side. He wasn't hiding behind a chair, and he wasn't sitting on the balcony, either. Billington made sure of it. Still, he couldn't be certain that Larry wasn't tracking his every move. Larry was good—REALLY GOOD. So good, in fact, that there was no reason why he had to eavesdrop in person. From the security of his bedroom, Larry sat next to the cordless telephone on his desk, listening intently to the entire conversation over the phone's intercom system. It was so basic—so counter to the sophisticated eavesdropping techniques that Billington had come to expect from the twelve-year old—that he had overlooked it in each of his previous intelligence sweeps.

But needless to say, Larry was not a happy camper. *How could she marry this big oaf*, he wondered? *He's nothing like Dad. He's not a television celebrity. He has no sense of humor. All he's ever good for is an occasional free comic book.*

Billington returned to the living room empty handed. "All clear," he said. "I'm sure he's going to be fine with this, Maxxi. Now try to relax."

Maxine reluctantly agreed.

"Just one thing, Max," Billington said. "I don't want Larry to know what's going on at work. I can't chance Phil finding out any more about what we're up to. If word gets out about what we're really doing with the Centurion, it will be all over the airwaves."

Maxine frowned. "Who cares? You make it sound like that silly cartoon is a matter of life and death."

Billington gently squeezed her hand. "Maxxi, just go along with me on this—"

She rolled her eyes. "My lips are sealed. No one will hear from me that the Centurion is going to die, even though he never really lived and can't die anyway."

"Shall we get on with it?" he asked.

Larry turned off the intercom switch and jumped onto his bed. He already knew everything he needed to know.

By the time I arrived at Excelsior's headquarters in New York, I was two-and-a-half hours late and soaked to the bone. The weather not only delayed my flight to New York, but it had flooded many of the main arteries leading into Manhattan. To make matters worse, Matthews had left two ominous sounding messages on my answering machine at home. Our presentation to Sanborn had been moved up more than a week to nine o'clock the very next morning, leaving us only that evening to piece together rough story boards for the Centurion's final issue. I should have been upset about it. But I was too excited for that. I had a plan for pulling off the Centurion's demise that I could live with; a plan that would satisfy everyone—Sanborn, Wall Street, and most of all, the few remaining diehards who called themselves Centurion fans. There was more than enough time for the task force to piece together rough storyboards overnight.

"Jee-zus Christ, kid, it's Sunday night," said a crumpled old security guard at the front desk. "Don't you ever go home?"

"You know me, Charlie," I said, wet as a noodle. "I can never stay away too long."

"Go wan upstairs, Mac," he said. "Miss McKinney's been waiting up there all night for you."

I knew I could count on Julie. She was the best thing about this place, and as I headed for the elevator I could hardly wait to see her. Apparently the feeling was mutual, because when the giant doors swung open she was there.

"Rick! I was getting worried."

She wrapped her arms around me with a kiss that practically took my breath away.

"It's, uh, good to see you too," I said, "but—"

"Oh, Rick, I'm sorry. I shouldn't have done that here."

"It's okay," I replied. "But what if the others see us?"

Julie stepped back, as the doors closed behind us. "No one else is here."

"Did Mike and Vicki leave?" I asked.

"Mike said he had something really important going on that he couldn't get out of, and Vicki, well, I left messages on her answering machine all day but she never returned the calls."

"Just as well," I said. "Maybe we'll get just as much done without a crowd tonight."

"What do you mean?" she asked.

"Matthews moved Sanborn's presentation up to tomorrow morning. We go in at nine."

Julie shook her head. "We don't even have an outline done yet."

"We may have more than we think," I said. "Mike had the right idea in his last concepts. We have to soften it up—inject some of the Centurion's history in it—and set it up for a sequel where he comes back to life."

The elevator stopped at the lower level, and we made our way in the dark to the dungeon.

"There's something I have to tell you," she said. "We don't have Billington's concepts anymore." Then she gently nudged open the door to the conference room and turned on the lights.

I couldn't believe it. The dungeon looked like it had been hit by a tornado. Papers were strewn all over the floor. The conference table was covered with illustrations, and Mike's easel was empty.

"What happened?"

"I don't know," she said, "this is how I found it when it when I got here at six."

"Did you call Security?"

Julie nodded. "They came down, looked at it and said it didn't look much different from the way we left it. But all of Billington's sketches are gone. And from what I can tell some of Vicki's work is missing too."

I could feel a really bad headache coming on. "Damn. This isn't going to make things easier."

Julie fished through the mess. "Any idea what we're going to do now?"

"How good is your memory?" I asked.

"You talking about Billington's mockups?" Julie replied.

"Yep. How much of them do you remember?"

"It's hard to forget them. They were pretty grisly."

"Good," I said, "I'll write. You draw. What I've got in mind tracks pretty closely to Billington's original story line. The only thing that changes are the bad guys. We replace Billington's evil alien by borrowing a villain from the past."

I reached into my suitcase and retrieved one of the old comic books I had found in my bedroom.

"Here's our killer," I said, pointing to the cover. It was an early classic that featured a clash of the titans—the Centurion versus Hades.

"Hades?" Julie asked, with a puzzled look.

"Greek god of the underworld. It makes perfect sense. They fought for the first time decades ago and the Centurion stopped him, so it will appeal to the purists and collectors. Now it's time for revenge. The premise is almost exactly what Mike is proposing. Hades, an evil alien with incredible super powers, escapes from a desolate prison planet in another galaxy and heads straight for earth to conquer the world.

"But Hades has grown stronger and he's had a lot of time to plot his revenge. He engages the Centurion in a gruesome battle to the death that kids will love. The Centurion dies. And it ends with the dark knight taking over the world."

Julie flipped through the crumpled pages of the old book. "Then what?"

"Then we let everybody think it's the end of the line for the world's mightiest superhero. We don't tell them this is just part one, the set-up for a sequel where the Centurion returns from the dead a few months later to face his old nemesis. I know exactly what needs to be done to resurrect the old guy. It's all been done before."

Julie picked up a sketchpad and pencil. "All right, I'm ready to go. How gruesome do you want it?"

"You good enough to imitate the master?" I asked.

"Payne?"

"Payne circa 1945," I said. "It has to have a real edge to it."

"I can come real close," Julie said. "It'll be retro-hip. A 1940s look with a story that's very today."

With that, the two of us plowed into the story at a feverish pace, racing against time and the uncertainty of how my new plan would be received.

Chapter 12

Excelsior Headquarters
Manhattan

Our hour of reckoning—the big presentation to Sanborn—came soon enough the next morning, and the setting couldn't have been more ominous. The boardroom on the 26th floor looked like something out of an old horror movie. It was dark and musty; every corner of the room just seemed to ooze gloom. Outside, the torrential downpour from the night before continued, complete with a symphony of thunder and lightning that seemed to engulf the entire building. In a bizarre way it served as a perfect backdrop to plot the perfect crime; killing the world's greatest superhero and resurrecting him from the dead.

Had he known what Julie and I were up to, Matthews would almost certainly have called for our heads. But at that moment, Matthews was dying a slow death of his own. Trieste's stock was in a free-fall, thanks largely to Sanborn's highly publicized meltdown on the Children's Network. The company was teetering on the brink of financial ruin once more, and this time Matthews was being held personally responsible for the mess. He desperately needed a bone to throw to the lions—something big that would placate Sanborn, stop the stock's slide and spring him from the doghouse. The Centurion project was exactly what the doctor ordered. If we succeeded, he was a big hero. If we bombed, he'd make sure we would take the fall.

"This had better be good," he whispered into my ear as he slinked back into his chair. "*Reeeeeeal* good."

Matthews calmly adjusted his tie, brushed back his hair, and cleared his throat.

"Ah-hem. As you know, we are here this morning to pay our final respects to the Centurion."

Matthews paused and smiled, but Sanborn didn't laugh.

"Ummmm, the task force has been working on this night and day—"

"Yes, yes, yes," the Walrus anxiously chimed in, "night and day, day and night. We all know the drill, Mister Matttt-hews. Let's get on with it. Mister Mac-Alleeeeeester, what have you got to say for yourself?"

I took a deep breath.

"We've developed an exciting plan for the Centurion's final issue, Mister Sanborn. But first, I think you should know we've had a slight change in direction."

Matthews winced. It was the first he'd heard of my new plan. Julie and I had worked straight through the night, right up until the meeting started and there wasn't enough time to tell him. Mike didn't even know what we were up to. I'm not sure how much Vicki knew (probably more than I was willing to give her credit for) but she showed up for the meeting just the same.

"A new plan, Mis-terrrr Mac-Alleeester?" the Walrus asked suspiciously.

"Yes, and I want to put forth a new proposal for your consideration today. We still intend to kill off the character, but we've added another dimension to the story that could prove very lucrative to the firm."

Sanborn sat up in his chair. "Go ahead, Mister Mac-Aleeeester. You have my attention."

"If we simply kill the Centurion and stop there it's a one-shot deal. The issue makes a big splash. We get the shock value out of it. But once it's over it's over. We immediately lose fifty years of equity in the character. Revenues from endorsements dry up. We lose contracts with two big toy companies and a cereal maker. And they'd all probably sue us when they find out we're pulling the plug on the Centurion. Plus, we run the risk of alienating older readers—the baby boomers—who grew up with the character. They might just be upset enough to tell their kids to stop buying our newer titles."

Sanborn started scribbling furiously on a notepad.

"Beyond that," I continued, "who knows? Hollywood might even say, 'The character's dead. How are we going to make a movie about him if he's gone?'"

Sanborn looked up from his notepad and scowled.

"Nor-butttt!!!" he screamed, "This was your idea. Why the hell didn't you think about this?"

Matthews swallowed hard. "Well, uh, actually Sterling I did. I know we talked about this. We agreed that this would be a calculated gamble and—"

Sanborn pounded his fist on the table. "And did you bother to think about the lawsuits??" he demanded. "We've already got too many goddamned lawyers breathing down our bloody backs now."

Matthews sat down without saying a word.

"We think we have a way to avoid all that," I jumped in. "We can have our cake and eat it too."

"Exactly what are you driving at, Mis-ttterrr Mac-Alleeeester?" the Walrus asked.

"We're proposing a two-part solution," I said, handing out copies of the new sketches that Julie had developed. "First, we kill off the Centurion, exactly as you had envisioned.

"We polish him off in a final climactic battle with an evil Greek god who appeared in one of the very first Centurion comic books fifty years ago," I said. "And we let everyone think it's the end of the line for the Centurion. But it's really not over."

The Walrus sipped on a Coke and snickered. "This, Mis-terrr Mac-Alleeester, I would pay to see."

"Well, sir," I said, "if you think we'd stir up a lot of attention by killing the Centurion off, imagine what would happen if we do what no one has ever done before—at least not in the last two-thousand or so years."

Like a conductor at the end of a symphony, Sanborn held up his hand and I stopped. "Jez-us Christ, Mis-terrr Mac-Alleeeester! Are you suggesting that we kill the Centurion and then raise him from the dead?"

"Exactly," I smiled.

Matthews shook his head. "There's no way in hell we'd ever print that crap. Why, why, it's goddamned sacrilegious!!"

"Ahhh, but we have," I casually tossed my old copy of Excelsior No. 1 across the table. "Look for yourself. It all happened fifty years ago. The Centurion has amazing regenerative powers. He comes back to life whenever someone discovers his armaments and the powers that go with them."

Sanborn grabbed the book from Matthews' hand before he could even open the cover.

"I know this book, I read it as a kid in London."

"And just think," I said, "it can happen all over again. Picture it: The evil Hades returns, stronger and more powerful than ever. He succeeds in avenging his loss. And with the Centurion gone, the world plunges into a new dark age under Hades' rule.

"But then, just as it appears all is lost, someone new rediscovers the tomb of the Centurion and the Sentinel of Light is reborn, stronger and more powerful than ever before. He looks exactly the way he did when it all began, with bold lines, an angular physique, the classic square jaw and a no-nonsense attitude."

I pulled out a large sketch of the character, a brooding, heroic looking Centurion that captured the best of the old and the new.

"What we're proposing here are perfect book ends," I continued. "A bloody ending that will surprise, shock and anger people—so much so that the death of the

Centurion will become the collector's issue to end all collector's issues.

"Then, two months later, we react to the public outcry, change direction, and bring the Centurion back for the greatest rematch of the century. Centurion versus Hades—a knockdown drag out battle to free the world. This time, the Centurion comes back and wins."

"So instead of one big blockbuster sales event, you've got two mega-events, and a character that's infinitely more marketable as a movie and merchandising property."

An eerie silence fell over the room. Sanborn poured more Coke in his glass and studied the sketches. "The old boy was a bit of a bruiser in his day, wasn't he?"

"He was very much a reflection of the times," Julie replied. "But he hasn't aged well. He's lost his focus and the story lines have been weak for years."

"In other words," Sanborn rubbed his chin, "he's become a bloody wimp."

"In a manner of speaking, yes," Julie answered.

"But what makes you think this Centurion will fly, Miss McKin-n-ney?"

Before Julie could answer, Matthews jumped back in with a vengeance.

"She doesn't know the fucking answer!" he shouted, pounding his fist into the table like a jackhammer after every sentence. "Nobody does because it's never been done before! You're out of your mind if you think—"

And that's when lightning struck once more. With every fist to the table, Sanborn's Coke can inched precariously closer to the ledge until it finally slipped head first all over the Walrus's lap.

"Nor-buttt! You idiot!" Sanborn screamed. "Look at the bloody mess you've made!"

Matthews grabbed a napkin and lunged for Sanborn's lap. It was pure bedlam—right out of a Three Stooges movie. And while we were all scratching our heads, Julie was using hers. Matthews' mess turned out to be her inspiration.

"It worked for Coca-Cola," she said.

With all the commotion, no one heard her at first.

Julie cleared her throat and spoke louder. "I said IT WORKED FOR COCA-COLA."

Sanborn finally looked up at her and asked, "What are you talking about, my dear?"

"It worked for Coca-Cola. When they killed off old Coke a few years ago, it created such an uproar that the company had to bring it back."

"But we're not selling soda pop here, my dear."

"What's more American than Coca-Cola?" Julie asked.

Sanborn stopped wiping his pants and looked up. "The Centurion."
Julie nodded. "Exactly. Figure it out for yourself."
Sanborn looked at his pants, then at the sketches, and finally at Matthews.
"YOU IDIOTTTTTTT." He slapped Matthews on the side of the head. "Of course it worked for Coca-Cola. But it wouldn't have if they had just killed the bloody brand off and left it at that. How could you have overlooked this?"
Matthews stood there in a stunned silence, not knowing what to say or do.
Then the Walrus turned to Julie and me and smiled. "You kill the Centurion with an enemy that no one has seen in fifty years, you stir up all this outrage, then bring him back just as demand is peaking. It's brilliant, I say. BRILLIANT! Tell me more."
Julie and I continued to walk Sanborn through both stories—sketch by sketch, detail by detail—until we reached the very end. He took it all in, like a child in a toy store. And when we were done, he rose from his chair and leaned across the board table.
"All right, Mis-terrr Mac-Alleeester, I will give you your sequel, because I think it will sell and I think it will sell big. But I want both of these issues to be graphic novels. I want high gloss, hard covers, brilliant illustrations, and a bloody rich price tag on each one. I want those rotten fans of his to pay through the nose for it."
A graphic novel? My heart soared. It was the comic equivalent of playing a Steinway or hitting the jackpot.
"That certainly won't be a problem," I said.
"But in return I must have your absolute vow of silence," Sanborn continued. "That goes for everyone in this room. This is too big to wind up in the headlines. If it does and I found out who the source of these leaks are, I will have their head on a platter. Do you all understand?"
Before anyone could say a word, Vicki Connors stood up, grabbed her notes, and headed for the door.
"I've had just about enough of this," she yelled. "This is the most idiotic idea I've ever heard and I refuse to have anything to do with it."
Sanborn's brow arched above his forehead. "Missss Connorssss!! You will have something to do with this, by God. I own you!"
Vicki didn't care anymore. "Screw the fucking contract, Sterling!" She turned the doorknob and cracked open the giant oak doors. "I'd rather die than illustrate this garbage."
Sanborn's face grew red with rage. "Walk through those doors, my dear, and I can promise you that it will be certain death for your career!"

Connors tucked her pad and pencil under her arm and marched through the doors without hesitating. "I'd shoot myself before giving you the pleasure," she shouted from the hall and disappeared.

Matthews immediately jumped up and started to go after her.

"Nor-butttt, let her go," Sanborn commanded. "We don't need her anymore. I think we have all the talent we need right here in this room to pull this project off."

Matthews quietly returned to his seat and cowered.

"Now then," Sanborn continued, arms crossed from the head of the table. "Our most pressing concern is timing. We need to do this soon—very soon—to capitalize on the peak summer selling season."

"Fourth of July is coming up," Billington offered. "It's the character's fiftieth anniversary. What better day to kill off an American icon than Independence Day?"

"Yes, yes, yes," Sanborn nodded his head, "that would do very nicely. We'll bill it as a special Fourth of July birthday issue. A grand old cel-e-bration of traditional American values—mom, apple pie, and the Centurion—that no one will ever forget!"

Sanborn looked at his calendar. The Fourth was less than six weeks away. "We have to move quickly. I want to see final boards in ten days. Not a moment later."

My life nearly flashed in front of my eyes. "But I really don't think—"

"No buts about this, Mis-terrrr Mac-Alleeester," Sanborn said. "We will have this out on time or else. And it will be a complete surprise, do I make myself clear?"

We all nodded. We had little choice in the matter.

"Ex-celllllent," Sanborn proclaimed. "You've all performed splendidly. Now go to it!"

As we filed out of the room, Sanborn grabbed my arm and whispered into my ear: "Remember, Mis-terrr Mac-Alleeester. Ten days."

Matthews, his ego deflated like a punctured raft, stayed behind.

"Well, Nor-butttt," Sanborn said as he closed the door behind us, "you made quite a spectacle of yourself this morning."

Matthews gazed up at the Walrus from his chair, unsure of what to say and how long he could contain his stomach from imploding.

Sanborn sat down next to him. "Listen very carefully to what I have to say if you want to save your career. We have two eee-mmediate problems on our hands, and you've just inherited them. The first is Miss Connors. She could blow this whole operation if she opens her big mouth.

"The last thing we need is her running all over the country telling everyone—most especially Lock-jawwww—what we're planning to do."

"What would you suggest?" Matthews asked.

"Cut a deal. Promise her lots of money. But don't put a goddamned thing in writing. Put somebody on her titles right away, and don't take her name off a single one. We can't afford to let her books sit around unfinished."

Matthews took down every word in his notepad.

"What if that doesn't work?" he asked.

Sanborn leaned toward him and whispered into his ear. "I want that bitch silenced."

He handed Matthews a folded sheet of paper. "If you can't buy her, call this number."

Matthews unfolded the sheet. 668-5129. It was Jimmy Montana's number.

"Ask for James," Sanborn said. "He'll make her go away permanently."

A cold chill raced up and down Matthews' spine. He knew Sanborn was ruthless, but he had no idea that he and Montana were connected.

"Now, there's one more thing," the Walrus continued, "I want some of those illustrations."

Matthews stopped writing. "My mole was down there Saturday night. I'm expecting a delivery this morning."

"No, no, no," Sanborn insisted. "I don't want the shit that's lying on the floor. I want the illustrations he showed us this morning."

"But why?" Matthews asked. "Why do you need those particular sketches?"

Sanborn rubbed his hands together. "We've got a spy in our midst. Connors has just walked out. We're racing against time on a daring new secret plan. And I can't trust you to keep on top of things. You figure it out."

Matthews didn't have to. Sanborn wasn't looking for an heir to succeed him. The Walrus needed someone to do his dirty work—lying, spying, and now apparently murder for hire—so he could concentrate on his own agenda, which Matthews hadn't quite figured out yet.

Though he was uniquely well suited for the task, Matthews wanted no part of it unless there was some big payoff in it for him. His disappointment showed.

"Don't look so perplexed, Nor-butttt," Sanborn said, as he gathered his notes and waddled out of the room. "Dying isn't so bad. It's coming back from the dead that will kill you! HAW, HAW, HAW!!!"

Chapter 13

Excelsior Headquarters

The turbulence in the boardroom didn't end once we had all left. Vicki made sure of it. She should have marched quietly out the door and never looked back. But that wasn't Vicki's style, even under the best of circumstances. This was personal, and as usual she intended to have the last word. So she whirled out of the boardroom like the Tasmanian Devil and continued ranting and raving all the way back to her office.

"That bastard!!" she screamed at the top of her lungs. "You wouldn't believe what Sanborn wants to do now. He's out of control and I'm not putting up with it anymore!"

Over the years, Vicki's tirades had become more or less an everyday occurrence, and hardly anyone paid attention to her—except for Mitch Gerber. As soon as he realized it was Sanborn that she was screaming about, he crawled out of his tiny office and discreetly stationed himself outside of Vicki's glass door.

"Who ever heard of such a stupid fucking idea? My grandmother could have come up with a better story line!"

Vicki stormed past her secretary, Gloria from Queens, who had been with her for years, raced into her office and slammed the door.

"Vicki?" Gloria banged on the door right behind her. "Vicki? What happened? Let me in."

She carefully twisted the knob, and finding it unlocked, walked in.

"Gloria," Vicki said, tears streaming down her face. "This time, that crazy son-of-a-bitch has gone too far. And I'm quitting."

Gloria reached over and put her arms around her. "Now, now, now," she said, "just calm down and everything will be fine."

Vicki shook her head. "No. It's not going to be all right. He wants me to put my name on a story concept that's an absolute piece of garbage and I won't do it."

"What was so bad about it?" she asked.

Vicki reached into her purse for a Marlboro. "I, I, I don't want to get into all the gory details. But it was bad enough that I just walked out of the presentation and quit."

"You walked out of the board room?" Gloria asked. "Just like that?"

"He gave me no choice. I won't put my name on it and give it credibility. It'll ruin my reputation before he does. But don't worry, I'm not going to let that happen—"

Just then two beefy uniformed security guards—quite unlike anything in Excelsior's regular rent-a-cop brigade—approached her office and barged through the door.

"Is one of you Vicki Connors?" the tallest guard asked.

Vicki looked the guard straight in the eye. "That's me, Frankenstein." "I'm afraid I'm going to have to ask you to leave the building now, Miss Connors."

Connors couldn't believe it. "Without packing?"

"I'm sorry, Miss Connors. We'll pack for you. You're going to have to vacate the premises now."

Gloria defiantly raised her hand to the guard. "This isn't a prison. You can't do this."

"It's private property. We can throw you out on your ass if you don't cooperate."

Vicki grabbed her purse. "It's all right, Gloria," she said, showing amazing restraint. They briefly hugged and Vicki was quickly escorted toward the back door with a security guard on each side.

They hadn't gone very far when Vicki spotted Gerber standing nearby, trying to appear as if he hadn't been watching the whole episode. But Vicki wasn't fooled. She knew exactly why Gerber was there, and how much the Centurion meant to him.

"This is a real classy outfit Mitch," she said, as they passed. "Just when you think you've got it all together, BOOOOOM—"

Gerber practically jumped out of his skin.

"—They cut you off at the knees," she continued. "And everything you've worked so hard for is destroyed."

Gerber closed his eyes and broke into a cold sweat. All he could think of was the grisly sketches he had found in our conference room. When he opened his eyes, the room was beginning to spin around him.

"What a shame to lose that kind of talent."

Gerber turned, half panicked. Matthews had found him again.

"So much potential. So much beauty. And so little brains," Matthews said shaking his head from side to side. "I had very high hopes for her, too. And now it's all over. Even before it began."

"What are you talking about?" Gerber asked.

"Well, Mitch, old buddy, you know how it goes. In this business you can be the very best. But if you say the wrong thing at the wrong time, or if you stick your nose where it shouldn't be, it can all end. Just like that."

Matthews quickly snapped his fingers. "Get my drift?"

Gerber nodded. "What dirty work do you want me to do now?"

Matthews was taken aback. *Was I that transparent?* He needed a pigeon like Gerber more than ever to buy time until he could figure out what Sanborn was really up to.

"Mitch, Mitch, Mitch, I'm surprised at you." He gently wrapped his arm around Gerber's shoulder. "I thought we were friends—comrades in a desperate mission to save a national treasure."

Gerber eyed him suspiciously. "That's what I thought, too. But nothing's changed. You heard her. Centurion's going to bite the big one. Some friend you turned out to be."

"Mitch, I'm doing everything I possibly can—you've got to believe me. But I'm going it all alone. People like Miss Connors are very formidable. They know things. They have connections. But now that she's out of the way conditions may be more favorable to us."

"Favorable?" Gerber scratched his head. "What do you mean?"

"Connors is gone. But her characters remain. They're all orphans now. Homeless waifs in search of a good parent. Someone who can nurture them. Someone who can make them what they really should have been all along—superheroes of the highest order."

Gerber started walking away. "Sorry. I know how it works. Sanborn will cave in. She'll come running back. All will be forgiven. And I'll be the one getting kicked out on my ass instead of her. No dice."

"Now, now, now," Matthews said, running after him. "Don't be hasty, Mitch. This time it's different. Much different. What Miss Connors did was irreversible. I don't think we're going to be hearing from her again."

But Gerber refused to bite. "I don't think so. Get yourself another patsy."

Matthews tried hard not to appear desperate. But it wasn't going to be easy. His stomach was queasy. His mind was on overdrive. And his heart was in turmoil over Connors' departure.

"Funny you should say that Mitch," he finally said, "that's exactly what Connors said about you, too."

Gerber stopped dead in his tracks. "What'd you say?"

"You heard me. Just before she stormed out of the boardroom she told Sanborn to get himself another patsy to do her work. Somebody like you."

"She said that?" Gerber asked.

"She said you were perfect for the job because you had no guts, no backbone and no talent. Then she told Sanborn the reason no one reads the Centurion anymore is because you and Payne are so out of touch with the real world."

Gerber's eyes welled up with anger.

Matthews had finally struck a nerve. "Are you surprised, Mitch? You know how jealous they all are of you. All she's ever really wanted was to get her little hands on the Centurion. Imagine what a prize it would be if she could take the Centurion and do with him as she pleased."

Gerber shuddered just thinking about it. "Yeah, I can see it now. She'd have him in motorcycle boots and spikes, with a whip and chains. That's her idea of a superhero."

"If it was only that simple," Matthews said.

"Whaddya mean?" Gerber asked.

"Mitch," Matthews whispered, "can you keep a secret?"

Gerber nodded.

"It was her idea to kill off the Centurion—"

"But you said it was MacAllister. He's the spy."

"He's not the only one," Matthews answered. "She was working for the other side long before he got here."

Gerber gasped.

"It's true, Mitch. Connors was Lockwood's first plant. She conceived the whole plan. Those drawings you found—they were all hers. Somehow, she managed to convince everyone—everyone except me, of course—that the only good Centurion is a dead Centurion. But she needed help to pull it all off, and she convinced Sanborn to bring in MacAllister to finish off the job. Then she got greedy. She saw what a plum assignment it would be to kill off the Centurion and she wanted it all by herself. She figured if she couldn't kill him, no one else would."

Gerber slumped to the floor. Matthews quickly sat down beside him.

"The problem doesn't end with her departure," he said quietly. "MacAllister and the others are still behind it. And he wants to bring the Centurion back to life as an entirely different kind of superhero."

"What do you mean, 'different?'"

Matthews winked. "You know, different. Not like you and I, Mitch." And then he winked again.

"I don't get it." Gerber replied.

Matthews leaned closer and spoke so softly Gerber could hardly hear him. "Mitch, this can't go any further than right here. Understand?"

Gerber frowned. "I'm listening."

"Mitch, he wants to make the Centurion GAY."

Gerber started gagging. "NOOOOOOOOO."

"Oh yes," Matthews consoled him. "MacAllister wants to call him the Mercenary. Think about it. The world's first gay superhero. He runs around in his tight little leotards saving gays from oppression. He goes home at night to his boyfriend, and he becomes an advocate for gay rights and safe sex."

"And Sanborn bought into this crap?" Gerber asked.

Matthews nodded. "All he sees is money, Mitch. It would open up a completely untapped new market for us. The promotional opportunities alone are enormous. Think of it—Mercenary condoms. Mercenary vibrators. Mercenary lubes and jellies. Who knows? Maybe someday we'll even see Mercenary McNuggets at McDonalds. It's endless."

"That's insane," Gerber snapped. "You're not going to let them do it, are you?"

Matthews shrugged. "It's not my decision. I told them they're making a big mistake. I said there's just some things in this country you don't mess with—the American flag, Coca-Cola and the Centurion. But they wouldn't listen.

"MacAllister's the real power broker now. He wants to do it. So does Billington and their perky little understudy. They think it's the 'socially responsible' thing to do. That's what I'm up against. Just one little guy against their powerful little clique. I'd say the situation is rather desperate."

Gerber felt sick inside.

"But-t-t-t-t," Matthews continued, "in light of Miss Connors' behavior this morning, I was able to persuade Sanborn to at least think the whole Mercenary idea over before committing to it."

Gerber, who was practically in tears, sighed. "Thank God. What do we have to do to stop this?"

"The task force is up against some real tight deadlines, less than two weeks for the first issue, and it's a graphic novel format. What's the toughest thing they gotta produce?"

Gerber thought for a second. "Front cover. They gotta push like hell to make that kind of timetable for the printers."

"Exactly," Matthews said. "But if all their best front cover designs should suddenly disappear, they'd never make it in time for a Fourth of July issue would they?"

Gerber smiled. "It would definitely slow them down."

"Yes, that's the idea, Mitch. It would buy more time so I can persuade Sanborn to abandon this crazy idea. Are you game?"

"It's risky," Gerber said. "Especially now that they've tightened security downstairs."

Matthews smiled. "Perhaps all of Miss Connors' old titles would be enough to compensate you for the risk."

Gerber hesitated. "It's not enough. I want the Centurion—all to myself—if we pull this off."

Matthews pretended to struggle with the decision. "All right Mitch," he finally said, "you win. By the authority vested in me, I hereby grant you complete and total creative control over all of Miss Connors' titles and the Centurion, if you can wrestle control of this project from the evil forces of doom and destruction."

"The world's mightiest superhero must be saved," Gerber said.

"We can't fail," Matthews replied.

"We won't fail," Gerber nodded.

Then Matthews hugged him. "Just get me those cover sketches otherwise we're both out of business, Mitch."

Chapter 14

Puerto Vallarta, Mexico

Nearly twenty-four hours had passed since Matt Payne had been rushed from the Royal Oaks to Our Lady of Victory Hospital in Puerto Vallarta, but for his wife, Alix, it seemed like forever. Payne's condition was critical. That he was even alive was a miracle. When she had discovered him shortly after he had collapsed on the floor of their cabin from an asthma attack, she was convinced he was gone. Now, as he lay motionless in his bed, tethered to a breathing machine and IV's, she couldn't help wondering what it was that triggered this latest attack.

Those rotten cigars, I told him to lay off those cigars, she thought. But there was more to it than that, and she knew it. Matt couldn't let go of the past.

He was consumed by the events surrounding his retirement, the future of his beloved Centurion.

Alix reached over the edge of the bed and touched his hand. It was cold. *Ice cold.* She had seen him like this before—seven years ago when he'd had his first attack, following a stormy confrontation at work over story line changes that he didn't want to make. It would take something like that, something sudden and shocking to push Matt Payne over the edge. Once the retirement party was over, she figured he was home free. She figured wrong.

"Señora Payne?" A slender Mexican doctor, with a reassuring voice, walked into the room and extended his hand toward her.

"I am Doctor Cancionnes, head of Respiratory Care. I treated your husband when he came in yesterday. Can I speak to you outside for a few minutes?"

Alix left her book on the seat and accompanied the doctor into the hallway. He looked so young. She wondered if he was even thirty years old.

"Can I get you something to drink?" the doctor asked.

"No, thank you, doctor," she said, "Just tell me what's going on."

The doctor smiled. "Your husband has a very strong will. We thought he was gone when they brought him in here. No pulse. Vital signs were extremely weak. But just when we were about to give up all hope, he responded. It was as if he had come back from the dead."

"How bad is the damage, doctor?"

"It's too early to tell," he replied, "We don't believe there was any substantive brain damage—

Thank God, Alix whispered silently to herself.

"He sustained a fairly severe concussion when he fell, and we're not sure how long he went without breathing. But we can't be absolutely sure because we don't have the kind of sophisticated equipment that you have back in the States.

"The next twenty-four hours will be critical. He was very lucky you came along when you did."

Alix closed her eyes and fought back tears.

"Will he recover?"

The doctor didn't answer. "Is he under a lot of stress? Or has he received some bad news recently?"

Alix hadn't discovered the sketches from New York in their cabin, so as of yet she knew of no smoking guns.

"Matt just retired," Alix said at last. "And the last few months haven't been easy for him. I was hoping he would unwind on the cruise."

The doctor walked over to an open window overlooking the town.

"There's no question he needs rest. But when he's healthy enough to travel, get him back to the States. He'll get much better attention in an American hospital.

"Meanwhile, we will do everything we can for him, I promise. But for now no excitement. No stress, Señora Payne. Absolutely no stress of any kind. And no visitors, outside of immediate family. Do you understand?"

Alix wiped a tear from her eye. Matt's doctor in Connecticut had said the same thing—practically word for word—many times before. And God knows, she had tried her best over the years to keep him from driving himself into the ground. But Matt's work always came first.

"I'll see to it that he complies, doctor," she said. "Thank you for being so kind."

Doctor Cancionnes extended his hand to Alix. "If you need anything—anything at all—my office is just down the hall."

As he walked away, Alix slowly gathered herself together and made her way back to her husband's room.

Even here, she thought, *Excelsior still haunts him.*

But there was little she could do now except sit, wait and pray. She tried to focus on something—anything to take her mind off Matt's condition. Finally, she reached into her pocket bag and pulled out the day-old copy of *The New York Times'* that she had found for Matt at a newsstand in Puerto Vallarta.

Alix nervously flipped through the first section, paying more attention to the ads than the headlines. Finally, a tiny headline at the bottom of page thirty-one caught her eye.

Excelsior Publisher Settles Centurion Flap; But Can New Blood Make the Character Fly Once More?

Alix wanted to stop reading right there and then, but somehow she couldn't.

"NEW YORK—*Excelsior Comics Publisher Sterling Sanborn III, promising to inject new life into the company's floundering Centurion comic book line, is handing the character over to one of the industry's hottest young writers for a face lift.*

"At a hastily called news conference at Excelsior's Manhattan headquarters yesterday, Sanborn named 33-year-old Richard MacAllister as the new senior story liner..."

My God, she whispered to herself, *they didn't give it to Mitch. How could they do this?* She quickly skipped down to the end of the story.

"Sanborn denied that the move was motivated by a precipitous slide in the company's stock price in recent weeks. He also declined to comment on recent broadcast reports indicating the company's financial health is deteriorating."

Alix looked up from the story and stared blankly at her husband. *Good Lord, that's all he needs to hear, being replaced by a kid who'll undoubtedly give the character a complete makeover. The mere thought of it would kill him.*

But amid the methodical hum of the respirator, she could only think of one thing—the doctor's voice whispering into her ear. "*No stress, Señora Payne. Absolutely no stress of any kind.*"

Alix quietly closed the paper and folded it in two. *Matt mustn't find out about this*, she thought. *Not now, not as long as his recovery is in doubt.*

"Let someone else go crazy," she said finally, as she gently stroked her husband's hand. "That nut house has done enough to you for now."

Then she calmly walked out of the room and across the hall until she found a garbage can.

"This is one place where you should feel at right at home Sterling Sanborn the Third." And with that, she neatly deposited the paper into the trash and walked away.

Chapter 15

Scout Headquarters

In a city that thrives on loose lips it didn't take long before word started to leak out about what we were up to.

"Are you sure about this?" Phil Plunkett asked.

The voice on the other end of the phone was adamant.

"I've never been so sure about anything in my life."

Plunkett underlined the words in the spiral notebook twice. *ABSOLUTELY CERTAIN.*

"Does anyone else know about this?" he asked.

"A small inner circle of people at Excelsior, that's it. The proposal was presented to Sanborn yesterday. He's the one who's crazy about the idea. That's all that matters. Sanborn pushes all the buttons."

"So how's it happen?"

"It's pretty gruesome," the voice continued. "Not at all like anyone would expect. The Centurion meets up with this really bad alien dude. Evil guy. They have an intense battle. The alien rips the Centurion apart and the Sentinel of Light gets the deep six."

Plunkett stopped writing. "He dies?"

"Finito. He's dead as a door nail, forever and ever."

Plunkett exhaled and a cloud of smoke rose above his head.

"Isn't that a little harsh?" he asked. "Kind of like throwing the baby out with the bath water?"

"Something like that," the voice responded. "But they're desperate. The company's in worse shape than anyone suspects."

"But that's not what they said at the press conference. Sanborn said the plan was to revitalize the character, bring in a new team and pump some life into the old boy."

"It was all a smokescreen," the voice said. "I don't know why they're going this route. Obviously, Sanborn thinks the old guy is worth more dead than alive. Otherwise, he wouldn't be wasting his time."

"What do you think?" Plunkett asked.

"He's going for broke. Cutting his losses while he still can in hopes that he can get something back for it. It's risky."

HMMMM. Plunkett cracked open a fresh bottle of beer.

"When's all this gonna take place?"

"Six weeks. Come Fourth of July weekend, Centurion's a dead man."

Plunkett scribbled as fast as his hand would go. CENTURION DEAD ON JULY 4.

"Do you know what the alien's name is?"

"Nope. Didn't get that."

"What about the Centurion's secret identity?"

"What about it?"

"Does he die too?"

"I, I suppose so…"

"And your sure your information is good on this one?" Plunkett asked. "Really solid?"

"Yep. Got it right from the horse's mouth. He was here for dinner the other night."

"Dinner again?" Plunkett asked, putting his pen aside. "That's two nights in a row."

"Three if you count Saturday," the voice said. "You'd think we're running a boarding house here."

Plunkett rubbed his chin. "He told you all this?"

"Are you kidding? He only talks to me when he has to. I overheard the whole thing."

"Just like that while you were eating dinner at the kitchen table?" Plunkett asked.

"Nooo. I got the whole house bugged."

"Very nice," Plunkett said. "Very nice."

"It was nothing. I used the electronic eavesdropping equipment you gave me for Christmas."

Plunkett smiled. "Works pretty good, huh?"

"Yeah, except the batteries went dead on me before the big idiot finished talking."

"Were you able to make out anything else?"

"There was a lot of static. The conversation kept fading in and out, but it sounded like there's this big rush on to get this done by the Fourth of July so it will hit right on the Centurion's fiftieth anniversary celebration. And they're gonna do it in a graphic novel format, too."

"What kind of format?" Plunkett asked.

"Graphic novel—a big, glossy, hard cover book with great visuals and lots of flash. Trey-expensivo."

"How expensive?"

"Six, maybe seven bucks to start."

"For a comic book?" Plunkett asked.

"It's a guaranteed collector's item. Once it hits the streets it will automatically double in price. Then in a few months, you'll see prices of fifty or sixty dollars an issue. You're talking some serious bucks here."

"What about the old comic books?" Plunkett asked. "Payne's old books?"

"They'll be worthless junk after this."

"You sure?" Plunkett asked.

"The real old stuff might be worth something," the voice answered. "But the newer books are all junk—it would be like paying money to watch reruns of *The Partridge Family.*"

Plunkett took the last drag on his cigarette and threw the butt into his empty beer bottle. It had been a very productive talk.

"Anything else you wanna tell me?"

"Well, there is something else," the source said, sheepishly. "But I'm not so sure you wanna hear it."

Plunkett sat up on the edge of his seat. When his number one source held back information it made him all the more eager to hear.

"Out with it," Plunkett said, "you know I don't like secrets."

"Yeah, I know, but stillll—"

"Just spit it out," Plunkett said, "I don't want any other reporter in town to hear this before I do."

"Okay, Dad. The big jerk asked Mom to marry him."

Plunkett felt like he had just been run over by a freight train. "He did?"

"Uh-huh."

"She didn't say 'yes' did she?"

This time there was no response.

"Umm, Dad, I, uh, well, you know how it is. That's it for now. I gotta go. Good luck with the story."

CLICK.

Chapter 16

Scout Network Headquarters

Later that day half of Scout's newsroom staff was huddled around a black speakerphone in a tiny studio conference room contemplating Sanborn's next move.

"G'day, Mister Lockwood's office. May I help you?"

"Matilda, this is Manny Schaffi calling from New York. We're working on a news story here that Sydney should be aware of. Is he available?"

"He's in an early morning conference right now, Mister Schaffi," Lockwood's secretary replied from Scout's international headquarters in Brisbane. "And he asked not to be disturbed."

Schaffi frowned. He had his orders. "I think you should interrupt him for this. It's about the Excelsior Comics story. Sydney asked us to keep him informed whenever there are any new developments."

"Very well. Just a minute, please."

Schaffi, on his first day back from extended sick leave, nervously fingered the script for the eleven o'clock newscast.

"I still don't see the story here," he said. "Who cares if this Centurion character gets killed off on the Fourth of July? So what if the world loses another goddamned cartoon?"

Plunkett gave him an icy stare from across the room.

Then the speakerphone suddenly crackled to life.

"Sydney Lockwood here."

Schaffi immediately sat up straight in his chair.

"Sydney, this is Manny Schaffi—"

"Who?" Lockwood asked in his thick Australian accent.

"Manny Schaffi, news director."

This time there was no response from Lockwood.

Schaffi cleared his throat. "Ah-hem. Manny Schaffi, Scout's news director in New York. Phil Booth suggested I call."

"Oh, of course," Lockwood replied. "I hope this is important."

Schaffi bit down hard on his pencil. "Umm, Sydney, there's been some new developments in the Centurion story that we thought you should be aware of before tonight's newscast."

"Oh for God's sake, why didn't you say so?" Lockwood replied. "Hang on a minute. Let me clear my office."

Lockwood quickly shuffled everyone out of the room and shut the door.

"All right now, what's going on?" he finally asked.

Schaffi leaned closer to the speakerphone. "Phil Plunkett has some new information he's uncovered. It appears that Excelsior is planning to kill off the Centurion."

"Good Lord," Lockwood replied. "That snake! I knew Sterling was up to no good."

"Word is he wants to do it on the Fourth of July holiday to coincide with the character's fiftieth anniversary," Schaffi added.

"Pretty ball-zeee, don't you think?" Lockwood asked.

Schaffi shrugged. "If you say so—"

"Hell, Manny, if he goes through with this people are going to go fucking wild," Lockwood said. "Where's Phil?"

Plunkett's eyes lit up. "Right here, Sydney."

"What's your take on this, Phil?"

"He's definitely rolling the dice big time," Plunkett said. "If he guesses wrong, everything around him could crumble. But if he wins, he wins big."

"How so?" Lockwood asked.

"If he creates an uproar, new issue sales will immediately spike up. The Centurion's death will almost certainly become an instant collector's item—maybe the biggest of all time. And then Sanborn will be making money hand over fist—exactly what Wall Street wants to see."

"That's why he's doing this," Lockwood said. "He needs to turn that stock price around otherwise his empire is going to fold like a cheap deck of cards."

"Somebody's placing big bets ahead of time, too," Plunkett said. "I have a source at the SEC who's telling me that insider trading on the stock has been very heavy all week. We don't know who's doing all the buying yet, but you'd have to think it's either Sanborn or someone in his inner circle."

Lockwood rubbed his chin. "If this thing takes off, it could damn well run Renegade right out of business. All Sanborn needs is one big hit and he'll be killing off all of his characters. Then he'll drag our titles down with him. We've got to move fast."

"His biggest weapon is surprise," Plunkett said. "If we break the story—really pound away at it—we might just take all the wind out of his sails."

"Hit them before they hit us, eh?" Lockwood asked.

"Nobody could blame us for breaking the news," Plunkett replied. "It's a huge story."

Schaffi stood up and groped around the room in a fit of exasperation.

"Now wait a minute. Doesn't this seem a little silly? Going after a comic book story like it was Watergate? I'd hate to see us turn Eyewitness News into Entertainment Tonight over this thing."

Everyone in the room stared blankly at each other without saying a word.

"May I remind you, Manny, that we were the inspiration for Entertainment Tonight," Lockwood finally said.

A subtle chorus of laughter ringed the room.

"Go with the story tonight," Lockwood continued. "Lead off the newscast with it and promo the hell out of it. We'll pick up the feed worldwide. I want this on every single affiliate in every major market around the globe."

Schaffi's jaw nearly dropped to floor.

"And Phil," Lockwood added, "I want you to go after this story with a vengeance until we figure out a way to counter it. With any luck, Sterling will solve the problem for us. Give him enough rope and eventually he'll hang himself."

CLICK.

By ten-thirty that evening, Manny Schaffi wasn't feeling any better about his lead story. The fact that he saw no news in the story was merely the tip of the iceberg. The death of the Centurion lacked what television needed most—dramatic visuals. Ordinarily, he wouldn't even consider a news story for the top slot unless it included video featuring at least one of the standard visual elements that viewers liked to see—rampant teenage sex, street violence, drug addicts, oppressed minorities with victimization complexes, bigots shouting racial slurs, scaffolding falling off high rises, or talk show hosts fighting with their guests.

Schaffi slapped the script down on the control panel in disgust. "All we've got is a sappy picture of this costumed clown jumping up in the air. If we don't get something better no one's going to watch it."

The assistant shrugged. "Booth is on the line. He wants to talk to you. Pronto."

Schaffi took a long drag on his cigarette and grabbed the phone. "Yeah, Will, what's up?"

"Sydney wants to break into programming with a live bulletin on the Centurion story as soon as it's ready."

"You can't be serious," Schaffi said.

"Year heard me, Manny. As soon as Plunkett's ready, let's do a run through."

"Jez-us Christ, Will. Do you know what we're putting aside for this? We've got nude pictures of the actress who played Marcia Brady. Plus, we've got eye-popping visuals of half-naked people from the Gay and Lesbian Day Parade downtown. And we're doing a bulletin on this piece of garbage with no decent visuals."

Booth bit his lip. "Manny, I don't care if you've got footage of mannequins whacking themselves off in the goddamned window displays on Fifth Avenue! This is what Sydney wants and this is what we're doing. And we're going to have it on the air before the other eleven o'clock newscasts get started. So just run the damn thing."

Schaffi slowly rubbed his forehead. He could feel a migraine coming on. "Fine," he snapped. He leaned over the control panel and flipped on the intercom switch to the studio.

"Listen up for a minute, everyone. We're breaking into the network with a special report on our lead story. I want the affiliates alerted, somebody get a bulletin graphic up and ready, and let's have a script set to go in five minutes."

The newsroom, already a frenzy of deadline activity, jumped to battle stations. And Plunkett positioned himself at the anchor desk directly in front of the camera.

"When we break from the commercial, Phil, all you have to do is say, 'We interrupt our regularly scheduled programming to bring you this special report.' Then just read the script. There's no intro and no music like we normally do for the opening of the newscast. Just the cue and you launch into it. Got it?"

Plunkett nodded. "Got it."

Five minutes later everything was set to roll.

"Everyone look sharp," Schaffi said, "we go live in sixty seconds."

It was just enough time for Plunkett to check in with his favorite source. So he quickly reached behind the anchor desk, grabbed the phone, and dialed his old number.

"Hello?"

"Larry, is that you?"

"Yeah, Dad. Whatcha doin'?"

"Can't talk long son. You near a TV?"

"Uh huh. I'm in my bedroom."

"Good, turn it on. I'm going to hit a big homerun with your Centurion story in less than a minute."

"Oh boy!" Larry said.

"Um, by the way, son, where's your mother?"

Larry suddenly turned quiet.

"Downstairs," he finally said.

"What's she doin'?" Plunkett asked.

"You know. Havin' dinner."

Plunkett looked at his watch. Ten forty-five p.m.

"At this hour?" he asked.

"Oh yeah," Larry replied.

"With who?"

"Who do you think, Dad?"

Plunkett twisted a pencil between his fingers.

"Do me a favor, son."

"Go watch TV downstairs in the family room. Turn it up good and loud."

"Really?" Larry asked.

"Absolutely, you have my permission. Just don't tell your Mom I said so."

"Okay, bye!"

CLICK.

Plunkett stared straight into the camera, as serious and solemn as he'd ever looked on the air, took a deep breath, and broke the news like a sledgehammer.

"We interrupt our regularly scheduled programming to bring you this special report," he said.

Schaffi studied the bank of television monitors arrayed in front of him. "Cut to Camera Two."

Camera Two zeroed in on Plunkett's face.

"America's legendary super hero—the mighty Centurion—will fly for the last time on the Fourth of July. The Scout Network has learned exclusively that the character will be killed in a bloody battle to the death with an evil alien on Independence Day."

Schaffi adjusted the microphone on his headset. "Bring in an over-the-shoulder graphic of the Centurion and tighten the head shot."

At Plunkett's Westchester home, Billington suddenly stopped eating. "What did he say?"

"This dramatic move is seen as a desperate attempt by Excelsior's floundering parent company—Trieste Communications—to revive interest in the character and bolster the company's stock price," Plunkett continued.

Larry did his best to act completely surprised.

"Is this true, Mike?" he asked. "Is the Centurion really going to die?"

Billington walked over to the TV without saying a word.

"Company officials couldn't be reached for comment," Plunkett reported. "Once again, the Scout Network has learned that come Independence Day the Centurion will fly no more. Stay tuned to your local news for more on this story at eleven."

Plunkett shuffled his script, just like Dan Rather, and cocked his eyebrow. His voice plunged three octaves lower to his most melodramatic tone.

"This has been a special report from the Scout Network. We now rejoin in progress Sissy and the Gargoyle Killers."

"Pull up the closing graphic and fade to black before I throw up," Schaffi said.

So the news was finally out; the biggest story of Phil Plunkett's career began to unfold right before his very eyes. But as luck would have it, he only got it half right. Had it not been for a dead battery in his son's electronic eavesdropping bug, he would have known that the Centurion's death was only a ruse; part one of a two-part saga that would rekindle the Sentinel of Light's flame by the end of the summer. But the truth didn't matter now. The story was taking on a life of its own. Everyone who heard it automatically assumed it was true.

At Excelsior headquarters, a group of artists stood stoically in front of a tiny television monitor in the employee lounge, at a complete loss for words. On the Belt Parkway, just outside Brooklyn, Norbert Matthews slammed on the brakes of his shiny new BMW and pondered Wall Street's reaction to the news. In Mexico, Alix Payne stopped dead in her tracks and started crying, after hearing the news in a lounge just outside her husband's hospital room. And in Times Square, just above the entrance to the Times Square Shuttle, an angry Mitch Gerber watched the electronic tickertape flashing around the perimeter of the old Newsday Building.

REPORT SAYS SUPER HERO CENTURION WILL DIE ON JULY 4TH....

Chapter 17

Our Lady of Victory Hospital
Puerto Vallarta, Mexico

Sister Carol Howard wheeled her food cart up to the door of room 176 with the greatest of reluctance. It was the last stop in a long night of deliveries—and this was the final patient to be fed on the entire floor—but it might as well have been the gorilla cage at the zoo.

"Dear Lord," she prayed, "give me the strength to resist strangling the living daylights out of this man tonight."

Then she slowly opened the door and peered inside. "Mister Payne. Youuuuuuu whooooooo...."

Dead silence. Good, she thought, *maybe the old coot is dead.*

A hefty black woman with arms as big as cannons, Sister Carol slipped quietly into the room, carrying a dinner tray filled with the usual weeknight fare—a half-baked burrito, anorexic string beans, slightly sour milk, and a fruit plate drowning in syrup.

She gently placed the tray on a serving table next to the bed, opened the milk carton, and made a mad dash for the door.

"MADAM!"

Sister Carol nearly jumped out of her uniform.

"What manner of poison is this?"

Having grown up in the slums of the South Bronx, there was little in life that could rattle Sister Carol. But the sound of Matt Payne's voice grating on her night after night, was enough to make her forget her vows.

"This food is not fit for an animal," Payne bellowed, as he bexamined the tray.

"Listen up," she said, "I tol' you las' night, I tol' you the night befo', and I tol' you the night befo' that—I don't grow it, I don't cook it, and I don't make you eat it. I jus' deliver it!"

Payne poked at his burrito with disgust. "How do you expect a man to get well on a steady diet of poison?"

Sister Carol pressed her fingers against her wrist until she felt a pulse. *Ninety-six, ninety-seven, ninety-eight....*

"Damn you!" she yelled. "You scared the livin' wits outa me."

Payne looked up from the plate and smiled. He had waited all day for her to walk through that door, and she knew it.

"Now you see here, Mista Payne in the ass," she scolded. "If you don't like the food, you fill out the form on the back of the menu. Understand?"

Payne glanced at his watch and snarled.

"My good sister, everyday at precisely this very moment I fill out this form and then you return twenty-four hours later with another generous helping of Alpo."

Howard looked at the plate. "I don't see no dog food on your plate when it comes back to the kitchen," she said. "It's dry as a bone."

Payne adjusted the oxygen tube ringing his nose, and tossed the cover back over his dish.

"My dear, if you were smart, you would see to it that I am served the finest food in the country. Because the quicker I recover, the quicker I can leave this God-forsaken paradise and be out of your hair forever."

Sister Carol defiantly placed her hands on her hips. "I've been doing more than that," she said. "Everyday I pray to the Lord that he'll make you well enough to go home. And you know what?"

Payne shrugged. "It worked. The doctors are gonna discharge you tomorrow. It's a miracle. God help your poor wife!"

Then she turned, like a sixteen-wheel truck backing out of a loading dock, and thundered out of the room.

It was exactly what Payne wanted to hear. Just a few days ago, he hovered close to death. But not anymore. His recovery continued to amaze the doctors. He wasn't quite one-hundred percent yet—he couldn't remember anything that happened before his attack, so he had no idea what was going on with the Centurion, and Alix was determined to keep it that way. She banned all newspapers and magazines from his room. She had the TV removed. And the sketches she had found in their cabin were history.

All of which gave Payne a bad case of cabin fever. So he immediately took Sister Carol's news as a green light to start packing. When no one was looking, he removed the oxygen tube from his head—something his doctors specifically warned him not to do—slowly wobbled across the room and poked his head into the hallway.

"Señor Payne, where are you going?" an orderly asked.

"I'm looking for my wife," he said. "The doctor's discharging me. We're getting the hell out of here. Have you seen her?"

"The doctor is releasing you?"

"I swear to God," Payne replied. "I just found out from Sister Carol. I've got to tell Alix the good news."

The orderly thought for a moment.

"I passed her in the lounge," he said. "Looks like she could use some good news. I think she's watching TV. You still might find here there."

Vicki Connors wasn't watching television that night, and even if she had Plunkett's news bulletin wouldn't have made much of an impression on her. Excelsior was almost history—bad history. And the sooner she put it all behind her, the happier she'd be. Vicki had already lined up another job, and to no one's surprise, her new boss was Sydney Lockwood. No, Vicki had never been Lockwood's spy. But as soon as she realized her contract with Excelsior was little more than a straight jacket, she ran straight over to Renegade and asked Lockwood for a job.

Lockwood was no dummy. He threw out the red carpet. He gave her a fat raise, an exclusive contract, total control over her characters, a cut of the profits from merchandising and licensing fees, her own logo, and loads of stock options. He also promised to defend her against any legal action by Sanborn—a virtual certainty—since she'd be working for Excelsior's biggest competitor. And he didn't stop there. If Vicki could persuade any of us to join her, she'd get a cut of the profits from our characters as well. That's how anxious Lockwood was to see Sanborn die on the vine.

Vicki feared the whole deal would fall apart if her name was connected in any way with a blockbuster issue that might cause problems for her new boss. So she did what any of us would have done under similar circumstances. She walked out.

All she needed to stage the largest talent raid in comic book history was her old Rolodex—complete with names and home phone numbers of every disenchanted Excelsior employee in New York. But it was still in her old office. And she knew she'd never see it again, unless she retrieved it herself. So later that night, under cover of darkness, Vicki snuck back into the building on a daring rescue mission.

"C'mon, c'mon, open up for Chrissakes!" Connors pounded on the delivery door at the back of the building until a scowling security guard finally emerged.

"You Vicki Connors?" the guard asked.

"That's me," she said.

"Okay, go on up, but don't stay there too long. You know what it's like around here."

Bless you for arranging this, Gloria. What would I do without you?

Vicki scurried up a back stairwell and made her way through the shadows to her old office several floors above. Only a few lights were on and she was certain that no one else had seen her. Her office—as she expected—had been trashed by Sanborn's goons. Brushes and inks and shredded papers were scattered all over the floor. But her precious Rolodex was still sitting on her desk—exactly where she had left it.

"Sloppy, Sterling," Vicki whispered to herself, "very sloppy. Details will kill you every time."

Vicki should have listened to her own advice. She didn't know it then but she wasn't alone. From a dark corner across the hall, a lone figure sat nearby in an abandoned cubicle next to an open window—clutching an old Centurion comic book—waiting patiently for her to re-emerge from her office.

"You should have stayed away, my dear," the figure whispered, gently stroking the book. "We could have avoided all this unnecessary pain."

Vicki eventually emerged from her office and a steely pair of eyes watched her tiptoe down the dark hall.

"Why the rush, my dear? You're going nowhere fast." The figure jumped up from the chair and followed her into the night, leaving the open comic book behind.

A moment later, a stiff breeze blew threw the window and flipped open the pages one at a time, offering a chilling moon-lit glimpse of the events which were about to transpire:

It's a late night at the LaBrea Science Lab for brilliant research scientist Dr. Dana Barnes. An exciting experiment of vast importance to America's war effort is on the brink of a breakthrough.

Weary and exhausted, Dr. Barnes finally packs away her experiment, locks her secret formula in a vault, and takes the keys.

Little does Dr. Barnes realize that she is not alone. Her every move is being scrutinized by an evil presence—the diabolical Dr. Terror!

Dr. Barnes has what he wants, and he'll stop at nothing to get it. Finally, she heads for the elevator, unaware of the danger that awaits nearby.

The doors swing open, revealing an empty elevator shaft. Then the unthinkable happens! A hand reaches out from behind her and Dr. Barnes is suddenly and violently thrown headfirst into the shaft.

This looks like a job for the Centurion!

Down the hall, the doors to the elevator bank opened and Vicki stepped toward the compartment without even thinking. But at the very last moment something inside her said *STOP.*

She looked down and saw nothing. No elevator compartment. No floor. Just a dark empty shaft. "Oh my God!" She quickly braced herself against the frame of the elevator, backed slowly away from the shaft, and collapsed on the floor.

When Vicki finally looked up, her heart was racing. Only the red light from the exit sign above a nearby door broke the stillness of the night. As far as she could tell, she was okay. Just frightened out of her mind.

Vicki shook her head and tried to catch her breath. She wanted to take the stairs but decided against it. The last thing she needed now was to bump into a security guard between floors. *Okay,* she thought, *let's try this again.*

She picked up her Rolodex from the floor, pushed the down button, and waited patiently for another elevator to arrive. But then—just as it appeared everything was fine—a gloved hand reached out from nowhere and covered her mouth like a vice. Vicki gasped.

"You thought you were so clever," a throaty, heavy breathing voice whispered into her ear. "But you can never extinguish the Sentinel of Light."

Vicki tried to scream, but couldn't. Then she tried kicking, but to no avail.

"The Centurion was sent here to protect mankind from the evil that lurks deep within his soul. Do you understand?"

Vicki could barely breath, and when she didn't respond it only angered her assailant even more.

"DO YOU UNDERSTAND?"

She managed to move her head up and down ever so slightly. Then the grip started to ease.

"You can't take away that which isn't yours, Miss Connors."

"It wasn't my idea to kill him off," she finally blurted out. "I wanted nothing to do with it."

"And I can promise that you shall have nothing to do with it," the voice thundered.

"What do you want from me?" Vicki cried.

The assailant laughed. "I want you to know what it's like to die a terrible death at the hands of someone you are powerless to stop."

Vicki gasped. Her attacker pushed her to the very edge of the open elevator shaft and forced her to her knees.

"The Centurion belongs to the ages!" Then with one hand holding her by the back of the neck, the assailant thrust her head over the open shaft.

"How does it feel to be so helpless, Miss Connors?"

There was no response. Vicki had passed out cold. The assailant pulled her head upright and listened. She was still breathing.

"You don't get off that easy, Miss Connors!" The attacker shook her by the shoulders until she regained consciousness.

"You wouldn't kill the world's mightiest superhero in just a couple of frames, now would you?"

Vicki coughed up blood and moaned.

"No. You'd drag it out slowly, frame by bloody frame. First, you'd shred his cape and rip his costume. Then you'd beat him to a pulp. And finally, you'd put our fallen superhero on display—like a dead carcass—that's what you'd do. You'd drape him over a grave stone, or impale him on a flag pole."

Vicki looked up in a daze. "Noooo, that's not the way it's going to happen—" For the first time in her life she felt fear—pure unadulterated terror.

"Come, come, now, Miss Connors. Don't deny it. It was all your idea. You did it all just to make the story more dramatic."

Then the attacker looked directly into her eyes.

"But did you ever stop to think about who you were hurting along the way? Have you ever thought about how others would feel when you take away their favorite superhero?"

Vicki blacked out again.

"Ah, what a pity. You're going to miss the special ending that I have planned for you, my dear. It's been in the making for almost fifty years."

With that, the assailant propped Vicki's limp body back over the elevator shaft. "NOW FEEL THE WRATH OF THE CENTURION!" And with one final push, Vicki plunged to the base of the shaft six stories below.

"My, how the mighty have fallen," the assailant said.

That anyone could have survived such a fall is nothing short of miraculous. But it's true. Vicki was alive—but just barely. A few moments later, her faint cries for help reached out from the cold concrete slab at the base of the shaft, but to little avail. Only her assailant was listening.

Slowly and very deliberately, the attacker reached up to the elevator wall plate between the two elevator shafts and depressed the lower button.

"Not even the Centurion can help you now, my dear."

A moment later, the elevator's motor sprang to life and the compartment began a slow descent to the bottom of the building.

To the very end, Vicki was every bit the fighter she made herself out to be. But it wasn't enough. She died the terrible death that her assailant had predicted, succumbing to a foe she could not possibly defeat. After a lengthy investigation, the police later rationalized it all away as the result of a tragic series of missteps in an elevator shaft that was supposedly closed for repairs. The official cause of death was eventually listed as accidental.

Chapter 18

I stretched out on my bed late that evening, completely unaware of what was transpiring at Excelsior, wondering why I had ever left Renegade in the first place. One by one, the reasons started coming back to me—more money, a bigger challenge and greater visibility. Throw in a lot more aggravation, relentless deadline pressure, and the nagging uncertainty that anything could change on a moment's notice, and I could truly say I had it all.

I looked at the clock. It was well past midnight, and I was wound up tighter than a drum. So I got out of bed and made my way into the mess that passed for my living room. *Ma would have croaked if she could see this,* I thought.

Newspapers and magazines were strewn all over the floor. Empty Coke cans and dried up ice cream dishes were piled on top of each other. Storyboards and illustrations that I had taken home to thwart our office thief covered the walls. In the middle of all this was my suitcase, still waiting to be unpacked from my trip back to Buffalo.

One side was filled with wrinkled shirts and jeans. The other half was stuffed with dirty socks, smelly underwear and something else, something really heavy that I didn't remember packing—my old Centurion comic books. Ma must have put them there, at least a hundred, maybe more, including a few that I actually remembered reading as a kid. On top of the pile was the first issue in a four-part series of murder mysteries involving Dr. Terror—a sinister looking serial killer in a long flowing cape, dark mask and a wide brimmed hat—that I would later learn served as the inspiration for Vicki's murder.

On a sleepless night, *Murder on the Sixth Floor* was too tempting a story to resist. So I indulged my curiosity and it wasn't long before I was completely lost in the details. When I finally came up for air, it was nearly two in the morning and I was even more wide-awake than ever. So I grabbed a beer from the refrigerator, and started reading the second installment of the series, *Murder on the Subways*. This time I didn't get very far. The phone rang and I jumped. It was Julie and something in the tone of her voice made me think something was very wrong.

"What's the matter?" I asked.

"It's Vicki," she said. "She... she's dead."

I laughed.

"No, no, Rick, I'm serious," she said. "Turn on your TV."

I flipped on the tube and up flashed Phil Plunkett's ever-so-serious face in the midst of a breaking news report.

"—police say the artist was crushed to death at the base of an elevator shaft by a descending passenger compartment—"

I turned up the volume. "Now for a live report from the scene, we take you to Jane Vasquez Mitchell. Jane."

Vasquez Mitchell's image quickly appeared in front of the Excelsior building.

"Phil, I'm standing outside the headquarters of Excelsior Comics where police and rescue teams are trying to piece together what caused this tragedy here tonight."

Vasquez Mitchell glanced down at her notebook and continued talking. "This is what we know so far. Vicki Connors, one of Excelsior's most popular artists and a central figure in the company's plans for the Centurion comic book character, was found dead about an hour ago in an elevator shaft—"

"I can't believe it," Julie said on the phone. "What was she doing there?"

"Hang on," I said.

"Yesterday," the report continued, "Vicki Connors resigned from Excelsior Comics in an apparent dispute over the Centurion. She showed up here late last night—for what we're not sure—but shortly afterward she fell six stories to the base of an empty elevator shaft, which was closed for repairs. Connors was later crushed when the elevator compartment descended to the basement level. She was pronounced dead at the scene a few moments ago by the Manhattan coroner's office."

A stretcher with a body bag made its way past the cameras into a waiting ambulance.

"Joining me here live is New York Police Detective Charles Gill. Detective how did this happen?"

Gill, a grisly plainclothes homicide veteran who had a real way with words, took a long drag on his cigarette.

"Don't know," he said, from behind a thick cloud of smoke. "It was very dark. She accessed the elevator shaft on the sixth floor. Next stop was the ground floor."

"How'd she die?"

"It was her heart. It stopped beating."

"Do you suspect foul play?"

"We suspect everyone until we find out differently."

"We're there any signs of a struggle?"

"Yeh," Gill said. "She lost. The elevator won."

"Could it have been an accident?"

"How many times you walk into an empty elevator shaft, sister?"

"What's the story on the elevator?" she persisted.

"That's what we'd like to know."

"What was she looking for in her office?"

"Whatever it was there's not much left of it now."

Gill looked at his watch. "Gotta go."

Vasquez Mitchell pulled back the microphone and stepped aside, just as a short, stubby man from the coroner's office ran up to the back of the ambulance carrying a sealed plastic bag.

"Is that what she was looking for in her office?" Vasquez Mitchell shouted in full view of the camera.

"No," the man held open the bag for the camera with a wicked grin on his face. "It's her head!"

The cameraman quickly circled back to a very flustered Vasquez Mitchell for a close.

"Uh, Phil," she said trying not to gag, "that's the very latest in the grisly details from here. This is Jane Vasquez Mitchell, reporting live. Now let's go back to the Scout Studios."

Plunkett's tired but well coifed face appeared on screen. "The death of Vicki Connors comes in the wake of a startling revelation that you heard first on Eyewitness News at eleven o'clock—Excelsior is planning to kill the Centurion on the fourth of July."

I nearly swallowed my tongue. The leaks were growing and now they weren't even close to being accurate.

"Vicki Connors was part of a crack creative team that was planning the final chapter in the character's illustrious career," Plunkett continued. "She was—"

CLICK. I couldn't watch anymore.

Julie was still with me on the other end of the phone. "Rick, this can't be an accident," she said. "Not with everything that's been happening in the office. I'm scared."

So was I. How many times do you read about a murder in an elevator shaft and then find out it really happened? The similarities were too close to be coincidences.

"Something's not right," I said. "Get in a cab and get over here as soon as you can. We've got to figure out what's going on."

Meanwhile, miles away in a dark, musty old room on the upper floor of his Brooklyn apartment, Mitch Gerber was also having trouble watching the same report on a small black and white set on his kitchen table.

Gerber tried to turn off the television but his hand was shaking so badly he couldn't grip the dial. Instead, he picked up an old comic book, one that he had worked on years ago as a young intern with Excelsior, and started reading it aloud.

"The evil reign of Dr. Terror grips Nickel City, and an another unsuspecting victim is about to die on the subway."

Chapter 19

Excelsior Headquarters

As Julie and I were trying to make sense of the events that were unfolding around us, Sanborn was already capitalizing on Vicki's death. He showed up at Excelsior at four a.m., a full half-hour earlier than usual, slipping in through a side entrance to escape the hordes of reporters hovering in front of the building. His entertainment empire had survived all kinds of bad news before, but nothing quite like the sudden death of an artist. As always, Sanborn's chief concern was himself. Amid all the chaos, he wondered if there was some way he could leverage this tragic event into his own personal gain.

We could say she gave her life for her company, he speculated. *Or better yet, we could let it leak out that she was killed by one of Lock-jaw's spies when she refused to divulge what she was working on. Now that's intriguing,* he thought. *Something right out of a Tom Clancy novel.*

"Mornin' Mista Sanborn sir." Excelsior's security chief, a short, stocky graduate of the Brooklyn Academy of Professional Security Services, snapped to attention as soon as the Walrus appeared through the revolving door.

"Would you like to see the crime scene, sir?"

Sanborn gazed across the lobby at the main elevator bank, which was still cordoned off by streams of shiny yellow police tape.

"I think under the circumstances, I'd prefer to take the stairs today."

Twenty minutes later, the Walrus emerged outside his office on the executive floor, out of breath and completely drenched.

"Miss Gott? What on earth are you doing here at this hour?" he asked, upon opening the door.

Gott peered out from behind a huge sack on top of his desk. "Unpacking, sir," she said, in her deep, droll voice. "The mailroom called me early this morning. We are being flooded by correspondence from all over the world. The pile was growing too big downstairs."

"Good Lord," Sanborn gushed. "All this came in overnight?"

Gott sliced open a Western Union envelope. "There are three more sacks in the hallway, sir."

"All condolences I would e-magine," he said.

"Oh no, sir," she replied. "They're not about Miss Connors at all. They're about the news report on the Centurion last night."

Sanborn's eyes grew wide with delight. "All this is about the Centurion?"

"Yes, sir. I've taken the liberty of opening a few dozen missives for you."

Sanborn flung his raincoat on the floor and raced to his desk. "Wel-l-l-l, what do they say?"

Gott began reading one of the letters aloud.

"Ahem. 'Dear Mister Sanborn, only a sick bastard like you would kill off a wonderful character like the Centurion. I hope you die, you blood-sucking worm.'"

Gott closed her eyes and braced herself for Sanborn to explode. But the Walrus merely smiled. "Really now. Someone actually wrote that?"

Gott examined the letter again. "Yes, sir. A Mister Thomas Borrelli from East St. Louis."

"Read me another one," Sanborn insisted. "And this time, Miss Gott, put some feeling into it, will you."

Gott unfolded a telex and began reading. "'DEAR ASSHOLE,'" she said with gusto. "'I just heard that you are plotting to kill the Centurion. How could you do such a terrible thing? I grew up with the Centurion. He represents all that is good about America. Go back to England and burn in hell. Signed Jason Cameron, Los Angeles, California.'"

Sanborn's smile grew wider. "That's wonderful-l-l-l Miss Gott! Absolutely wonderful-l-l-l. Are they all like that?"

"Those were the tamer ones, sir," she said.

Sanborn applauded and started dancing around the room like Feziwig on Christmas Eve. "I knew it! I knew it! It's happening. They're biting. Those rotten, miserable fans are finally starting to bite."

After a few moments he stopped in front of the aquarium in the center of his office and opened the lid of the tank.

"It's the start of a feeding frenze-e-e-e," he said, dangling a few pieces of frozen shrimp over the water. Several famished piranhas immediately shot up to the top and devoured the catch.

"You know, piranhas are almost human sometimes, Miss Gott. Take away their food and they will hunger for more. Lots more. Eventually, they will kill each other to get what they want."

Sanborn dropped what was left of the shrimp into the tank and watched with delight as it all disappeared in a whirlpool of churning water. Then he closed the lid and waddled back to his desk.

"Leave me now, Miss Gott," he said. "And hold all my calls. I wish to read my fan mail personally."

Gott retrieved another sack of envelopes from the hall and hoisted it atop Sanborn's desk. Then she headed for the door.

"Mister Sanborn…"

"Yesssss?"

"Do you wish to prepare a statement about Miss Connors, something acknowledging her loss or expressing condolences to the family, in case there are any inquiries?"

Sanborn gazed up at the ceiling, pondering a tactful way to address the situation.

"Hmmmmm, I suppose that would be in order."

He thought very carefully about it. And when he was done, he turned to Gott and said: "Post a note downstairs, Miss Gott. 'El-ee-vator temporarily out of order.'"

Then without skipping a beat, he plunged into a pile of letters on his desk like a kid unwrapping a candy bar.

"'Dear Excelsior Comics,'" he read aloud. "'My name is Jimmy. I'm ten years old and I love the Centurion. He's my best friend. He makes me feel good when I'm sad. Please don't kill him.'"

"How touching, little Jimmy," the Walrus said. "Unfortunately, my boy, life sucks sometimes."

Sanborn tossed the letter into the trash and retrieved another one from the pile.

"'Dear Shit-head. Hanging is too good for you.'"

Sanborn couldn't get over the passion. It was exactly what he had been hoping for. "Sydney," he said, "I ought to put you and that dumpy network of yours on the payroll. You're going to make more money for us than we could ever do on our own!"

Then the phone rang. Not his regular line. It was the VIP phone for special investors like Jimmy Montana, whose interest in the company was not entirely reflected on Trieste's balance sheet.

"Sir James," Sanborn exclaimed, "this a red-letter day for us all."

"I heard da news, Stoi-ling," Montana replied, in his heavy Brooklyn accent. "We're marking up every Excelsior title in da house BIG TIME."

"I must extend my compliments to your people for all the fine work they did overnight," the Walrus said.

"We didn't do nuttin'."

"You are too modest, old chap. The Scout report about the Centurion's death—it was a brilliant piece of covert news placement."

"We didn't do it."

"Come now," Sanborn chuckled. "Next you're going to tell me you had nothing to do with resolving the Connors situation either."

"You got dat right," Montana replied.

"Matthews didn't call you about the problem we had here yesterday?"

"Nope."

Sanborn hesitated. "You mean you didn't bump the bitch off?"

"No freakin' way," Montana said. "We'd never leave any evidence in an elevator shaft. Dat's sloppy workmanship."

"Then who did all this?" Sanborn asked.

"Whoever it is did you one hell of a favor Stoi-ling."

"Whaddya mean?"

"Connors is worth more dead than alive. She was the best in the business. The price on everything she did just tripled in value."

"Everything?" Sanborn asked.

"Every goddamned thing that's got her name on it."

"Good Lord," the Walrus exclaimed. "We've got a dozen of her titles sitting at the printer. And the last issue of the Centurion is going to have her name stamped all over it."

"Eggg-zactly. You're sitting on a gold mine dat's bigger than freakin' Fort Knox."

Sanborn was nearly delirious.

"Not so fast, Einstein," Montana said. "Don't count your chickens yet. If you wanna cash in on dis, you gotta fan the flames on da story until dose new issues come out."

Sanborn thought for a second. "We could announce that we're going to bring the Centurion back."

"Stoi-ling are you nuts?" Montana asked. "Don't breathe a word about any sequel. Dey find out da old boy's coming back too soon and we're right back where we started. All the prices go down. Da media thinks dey're onto somethin' here. Let 'em believe their own press."

Sanborn rubbed his chin. "Live the lie?"

"Call a press conference and deny everything. Then throw dis Plunkett guy a few more bones to keep da press off balance."

"How do we handle the Connors situation?" Sanborn asked.

"Dere's your hook, Stoil-ing. Spice it up. Tell everyone she was moidered. Offer a reward for the killer."

"How much?" Sanborn asked.

"A million bucks."

"A million bucks? Why in God's name would I do that?" the Walrus asked.

"Only one thing's better than a dead artist's name on your comic book."

"What's that?"

"A dead, martyred artist. If you make her out to be a goddamned saint you're gonna make a mint on dat last Centurion issue. Wall Street will eat it up and da stock price is gonna skyrocket."

Sanborn furiously scribbled down every word on his pad. "Anything else?"

"Cut me in on a piece of da action," Montana said.

"The usual twenty percent?"

"Nope. Double the press runs on the last Centurion issue, call it a "limited edition" printing, and send it all to me. I'll sell everything you print."

"You've got it, Sir James."

"Stoil-ing, I knew there was a reason why we made you chairman," Montana said. "Now I gotta go."

"Where to so early in the morning?"

"Gotta wake up my broker before you call dat press conference."

CLICK.

Sanborn looked at his watch. Four fifty-eight a.m. He knew he'd have to move quickly. So he picked up the phone and dialed Matthews at home. After twelve rings, he finally answered.

"Hullll-o?"

"Matt-hewssss," Sanborn said, "are you still asleep?"

Matthews peered out from under the pillow, all bleary eyed and groggy.

"Of course, I'm still asleep. Who the fuck is this?"

"Sanborn, you idiot!"

Matthews sat straight up in bed at a ninety-degree angle. "S-S-Sterling, forgive me. Is something wrong?"

"Did you hear the news reports last night?"

"Uh, yes, last night on the way home. The Centurion story. And they got it wrong—"

Sanborn shook his head. "Yes, yes, yes, I know they got it wrong. But it doesn't matter. The fans are going wild."

Matthews thought he was still dreaming. "What?"

"You should see the piles of faxes and tel-e-grams on my desk. It's unbelievable is what it is."

Matthews shook the cobwebs from his head. "If you say so—"

"But we have to move quickly if we're going to capitalize on this," Sanborn interrupted. "Did you get those sketches I've been waiting for?"

Matthews' mind went blank. "Sketches? What sketches?"

"The fucking front cover illustrations you promised me, you idiot!!"

Matthews' memory suddenly returned. "They're supposed to be in my office when I get in this morning. I'll bring them up to you as soon as I get there."

"And when might that be, Mister Matt-hewsss?" Sanborn asked.

Matthews' stomach started to twist like a knife. "Eight thirty, my usual starting time, Sterling. Is that a problem?"

"It will be Mister Matt-hews if those sketches fall into the wrong hands. I'm sending a car for you right away."

Matthews gazed at his alarm clock. "Sterling, it's five o'clock in the morning. Are you sure we have to do this right now?"

"Yes, immediately," Sanborn said. "I want you to get into the car. Don't talk to anyone. Don't listen to the radio or TV. And don't use the cell phone. Do you understand?"

"Yes, absolutely, Sterling."

"Just get those fucking drawings up to my office safely. Do I make myself clear?"

"I got it," Matthews said.

"Now then, Norbert, get to it. We have no time to waste.

CLICK.

Sanborn slammed down the receiver and pointed his remote at the television set on the wall across his desk.

CLICK.

"Overnight, trading on the Tokyo stock exchange was heavy," reported a stuffed suit anchor from the all-night cable business channel. "Topping the active list was Trieste Communications, up seven-and-a-half points on news reports that the company is planning to kill off it's flagship comic character, the Centurion."

The Walrus quickly grabbed the phone with his pudgy fingers and dialed the firm's chief financial officer, William Lederer, an old crony who'd been a part of his inner collective for years. In financial circles, Lederer was known as "Mr. Wizard" for his innate ability to manipulate currency markets and make red ink mysteriously disappear from balance sheets.

"Lederer here."

"Bill, my good man," Sanborn enthused. "I understand we did very well in Tokyo last night."

Lederer turned to his computer screen and adjusted his glasses.

"Hmmm, it would appear so, Sterling," he began. "Up seven-and-a-half points at—"

"I think this might be an opportune time to accelerate our corporate stock repurchase program," Sanborn interjected.

"What stock repurchase program?" Lederer asked.

"We don't have one?" the Walrus asked.

"Not that I'm aware of Sterling."

"Then let's create one," the Walrus said.

"Just one problem. Where we gonna get the money to buy back the stock?"

Sanborn deliberately hesitated. "How about tapping the employee pension fund?"

"The employee pension fund has a manager who's doing a great job," Lederer said. "Besides I doubt if he would go along with using pension fund assets to repurchase a shaky stock like Trieste."

"Very well then," Sanborn continued. "Fire him."

"Excuse me?" Lederer asked.

"You heard me. Fire him and start buying back the stock as soon the markets open this morning in New York."

"Sterling, you're not serious—"

"I'm very serious, Bill," Sanborn said. "If he won't do it, fire the son-of-a-bitch."

Lederer got up and closed his door. "Sterling, how much stock are you talking about?"

"I think three billion dollars worth would be a good start."

"Three billion dollars?" Lederer almost gagged. "Federal law limits the amount of company stock a fund can hold—

"And then," Sanborn continued, "say around eleven o'clock, I want you to buy another billion dollars in stock and put it directly in my name."

"Eleven o'clock? Why eleven o'clock?"

"Because I'm going to hold a press conference right after that and I want to buy it before the stock price really soars."

"Sterling, you can't do that," Lederer warned. "The SEC would be all over you in no time."

Sanborn rubbed his nose. "I don't intend to hold onto it very long. Just a few hours."

"Sterling, what you're talking about here is illegal. You're manipulating the stock price for your own personal gain."

The Walrus laughed. "Me? Pre-e-e-posterous!"

"And how do you propose explaining to the SEC that you're using employee pension funds to buy stock in your own name?"

"I'm an employee of the company. Am I not?" Sanborn asked.

"Yes…"

"I can take out a loan—borrow against my holdings—like any other employee. Can't I?"

"Yeh, but you're talking about a billion dollars here," Lederer said.

"Wellllll, I am the chairman. If I can't do it, then who should?"

Lederer threw his glasses across the desk and rubbed his eyes.

"Sterling, you can dress it up any way you want. The SEC isn't blind. You can't be that obvious."

"Williammmmmm, Williammmm, Williammmm. I'm not stealing money. I'm merely borrowing capital to enhance the company's stock repurchase program. It's a sign of management's conf-eee-dence in the company's future. Now that's something Wall Street can appreciate. Don't you think?"

Lederer banged his head against his computer screen. "You'll hang for insider trading—"

Sanborn slammed his fist against his desk in a rage. "Oh, the hell with the goddamned SEC! I'm not going to manipulate anything. I'm going to increase the stock's value and create more wealth for our shareholders. That's what I'm supposed to do!"

"But what if the stock goes down? You're responsible for the losses. Have you considered that?"

Sanborn had had enough. "MIS-TERRR LEDERER!!!!! HAVE YOU CONSIDERED WHAT YOUR LIFE WOULD BE LIKE WITHOUT YOUR JOB?"

Lederer's life flashed before his eyes. He was just eighteen months away from retiring and his self-preservation instincts kicked in.

"All right, Sterling, you win," he said. "I'll make sure the order goes through."

"Very good, old man. See how much more we can accomplish with a little cooperation?"

"All the same Sterling, you won't accomplish much if you're in jail. I hope you know what you're doing."

Sanborn grinned. "Ah, Wil-l-l-liam, my good friend. You're the best chief finan-

cial officer in the business. But you've got no balls. No balls at all."
CLICK.

Twenty minutes later, a bleary-eyed and out-of-breath Matthews stumbled into Sanborn's office, still wearing his monogrammed Ralph Lauren pajama top and slippers.

"Here's the sketches," he said, handing Sanborn an oversized envelope.

The Walrus grabbed the envelope like a hungry dog and peered inside to make sure the sketches were really there. They were all in perfect condition.

"Exxxxcellent, Mister Matt-hewssss. Excellent.

Sanborn waddled over to the door, closed it tightly and returned to his desk.

"Sit, Mister Matt-hewssss. Sit."

Confused and still half asleep, Matthews slumped into a chair.

"I did as you asked, Sterling," he began. "I jumped into that limo as soon as it showed up and got right over here."

"Yes, I know, I know," Sanborn replied. "And I'm sure you're aware of all that has transpired here over the past twelve hours."

"Damn Scout Network," Matthews replied. "I swear they've got spies all over the place. I shudder to think how this is going to play out once the markets open."

Sanborn couldn't believe it. Matthews didn't know about Connors yet. The Walrus knew he'd have to break the news to him gently otherwise he'd wind up having to do all his own dirty work himself.

"By God, we're going to find out who leaked the story and we're going to punish the perpetrators—I can promise you that! But right now, there's something else I have to talk to you about. Something that I've been wanting to discuss for some time."

Matthews braced for the worst. He had been expecting the ax to fall ever since the Maria Bartiromo fiasco.

"My boy, your work here over the past few days has been just extraordinary!"

Matthews sat there stone-faced. "It has?"

"Of course, my boy. Your counsel has been in-val-U-able. And your discreet acquisition of these illustrations means more to me that you could possibly e-e-e-magine."

The Walrus smiled and pulled out a checkbook from his top drawer.

"Ah, such modesty. I shouldn't be surprised. All the great ones are like that. Always thinking of others first. Performance like yours deserves to be rewarded.

So today, my good man, I'm writing you a personal check—a reward—for ten thousand dollars."

Ten thousand dollars? Matthews was mystified. He still hadn't figured out Sanborn's agenda. But he figured there had to be a lot more to it if Sanborn was willing to part with money. So he decided to play along for the time being.

"I don't do this for just anyone," the Walrus said, signing the check. "But I just want you to know how much I value your counsel."

Matthews reached for the check and pretended to fight back tears. "I don't know what to say, Sterling."

Sanborn's bushy white eyebrows poked up over his forehead and his eyes grew wide with delight.

"Just say you're with me, son. At least that's how I'd like to think of you. The son I never had. We're family. We stick together through thick and thin. We go the distance for each other, no matter what."

Matthews looked at the check. It was postdated by a good two months, and Sanborn hadn't signed it.

Matthews bit his lip. "Sterling, I'm with you. Tell me what to do."

"We have to hold a press conference to clear up this mess about the Centurion this morning," Sanborn said. "I want you to make all the arrangements. Invite everybody. I want every newspaper, radio and television station in town here by noon. I'll begin working on my statement."

Sanborn put his arm around Matthews' shoulders.

"Northrup, my son, do this well and you will become rich beyond your wildest dreams."

Matthews reached for his hanky.

"You can count on me, Sterling."

With that, Matthews walked out the door. But before he could go very far, Sanborn called out to him.

"Oh, by the way—"

Matthews turned, still all misty eyed. "Yes?"

"I'd try the stairs if I were you," Sanborn said. "We wouldn't want you to wind up on a cold slab like Miss Connorsssss did last night. Terrible things, these industrial fatalities you know."

Then Sanborn turned and slammed the door behind him.

Chapter 20

New York

Julie and I spent what was left of the early morning hours huddled together in my apartment watching news reports of Vicki's death. The story grew more dramatic with each passing hour. By dawn, Scout was hyping it as the "tragic death of a comic book queen." But the basic facts hadn't really changed. Vicki was gone. The circumstances surrounding her death were suspicious. And we couldn't help wondering if one of us would be the next victim.

The police were clueless. In the rush to find a cause, they had overlooked the most telling piece of evidence aside from the murder scene itself—the old Centurion comic book that the assailant had left on the sixth floor. Of course, the entire building was literally stuffed with comic books, so one old issue on an empty desk wouldn't have caught my attention either. But since I had just read the exact same issue at home, it was hard to ignore the similarities between Vicki's death and the fictional account of Dr. Dana Barnes.

"What are you going to tell the police?" Julie asked.

I shrugged. "How about 'the answers you're looking for are in this comic book?'"

Julie shook her head. "You do that and they're going to wonder what planet you came from."

She was right. But at some point, the police would undoubtedly want to talk to us and I could at least plant the seed. In the meantime, all we could do was return to work and watch our backs. So later that morning, Julie and I made our way back to Excelsior, arriving just in time for the start of Sanborn's press conference in the lobby. It was bedlam. Hordes of jumpy reporters and camera crews had jammed the entrance and they were all jockeying for position.

"Mister Sanborn! Mister Sanborn!"

The Walrus, standing behind a podium on a makeshift stage, pointed his index finger at a reporter in the front row.

"Is it true you're planning to kill off the Centurion?"

"Reports of the Centurion's demise have been greatly exaggerated," Sanborn replied.

"Are you saying you're *definitely* not going to kill the Centurion?"

The Walrus chuckled. "I can assure you the Centurion's vital signs are all very healthy, and we have not changed our plans to re-invigorate the character one iota."

"But what about the Fourth of July?" another scribe asked. "Isn't that D-Day for the Centurion?"

Sanborn put his hand over the microphone and conferred with Matthews.

"The Fourth of July is an official hol-ee-day. Excelsior is closed. Our people will be enjoying the fireworks with their families," he responded.

But no one laughed.

"What about the Scout reports on TV, Mister Sanborn?" a reporter from another network finally shouted back.

Sanborn looked at his watch. Eleven thirty-five. His stock manipulation scheme was on time.

"Miss, I don't know where the information for that report came from. And I'm not going to dignify it with a comment here."

"Then why'd you bother calling a news conference if you're not going to say anything?" she asked.

Sanborn cleared his throat. "Good Lord, people. Have you no respect for the dead?"

An air of silence suddenly descended over the room. Sanborn retrieved a prepared statement from his breast pocket and began reading.

"Last night, not far from this spot, one of the brightest lights in our business was sudden-leeee and violent-leeee extinguished. Vicki Connors was an artist without peer. Her work was extra-ordinarrrrry. Her contributions to her profession were eee-mense. And we—her grieving colleagues—will not rest until the perpetrator of this heinous crime is brought to justice.

"I have called this news conference today to offer a one million dollar reward for information leading to the capture and conviction of her killer."

Sanborn paused and pretended to wipe a tear from his eye. "Now are there any further questions?"

"So you think it was murder, Mister Sanborn?" one journalist asked.

"Indeed I do," the Walrus said. "Over the past several days our headquarters facility has been repeatedly vandalized and important documents have been removed from our offices. We believe there is a connection between these late-night thefts and Miss Connors' death."

"What about her titles?" shouted a wire service reporter from the back of the room. "What will become of her characters?"

"Her final titles are in production right now. As you know, Miss Connors was also heavily involved in the Centurion project. All the preliminary artwork is hers. We are dedicating this issue—a limited edition run—to her loving memory."

Up until this point, Phil Plunkett had been content to stand by silently on the sidelines. The real story here was Vicki's death. And now that Sanborn was talking about it, he sensed the moment was right to jump into the fray.

"Didn't Vicki Connors resign yesterday because she objected to your plan to kill the Centurion?" he asked in his best Mike Wallace voice.

The Walrus grabbed his suspenders and glared back from the podium. He recognized Plunkett's face instantly.

"Mis-terrr Plunketttt. Seeing as the matter is currently under invest-e-gation, I do not think it would be appropriate for me—"

"But," Plunkett interrupted, "she was thrown out of the building yesterday by your security guards and told not to return, wasn't she?"

Sanborn bit his lip and forced a smile.

"Miss Connorssss was escorted to the parking lot. It's a courtesy service we gladly provide to any of our employees who ask for it, Mister Plunketttttt."

Plunkett rubbed his chin. "Doesn't the timing seem a little strange, Mister Sanborn? First you throw her out on the street like a piece of trash and now she shows up dead in your building. Are you going to stand there and tell me you didn't know anything about this?"

Sanborn grabbed onto the edge of the podium to contain his anger.

"Now see here, Mister Plunkettttt! Eggg-zactly what are you implying here?"

Matthews quickly grabbed the Walrus from behind. "Don't let him bait you, Sterling. It's best not to say anything at all."

Sanborn paused, closed his eyes, and counted to ten.

"As I was saying, Mister Plunketttt. The police are investigating this matter and I think it's best that I not comment any further."

Plunkett wasn't satisfied. He hadn't grilled anybody like this in years, and he wasn't about to let up now.

"Mister Sanborn, were you here last night?"

Sanborn's nostrils flared. "Why you miserable little son-of-a-bitch!" He shoved the podium to its side, jumped off the stage like a raging bull and headed straight for Plunkett.

"I'll tell you what's strange!" he screamed. "Your line of questioning is strange!"

"Harry," Plunkett yelled to his cameraman, "back up and get this all on tape."

Before he could even move, Sanborn lunged for his throat.

"Who's putting you up to these questions, Mister Plunkettttt? It's Lock-jaw isn't it?"

Plunkett grabbed Sanborn by the arms and broke his chokehold. The two then circled around the floor like a pair of wrestlers in a ring.

"I'm just looking for the truth, Mister Sanborn! Do you have a problem with that?"

Sanborn's face turned red as a beat. "If I wanted the truth, Mister Plunketttt, the last place I'd look for it is the Scout Network."

The Walrus shoved Plunkett to the floor then charged after his cameraman. "Don't move," he said. Sanborn clutched the end of camera like a megaphone and peered into the lens.

"Listen to me, Sydney! I know you're watching and this is driving you crazy. But if you want to find out what's happening to the Centurion you'll have to buy the comic book like everyone else!"

Matthews watched the exchange from atop the stage, completely horrified. "Get in there and get him away from the cameras," he yelled to the security chief.

Two burly guards immediately jumped into the crowd and pried Sanborn away.

"Your spies won't find a goddamned thing here, Sydney," the Walrus screamed, as they dragged him down a long, narrow corridor and into a small conference room.

Plunkett finally picked himself off the floor and rushed to his cameraman's side.

"Did you get all that on tape?" he asked.

The cameraman nodded. "The whole thing, Phil. I can't believe it. It's gonna be great footage."

Away from the spotlight, Matthews pleaded with Sanborn not to return to the press conference.

"Sterling, it's not going to help our cause if you're always out of control on camera." Sanborn suddenly stopped yelling and smiled.

"The hell it won't Norbert," he said, breathing heavily. "You watch. It's going to make great footage."

"What???" Matthews asked. "It's going to be great footage on the news. They'll play the hell out of it. You'll see."

"You mean you staged the whole thing?" Matthews asked.

Sanborn straightened his tie and thanked the security guards for their help.

"Staged, Norbert? I just gave the tel-ee-vision networks what they want. Stay tuned to Eyewitless News at six for more details. HAWWW! HAWWWWW! HAWWWW!"

Redding, Connecticut

Matt Payne hobbled from his bed to the bathroom and peered cautiously in the mirror. He had been home all of twenty-four hours now, but he looked worse than he did in the hospital in Mexico. Three flights, three separate time zones, and enough bad airline food to kill a horse, had left him weak and irritable, not to mention, constipated.

All things considered, however, it could have been much worse. As luck would have it, he never saw Plunkett's latest news report on the Centurion in the hospital. Alix had changed the channel to a soap opera just moments before he found her crying in a lounge. And since he still had no memory of the incident that triggered his asthma attack, he was completely in the dark over the Centurion's fate. Nevertheless, Alix wanted no more close calls, so as soon as they got home she promptly clamped a news embargo over the entire house.

"The doctor said rest," she lectured him before leaving the house to restock the refrigerator. "No TV, no radios, no newspapers, no magazines and no mail until you're feeling better. Now try to relax."

Payne sighed. Relaxing wasn't his style. As soon as Alix left the house he made a beeline for the television set. But when he turned it on—much to his surprise— there was only static on the screen. "Damn cable company," he muttered.

He carefully checked and re-checked the cable connection. But it didn't make any difference. All he could see was snow. Finally, in a pique of exasperation, he picked up the phone and dialed directory information.

"What city please?" the operator asked.

"How the hell do I know?"

"What listing are you looking for?"

"The cable company."

"Is that cable with a 'c' or a 'k'?"

"Cable with a 'c'," Payne answered. "How else would you spell it?"

"I'm sorry, sir. I have no listing for A Cable Company."

"No, no, no, madam. I'm not looking for 'A Cable Company'. I want the cable company."

"Is that 'The' with a 'T'?" the operator asked.

Payne bit his lip. "My good woman, I'm looking for the company that provides local cable television service to my home."

"Is your service out?"

"No, I'm just calling them for my own health," Payne said in exasperation.

"Did you check your cable connection?"

"Of course I did!"

"Is your television set plugged in?"

Payne looked at the TV and saw plenty of snow.

"Yes, Goddammit! I'm not feeble."

"Do you know what cable company serves your area?"

Payne rubbed his forehead. "No, that's what I'm trying to get from you."

"Where do you live?"

"Redding."

"Is that with one 'd' or two?"

"Two 'd's," he said, "as in 'dumb' and 'dumber.'"

"That must be Connecticut Cablevision then," the operator finally said.

"What's the number?" Payne asked.

"I wouldn't hold your breath waiting for 'em," the operator said. "It's gonna take at least two weeks before they got out there, trust me."

"Just give me the goddamned number!"

"773-3265," the operator responded. "Will there be anything else?"

"Not unless you can fix my cable."

CLICK.

Payne dialed the number and waited patiently on hold for another fifteen minutes.

"Are you calling about a service related outage?" a voice finally asked.

"As a matter of fact—" Payne started.

"Then press two now."

Payne pressed the number two button on his phone.

"Is the nature of your service interruption related to any downed trees or severe weather conditions?"

"Not that I'm aware of—"

"Then press three now."

Payne pounded the number three button with his finger in frustration, and was connected to a service representative.

"How may I help you?"

"Are you alive?" Payne asked.

"Excuse me?"

"Are you for goddamned real?"

"Last time I looked," the service rep answered.

"Well what does it take to get some service around here?"

"How long has your service been out?"

"Ever since I got home," Payne responded.

"You have no picture at all?"

"That's right," Payne answered.

"Did you check your cable connect—"

"Yes, damn it. And the TV is plugged in too."

"I'm looking at your record, Mister Payne. It doesn't appear to be a service problem."

"What do you mean?" Payne asked.

"Your service was suspended."

"By who?"

"Alix Payne."

Now why would she do that? Payne wondered. Then the answer came to him.

"She must have done it before we went away on vacation."

The service rep looked at Payne's record again. Alix had suspended service as soon as they had returned from Mexico.

"Actually," the rep started, "she called about it yester—"

"No matter," Payne cut in. "When can you have service restored?"

"We can have it back up within the hour, just in time for the six o'clock news."

Payne looked at his watch. Five o'clock.

"That's the best you can do?"

"I'm afraid so, sir."

"All right, I'll take it," Payne said. "But it better work. I'll be watching."

CLICK.

A few minutes before six, Payne picked up the remote and turned his television set on. Much to his relief, the snow was gone and the reception was clear. Sally Jesse Raphael was wrapping up her afternoon talk show, an intensely revealing expose entitled, "bitchy women and the men who love them." So he sat back in his easy chair and waited for Eyewitness News to begin.

On the other end of the camera, Phil Plunkett shuffled his manuscript between his hands and waited patiently for the cue to begin reading his promo.

"Are you sure you didn't sustain any injuries during the scuffle?" Schaffi asked over the intercom.

"For the last time Manny, I'm fine," Plunkett answered.

"What about the scrape on your face? Is it still bleeding?"

A messenger handed Plunkett a special delivery package.

"Manny, I'm fine," he said, slipping the package under the anchor desk. "Don't make a bigger deal out of this than it already is."

Schaffi cut the intercom off from the production booth and turned to his assistant.

"I want some goddamned blood in this thing. When I give you the signal I want you to zoom in on his chin, real tight."

Schaffi flipped the intercom switch back on.

"Standby promo on my cue. Five, four, intro music, two, one. You're on, Phil."

Plunkett's face beamed directly into the living rooms of millions of homes, including Payne's.

"Coming up tonight on Eyewitness News ... leaping lizards, Batman! We'll show you how comic book publisher Sterling Sanborn the Third reacted today to our exclusive report that the Centurion will soon die."

Videotape of Sanborn lunging at Plunkett during the press conference filled the screen and Payne gasped.

"We'll have exclusive details of the violent scuffle that erupted during a televised news conference—"

Off camera, Schaffi screamed to his assistant. "Now, now. His chin!!!"

Camera Six immediately locked in on Plunkett's bruised chin, as he continued reading.

"—along with the latest on the real-life death of American comic book queen Vicki Connors, right after these words from the makers of Gynoloteriman."

"Cut to commercial," Schaffi barked at the studio. "Phil, you looked great."

As Plunkett's image slowly disappeared from the screen, Payne put his head in his hands and started crying.

Chapter 21

Excelsior Headquarters

Videotape of Sanborn scuffling on the floor with Plunkett became instant headline news on virtually every major network and front page around the world. Wall Street, as the Walrus had predicted, loved every minute of it—especially the part about the upcoming limited edition Centurion issue—and promptly sent Trieste's stock soaring.

"The stock of Excelsior's parent company—Trieste Communications—jumped more than forty-five points this afternoon on increased earnings expectations," Plunkett said during his newscast, "a new all time high."

Sanborn couldn't have been more pleased with himself.

"Did you hear that, Misterrrrr Ledererrrr?"

Lederer pulled his chair up closer to the television set in Sanborn's office.

"Several analysts upgraded the stock to a strong buy," Plunkett continued.

"Unbelievable," Lederer mumbled to himself. "Un-fucking believable."

"How much does that give us now, William?" Sanborn asked as he puffed away on a smoky Cuban cigar.

Lederer poked away at his calculator.

"The three billion dollars we invested in the pension fund is now worth more than five and a half billion," he began.

Sanborn's eyes grew as big as melons.

"And the one billion dollars that we invested in your name is worth about one and a half billion," Lederer continued.

"For a grand total of seven billion dollars," the Walrus crowed. "Not bad for a day's work. And we're not done yet."

"Oh yes, we are," Lederer said, shaking his head. "You're playing Russian Roulette with the stock, and I have no intention of spending my retirement as your cell mate in Sing Sing."

"Spare me the speeches, Wil-l-l-l-iam." Sanborn took a long drag on his cigar and slowly exhaled.

"I recognize that there is a certain, shall we say, el-eee-ment of risk here, Wil-l-l-liam. And I'm willing to see to it that you are fairly compensated for your loyalt-eeeeee."

"Loyalty?" Lederer responded. "This has nothing to do with loyalty. What you're talking about is an outright bribe."

"All right, Wil-l-l-liam, if that's what you'd prefer, I'll call it a bribe."

Lederer's mood suddenly shifted. Now the Walrus was talking his language.

"How much is my 'loyalty' worth to you, Sterling?" Lederer asked.

"Shall we say, perhaps, twenty percent of the bount-eeeee on this profitable day?"

Twenty percent? Lederer did a quick calculation in his head and it wasn't enough. "That might cover the bail bond and a good lawyer," he said.

"Thirty-five percent and not a penny less, Sterling."

Sanborn frowned. "That's too much."

"Not if you don't want to get caught, Sterling. Thirty-five percent is a bargain compared to thirty-five years in the slammer. Think of it as disaster insurance."

Sanborn didn't like it when others played by his rules. But this time he was in no position to disagree. "Very well. Wil-l-l-liam," he said, reluctantly. "Thirty-five percent it is. But tomorrow at the opening bell I want you to sell our new equity position."

Lederer nodded. "The sooner the better—"

"Then at four o'clock I want you to go back in with another ten billion from the pension fund and buy an even bigger stake in my name."

Lederer nearly gagged. "Are you out of your mind? Two major trades in less than seventy-two hours? You might as well take out an ad in *The Wall Street Journal* if you're going to be that obvious."

"I don't care if Jesus H. Christ himself gets wind of it," Sanborn replied. "I want this done and I want you to do it."

"Why tomorrow?" Lederer asked. "Why can't you wait a few weeks until things settle down?"

Sanborn reached into his desk drawer and pulled out a heavy loose-leaf binder.

"Feast your eyes on this, my boy," he said, tossing the book in Lederer's lap. It was a confidential internal report from Scout.

"Scout's Global Entertainment Network: Analysis and Prospectus," Lederer read aloud. "Where did you get this?"

Sanborn laughed. "Lock-jaw's not the only one with spies."

Lederer started to thumb through the report.

"Take a look at the last page," Sanborn said, exhaling slowly.

Lederer quickly turned to the back of the book.

"Conclusion: The downturn in worldwide advertising revenues, coupled with severe currency devaluations in key overseas markets, has negatively impacted Scout's network earnings potential. Non-performing acquisitions in continental Europe and Australia are draining cash reserves, and have pushed debt ceilings beyond acceptable comfort levels. Program ratings in several key developed markets have declined. These factors cast a cloud over the company's ability to maintain the kind of earnings growth and investments required to expand the network's programming to new geographies. In this weakened position, Scout's ability to fight off potential suitors is in doubt."

Lederer looked up from the page and removed his glasses.

"Sterling, you're not seriously thinking of making a hostile takeover run at Scout?"

"What's wrong with that?" Sanborn asked.

"Even if we were able to pull it off we'd never be able to service the debt level. We're barely making a go of it now."

"I don't want to service any debt whatsoever," Sanborn said. "I want to sell the company off one piece at a time. It's worth a king's ransom."

"That's what it will take to do this," Lederer said. "A huge war chest."

"But we're seven billion dollars closer to it now than we were twenty-four hours ago, Wi-l-l-liam."

"You'd need ten times that much," Lederer countered. "Maybe more. And you'd still have to sell off half the crown jewels to pull it off. The publishing companies, the comic books, your yacht, and all your real estate holdings."

"I'm well aware of that," Sanborn said.

"And then what have you got?" Lederer asked. "He's as overextended as we are. Maybe more. Why would you want to risk everything you've worked so hard for, plus a possible jail term, for a company like Scout?"

"Because, my dear Wil-l-l-liam, that 'company' is owned by Sir Sydney Lockwood. He has hounded me all my life. I intend to put that bastard out of business once and for all, and I don't care if it takes every fucking shilling I've got."

Sanborn took the report back and cradled it in his arms.

"But we have to strike NOW when he is most vulnerable and least expects it. Surprise is our greatest ally."

"That's what the Japanese said before Pearl Harbor," Lederer said.

Sanborn scowled.

"Sell at the opening bell and then go back in with a buy order at four for ten billion dollars. Do I make myself clear?"

Lederer nodded. "It's your life."

Rooty's Pump Room was as unlikely a place to hold a staff meeting as any in New York. The beer was flat, the food was stale, and the atmosphere was just one notch above a morgue on a chilly night. Not surprisingly, it was Mike Billington's kind of place.

"Whaddya have?" the bartender asked.

"Jack Daniels on the rocks," Billington said. "Give my friends here two drafts."

The waiter looked at me and Julie sitting there together like timid rabbits and laughed.

"First time here?" he asked.

Billington nodded. "I'll vouch for 'em."

"Don't worry," the bartender said, "everything's well preserved."

"You really think Sanborn was behind Vicki's death?" I asked.

"The Walrus is capable of anything," Billington replied. "Especially when he's backed into a corner."

"Even if he did," Julie began, "where would it get him? Vicki was already gone. Why kill her?"

Billington didn't say a word. He was too busy watching a roach crawling across the table, just behind Julie's arm.

BLAMMMMMM!

Billington peeled his hand off the tabletop and brushed the flattened bug onto the floor.

Julie nearly died.

"Sanborn didn't do it," Billington said. "He's too smart for that. He'd pay someone else to do the job. And then Vicki would have just disappeared."

"What about Matthews?" I said.

"Too jumpy," Billington said. "Besides, he worshiped her. More likely it's some sick-o."

"A fan?" I asked.

"Could be," Billington said. "Lot of old timers out there love the Centurion."

"Enough to kill?" Julie asked.

Billington downed his shot glass. "More likely it's somebody inside."

"You mean somebody we work with?" I asked.

"Do the math. Illustrations are disappearing from right under our noses. Word keeps leaking out about our work. Now Vicki is gone. And it all happens right in the building."

"How about the old comic book I read?"

Billington rubbed his chin. "I'd say somebody we know isn't very happy about what we're doing."

"Any idea who?" Julie asked.

"Sanborn's pissed so many people off, it could be anyone," he said. "But whoever it is knows how to kill."

"What about going to the cops?" I asked.

"Waste of time," Billington said.

"How can you be so sure?"

"They hate us," Billington said. "Sanborn backed the wrong horse in the last election. Donated millions to the guy. He ran on a platform to reform the NYPD. They're not going to be any help to us now."

"We've got to do something," Julie said.

Billington leaned over and lowered his voice. "Watch your backside, watch what you say, don't go out alone, and keep working."

Just then the waiter reappeared alongside the table. "You want anything to eat?"

I looked at the menu but I really didn't have much of an appetite.

"What would you recommend?"

Billington smirked. "Prayers, Rick. Lotsa prayers."

Chapter 22

Brooklyn

Mitch Gerber folded up the evening newspaper and pinned it to the drawing table in his apartment. Then with a razor sharp knife he carefully cut out a picture of Vicki Connors from the front page and pasted it onto a blank sheet of paper.

"So tragic," he wrote in his best long hand, next to Vicki's photo. "But it's not like she didn't have it coming."

Gerber was supposed to be finishing up one of the titles he had inherited when Vicki quit, but with all that had happened over the past twenty-four hours his mind clearly wasn't on his work.

He had read the story of Connor's death at least a dozen times during the day, and each time he had felt a deeper sense of satisfaction. That her death should come at the bottom of an elevator shaft—nearly mirroring the fate that nearly doomed Dr. Dana Barnes all those years ago—was poetic justice. More than any other issue, *Murder on the Sixth Floor* had launched the Centurion to fame. It was one of his personal favorites; the pride of his own privation collection. And he instinctively knew that the circumstances surrounding Vicki's death were strikingly similar to the events that played out in this long forgotten issue.

"She should have left us alone, and none of this would have happened," Gerber wrote. "But she had to learn the hard way."

Gerber placed the note in an overnight envelope, along with a dozen discarded sketches he had found in our conference room. He flipped through his little black book until he found Matt Payne's home address.

"Sleep better tonight, my friend. The Centurion isn't dead yet."

When he was done he carefully returned his copy of *Murder on the Sixth Floor* into its plastic sleeve. Then he picked up the next installment in the old series and blew the dust off its clear jacket. The title—*Murder on the Subways*—eventually appeared in bold colors and it made him smile. Gerber had come to the right place for inspiration. In the dim light of his apartment, he opened the issue and began reading the story aloud.

"*Midnight and Nickel City is shrouded in a deep fog. The streets are still, for few* are brave enough to venture where they cannot see. John Sullivan is not so easily dissuaded. He does not fear the night.

"Heading home from work—an unusually late evening at the office—Sullivan walks through the turnstile into the musty subway station below Genesee Street and waits quietly for the subway home."

Gerber took a long, slow drag on his cigarette.

"His mind is preoccupied with the manuscripts he must still edit, the pages he has yet to read. He is not at all aware of the dark and foreboding presence that lurks closely behind."

With each line he could feel his heart pounding stronger. He gazed at a picture of the Centurion hanging on the wall over his bed like a shrine. "The gods are with us. I can sense it."

Time? Gerber looked at his watch and nearly panicked. Eleven twenty-three. He quickly packed up his knife, shut the lights and raced out of the building.

Midtown Manhattan
Midnight

Even on a good night, the 38th Street subway station looked like it had been through a war. The walls were covered with graffiti. The stairs were cracked and crumbling. The platform reeked from urine. And when it poured, as it did that evening, water cascaded through the ceiling and down the walls. But for someone like Mike Billington, who instinctively preferred the road less traveled, it was the perfect way to end a less than perfect day.

As soon as he got past the turnstile, Billington went through his usual security checks, carefully scoping out the station, section by section, for any signs of trouble. Mike was always prepared for the worst. His handgun—a potent Charter Arms & Bulldog forty-four caliber revolver—was loaded and carefully concealed on his belt holster. But he doubted if he'd need it. The station was completely empty. So he waited quietly on the platform for a downtown subway with his nose buried in the latest issue of *Soldier of Fortune*.

Maybe he had too much to drink at dinner with us, or perhaps it was because he had grown so accustomed to the surroundings. Then again, maybe it was just fate. For whatever reason, Mike didn't follow his own advice that evening and openly courted danger. He traveled alone. He didn't watch his backside. His mind was preoccupied with work. And like John Sullivan, he never saw the lone figure moving slowly toward him from behind. Nor did he see the first blow coming straight at him. All he felt was a sudden and sharp surge of pain racing across the back of his neck. It was a powerful jolt, enough to knock the wind from his lungs and force him to his knees. An instant later he was struck once more—this time on the side of the head—with such force that he hit the concrete platform face first and blacked out.

"Wake up, oh mighty warrior." At first, the voice was faint—deep and raspy and barely audible. But little by little it grew more insistent. As Billington regained his senses, each syllable brought forth more pain.

"WAKE UP, MIGHTY WARRIOR!!!" A strong, willful hand grabbed a clump of Billington's hair from behind and lifted his head off the platform.

Blood trickled down his face, blurring his vision, and he could feel the cold blade of a sharp knife against his throat.

"B-b-b-back pocket," he moaned. "T-t-t-take it. The money's yours."

"I don't want your money," the voice whispered into his ear. "No amount of money can undo what you've done."

"What do you want then?" Billington asked.

"I want you," the assailant answered. "You and you alone must atone for your sins."

Billington couldn't move. The attack had been so quick and so debilitating that he had no strength to fight back.

"Why are you doing this?" he finally asked.

"You of all people should have known better," the attacker answered. "You can't kill a warrior like the Centurion."

Billington started to black out again.

"Oh no you don't!" the assailant pulled Billington's heavy frame from the floor and shook him by his shoulders. "You're going to listen to this even if it kills you. Do you hear me?"

Billington inhaled slowly. "I-I-I hear you," he muttered.

"Now listen carefully," the assailant said. "What sound do you hear?"

The telltale rumble of an approaching subway train loomed in the distance.

Billington coughed. "The A Train," he said, "track three."

"Very good," the voice whispered into his ear. "In about two minutes it's going to come barreling past this stop at eighty-six miles an hour and you're going to meet it. Head on."

The assailant grabbed Billington by the neck and dragged him to the edge of the platform, forcing his head out over the tracks.

"But before you cross over to the other side, I have to help you see the light, Mister Billington. I want you to repeat after me. Killing the Centurion is wrong."

Billington didn't respond. The assailant immediately pulled him onto the platform and forced the knife back into his chin.

"I don't hear you big fella. Let's try again. Killing the Centurion is wrong."

Billington played along. He had no other choice. "Killing the Centurion is wrong."

"Very good," the assailant said. "The Centurion is a hero to millions."

Billington obediently repeated the words.

"He was sent here to protect mankind from the evil that lurks within…"

Billington coughed up blood and forced out the words. "He was sent here to protect mankind from the evil that lurks within."

"No one," the assailant continued, "not even me is going to stop him."

"No one," Billington slowly repeated, "not even me is going to stop him."

"Now isn't that better?" the assailant asked. "Do you see the light?"

Billington looked up and saw a single headlight heading straight toward him on the track.

"DO YOU SEE IT?"

"I see it."

"Do you understand what it means?"

"I do," Billington said.

"Good," the assailant said, pulling Billington back onto the platform. "I was afraid you might need more convincing."

"You've convinced me," Billington responded.

"Such a pity you didn't see it sooner."

"What do you mean?" Billington asked.

"You didn't think it was that easy, did you? First, you impale the Centurion. Then you have him ripped to shreds by flying monkeys. You still have to pay for all that."

Billington struggled to free himself. But it was no use. The assailant was too strong, he was too weak, and the knife was too close for comfort.

"Ah, but I promise you it will be quick." The assailant thrust Billington's head back out over the platform. "Not at all like what you had in mind for the Centurion."

The subway line was much closer now—so close that Billington could almost make out the train's call numbers on the head car.

"You're making a big mistake," Billington pleaded. "Don't do this."

"Au contraire," the assailant yelled over the rumble of the tracks.

"I should have done this a long time ago."

Billington knew he had just a split second to act or it was all over. As the train surged forth, he summoned up every last ounce of his strength and hurled himself away from the open track, back into the arms of his surprised assailant. The two tumbled backwards, rolling over each other several times until a turnstile finally stopped their momentum with a thud.

Billington made it to his feet first, quickly kicked the knife from the attacker's hand, and then staggered for cover behind the ticket booth. His head was throbbing, and his heart was racing like an engine. But he was still a soldier at heart, and he had the presence of mind to draw his gun and wait silently in the shadows for the assailant to make the next move.

But nothing happened. Billington poked his head out from behind the ticket booth. From where he was, he could see the assailant lying face down and motionless near the turnstile. Eventually, when he had caught his breath, Billington picked himself up and stumbled toward the figure.

The assailant was average in size, no more than five feet eight, if that tall, and was wearing a green army jacket, leather gloves and a black ski mask. *A masked avenger.* Billington couldn't believe it. *How could someone this small have inflicted so much pain?*

"Get up," he yelled, with his gun leading the way. "Let's see how brave you are now."

Still the assailant didn't move. *Something's not right,* Billington thought at first. *We didn't hit the turnstile that hard.*

He poked at the figure with his foot, and when nothing happened he flipped the body over. There were no signs of life anywhere. No breathing. No twitching. Nothing. Billington had seen Viet Cong fake death before in battle, but never quite this well. Nevertheless, he had to be sure, so he tried an old trick from the jungle. Billington spotted the assailant's knife about ten feet away. He quickly retrieved it and poked the figure sharply in the arm. There was no reaction. Just a tiny stream of blood trickled to the floor.

"Looks like you got run over by a freight train," Billington said when he was certain there was no fight left in his foe. He tossed the knife to his side and took a deep breath. The pain had subsided, but his curiosity hadn't. He wanted to know who had attacked him and why before the police got there. So he knelt down beside the body, his gun still pointed directly at the assailant, and carefully started to remove the mask with his left hand. But then something went wrong. Terribly wrong. The lifeless figure below him suddenly gasped for air and bolted up from the floor with a concealed switchblade that found its mark just above Billington's belt, carving a bloody path toward his heart. It happened so swiftly and so suddenly that Billington couldn't react.

"What is it they say, Mister Billington, about curiosity killing the cat?" the assailant asked.

Billington screamed, as the knife slowly twisted inside him and his life started slipping away.

"You call yourself a warrior?" the figure yelled. "You should have finished me off when you had the chance. Now you will feel the full fury of the Centurion!"

A moment later, just as the lights from another subway train emerged from the tunnel at the edge of the station, Billington collapsed.

The assailant quickly grabbed Billington's coat by the collar and dragged his two-hundred sixty-pound frame toward the edge of the platform. "I'm afraid it's lights out, old warrior."

Then with one final heave from behind, the assailant pushed Billington's bloody body over the edge of the platform directly onto the railway bed. A few seconds later an express train sped by and it was all over, exactly the way it had happened in the pages of an old comic book that hadn't seen the light of day in half a century.

When the last car disappeared into the northbound tunnel, the assailant peered over the platform at the tracks below and saluted.

"Farewell old soldier," the assailant said. "You made the ultimate sacrifice. You gave your life for your company."

Chapter 23

Aboard Sanborn's Yacht
New York Harbor

A few hours later, Sanborn was aroused from a deep sleep aboard his private yacht, *"The Relentless."*

"I'm so sorry to disturb you sir," his butler said. "But you have an important call from Mister Montana."

Sanborn sat up in bed, not completely coherent, and nodded. He knew Montana would only call at this hour if it was urgent, so he quickly reached for the phone. "Thank you, Alfred."

"Stoi-ling, wake up." Montana said.

"What is it James?"

"I just got a call from our guy in da Thirty-Eighth Precinct downtown," Montana said. "One of your people has turned up in da subway station."

Sanborn looked at the nautical clock on his night table. *Three A.M.*

"Probably couldn't find any cabs at this hour, I would eeee-magine," Sanborn said.

"No, Stoi-ling, it's not like dat," Montana replied. "Dey found him dead."

"Dead?"

"Dat's right. Cops peeled what was left of him off da front of da "A" train about twenty minutes ago."

"Who is it?"

"Does the name Michael Billington mean anything to you?" Montana asked.

"Good Lord, Bill-eeeng-ton?" the Walrus asked. "Are you sure?"

"Dats what his license says. Dey found it in his wallet on da track."

Sanborn threw off his blanket and sat up in bed. "Let me guess. Your people had nothing to do with this, right?"

Montana cracked his knuckles. "You got it, Stoi-ling. We don't leave no evi-dee—"

"No ev-eee-dence," Sanborn finished the sentence, "I know. I know. Was it su-eeee-cide?"

"Not likely," Montana said. "Dere's blood all over da freakin' platform. Really pisses me off."

"Why's that?" the Walrus asked.

"Whoever is doing dis is making it difficult for professionals to make a living. It's getting so you don't know who's coming or goin'. And now the cops are puttin' da heat on us and we didn't even do it."

"Quite disconcerting," Sanborn said.

"How 'bout you, Stoi-ling? You wouldn't be using another service, would you?"

Sanborn shook his head. "Heavens no, Sir James. Besides, I didn't want him dead. He was a pain in the ass with that rotten att-eee-tude of his, but his books are big sellers."

Montana laughed. "You ain't seen nothing yet, Stoi-ling."

"What do you mean?"

"C'mon Stoi-ling. He's a big name. His characters have strong followings. Now he's dead. We've been through dis drill before."

"Oh, Christ!" Sanborn exclaimed. "We have another dead martyr on our hands, don't we?"

"My boys are raising all da prices on his stuff as we speak."

"Everything he did is an instant classic now, right?"

"Egg-zactly Einstein."

"Not to mention," Sanborn added, "Billington's name is all over the Centurion project."

"Are you thinking what I'm thinking?" Montana asked.

Sanborn started to choke up. "Death to the Centurion, dedicated in loving memory to Vicki Connors and Mike Billington."

"Stoi-ling, it's gonna be historic," Montana said. "Play this right and we could make more money in da next few hours than when did in da last few days."

"Has Plunkett gotten wind of this yet?" the Walrus asked.

"Nah. My boys are gonna keep dings quiet until we finish marking up da inventory, Stoi-ling."

"Then we'll have to move fast," Sanborn said. "I would assume another press conference is in order?"

"Yes," Montana said. "But it can't looked staged dis time."

Sanborn retrieved his notepad from his night table and started scribbling. "What do you suggest?"

"Go in a little late. Use da front entrance and let da cameras corner you when you get out of the car."

"Got it," Sanborn said. "Same formula as the last time? Shock, outrage and mourning?"

"Dat's good," Montana said. "But no prepared statement. Just take questions."

"Should we increase the reward?"

"Double it."

Sanborn gasped. "Double it?"

"Even dat's not enough," Montana said.

"Two million dollars isn't enough?" Sanborn asked.

"We've done it before," Montana said. "We need something else to go with it dat will really blow everyone away."

"Any suggestions?"

Montana thought for a moment. "Put a bounty on da killer's head."

"A bount-eeee?" the Walrus asked.

"You heard me Stoi-ling. A bounty."

"You mean like bring him back dead or alive?"

"Let's be more specific," Montana said. "How about, 'two million dollars to the first person who brings me his head!'"

Sanborn paused. "It has a nice ring to it."

"You bet it does," Montana said. "Da TV stations will eat it up."

"But are you sure we can do that, Sir James?"

"Dis is America, Stoi-ling," Montana said. "You can SAY anything you like and always take it back later."

"But aren't there laws against that sort of thing?"

"Can you help it if you're all overcome by da emotional trauma of da moment?" Montana asked.

"No, I, uh, suppose not—"

"Can you help it if you temporarily lose control of your senses when a reporter asks, 'What are you doing to stop da killer from attacking again?'"

"Now that you mention it—"

"No one could blame you, Stoi-ling, if you just blurted it out—da perfect sound bite—raced back into da building, and issued a very contrite clarification after every freakin' network in da world broadcasts it."

"Hmmm, quite true," the Walrus mused. "But how do we know a reporter will ask the question?"

"Don't worry about it, Sterling. Half da reporters in town are on my payroll."

"What about Plunkett?" Sanborn asked. "He'll be all over this thing."

"Did you send him da sketches of da Centurion?"

"Indeed I did."

"Good" Montana said. "Let's give him da exclusive on Billington too. That'll keep him and Lockwood guessing."

Sanborn rubbed his hands together with glee. "If they only knew what we're really up to. Old Sydney would go into convulsions."

"I take it you've made all da necessary arrangements to capitalize on our good fortunes?" Montana asked.

"We'll have to adjust our timetable a bit now, but we'll be playing the market for all it's worth today."

"If Wall Street cooperates, we could lower da boom on Lockwood next week," Montana said.

"What a glorious day that will be," the Walrus gushed.

"True. But we still need something big to finish Lockwood off after we make our bid for Scout," Montana added. "Is da Centurion finale going to be ready on time?"

"I believe so," the Walrus said, "providing we don't lose any more talent."

"You better light a fire under dat task force of yours before dey disappear, too, Stoi-loing."

"Oh, I will," the Walrus replied. "You can count on it."

"And you might wanna consider more protection for yourself while you're at it," Montana said.

"Protection, James?"

"With all that's going down, you can't be too careful nowadays."

"I appreciate your concern," Sanborn replied, "but at the moment I'm rather unattached."

Montana rolled his eyes. "Stoi-ling, your people are dropping like flies. The last ding you want is to meet dis killer face-to-face."

"Meet him," Sanborn laughed. "With all the money he's making us, I'd like to put him on the payroll."

Two hours later, the phone in Phil Plunkett's apartment started ringing.

"Yeah, what is it?" Plunkett said when he finally answered it.

"Plunkett? Is this Phil Plunkett?"

"Who's calling?"

"A friend," the voice said.

"It's five o'clock in the morning, *friend*."

"Early bird gets the worm, Phil."

Plunkett rubbed his eyes. "Whaddya talking about?"

"There's a big story waiting for you in the Thirty-Eighth Street subway station and it's all yours. But you better hurry."

"Story?" Plunkett quickly shook off the cobwebs and sat straight up in bed. "What kind of story?"

"You'll see when you get there. But I'd bring a camera crew if I were you."

"Why?" Plunkett asked. "What kind of story is it?"

"It's bigger than a bread basket."

"You're going to have to do better than that," Plunkett said.

"Its got lots of great visuals—blood, gore, violence—you name it," the voice continued.

"You've got my attention," Plunkett replied.

"If you look hard enough you might find a connection with the Centurion story you're so hot and bothered about. And right now you're the only reporter in town who knows about it."

Plunkett jumped out of bed. "I'm on my way."

Over the next three hours, all the elements of Sanborn's plan began to fall into place. Plunkett arrived at the subway station with his camera crew just in time to be personally escorted to the crime scene by a contingent of New York's finest. Matthews coached Sanborn's limo driver through a series of early morning drive-by maneuvers in front of Excelsior's headquarters. And Lederer rushed to Sanborn's yacht to choreograph the timing of his market trades. "Buy at the opening bell before the market can react to Billington's death," Sanborn ordered. "Then lock in the gains and sell as soon as I announce the bount-eeee offer. When the stock has dropped back down, we go back in again and buy it on the upswing."

At nine-thirty, Lederer executed the first buy order for ten million dollars. Fifteen minutes later, shortly after Trieste's stock opened for trading on Wall Street, the Scout Network interrupted its regular programming for a news bulletin announcing Billington's death. A half-hour later, just as Julie and I were approaching the office—completely unaware of what had happened—Sanborn's black limousine pulled up to the front entrance of the building and was immediately surrounded by a horde of ravenous reporters and camera crews.

Before he stepped out of the car, the Walrus donned a pair of dark sunglasses and put on his most dour face. Then he forced open the door and emerged from the limo, the very picture of a grief-stricken chief executive.

Dozens of reporters shouted out to him all at once. "Mister Sanborn, Mister Sanborn?? What is your reaction to Michael Billington's death?"

Sanborn stopped dead in his tracks and looked directly at the cameras. "I can not find words to express my grief over this unsp-eeeee-kable tragedy."

Then he removed his shades and pretended to wipe a tear from his eyes.

"Michael was so young, so brave, so talented," he said. "And he had so much to live for."

"What have the police told you?" asked one reporter standing directly in front of him.

"What else could they say? He's dead. Does anything else really matter?"

"Do you see any connection between this and Vicki Connors' death, Mister Sanborn?"

"Forty-eight hours ago they were two of the most talented ind-eeee-vidiuals in our business," he said with a sniffle. "Now they're dead."

"How will this effect your operations, Mister Sanborn?" another voice called out from the pack.

Sanborn shrugged. "We haven't even given it a thought yet. Mister Bill-eee-ngton's story lines and characters were very popular. We'll do our best to carry on without him and get his last nine issues printed and published."

Sanborn paused. "All *NINE* of them. They are the last of their kind. And once they're gone, that's it. Forever."

"What about the Centurion project?"

"I haven't had a chance to discuss it with his remaining colleagues," Sanborn said. "But in light of the circumstances, I'm sure we will certainly consider commemorating the upcoming Centurion's collector's issue to the memory of both Vicki and Mike."

Then, sensing it was time to deliver his finale, the Walrus started heading toward the building. The sea of journalists surrounding him surged forth as well.

"Are you going to increase your reward, Mister Sanborn?" someone called out to him.

"That I can answer," he replied forcefully. "I am doubling the reward for information about the killer to two million dollars."

"But what are you doing to stop the killer from attacking again, Mister Sanborn?"

That was his cue—the question he had been waiting for to shift into high gear. True to form, he promptly turned toward the cameras, like an angry tiger and roared.

"I'll tell you what I'd like to do," Sanborn said. "I'd like to give that two million dollars to the first person who brings me his head!"

A curtain of silence suddenly descended over the scene. Then, after what seemed like an eternity, Scout's Maria Vasquez Mitchell stepped forward and shoved her microphone under Sanborn's nose.

"Are you saying you're offering a bounty on the killer's head?"

Sanborn's face grew even more determined. "Call it what you'd like, my dear. If that's what it takes to stop this madness, then so be it."

Before anyone could ask another question, Sanborn turned quickly and disappeared into the building.

Lederer, who had been watching the proceedings on CNN in his office twelve stories above, picked up the phone.

"Harry," he said with a sigh, "sell our position. All of it."

"Are you nuts?" the broker asked. "The stock is up forty-five points and the momentum is incredible."

"I know Harry. But those are my orders."

Across town, Sanborn's comments were already causing a stir in the *Post's* newsroom. As soon as he saw the television report, Foster Spencer, the paper's chief copy editor, picked up the phone and called downstairs to the Composing Room.

"Hold page one for a picture of Sanborn and a new banner headline."

"What's it gonna be, chief?" the foreman asked.

"How's this sound? Off With His Head!"

Chapter 24

Greenwich, Connecticut

Through nobody really noticed, Phil Plunkett was missing in action at curbside that morning. Having scooped the entire town with word of Billington's death earlier in the day, he quickly jumped into a news cruiser and headed for Connecticut to tell Maxine about Billington's death, since he was certain she hadn't seen it on the news.

Breaking bad news on television was never a problem for Plunkett. Doing it in person was an entirely different matter.

"What am I going to say to her?" he asked. "They just got engaged."

Arty Crenshaw, Plunkett's cameraman and driver for the day, pulled the van up along the gravel driveway that circled in front of his old house, and stopped.

"Take her hand and break it to her gently, Phil," he said. "That's all you can do. When she gets all emotional offer her your shoulder to cry on."

"Which one?" Plunkett asked.

Arty looked at him for a moment. "Your right side. That's definitely your better shoulder."

"And what do I do if she gets hysterical?"

"That's what you want. Hysterics plays well on camera. If you need me, I'll be right out here. I know CPR."

"Thanks," Plunkett said. "That's reassuring."

Arty jumped out of the van and lit a cigarette, while Plunkett rang the buzzer. Several minutes later Maxine opened the door.

"Phil, what are you doing here?" she asked. "It's not Saturday and Larry is in school."

"I know, Max. I have something to tell you. You might want to sit down."

Maxine looked at the serious expression on his face and hesitated.

"Phil, it'll have to wait. I've got a hair appointment in ten minutes."

"You're going to have to reschedule—"

"Are you crazy?" she said. "Do you know how long I had to wait for this appointment?"

Plunkett held up his hand. "Max, there's no easy way to tell you this," he said. "It's Michael. He's dead."

She looked at him for a second and then laughed. "Don't you wish, Phil. I know you don't like him but—"

"No, no, no, Maxie," he grabbed her by the hand. "It's nothing like that. I covered the story this morning. He was found dead on the subway tracks in Manhattan. I'm so sorry."

Maxine stared at him blankly. "You're serious, aren't you?"

Plunkett shook his head. "I'm afraid so."

Maxine froze, rock solid, like a marble statue.

"Max? Max? Are you all right?"

She didn't respond. She just stood there, completely numb.

Plunkett opened the door behind her and gently led her back inside to a comfortable couch in the living room.

"Max, say something," he said.

But she didn't budge. Plunkett waited patiently by her side. And then he waited some more. But it was no use.

"Don't go away," he said. "I have to get something in the van. I'll be right back."

Plunkett darted outside, half panicked. "Arty? Arty?" he whispered. "Where the Christ are you?"

Arty popped up from behind a shrub near the living room's main window, with his camera strapped over his shoulder.

"You gotta do something, Phil," he said. "What the hell are we gonna do with video of a zombie?"

"What am I supposed to do Arty? She's in shock. She's out millions. She could be like this for hours."

"Maybe that's how you get her to open up Phil," Arty said. "Take it all over again from the top and this time tell her how much money she's lost."

"Are you in a good position to get it all?" Plunkett asked.

"Windows's open. Don't worry about me. I've got the best seat in the house."

Plunkett marched back into the living room and sat down next to her on the couch.

"Maxine," he said, taking her hand. "Listen to me. I have some bad news. Michael's dead. The police found his body early this morning in the subway."

She still didn't react.

"What a terrible loss this must be," he said, shaking his head. "You had a wonderful life planned together. Not to mention all those *MILLIONS* you would have inherited someday…"

Plunkett stopped. A tear started rolling down her cheek.

"You would have been RICH," he continued. "*FILTHY RICH.* Independently SECURE..."

More tears.

"You'd never have to worry about *MONEY* for the rest of your life..."

Maxine started sobbing uncontrollably.

"You could have had a *FLEET* of cars. Jaguars, Mercedes, *BMW's,* in all your favorite colors..."

She buried her head in his shoulder and really started screaming.

"Not to mention a *BIGGER HOUSE.* Maybe a mansion next door to *KATHY LEE* on Long Island Sound..."

That did it. Maxine began sobbing hysterically. "Oh my God!" she screamed. "My life is over!"

Plunkett held onto her tightly, the way he had years ago when they fell in love. Then, in the sheer emotion of the moment, he gazed out the window and Arty gave him a hearty "thumbs up." His second exclusive of the day was in the bag. And this was one story he was absolutely positive no one else would have at six o'clock.

"Now, now, now," he said, "Let it all out. I understand and I'm here to listen."

Neither Julie or I remember the elevator ride down to the dungeon, but I do remember who was waiting for us when we got there.

"Mister MacAllister," Matthews said. "This is Detective Charles Gill from the New York City Police Department."

Gill peered out from beneath his wide-brimmed hat, looking every bit as imposing as he did on television, and nodded.

"Detective Gill is investigating the unfortunate demise of your two colleagues," Matthews said. "He'd like to spend a few minutes with you."

"Be happy to," I said.

"By the way," Matthews added as he walked out of the room, "as soon as you're done let's talk about where you stand on the Centurion issue."

Gill removed his trench coat and sat down. "You work for him?" he asked.

"Some days more than others," I said.

"Lucky you," he replied. "I understand both of you were with the deceased last night?"

"Until about eleven o'clock," I answered. "We went out for drinks and a bite to eat."

"Where?"

"Rootie's Pump Room."

Gill made a notation in his notepad. "Good burgers," he said. "Atmosphere stinks."

"Michael liked to go there," Julie said. "He knew everyone."

"Anything suspicious happen while you were there?"

"Like what?"

"Did he have words with anyone?"

"Nope."

"Anybody strange show up—an ex-girlfriend, his bookie?"

"No."

"Any hookers?"

"Hookers?" I asked.

"Gotta ask," Gill replied.

"No hookers that I'm aware of."

"Did anybody come up to you and start talking?"

"Just the bartender," Julie said. "He took our order."

"How did Mister Billington seem?" Gill asked. "Was he troubled?"

"Mike wasn't the type to commit suicide, if that's what you're inferring," I answered. "He was concerned about Vicki's death. Just like us."

"Did you talk about it?"

"Yeah. Michael thought the killer might be somebody on the inside," Julie said. "Someone who knows what we're up to."

Gill looked around the room. "And what might that be?"

"We're working on the final Centurion issue."

Gill stopped taking notes. "You really gonna kill him off?"

Julie and I looked at each other.

"Do I have to answer that?" I asked.

Gill glared at me. "Do it here or do it downtown."

"He's going to go away for the time being," I said. "But in the comics nothing is forever—"

Gill shook his head. "This is why kids are shooting at cops."

"Excuse me?" I asked.

"They see it happening in the funny pages. All the killings. The violence. And they think it's okay. Like this is how it's supposed to be in real life."

"Michael warned us to be careful," Julie said. "And he said he didn't think the police would be much help."

Gill rubbed his chin. "Sounds like your dead friend was pretty perceptive."

"But you can't just let the killer go on a rampage," Julie said. "Vicki and Mike didn't deserve to die."

"Did they piss off a lot of people like your publisher?"

"Not like that," I said. "But there are so many strange personalities around here it's hard to tell who's upset with who sometimes."

"Do you know if they had received any threats recently—crank phone calls, harassing letters, or the like?"

"No," Julie said. "Both of them got lots of fan mail. But it wasn't hate mail."

Gill wrote it all down on his pad. "What about the break-ins you reported? Are they still occurring?"

"Yes," I replied. "Illustrations are disappearing every day. A lot of what's missing was done by Mike and Vicki."

I showed Gill one of Vicki's old sketches. He winced. "Cute."

"Anything else unusual going on?"

"Now that you mention it," I said. "This could be something, or it could be nothing. But I was reading some of my old comic books recently and in a couple of cases I noticed some similarities between the stories in a couple of them and Vicki and Mike's deaths."

"How so?" Gill asked.

I retrieved both issues from my backpack and handed them to Gill. He flipped through each one for several minutes with more than a casual interest.

"Do you see how close they are to what really happened?" I asked.

Gill nodded.

"How old are these?" he asked.

"They go back to the 1930s," I said. "At least fifty years old."

"Probably worth some bucks," he said.

"Do you think someone could have used these as blueprints to kill Vicki and Mike?"

Gill laughed. "I think you've been reading too many old comic books."

Julie flashed me a look that said "I-told-you-so."

"You don't see any connection here whatsoever?" I asked. "How often do two people in the same business die, one right after the other, in an elevator and on a subway in exactly the same fashion it happened in these two comic books?"

"This is New York," Gill said, very matter-of-factly. "Happens every single day."

"Maybe so," Julie replied, "but for all we know, we could be next."

"No need to panic, Miss," Gill responded. "We're on the case. We're talking to people. We're tracking down leads."

"But you don't have any suspects yet, do you?" Julie asked.

Gill bristled. "I'm talking to the two of you."

"You don't think we had anything to do with this?" I asked.

Gill eyed us cautiously. "Nah. But I know your work. You're pretty good with murder stories. So I gotta ask."

"What are we supposed to do now?" Julie asked. "Wait here like sitting ducks?"

Gill closed up his notebook, handed back my old comic books, and headed toward the door.

"If you're that concerned about it, you could always read the next installment in the series," he said.

"And then what?" Julie asked.

"Don't forget to duck."

Chapter 25

Scout Network News Studio

At six o'clock that evening, the largest audience ever to watch a network newscast in New York tuned into Eyewitness News. Scout had been updating the story all day with special reports and tantalizing promos promising the latest and greatest on "New York's comic book serial killer." And Manny Schaffi intended to deliver. In less than forty-eight hours, he had converted from skeptic to believer, largely because the story now featured every imaginable dramatic element he could have possibly hope for—blood, murder, mayhem, greed, shock and mourning, not to mention Sanborn's outrageous bounty offer. Schaffi was so sure it would be a ratings blockbuster he did something he had never done before—he chucked his regular news budget and devoted the entire newscast to the story.

"Everyone look sharp," he barked out from the production booth. "This could very well be our finest half-hour."

Plunkett stacked his news script neatly together and positioned himself squarely in front of Camera Seven while the Eyewitness News introductory sequence rolled out across the screen.

"Ready on my mark," Schaffi commanded. "Three, two, one—go, Phil."

"Topping tonight's Eyewitness News: Has New York's comic book killer struck again?"

A head-and-shoulders shot of Plunkett filled the screen.

"Good evening. Police have now confirmed what we told you exclusively on Eyewitness News at six a.m.: Comic book writer Michael Billington—the son of billionaire investor Warren Billington—was killed by an oncoming subway train shortly after midnight, following a bloody struggle on the platform of the Thirty-Eighth Street Subway Station."

Video of paramedics wheeling a yellow body bag out of the subway on a gurney soon appeared on screen.

"This was the scene early today as police investigators made the gruesome find. Billington, a decorated Vietnam veteran and one of the principal players involved in scripting the final chapter of the Centurion, was waiting on the platform when he was viciously attacked and brutally hurled into the subway's path.

"Billington's death comes a little more than twenty-four hours after Excelsior's superstar artist Vicki Connors was found dead at the base of an elevator shaft at the company's midtown Manhattan headquarters. As police try to piece together the puzzle surrounding these senseless slayings, the impact of Billington's death is being felt here in New York and among comic book fans around the world.

"Now for live team coverage let's go to Maria Vasquez-Mitchell for the latest. Maria…"

Vasquez-Mitchell appeared on screen standing next to the closed subway entrance where Mike had been killed.

"Phil, Michael Billington walked down these steps late last night expecting to board a subway for home," she said, heading solemnly toward the steps. "But little did he know that this would be his final stop."

The camera closed in tightly on Maria's face. "Before we continue, we must warn you that you may find portions of this report very disturbing."

Schaffi adjusted his headset. "That's our cue. Roll the video of the blood-splattered subway."

Sure enough, the next image that appeared on the screen was that of the bloody subway car that had struck Billington head-on—footage that no other network had or would dare show.

"Michael Billington died instantly when he was struck by this subway train speeding by at more than seventy miles an hour," she continued. "But judging by all the blood on the platform, police sources tell us he may have been fighting for his life even before that."

"With me here live is Homicide Detective Charles Gill, the lead investigator on the case. Detective, is this the work of a comic book killer?"

Gill stared into the camera. He hated interviews, especially when the reporters had more information than he did.

"If it is, we have no idea what this person's reading preferences are."

"Well then, who could have done something like this?"

"Dunno. In a city of seven million people, there are a lot of possibilities."

"Then it's definitely murder," she said.

"Would you beat yourself up on a platform and then throw yourself into an oncoming train?" Gill asked.

"It appears there was quite a struggle on the platform."

"Appearances can be deceiving," Gill said. "We're testing for blood types now. We'll know for sure when the results are in."

"Why would someone want to kill Michael Billington?"

"You tell me."

"Could it be a stalker?"

"Could be," Gill answered.

"Maybe a fan?"

"Maybe."

"Someone just begging for attention?"

"What is this," Gill asked, "multiple choice?"

"How is this connected with Vicki Connor's death?"

"We haven't established a connection yet."

"What about suspects?"

"There are no suspects."

"So it's very possible then that the same person could be responsible for both deaths?"

"Read my lips," Gill sneered. "We don't know yet."

"What about witnesses?" Vasquez-Mitchell asked.

"The walls don't talk," Gill replied.

"What about sketches?" she persisted. "Have you come up with any sketches of possible suspects?"

"As soon as a suspect sends us one I'll let you know."

"Have you started a manhunt yet for the killer?"

"We'd like to start taking applications for a posse right now, but like I said, sister, we don't even know who we're looking for yet."

"Thank you, Detective Gill." Vasquez-Mitchell pulled back the microphone and cocked her eyebrow for the camera. "Obviously, as you've just heard, the police don't have a clue about what's going on. Perhaps that's why earlier today, British publishing magnate Sterling Sanborn the Third made a stunning offer outside Excelsior Comics headquarters."

"Cut directly to Sanborn's soundbite," Schaffi barked.

Videotape of Sanborn's latest audience with the press popped up on the screen for the world to see, just as Montana and the Walrus had planned.

"I'd like to give that two million dollars to the first person who brings me his head!" a distraught Sanborn yelled out to the cameras.

"Are you offering a bounty on the killer's head?"

"Call it what you'd like, my dear. If that's what it takes to stop this madness, then so be it."

Sanborn, who was watching it all unfold on a television in his office in Excelsior's headquarters, slapped his knee and howled with delight.

"Two million dollars to the first person who brings me his head," he said.

"Thank you Lock-jaw. You've just made that one of the most memorable lines of the year."

Matthews looked up from his notepad.

"How is my mea culpa coming, Norbert?" the Walrus asked.

"Listen to this," Matthews said, clearing his throat. *"The events of the past forty-eight hours have been extremely trying. Unfortunately, I was so overcome with grief this morning by the news of Michael Billington's death that I misspoke.*

"I would never knowingly put a price on another life. Under the circumstances, I would ask for everyone's understanding and prayers, especially for the families of the victims."

"Very good, Norbert," the Walrus said. "Never hurts to bring God into it."

"There's more," Matthews added. *"Meanwhile, we're continuing to offer a reward for information leading to the capture and arrest of the person or persons responsible for Michael and Vicki's death."*

"Exc-eeee-lent," Sanborn said. "Issue that statement to the wire services immediately, and have it messengered over to all the networks."

Matthews, notepad in hand, dashed out of the room. Then Sanborn turned to Lederer.

"I take it we achieved our daily investment objective?"

Lederer punched up the closing quote on Trieste. The stock's stunning early morning rise had quickly evaporated by the close of trading. "We got out when it was up forty-five points," he said. "It finished the day down sixty-two. We made a cool twenty-eight billion dollars."

"How much does that give us now?" the Walrus asked.

"Sixty-two billion dollars, give or take a few million."

Sanborn rubbed his chin. "It's not enough. Lock-jaw's shareholders could still put up a fight. We need at least seventy billion dollars to make them capit-uuu-late. Let's jump back in again first thing in the morning while the stock is down, and then get us back out by noon."

Lederer shook his head. "We've gone to the well too many times, Sterling. If you do this the buy order's got to go under somebody else's name or you're going to have the Feds here tomorrow seizing our records."

"Damn," Sanborn said. This was a real problem. None of his relatives were speaking to him. A restraining order prevented him from even calling his ex-wife. And he had no close friends whatsoever.

"I've got it," he finally said. "I was just telling Matthews he's like the son I never had. Let's place the entire bet under his name."

"He didn't believe that nonsense, did he?" Lederer asked.

"He's still with us isn't he?"

"If we're not careful he could wind up in jail, Sterling. Are you sure he'll be okay with this?"

Sanborn shrugged. "Of course, Wil-l-l-iam. Norbutt will do anything I tell him to. He adores me."

"Fine. How much do you want to put at risk under Matthews' name?"

"All of it," the Walrus commanded.

"Sixty-two billion dollars, Sterling?"

"Only big bets pay big returns."

"Sometimes," Lederer said, "big bets turn into big busts, too."

Sanborn frowned. "Don't worry, Wil-l-l-iam. As soon as Plunkett shows those sketches I sent him, the stock's going to soar once again."

"All right," Lederer replied. "You're the boss."

Sanborn puffed on his cigar and smiled. "And I know how to take care of my people. In fact, I'm planning a little cel-eeee-bration tomorrow night on my yacht with a few of our closest investors. Why don't you join us?"

"I don't know," Lederer said. He hated social events.

"Come now, Wil-l-l-liam. By this time tomorrow night, you're going to be rich beyond your wildest dreams. Why don't you loosen up and live a little? Tell Irene you're going to be a little late."

"What time?" Lederer asked.

"Dinner starts at seven," the Walrus said. "The party starts at nine."

Lederer finally relented. "I guess it wouldn't hurt—"

"Splendid! We can count our fortune and plot our big move against Lock-jaw," the Walrus said, adjusting the volume on the television monitor.

At that very moment, Maria Vasquez-Mitchell was just wrapping up her live remote report from the subway. Scout's coverage, however, was far from over. In fact, for Sanborn the best was yet to come.

"Now back to you, Phil, for more on this unfolding story."

A head-and-shoulders shot of Plunkett appeared on the television screen. "In Connecticut, news of Michael Billington's death hit like a thunderbolt.

"In a story you'll see only on Eyewitness News, this is how Billington's fiancée reacted when she learned of the tragedy."

In the production booth, Schaffi quickly snapped to attention. "Cut to tape of Maxine screaming."

Maxine's frantic image quickly popped up on his monitor. "Oh my God! My life is over!"

"Lower the sound and rerun it four or five times," Schaffi yelled.

The video replayed over and over while Plunkett continued narrating.

"Relatives weren't the only ones who were shocked by the news. In Japan, a distraught fan committed suicide as thousands of college students protested against American violence in front of the U.S. embassy in Tokyo. Here in New York, bystanders lit candles outside the subway station where Billington was killed, while comic books fans bid up prices on Billington's work to unheard of levels. Lines stretched for blocks around several Manhattan comic book stores."

Schaffi tapped his director on the shoulder. "Roll the fan interviews."

Plunkett's image disappeared, and up popped a wide shot of a crowd of people—mostly young boys and their fathers—lined up outside of the Forbidden Planet, one of city's largest comic book dealers.

"How long you been here?" a cameraman asked one boy at the head of the line.

"Six hours," the youth replied. "His books were awesome."

The camera focused on the boy's father. "How about you, Dad?"

The father put his head in his hands and turned away from the camera.

"I've never seen my Dad so upset," the boy said. "When he heard the news this morning he told me, 'To hell with work. We have to go to the comic book store today.'"

"Figured he'd feel better if he could express his grief here with other fans?" the cameraman asked.

"Nah," the boy said. "He figured this would be a good place to scalp some of his older books once the prices went up inside."

The cameraman quickly moved down the line. "What about you?" he asked. "Why aren't you in school?"

The boy shrugged. "They closed down our school for the day," he said.

"Really?" the cameraman asked.

"Yeah. Half my class is here with me."

As the interviews were ending, Schaffi ordered up the next video sequence. "Ready video of Wall Street traders," he said.

Plunkett swiveled to his left side, leaned gently on his elbow, and waited for the signal light atop Camera Five to flash on.

"Camera Five on my mark," Schaffi yelled. "Three…two…one…go, Phil."

"Wall Street was also rocked by the news of Billington's death," Plunkett said, as a shot of frantic traders scurrying about behind a bank of computer terminals appeared on screen.

"Trieste's stock hit a new fifty-two week high early this morning, jumping forty-five points at the opening bell. Volume was extremely heavy, with more than seven million shares trading hands. But in the afternoon, investors became nervous, following comments by Trieste's Chairman Sterling Sanborn the Third, and the stock plunged sixty-two points."

Plunkett paused and looked to his left. "Joining us here for an analysis is Scout's chief business editor, Stuart Carney."

Carney, a strapping Australian with a twangy accent and receding hairline, peered into the camera.

"G'day, Phil," he said. "It was an incredible roller coaster ride for Trieste today, as the stock gyrated wildly with each new development in the Billington murder. Trieste has been on an upswing in recent days, as investors have generally applauded the company's Chairman, Sterling Sanborn the Third, and his handling of the murder crisis.

"But the run-up in the stock came to a screeching halt this morning when Sanborn posted a bounty for the killer. The stock promptly gave up all of its gains and lost more than a third of its value in heavy trading. The depth of today's plunge was an absolute stunner, and a lot of people are wondering what's going on in the house that the Centurion built. Phil…"

The camera pulled back for Q&As. "What are analysts who follow the stock saying, Stuart?" Plunkett asked.

"There's a lot of genuine concern out there about the wild swings in the stock price," Carney said. "One analyst I spoke to put it this way, Phil: 'Somebody out there is getting rich, and it isn't me.'"

The camera tightened back in on Plunkett. "Well, Stuart, here's some news that's may make investors smile when trading resumes tomorrow. Apparently the murders of Vicki Connors and Michael Billington aren't delaying Excelsior's plans to kill off the Centurion. Eyewitness News has obtained exclusive sketches from the last issue of the Centurion, providing the most detailed evidence yet that the Mighty Sentinel of Light is about to bite the bullet. But before we show them to you, we must warn you that these illustrations are extremely graphic."

"Here it comes, Wil-l-l-l-iam," Sanborn said in his office. "Mister Plunkett is about to hand Wall Street our next feast on a silver platter."

Schaffi pushed a button on the control panel and a series of sketches slowly cascaded across the screen; they were the most violent and bloody illustrations that Vicki had done. All had come from the wastebaskets in our conference room, and none of them were ever supposed to see the light of day. But to the millions of people who were watching them on television that evening, the sketches were the real things; proof positive that an American classic was about to bite the dust.

In New York, Matthews gazed at the tiny television set in his office and promptly threw up. Not because the pictures were so explicit, but because he realized he was still being used like a pincushion by Sanborn.

In Connecticut, Matt Payne stared at the television in disbelief.

In Australia, Sydney Lockwood cursed Sanborn and threw his shoe at a dartboard picture of the Walrus mounted on the wall in his office.

In Brooklyn, Jimmy Montana immediately closed the Comic Cave and ordered another round of price increases on all remaining copies of the Centurion.

And a few blocks away, in the shadows of his creaky old apartment, Mitch Gerber tended to his bruise and returned to his drawing table. "Two million dollars to the first person who brings me his head," he uttered to himself. "Now there's an interesting proposition."

He carefully cut Sanborn's picture from the front page of *The Post*, cropped it above the shoulders, and pinned it up on his bulletin board next to the other black and white pictures he had clipped of Mike and Vicki.

With little effort, he retrieved another old comic book from his collection and headed to his bedroom. In the dim light, he pulled the book from its sleeve, inhaled deeply, and smiled. Murder on the High Seas was the perfect prescription for a sleepless night.

Chapter 26

Excelsior Headquarters

Lederer retreated to his office, his head still spinning from the day's events, and closed the door. Insider trading was a tough business, even for an experienced pro and he knew that too many moves—no matter how well disguised—would eventually be detected by the Securities and Exchange Commission. The only way to escape was to leave the country. And that's exactly what Lederer intended to do. He'd stick around long enough to place Sanborn's "big bet" on the table and collect his portion of the winnings. But then he'd cash out his chips and take his wife and newly minted fortune somewhere overseas—someplace exotic—where the Feds couldn't possibly touch him.

Lederer sat down at his desk, sipped his coffee the same way he had been taking it for more than forty years, black—no cream, no sugar—and called home.

"Irene?"

"How's it going?" she asked.

"As expected," he said. "If it goes well we could be millionaires tomorrow."

"And if it doesn't—"

"Don't worry," he said. "Sanborn's stacked the deck again. The stock's probably going to light up like a Christmas tree because of the sketches on tonight's news."

"I saw them," she said. "They didn't look like such a big deal to me."

"The analysts eat the stuff up," he said, "which is why I'm calling. Sanborn wants me to have dinner with a group of investors tomorrow night on his boat. Sort of a victory celebration. So I'm going to be late."

"Oh, no," she said. "We're supposed to have dinner at the Paynes' house tomorrow night. They'll be so disappointed."

Lederer looked at his calendar. *Dinner at Payne's, 7:30*. They had been friends for years.

"How's Matt doing?" he asked.

"Not well," she said. "He apparently saw some of the news reports on TV when they came back from the cruise and he's been really depressed. Alix is beside herself."

"Don't blame him for being upset," Lederer said. "See if you can reschedule and tell Alix I'm sorry about canceling."

"Bill, are you sure you're all right?"

"I'll be better when this is all over," he said. "We should take a long vacation."

"You have any particular place in mind?" she asked.

"Pick an island in the South Seas," he said. "We'll buy it."

Julie and I raced back to my apartment shortly after our conversation with Detective Gill to dig through my comic book collection. He did us both a big favor by suggesting we read the next installment in the murder mystery series. Neither one of us were thinking clearly enough that morning to ask the obvious question—*where will the killer strike next?*

It took us a while to figure out the answer. We had a ton of comic books to go through, thanks to Ma's clever packing skills. To make matters worse, the issue we were looking for was buried at the very bottom of my collection, and unlike its predecessors, it hadn't aged well. The front cover was missing and without the title page we couldn't tell if the book was part of the original series. We completely overlooked it the first time we went through the pile. Finally, after two hours of searching, Julie figured it out.

"This is it," she said. "Listen to this: *'Who knows what evil lurks in the soul of mankind? Doctor Terror does, as he takes dead aim on his next victim—international publishing magnate Mitchell Powers, in a tale of murder on the high seas!'*"

This time there was no elevator or subway. Doctor Terror's victim wound up swimming with the sharks alongside his luxury yacht.

Julie flipped the page and read some of the dialogue aloud. "*'You laughed at me, you scoffed at my ideas, now who's going to have the last laugh?' Dr. Terror asked, as Powers became fodder for the sharks.'*"

"Sanborn's next on the list," she said when she finished.

"Does he have a yacht?"

"One of the most expensive in the world."

"So what do we do now?" I asked.

"We can't go back to the police," Julie said. "Gill's not going to believe us, let alone do anything."

"We've got to call Sanborn and warn him."

"He won't believe us either," she warned.

"But we've got to try." I immediately picked up the phone and started dialing Sanborn's number. It was late and chances are he wouldn't even be in his office.

"Hel-l-l-l-o?" It was Sanborn's voice.

"Mister Sanborn?"

"Who's this?"

"Rick. Rick MacAllister."

"Misterrrrrrrr MacAll-eeeee-ster," the Walrus replied. "So good of you to call."

"I'm glad I caught you in, sir. There's something I need to talk to you about."

"Yes, yes, yes, I know."

"You do?"

"Of course, my boy," the Walrus replied. "I know you and Mister Bill-eee-ngton were close. And now that he's gone, the burden of finishing the Centurion project really falls on you and Miss McKinney."

"No it's not that," I said.

"I realize, too, that your deadline is looming larger and larger everyday," he continued. "And I don't mean to add to the pressure. But it's more important than ever that this issue be ready on time."

"Yes, I know that, but—"

"Ah, tut, tut, tut, Mister MacAll-eee-ster. There will be no buts and no delays. Do I make myself clear?"

"Yes, I hear you—"

"Splendid, Mister MacAll-eeeee-ster," Sanborn said. "Then I know we can count on you to be ready to go as we had planned."

"Yes, but there's something even more important to tell you," I said.

"More important than the Centurion project?"

"I think we've uncovered a pattern to the murders. They match up closely to the stories in some of the old Centurion comic books I have at home."

"Reall-eeeeeeee now?" the Walrus asked.

"In the first comic book the victim dies in an elevator shaft, just like Vicki did. In the second book, the victim gets killed when he's pushed into the path of a speeding subway."

"Yes, yes, go on," the Walrus said.

"We just found the third book in the series and the victim is a publishing executive. He gets killed on his yacht and dumped overboard."

"Oh, my," the Walrus said. "How positively dreadful."

"We don't want to alarm you—"

"Oh no, not at all," Sanborn said. "I'm glad you called."

"We know you have your own private yacht, and with all that's going on—"

"I will definitely act on this at once," he said. "Now tell me again where you found all this."

"It's in some of the very first Centurion comic books," I said. "Mine are all reprints. But they go back a long way. The first one was printed in nineteen thirty-nine."

Sanborn took it all down in his notepad. "Very good," Sanborn said. "Now I don't want you or Miss McKinney to worry about a thing. We're going to see to it that you are protected. Concentrate on your work and if you need anything—anything at all—you just call me."

"I appreciate that Mister Sanborn."

"I know you do my boy," the Walrus said. "Now do me a favor."

"What's that?"

"Don't say another word about any of this to anyone. Do you understand?"

"Our lips are sealed," I replied.

"Exce-e-e-elent. You're going to make history, my boy. And we're behind you all the way."

CLICK.

Sanborn hung up the phone and called Matthews at home.

"Norbert," he said, "we have another potential marketing opportunity that requires your imme-e-e-ediate attention."

"What's that?" Matthews said, rubbing the sleep from his eyes.

"MacAllister tells me that some of the early Centurion books bear a striking resemblance to the murders of Miss Connors and Mister Bill-eee-ngton. I want you to see if we can find them."

"Any idea when they came out?"

The Walrus looked at his notes. "They're ancient. Nineteen thirty-nine, nineteen forty-nine, maybe fifty-nine. Something like that."

Matthews jotted down the dates and a short description on a pad he kept on his night table.

"And if I find them?"

"Let's see about getting them reprinted and into circulation. The collectors will go wild. With the right spin it could give us a hell of a lot of exposure."

"What'd you have in mind?" Matthews asked.

"Hmmm. How about this: 'Read the classics that inspired the murders.'"

Chapter 27

New York Pier

The next afternoon around four-thirty, a caravan of trucks from Nola Brothers Catering in the Bronx pulled up alongside Sanborn's yacht with enough food and liquor for a feast. It had been that kind of a day on Wall Street and Sanborn was in a partying mood. At nine forty-four a.m., just minutes after Sanborn's buy order was executed under Matthews' name, Trieste's stock opened up a whopping seventy-three points higher. At eleven o'clock, with volume surging, the stock climbed another forty-two points as institutional fund managers—always afraid of being left out of a sure thing—started gobbling up the stock like there was no tomorrow. By two o'clock, program trading kicked into high gear and Trieste rose thirty-three more points to a new high of $325 a share. Then by three-fifteen, as word spread about the stock's performance, small investors jumped into the fray, and the buying frenzy continued to accelerate. Twenty minutes later, Trieste topped an unprecedented $450 a share, and Sanborn locked in his gains.

By the end of the day, he had seen his sixty-two billion dollar war chest more than double. He now had more than enough cash on hand to launch a hostile takeover bid of Scout and force Lockwood to his knees.

A burly deliveryman knocked on the cabin door.

"Delivery for Mista Sanborn, Mac."

Sanborn's stately British butler, Alfred, eyed the enormous collection of crates and tins suspiciously. "My, that's quite an order."

The deliveryman looked at his order form. "Came directly from Mista Sanborn himself. Something about a big party tonight."

"A party?" Alfred asked. As usual, he was the last to know.

"Says right here, provisions for two hundred people. Food, booze, you name it, and a cake that'll really blow your mind, Pop."

Alfred frowned. "Bring everything around to the galley and we'll stow it all there."

Sanborn—with Lederer in tow—finally made an appearance around six-thirty.

"Break out the bubbly, Alfred," the Walrus said once he had waddled up the gangplank with Lederer close behind. "Our ship has come in. A cel-eeee-bration is in order."

"The caterer informed the staff, sir," Alfred said. "The Estate Room is all set up. When can we expect the rest of the guests to arrive?"

"The party isn't until nine, Alfred. But I'm having a private dinner before hand with Wil-l-l-liam here and Mister Montana. He should be arriving shortl-eeeeee. Haul out the red carpet."

"And may I inquire as to the nature of this celebration?" Alfred asked.

Sanborn took a big puff on his cigar. "It's the end of an era, Alfred. We're cel-eeee-brating the impending demise of the Scout Entertainment Network!"

"My word," Alfred said. "Has some great misfortune befallen Mister Lockwood?"

A big grin came over Sanborn's face. "No, but it's about to."

As Sanborn and Lederer made their way to the banquet room, one of the crates in the galley began to stir. Eventually, the top sprang open and a slender figure emerged from inside wearing a black face mask—an ominously foreboding mask—and olive green fatigues. It was the same outfit that had struck terror in the hearts of Vicki Connors and Mike Billington in their final moments on earth. This time, however, the Mask had bigger fish to fry. As Julie and I had guessed, it was none other than Sanborn himself.

Slowly, and with the utmost caution, the Mask cut a path through the dark room and wandered about the lower decks without attracting attention. Sanborn and his guests were upstairs in the Estate Room—the site of many of the world's most extravagant affairs—standing at the end of a formal dining table nearly half a mile long. To his right stood Lederer. And on his left, occupying almost the entire quarter of the table, was Montana.

Lederer was nervous. He had seen pictures of Montana before on mug shots in his local Post Office. But he had no idea he was one of Trieste's top investors.

"Sterling," he whispered, "where are the other investors?"

"Others?" Sanborn replied. "What others?"

"The investors, Sterling. Where are the other investors?"

Sanborn looked at Montana with a pretentious smile. "Wil-l-l-liam here wants to know where the other investors are, Sir James."

Montana grinned back. "I represent all da other interests."

"Mister Montana came to us as a venture capitalist," the Walrus added. "He gave us seed money for the Excelsior acquisition in exchange for a rather sizable equity interest in Trieste."

"Surely we should be consulting with the other senior executives before we embark on this path—"

Montana shook his head. "Nah. Dey ain't gonna give us no problems."

"What about the board of directors?" Lederer persisted.

"Dey've given me full proxy power to vote on dere behalf," Montana smiled. "Trust me."

Sanborn raised his glass. "Enough idle chatter. Gentlemen, a toast. To our new acquisition."

"Hear, hear," Montana added.

Sanborn downed the champagne and promptly hurled the glass into a magnificently lit marble fireplace just to the left of the table.

"Old Greek tradition," the Walrus crowed. "It's supposed to bring good luck."

Montana tossed the glass in the air, quickly pulled a revolver from his holster, and pumped several rounds into the air.

"Divide, conquer, rape and pillage!" he said, as the glass shattered into hundreds of tiny pieces. "Old Roman tradition."

The Walrus laughed.

"With the kind of capital we've raised," Montana continued, "we're not going to need any luck. Scout's shareholders would be crazy to reject the offer we're going to make. And if they do—"

Montana kissed his gun and gently returned it to his holster.

"It really isn't a question of why but when," Sanborn said. "When should we strike? When can we get the deal wrapped up by? And when can I have the pleasure of throwing Lock-jaw out on his ass?"

Montana rubbed his belly. "Save it for dee-zert, Stoi-ling. I'm famished."

As the trio ate, the Mask inched closer and closer to the Estate Room, moving freely about the ship like a stealth fighter. Of course, Sanborn made the hunt very easy. He had done nothing to bolster his security detail beyond the lone rent-a-cop who worked on board and rarely strayed from his station next to the ship's bridge.

Montana always traveled heavily armed. His contingent of well dressed thugs were stationed at key positions around the perimeter of the boat. But none of them had bothered to search inside the ship beforehand, and there were no sentries below deck. So getting into the Estate Room wouldn't be hard. Since Sanborn had planned to one day turn the ship into a floating casino for his guests, the room was surrounded by a vast network of empty corridors and air conditioning ducts that snaked through the walls, under the raised floor, and in between the decks. Many, in fact, were big enough to crawl through. And that's exactly what the Mask did. After gaining access through an unlocked electrical room just a few doors down the hall, all it took was a good ear to follow the rumble of laughter and small talk directly to the Estate Room.

Within minutes, the figure was stationed just below the dinner table in the narrow gap under the raised floor, peering out through an air conditioning vent at the scene above.

"Alfred," Sanborn said, "how much more do you have to do before we're all set for the party?"

"We're almost finished here, sir," the butler said. "We're bringing in the cake you ordered now."

A moment later, three busboys wheeled a towering six-foot tall cake into the center of the room.

"Good. As soon as they're finished, dismiss the staff and lock the doors. We have business to discuss."

"Very well, sir," Alfred said. "What time shall we start letting people in for the party?"

The Walrus looked at his Rolex. "Throw open the doors at nine, Alfred. Not a moment before. We'll be here waiting for them."

As soon as the caterers had left the room and the doors were secured, Sanborn got right down to business.

"Now then, let us turn to the matter of the Scout acquisition," he said. "When do we make our move?"

"I would wait a bit, Sterling," Lederer said. "Let all the commotion die down and then make a move when he isn't expecting it."

Montana nodded in agreement. "Lockwood's clever, Stoi-ling. He ain't going down for da count without a fight if his back is against da wall. We need to hit him hard with a combination of punches. When will da Centurion finale be ready?"

"Two weeks, as promised," the Walrus said. "I spoke with MacAll-eee-ster today. The old boy will be as dead as a doornail on the Fourth of July."

"Good," Montana replied. "If Lockwood offers any resistance at all, this will put an end to it."

The Walrus looked at Lederer. "How do we tender the offer?"

"Our attorneys would send Lockwood and each of his board members registered letters notifying them of our intentions," Lederer said.

"Not dramatic enough, Wi-l-l-liam," the Walrus replied.

"We're required by law, Sterling."

"Yes, yes, yes. I know. But we ought to have some fun. It's Sydney we're talking about here. He's a snake in the grass. He's given us all fits over the years. The least we can do is make his life a living hell."

"Well, Sterling," Lederer said, trying hard to be funny, "we could always make him an offer he can't refuse."

Montana shook his head. "Been done before. It's too Hollywood. Besides, it's much easier to mess with his head den it is to blow it off."

"Do you have anything special in mind, Sir James?"

Montana rubbed his chin. "How 'bout we let Plunkett break da news to him on TV about our bid? What could be worse den finding out your kingdom is about to be overthrown from your own talkin' heads?"

Sanborn smiled. "That's eggg-zactly what I was thinking, Sir James. Plunkett's done so much for us already, why shouldn't we give him another 'Eyewitless News exclusive' gift wrapped for his boss?"

"I can see it now," Montana exclaimed. "Topping tonight's broadcast—*Scout Gets Scalped!*"

The Walrus roared. "And when they stick the microphone in front of my face, instead of 'Off with his head', I'll say, 'We're going to cut Sydney off at the knees'."

Under the table below the floorboards, the Mask heard the laughter too. Finding Sanborn, Montana and Lederer all in the same room was a real surprise. Killing them in one fell swoop would leave Trieste a rudderless ship, and it would almost certainly derail any plans to bump off the Centurion. Montana posed the biggest challenge. Physically, he was too fat to offer much resistance. But the gun he was packing could certainly make things tricky.

Then came an unexpected break. First, Lederer excused himself to go to the bathroom. Shortly after he left the room, the chandeliers in the room started flickering. A moment later, an old Con Ed Transformer that supplied AC current to all the docked boats in the harbor gasped its last breath and died, leaving the ship completely dark from stem to stern. The Estate Room had an ample supply of emergency backup lights—as state law required—but Sanborn was so cheap that he never installed batteries in any of the units. Were it not for a few flickering candles atop the dinner table, the giant dining room would have been completely black.

"Stoi-ling!" Montana jumped. "What da Christ is goin' on?"

"Blasted power company," Sanborn fumed. "This happens here all the time. If it doesn't come back on in a few moments, we'll power up the ship and everything will be restored."

"I don't like dis," Montana said, peering into the darkness.

"Neither do I, Sir James, but there's not much we can do to—"

Montana grabbed Sanborn's arm. "No, Stoi-ling. You-you-you don't understand. It's da dark."

"Da what?" Sanborn asked.

"Da dark, Stoi-ling. I hate da dark. Strange dings happen in da dark, especially in my line of woyk."

"Never fear, Sir James," the Walrus said. "Sanborn is here. I'll retrieve a candle and everything will be just fine. You'll see."

Montana sat paralyzed in his chair while Sanborn disappeared into the shadows. A few seconds later, a flickering flame emerged from the other end of the room and moved closer toward him.

"Hurry up Stoi-ling. Dis is making me very noy-vous."

The candlelight moved closer; so close in fact, that it practically blinded Montana's view.

"Stoi-ling, don't play games. Just give me da freakin' candle."

Then a husky voice he didn't recognize broke the silence. "Care for a light, big boy?"

Montana slowly rose from the table and started to draw his gun, but he wasn't fast enough.

A sudden sharp kick to the groin brought him to his knees, and another quick blow to the back of his head sent his hulking frame crashing to the floor.

Sanborn, hearing the commotion, grabbed a candle from the table and waddled back as fast as he could to Montana's aid. He found him lying face down on the floor, alone and unconscious.

"James!" he shouted. "Are you all right?"

Sanborn shuddered when there was no response. "Damn! I told the cleaning crew not to put too much wax on the floors!" He quickly knelt down beside Montana and tried to rouse him. When that didn't work, he tried turning him over. But three hundred-sixty pounds of dead weight was dead weight.

"What a fine pickle this is," Sanborn muttered.

Then a voice reached out to him from the dark.

"Can I give you a hand?"

"Yes, thank goodness you're here," Sanborn said, thinking it was one of the busboys. "Let's try turning him over."

Sanborn grabbed Montana's shoulder. "Push at the waist and I'll give it a go from here."

But nothing happened. Sanborn turned around to find out what was causing the delay, but all he could see was the flickering flame of another candle behind him.

"Are you going to give me a hand or not?"

"Here it comes," the voice responded. Seconds later a clenched fist slammed into Sanborn's face like a sledgehammer, sending him sprawling across the floor. Then before he could react, the masked figure grabbed him by the back of the head and shoved him head first into the deck.

The Walrus cried out at the top of his lungs. But there was no one nearby to hear him.

"How pathetic," the Mask said. "Here lies the master of manipulation alone and helpless with little ol' me."

Sanborn couldn't move. The figure had him pinned down by the back of the neck, and he could feel the imprint of a cold Army boot digging into his skin.

"Whoever you are," Sanborn struggled to spit out the words, "whatever you want—it's yours. Just name it."

"Amazing," the Mask responded. "I've been dropping some pretty heavy hints the past couple of days. How many more people must die before you finally figure it out?"

"It's the Centurion isn't it?"

"Oh you're getting warmer."

"What eggg-zactly do you want us to do with the Centurion?" the Walrus asked.

"Do I have to spell it out for you?"

"Yes."

The Mask gazed into the candlelight and sighed. "Don't play games with me, Sanborn. What I want is what I've always wanted—the Centurion must live."

This time, Sanborn didn't say a word.

"My goodness," the figure finally said, "no pithy soundbites for the cameras?"

"The Centurion must die," Sanborn said. "It has to happen otherwise we can't bring him—"

Sanborn stopped, as the pressure from the Mask's boot grew even more intense.

"That's not what I want to hear, big boy."

"Wait, you don't understand." Sanborn struggled.

"I've waited long enough! And it's obvious you're not going to change your tune. Not when there's a fast buck to be made."

"You won't get away with this," the Walrus charged.

"The hell I won't!" The enraged assailant grabbed Sanborn by the back of his head and threw him into a sharp corner of the dinner table. The impact opened up a huge gash in his forehead and he slumped to the floor.

"You've given your last order Sterling Sanborn the Third," the Mask said over Sanborn's tortured cries. "You'll never hurt anyone again."

The attacker rolled Sanborn on his back and jammed a knife up against his throat. "Now it's time for you to see the light."

But then, just as suddenly as they went out, the lights aboard ship returned with a blinding intensity. Before the killer could adjust, the door handle turned and Lederer waltzed back in from the men's room, completely unaware of what was happening.

"My God," he gasped at all the carnage. On one side of the dinner table, Montana was lying motionless in a pool of blood. On the other, he saw the masked figure hunched over Sanborn's battered body with a knife.

Lederer's first thoughts were to turn and run. And he did. But in his rush, he bumped into the door behind him and it closed in place. The delay was just enough time for the Mask to hurl the knife directly at him. But the blade missed its mark, hitting the door just above the handle.

"You're not going anywhere," the attacker charged. "You, of all people, should have known better!"

The voice sent a chill down Lederer's spine. Slowly he turned in place and faced the masked figure. "W-W-What are you talking about?"

"The Sentinel of Light can't be extinguished. You know that!"

Lederer took a deep breath. *Talk*, he said to himself. *The longer you talk the longer you stay alive.*

"W-W-Who are you?" he asked. "Why are you doing this?"

The assailant laughed. "Who am I? WHO AM I??? You know damn well who I am."

The figure reached up with one hand, yanked off the mask and threw it to the floor.

Lederer gasped. He recognized the face instantly. "You? How could you do this?"

"Very easily, William. You've given me no choice. You're destroying something that is more precious to me than life itself."

"But you've got it all wrong," Lederer replied. "It's not going to happen the way you think—"

"Spare me the lies, William! I've heard them all before. Now you expect me to trust you?"

"You've got to," Lederer said. "I'm telling the truth. The Centurion is not going to die."

"But I'm afraid you are, my friend," the attacker said.

Lederer closed his eyes, and braced for the worst. "Make it quick."

Then, suddenly, a loud pop rang out from across the room and the assailant immediately fell flat on the floor.

Lederer opened his eyes. "Oh, God," he said. A split-second later a bullet struck his forehead, and he died instantly. Montana had come to and fired his revolver from the floor. But his arm was shaky and his aim was way off.

"Stoi-ling, I got him!" Montana yelled. "I got him!"

Sanborn didn't respond. He was out cold. Montana looked around but the Mask was nowhere to be seen. When he realized that he had missed the attacker, he fired off several more rounds at random.

"You ain't leaving here alive," Montana yelled.

In the distance, he could hear the ship's engines humming. But that was all. Now it had come down this—a duel to the death, one on one, predator against predator, criminal against criminal. It was exactly the kind of action Montana lived for.

"You can make dis easy or you make dis hard," Montana cried out. "Eider way you're gonna die."

Montana fired off several more rounds in every conceivable direction. But his back was so sore, he couldn't turn completely around. As a result, he never saw the floor board sliding open behind him, or the figure emerging from beneath the floor less than a few feet away, brandishing a deadly Gurkha knife.

"I know you're in here," Montana yelled. "I can hear ya breadin'—"

Suddenly he felt a sharp piercing pain in his back and it was over. "You talk too much, fat man." In the end, Montana died a death that he feared most—stabbed in the back with his eyes wide open. It went against everything he stood for. But how it happened made little difference to the attacker, as long as he was dead.

Exhausted and exhilarated, the assailant retrieved the bloody knife from Montana's back, put the ski mask back on, and turned next for Sanborn, who was still breathing.

In the far corner of the room an antique grandfather clock sprang to life; its chimes tolling eight o'clock.

The assailant unbuttoned Sanborn's bloody shirt and smiled.

"Wait 'till you see the seat I've saved for you at the head table."

At exactly nine o'clock, Alfred made his way through the crowd of guests waiting outside the Estate Room and opened the doors, just as Sanborn had ordered.

They all piled in—cocktails and hors d'oeuvres in tow—an eclectic collection of well-heeled executives, flashy mobsters, and affluent comic book collectors who all knew that Sanborn liked to have a good time.

"Give them a couple of minutes to find their seats and turn the spotlight up on the front of the room," Alfred told the headwaiter. "You know how he likes to make dramatic entrances."

A few minutes later the spotlight came to life and the talking stopped. The room was immaculate. Every piece of china was in place. The champagne glasses sparkled. Dozens of dinner tables were all arranged neatly in a semi-circle around the head table. And at the center of it all—sitting atop a well-polished parquet floor—was Sanborn's giant cake, all lit up with sparklers from the Fourth of July.

And then, suddenly, there was laughter. First one table, then another, and another, until eventually everyone in the room was howling.

"Will you look at that!"

"Sterling, what a card!"

"Anything for a laugh!"

"You tell 'em Sterling," shouted one executive from the back of the room. "Off with their heads!"

Lined up side by side atop the cake were three heads that looked exactly like Lederer, Sanborn and Montana. Of course, nobody in the room thought for a moment that they might be real. Everyone just assumed Sanborn was poking fun at himself and his well-timed bounty threat with some very realistic-looking props from the local wax museum. But a hot spotlight and sparklers can do funny things to a cake with whipped cream filling. Eventually, the center of the cake started to soften up, and it wasn't long before the three heads started to wobble and teeter from their perch.

Montana's went first—at one point it starting sinking into the cake like it was quicksand. Then Lederer's head tipped to the left and dangled precariously over one side. But it was Sanborn's head that actually toppled over the edge and bounced from one layer to another like a basketball. And it continued rolling across the floor, leaving a trail of frosting in its wake, until it came to a dead stop at the foot of a nearby dinner table.

Carmine Ipollitto, Montana's top lieutenant, reached over from his seat, picked up the head and examined it. Like most of his colleagues in crime, Ipollitto was no stranger to the finer art of decapitation, and he immediately realized that this was no joke.

"Jez-us Christ, Stoi-ling," he said, very matter-of-factly. "I never figured you'd be the type to lose your head over a silly comic book."

Chapter 28

Manhattan

The next twenty-four hours were indescribable. As soon as everyone realized what had really happened, Sanborn's guests stampeded out of the Estate Room and off the boat in a panic. Within minutes, a squadron of police cars descended on the harbor from every conceivable direction, just as Montana's goons were speeding off the pier. The police were followed by an aerial convoy of television news helicopters and floodlights. And it didn't take long for the cameras to find what the police couldn't locate—three headless bodies scattered in and around the ship. Lederer showed up in the water, floating off the port side of the boat; Montana's decapitated form was dangling from the ship's anchor; and Sanborn's body was impaled on the boat's bow, almost exactly the way Billington had envisioned one of the Centurion's early death scenes.

Ipollitto, anticipating the start of a new mob war, immediately assumed control of Montana's comic book empire and beefed up security around each one of the Montana family's Comic Cave locations.

Amid all the turmoil, the mayor of New York appealed for calm and did what mayors are supposed to do in crisis situations—he put pressure on the police commissioner for action. The police commissioner, in turn, demanded that the homicide squad make an arrest. The homicide chief read the riot act to Detective Gill, and he, in turn, had the most senior surviving senior officer at Excelsior hauled in for questioning—Matthews.

Lockwood, who was watching live coverage of the event from his vacation resort in the Australian coastal town of Broome, took advantage of the chaos and did something he'd been wanting to do for a long time—launch a hostile takeover bid of Trieste that would make Sanborn turn over in his grave even before he was in it. Plunkett, of course, broke the story.

Then the SEC, citing "insider trading irregularities," immediately launched an investigation into Trieste's stock. Wall Street responded by halting all trading in the company until the probe was complete.

Meanwhile, Julie and I watched the entire scene unfold once more on television in my apartment behind locked doors. This time, however, we weren't surprised. I think we both instinctively knew that we were next on the killer's hit list. But without police support, our only hope of surviving was to find the fourth and final installment of the old comic book murder series before the killer could strike again.

"Are you sure there even is another issue?" Julie asked, as we frantically tore through my comic book collection for the fifth time.

"Positive," I said. "The series is called Death Knocks Four Times. Everything gets all wrapped up in the final installment."

Julie shook her head. "It's not here, Rick. Could it be at your mother's?"

"No. Every one of my old Centurion books is here. I don't think I ever had that issue in my collection."

"We've got to find it," Julie said.

"We could always try a comic book store," I said. "One of the big houses in town might have it in their back issues."

"Not today," Julie said. "Every comic book store in Manhattan is going to be jammed."

"What about Excelsior?" I wondered. "We must have old issues stored away someplace."

Julie thought for a second. "There's an archives section on the third floor, and I know the guy who runs it. It's worth a shot."

We quickly gathered our things and hopped into a cab. By the time we arrived, Excelsior looked like a war zone once more. Cops were crawling all over the place. Crowd barriers were set up around the building. Metal detectors were installed at each entrance to screen for weapons. And news crews were camped out all around the building, practically fighting each other for interviews.

"Got any ID, Mac?"

I handed my badge to the cop at the front entrance.

"You Rick MacAllister?" he asked.

I nodded.

"My kid reads your stuff all the time."

"What's your kid's name?"

"Jack," he said. "Jack Larson. He's twelve years old. I think he's got every one of your Intruder issues."

I stepped through the metal detector. "Tell him I said hi."

"Not so fast," he said.

I froze.

"Would you mind signing an autograph for my kid? It would make me a big hero at home tonight."

He handed me his note pad and a pen and I obliged.

"Thanks, Mister MacAllister," the officer said. "Proceed through."

A few moments later, as Julie and I were waiting nearby for the elevator, I overheard the same cop talking to one of his buddies on the force.

"Know who that was?"

"Nope."

"Rick MacAllister."

"Rick who?"

"You know, MacAllister—the guy who's doing the Centurion."

"That's him?"

"You got it," the cop said. "He just gave me his autograph for my kid."

The other cop looked at my signature. "I'd hang on to that if I was you," he said. "That's gonna be worth a fortune when he's dead."

Excelsior's Archives Department was affectionately known as "the Morgue." It was literally stuffed with the ghosts of comic books past—thousands of them, all wrapped in plastic, occupying every inch of space between the floor and the ceiling.

"You whooooo, Miss Julie," a high-pitched voice called out from nowhere. Staring back up at us from behind the counter with a wide grin, bulging muscles and a microchip memory, was "Butch," the Morgue's munchkin-sized curator.

"All this violence. It's just terrible. How are you holding up?"

Julie shook her head. "We've had better years," she said.

"Could be worse, my dear. Think about the headache our dearly departed fearless leader must have had when he went to bed last night."

Julie forced back a smile. "Butch, I want you to meet a friend of mine. This is Rick MacAllister—"

"Say no more," Butch replied, his bald head barely clearing the counter top. "I know your work. We've kept a file on you since you were at Scout. Very impressive."

I reached over the counter and extended my hand. "Thanks."

"Butch," Julie interjected, "we've got a little problem, and I was hoping you could help us out."

"The Archives are at your disposal, Miss Julie."

"We're trying to track down an old Centurion issue."

"Then you've come to the right place," he said. "We've got an entire room devoted to the Centurion."

"The one we're looking for is really old and it's part of a series," I said. "It's called *Death Knocks Four Times*."

Butch thought for a second. "March, nineteen thirty-nine. Issue number six. Doctor Terror versus the Centurion."

"That's the series, but we're only looking for the fourth installment."

"Gotta name on that?" Butch asked.

"No. But we know it follows Murder on the Subway and Murder on the High Seas."

"That shouldn't be too hard to find." He led us down a narrow corridor to an old room behind the Morgue and opened the door.

"Behold the Centurion room," he said. "Over ten thousand back issues, preserved, catalogued and filed; the largest Centurion collection in existence today."

Julie and I looked around. The room was overwhelming, sort of like a Home Depot for comic books, covered by an inch of dust.

"We don't get many visitors here anymore," Butch said. "In fact, you're the first since Matt Payne retired."

"This must be worth a fortune," I said, taking it all in.

Butch shrugged. "Maybe half of it is," he said.

"Whaddya mean?" I asked.

"The older stuff is pretty rare," he said. "The rest of it is all shit."

"Why's that?"

"It's been years since Payne put out a good book. That's why the collection is so large. Everything we couldn't sell got dumped in here."

"The issue we're looking for is definitely one of his earliest books," I said.

Butch picked up a binder that listed all the issues by dates and began searching for the issue.

"Nineteen thirty-nine was a very good year for comics. Excelsior controlled every newsstand in town. Nobody could touch us. Artists were treated like gods. It was truly a golden age for Excelsior."

"What a difference fifty years makes," Julie said.

"Here it is," he said finally. "Nineteen thirty-nine. *Death Knocks Four Times*. The first issue was in March, *Murder on the Sixth Floor*. In May came *Murder on the Subway*. In June, *Murder on the High Seas*. July was the last installment—*Murder at the Coliseum.*"

"That must be it," I said, "Can we see it?"

Butch scrambled up a portable ladder to the very highest shelf in the room. He remained there for several minutes, frantically scrambling through old boxes and jammed drawers. "That's strange…"

"What's wrong?" Julie asked.

"It's not here," he yelled down to us.

"What do you mean?"

"All four issues in the collection are gone. Somebody must have signed them out."

"Who?" I asked.

Butch scurried down the ladder and started rifling through another logbook.

"Only one person ever borrowed copies from this room," he said. "And he always brought them back."

"Who's that?" I asked.

"Just as I thought," Butch answered. "Matt Payne took all these books out before he retired. His initials are right here. He hasn't sent them back to us yet."

Julie and I looked at each other, thinking exactly the same thing. Could Payne possibly be the killer?

"Did he take out any other books before he left?" I asked.

Butch eyed the log. "Nope. Just those four. But I don't know why he'd take them. He's got quite an extensive collection at home."

"Do you know where Payne lives?" Julie asked.

"Up in the woods in Connecticut. I think the town is Redding."

"Can you think of anyplace else where we could find the last issue?" I asked.

Butch scratched his head. "All four of these issues are extremely rare. You'd have to go to a big collector, and if you found them you'd have to pay a pretty steep price."

Julie cast a suspicious eye in my direction. "You're not thinking of going up to Payne's house are you?"

"Either that or we wait and see if he comes for us."

Getting grilled under hot lights by an ornery cop first thing in the morning like a two-bit thug in an old gangster movie wasn't exactly what Matthews had in mind when he realized he was Excelsior's new chairman. He hadn't even shaved and showered when the cops forced their way into his apartment and dragged him into the station house for questioning. But it didn't matter how he looked. As Trieste's new chairman, Matthews knew he had a responsibility to do everything he could to put the right spin on the situation and save his own ass.

"Whaddya take us for?" Gill asked him. "Fools?"

Matthews shook his head. "Certainly not—"

"We know how corporate politics works," Gill interrupted. "You're on a fast track. You wanna be the top dog. But it wasn't happening fast enough. So you got rid of everyone in your way. You just rubbed 'em all out. Isn't that right?"

"No, I had nothing to do with this—"

Gill blew smoke in Matthews' face. "C'mon, I wasn't born yesterday, pal. How do you explain the fact that a day after your boss turns up dead you're not only running the company, you're one of the wealthiest men alive?"

"I am?" Matthews asked.

"Don't tell me you overlooked the cool one-hundred and twenty five billion dollars you made yesterday on the stock market before you killed Sanborn?"

Matthews couldn't believe it. "One-hundred twenty-five billion dollars?"

"Give or take a few billion," Gill replied.

"But I didn't make that kind of money yesterday."

Gill slapped a computer printout of Matthews' brokerage account on the table. "Maybe with your busy schedule it slipped your mind."

"No, detective, there has to be some mistake," Matthews replied.

"It looks pretty cut and dried to me," Gill said. "You kill one of your colleagues before you go to bed. Then you call your broker in the morning. You put in your buy order. You make a mint. You sell before the stock plunges. Then you go out and kill your boss at night, and start the whole process all over again. Am I right?"

Matthews' head started spinning. "I don't know what you're talking about—"

"You had access to the building, you had access to the boat, and from what I can tell, you've had access to everyone at Excelsior who's died around here lately. Isn't that right?"

"Well, it's true I do get around—"

Gill slammed his fist into the wall, causing Matthews to jump. "Bein' a wise ass isn't gonna help your cause, Matthews," he said. "We been watchin' your sorry ass for some time now. We know you work some pretty strange hours and you've got a real warm way with your people."

Matthews swallowed hard. "But I'm innocent I tell you. You have no motive—"

"Motive?" Gill laughed. "You want a motive? I'll give you a motive—revenge."

"That's rich," Matthews laughed. "Like I killed my boss because he wouldn't give me the day off."

"Nah," Gill said. "But maybe—just maybe—you did it because Vicki Connors wouldn't give you the right time of day."

Matthews swallowed hard. He couldn't help but look guilty.

"You don't deny havin' the hots for Vicki Connors, do you?"

"I-I-I admired her work," Matthews stammered. "It was strictly professional."

"But the feelings weren't reciprocal, were they Romeo?"

Beads of sweat started building up on Matthews' forehead, and his stomach rumbled even more.

"You know what I think, tough guy? I think you couldn't handle it when she rejected your romantic overtures. And you figured if you couldn't have her nobody would."

"No I didn't—"

"And once you killed her, you couldn't stop. You pushed Billington into that subway car. And then you brutally sliced and diced your boss and his senior management team so you could take control of the company—all by yourself. Isn't that so?"

"NO, NO, NO, NO!" Matthews yelled. "I didn't kill them! I had nothing to do with their deaths."

Gill grabbed Matthews by the shoulders and eyeballed him at close range. "Your lips say 'no' but your eyes say 'yes, yes, yes.' "

"You've gotta believe me," Matthews pleaded.

Gill scratched his head and lit another cigarette. Matthews wasn't smart enough to be the killer. He knew that even before he had him hauled in for questioning. But Gill also knew that Matthews was close enough to Sanborn to point him in the right direction. With a little more softening up, he figured Matthews would sing like a bird.

"I'd like to believe you, Slick. I really would. But we found this little note in your bedroom."

"A note?"

Gill unfolded a piece of notepaper with Matthews' handwriting on it. "Does this ring a bell? 'Old comics resemble the murders...read the classics that inspired the murders...'"

"Wait a minute," Matthews interrupted. "That's not what you think it is."

"What am I supposed to think, Matthews, when I see something like this?"

"But I can explain—"

Gill cut him off. "That's what I'm hoping for, Matthews. Because if you don't explain what this means I'm just going to conclude that this is nothing more than another case of an angry, rejected white guy on a rampage. Five murders, all premeditated. You're looking at the death penalty here. Unless you know somethin' we don't know..."

"I think I'd like to consult with legal counsel now if you don't mind," Matthews said.

Gil laughed.

"No sweat, Slick. That's your right. And as soon as we're done here, we're going to call the American Civil Liberties Union. They love to represent rich white guys who've gotten caught with their hands in the cookie jar."

Matthews could hardly contain himself. His stomach was about to explode. The truth wasn't working. He had to think of something to divert the heat and fast.

"All right, I'm not your killer," he finally blurted out.

"Then who is?"

"It's, it's, it's MacAllister."

"Rick MacAllister?" Gill asked. "The young guy with the over-active imagination?"

"Yeah, that's him," Matthews replied. "He's telling everybody the murders are patterned after all these old comic book stories—"

"Yeah, yeah, yeah," Gill interrupted. "I know all about it. The killer reads 'em and then goes out and commits copy cat murders."

"That's it," Matthews said.

"Just one problem," Gill said. "We ain't got any card-carrying eighty-year-old serial murderers walkin' around New York who read comic books."

Matthews shook his head. "It's not some old geezer, detective. MacAllister's got all those books in his collection at home. He knows every one of the story lines."

"Yeah. So what if he does?" Gill asked.

"He saw more of Connors and Billington than I ever did. He was their boss. And he could get through to Sanborn whenever he wanted. It just makes sense. He killed them all."

Gill took a deep breath. "What about a motive? Why would MacAllister kill all these people?"

"He came to us from Scout," Matthews replied. "No one comes to Excelsior from Scout. It's like going from the Yankees to the Cubs. Some of us suspected he was a spy. We thought he was manipulating Sanborn—purposely trying to kill off the Centurion—to weaken us from within so Lockwood could run Excelsior out of business."

"Go ahead," Gill said, "I'm listening."

"Everything was going according to plan until Connors balked. She didn't like his plan for the Centurion project and stormed out. Then the leaks started, and pictures began showing up on TV. Sanborn started to question his plans. And everything was crumbling underneath him. So there was only one thing left for him to do."

"And what was that?" Gill asked.

"Kill everyone and anyone who stood in his way. First, Connors. Then Billington and Sanborn and Montana and Lederer. Now Lockwood's moving in for the kill—he's going to take over Trieste just like he's wanted to do all along. I'm the only one standing in his way. If I go, so does the company."

"Why didn't you say anything?" Gill asked.

"I had no evidence, detective," Matthews said. "You know this better than anyone else. What good are theories if there's no hard evidence?"

"You still don't have any evidence," Gill countered.

"That's true," Matthews said, "Unlike you and your storm troopers, I can't go barging into people's homes searching for answers. But if you were to pay MacAllister a visit right now, I'd bet you'd find him reading and plotting his next murder."

"Any theories on who that might be?" Gill asked.

Matthews swallowed hard. "Do the math, detective. There's one more book left in the series and I'm the only one left from Sanborn's inner circle."

Gill rubbed his chin and contemplated the possibilities. "If what you're saying is correct—and that's a big if—would you be willing to help us with the rest of the investigation?"

Matthews couldn't believe it. Gill actually seemed to be buying this nonsense.

"Of course I will help, detective," Matthews said, "The life you save may be mine."

Gill stood up and headed for the door. "Wait right here."

Homicide Chief Victor Barratto was waiting for him in an adjacent room behind a two-way mirror.

"Did you catch any of that?" Gill asked.

"Every word," Barratto said. "You believe him?"

"Nah. He'd sell his mother for a price if it would help him."

"Just the same, let's put a tail on MacAllister," Gill said. "I may have dismissed his story too quickly."

"What do we do with Matthews?"

"We oughta throw him back out there and see if his number comes up next," Gill said. "No great loss for mankind if he goes."

Barratto peered into the interrogation room, where Matthews was puking his guts out in a garbage can. "Yeah, but I don't want to have to answer to the mayor if we lose another one. Keep him locked up for his own protection and you better give him lots of barf bags."

Chapter 29

Redding, Connecticut

Matt Payne's house, as we had been told, was tucked away in the woods about an hour and a half north of New York City. Like Payne himself, the house was unique. It had very sharp, angular lines, an enormous front porch, and towering twin peaks, the architectural equivalent of Frank Lloyd Wright meets the Addams Family. A tiny stream circled around the perimeter of the property, which bordered an old cemetery that hadn't seen a new customer in decades. It didn't take much to envision Payne sitting upstairs in a drawing room overlooking the cemetery on a stormy night dreaming up those early Centurion tales with their sinister villains and diabolic plots. Then again, I wondered, could there be a better setting for a serial murderer?

"This place gives me the creeps," Julie said. "Lets go home."

"We're this close, we can't stop now," I said, looking in the rear view mirror. "Besides we have company."

Two New York City cops who had tailed us all the way from Manhattan were sitting in their unmarked car at the end of Payne's driveway trying hard to appear inconspicuous.

"All right, this was your idea," Julie said. "What do we do now?"

"We could just knock on the door and confront him," I said.

Julie frowned. "Just walk right up there, ring the bell, and say, 'Excuse me old man, but are you the guy who's trying to kill us?' "

"You got a better idea?" I asked.

Julie shook her head and opened the car door. "Yeah. Follow my lead and don't say anything until he shows us the comic books."

She rang the doorbell and waited. Several minutes later, Payne opened the door. He looked worn and haggard, nothing like the Matt Payne I remember from his retirement party.

"Hi, my name is Julie, and I'm a graduate student from Pratt. Are you Matt Payne?"

"Yes, but—"

"I'm terribly sorry to disturb you, Mister Payne. But I'm working on my graduate thesis—"

"This really isn't a good time, Miss," he said, closing the door.

"Oh, but Mister Payne, I've come all the way from Brooklyn and Professor Shayne thought you would be able to help me."

Payne eyed us both suspiciously.

"Shayne?" he asked. "Robert Shayne? He's still teaching?"

"He's dean of Graphic Arts," Julie said.

"What's your thesis on?"

"The Centurion. The making of the first American superhero."

"Ever hear of the phone, young lady?"

"You're not listed," Julie said.

"And who's this?" he asked, pointing at me.

I extended my hand. "I'm Rick—"

"Rick's my boyfriend. He's from Connecticut—he knows the area—and he accompanied me up from school. He won't be any trouble."

Payne hesitated. "Well, I really shouldn't do this. But if Shayne sent you I guess it's all right. C'mon in."

Inside, the house was enormous. But it had none of the trappings of a home. There were no pictures—no children or grandchildren—nothing that would indicate a family ever lived there.

Payne walked slowly ahead of us into the living room. His gait was shaky.

"Sit down," he said. "What do you want to know?"

Julie retrieved a pen and pad from her purse.

"My interest is mainly in the early years of the character. How he evolved, the thinking that went into creating the Centurion, and what you did to make him the icon he is today."

"Some icon," he said. "The way things are going maybe you oughta be writing an obituary on the old guy."

"I've seen the TV reports," she said. "I can't believe they're really going to kill him off."

Payne shook his head. "Don't underestimate the power of greed, young lady."

"What was the inspiration for the Centurion?"

Payne thought for a moment. "Believe it or not, my wife," he said. "When I met her she was an Olympic athlete in training. She had these amazing powers—at times I used to think she was super human—and when she performed she made people smile. That's what I wanted this character to do."

"But originally, the Centurion was a pretty tough guy."

"Those were pretty tough times," Payne said. "We were on the brink of war. People were looking for a leader who would stand up against the forces of evil."

"One of my favorite villains is Doctor Terror," she said. "I think he first appeared in nineteen thirty-seven."

Payne's eyes lit up. She was starting to win him over.

"Nineteen thirty-nine, to be exact, my dear," he said. "I named him after my wife's doctor. That was his nickname—he was always filled with gloom and doom."

"I understand some of those older books are pretty rare now," Julie said.

"I have them all in my collection," Payne said. "Every single one is in mint condition. Wanna see them?"

Bingo!

Julie smiled. "I was hoping you'd ask."

Payne led us to the back of the house, down a long, dark flight of stairs, to a locked room that ran beneath the house. As soon as he opened the door, the room seemed to spring to life. His collection was stunning and altogether different from the one at Excelsior. This one wasn't warehoused. It was a shrine. Prominent editions were framed and displayed in trophy cases. Pictures of the Centurion lined the room, almost like a family photo album.

"They're all here," Payne said. "Every single issue from start to finish."

"I had a reprint of the very first issue once," I said.

"Wanna see the real thing, kid?"

Payne opened a locked file cabinet drawer and pulled out a thick folder, stuffed with dozens of old issues. "Feast your eyes."

"They must be worth a fortune," I said.

"You can't put a price on these, son," Payne replied. "To me, they're worth a lot more than anything a collector could ever offer."

"Tell me more about Doctor Terror," Julie said. "How did he come into the picture?"

Payne returned the file to the cabinet and locked the drawer. "Evil villains were big sellers in those days. We needed a really sinister character who would stop at nothing to get what he wanted, particularly if it was a government secret."

"Do you have those issues in your collection, too?"

"Of course," Payne said, with a puzzled look on his face. He opened another file drawer next to his drawing table and pulled out several more folders that were filled with comic books.

"I haven't looked at these in ages," he said, handing them to me one at a time; *Murder on the Sixth Floor, Murder on the Subway, Murder on the High Seas*. And then he stopped.

"There was a fourth issue in the series, wasn't there?"

Payne looked at the folder and started rummaging through the file drawer. "Hmmm, that's strange. I'm sure there was a fourth installment. It should be here with all the others. I know I have that book in the collection."

My heart started racing. Was he onto us? Could he be covering it up?

Payne rubbed his chin. "My wife, Alix, was tidying up in here a few days ago. I wonder if she moved it."

A voice we weren't expecting to hear provided the answer.

"What are you blaming me for now, dear?"

All three of us jumped as Payne's wife appeared in the room.

"Alix, my dear," Payne said. "I didn't hear you come in."

"That's obvious," she said with a smile. "Whenever I need help with the groceries you're never around." Then she eyed us. "Aren't you going to introduce me to your guests?"

Julie extended her hand. "I'm Julie and this is my friend, Rick. I'm doing my graduate thesis at Pratt on the Centurion and your husband was kind enough to talk to us when I rang the bell—"

Alix gave us both a long, hard look. "And what can't you find?"

"She's interested in the Doctor Terror series, dear," Payne said.

"Everything's here in the file, except for the last issue. And I thought maybe—"

"Have you checked in the library?" she asked. "You brought a couple of boxes of comic books there the other night."

"By God, I did," Payne replied. "I'll go have a look. Wait here."

As soon as Payne was out of range, Alix's smile disappeared. "If you're here to dig up more material for the last issue of the Centurion, I'm going to have to ask you to leave, Miss McKinney—"

Julie nearly swallowed her tongue.

"There must be some mistake," I said.

Alix glared at me. "There's no mistake. I recognize you from television, Mister MacAllister. I don't know what you're up to, but my husband is not well and you're not welcome here. He almost died because of what you're doing to the Centurion."

"No, please listen to me," I said. "We're not killing the Centurion. But somebody is trying to kill us. That's why we have to find this comic book. All of the murders follow a pattern. They're happening exactly the way they did in the Doctor Terror series. We think we're next, and we have to find out what's in that final installment before the killer strikes again."

Alix hesitated. "You're not going to find any killer here. My husband isn't well enough to hurt a fly."

"We're here because we know Matt has the comic book we're looking for. He checked it out at Excelsior's morgue before he retired."

"He did?"

"That's what we were told when we went looking for it in the Archives."

"Matt never went there," she said. "Not with his asthma and all that dust."

"We saw his name on the sign-out sheet," Julie said. "If it wasn't your husband, than who was it?"

Before she could answer, Payne reappeared in the doorway, out of breath, carrying a large box in his hands. Alix quickly grabbed the box from him and helped him to his chair.

"I don't understand how things keep disappearing all the time," he said, trying to catch his breath. "I know the book is around here someplace."

"Take it easy, dear," she said. "I'll look for the book. It seems there's more to this mystery than meets the eye. Your friend here isn't working on her term paper."

Julie and I told him our story. At first, Payne was angry that we had deceived him, and even more upset that we suspected him as the killer. But then, when we explained why we were really there, his anger turned to concern.

"Do you have the issue from the morgue?" Julie asked.

"No," he insisted. "Never touched anything in that dirty ol' place."

"But why would Butch tell us that they were signed out under your name?"

Payne scratched his head and thought for a moment. "Mitch used to go down there all the time and retrieve old issues for me."

"Mitch?" I asked.

"Mitch Gerber, my assistant."

"Short guy with a beard?"

"That's him," Payne said. "I used to let him sign out books under my name. I bet he took them out."

"But why would he sign out the Doctor Terror series?" I asked.

"That's easy," Payne said. "He created them."

"He did?"

Payne nodded. "He did a lot of Centurion books for me. The Doctor Terror books were his first solo issues."

"But I didn't see his name in the credits," Julie said.

Payne shook his head. "It's a long story. Mitch was a young intern at the time and he needed some seasoning. Unfortunately, we were a union shop and guild rules prohibited interns from doing the work of full-timers.

"It was Catch-22. He needed experience to become a regular artist, but the stupid rules wouldn't allow us to give him the experience he needed to get hired."

"So what happened?" I asked.

"I told the union to fuck off and I let him do the issues all by himself. We didn't tell anyone it was his work until after the series turned out to be such a hit. Then he finally got hired."

"He was next in line to succeed you," Julie said.

"He should have gotten the job," Payne replied. "He deserved it. He produced some of the finest Centurion books around. He lived for the Centurion!"

"But then Sanborn came along and his career tanked, too—"

"Yeah," Payne said, "I guess so."

Julie thought for a second. "Let me see if I've got this straight. Gerber creates the murder serials. He plots out the stories and develops the villains. But he never gets credit for them. Then he spends three decades serving under you, and when his big moment comes, he gets passed over for promotion …"

"Now wait a minute, young lady," Payne interrupted. "Mitch is no killer. He wouldn't hurt a fly."

"But he had access to everybody," Julie said. "He sat near Vicki. He worked late at night. He knew where Michael lived. He could have followed him to the subway—"

"He could get to Sanborn as easily as anyone else," I added. "And maybe he thinks we're really going to kill the Centurion."

"You're not?" Payne asked.

"Not for good," I replied. "He's an alien. He comes back to life.
You know that. It's all based on your original premise."

Payne walked over to his desk, opened a drawer and pulled out a big overnight envelope. "What about these?"

He handed me several sketches—dozens of rejects from the dungeon.

"Where did you get these?" I asked.

"They've been coming in the mail from New York since I left."

"They came from the garbage," I said. "Sanborn originally wanted to finish him off for good. But I couldn't do it."

"Rick sold Sanborn on the idea of bringing the character back like he was in the beginning," Julie added.

"Then this has all been a setup for a sequel," Payne said.

"Labor Day," I said. "We bring back the original, in his classic form."

Payne looked at the envelope, then at Alix. "My God, that's Mitch's handwriting—he sent these."

Alix stopped digging through the box and held her hands over her mouth. "Oh, no. Not Mitch."

"It all makes sense," Payne said. "We've got to stop him."

"But he's got the final comic book from the morgue," I said. "So we don't know when and where he's going to strike next. Do you have any idea where we can find another copy of that issue?"

Before Payne could answer, Alix jumped in. "Is it *Murder in the Coliseum* you're looking for?"

"That's the one," I said.

She pulled the comic book from the box and handed it to me.

"Look no further."

Chapter 30

Murder in the Coliseum took place in an old Manhattan supper club on the East Side. In its time, the Coliseum was the place to be in New York, with big bands, swing dancers, lavish Roman décor and great food. All of which made it the perfect backdrop for a climactic confrontation between the Centurion and Doctor Terror.

This time, however, it was the Centurion who lured Doctor Terror into a trap. He showed up in place of the intended victim, cleverly disguised, and waited for the killer to make the first move. The ploy worked, setting up a battle that started in the Coliseum's ballroom and played out in an Excelsior duel to the death on the roof of the building.

"I remember this now," Payne said. "The Coliseum night club was Mitch's favorite hangout. We were concerned that the owner was going to sue us if we used it in the story."

"Is it still there?" I asked.

Payne shook his head. "It was torn down years ago. "There's a high rise there now."

"Then we have to find Gerber before he finds us."

"I know where he lives," Payne said. "Take me there. Let me talk to him. I can get through to him."

Alix grabbed him by the arm. "You're not going anywhere in your condition," she said.

"The only thing I'm suffering from, my dear, is cabin fever," Payne said. "I'm sick of being cooped up in this house with nothing to do. I'll be fine."

Alix's eyes welled up with tears. "But what if Mitch really is the killer and he goes after you?"

"Mitch won't hurt me," Payne said. "We've been through too much together."

"That's what worries me," she replied. "You've both had too much to deal with."

Payne took her hand. "Alix, I have to do this. I'll come back alive. I promise."

"I'll stay with her," Julie volunteered.

That iced it. Payne and I were joining forces.

"We'll call you from his apartment as soon as we know something," I said.

So off we went to Gerber's Brooklyn apartment, shadowed by two cops, hoping to find our modern day Doctor Terror before he came looking for us.

Meanwhile, inside the unmarked police car, Detective Joe Malone was growing concerned.

"He's just come out of the house with an old guy," he radioed back to police headquarters on his microphone. "Must be Payne. The girlfriend is still inside."

In New York, on the other end of the conversation, Gill took a long drag on his cigarette. "Which way are they heading?"

"South. Probably back to the city," Malone said.

Gill put the mike down and turned to his boss.

"Whaddya think they're up to?" Barratto asked.

Gill looked at his watch. Nine o'clock. "They ain't goin' to no comic book convention at this hour. That's for sure."

"Question is are they doing a little head hunting tonight?"

"Maybe we should offer them some bait once they get where they're going," Gill said.

Barratto scratched his head. "Matthews?"

"We could wire him up for sound."

"Sounds good to me," Barratto said.

"What about protection?" Gill asked. "Should we suit him up in a bullet proof vest?"

Barratto peered through the two-way mirror at Matthews, who was still puking his brains out in the interrogation room. "Nah," he said, shaking his head. "No sense messing up one of our new suits."

Gill picked up the mike. "Keep tailin' 'em, Joe. We may have the guy they're looking for and he's working for us. We'll deliver him to the party."

Malone stepped on the gas, while his partner, a red-haired recruit fresh out of the academy named Jim Szymanski, polished off the last bite of a jelly donut.

"What about the girl?" Szymanski asked. "We just gonna leave her there?"

"You heard the boss," Malone replied. "We're supposed to follow them."

"I don't know," Szymanski said, shaking his head. "We shouldn't leave her here by herself."

Malone stepped on the brakes. "You wanna stay here in the woods and watch her while I chase these clowns down?"

"No, but—"

"Then relax," he said. "What kind of trouble is she gonna get into in the middle of nowhere with Payne's old lady?"

It took us nearly two hours to navigate through the heavy traffic before we found Gerber's apartment in Brooklyn. But it gave us time to talk. Payne still had a real spark about him, and the more we talked, the more I liked him.

"I really thought you were killing off the Centurion for good," he said. "The pictures and the news reports were—"

"They were wrong," I said. "We had a leak someplace. But only half the story got out."

"Wouldn't surprise me if it was Sanborn, kid. He'd stop at nothing."

Gerber's apartment was dark and desolate. We rang the bell several times but there was no answer.

Payne looked at his watch. "Not like Mitch to be out at this time of the night."

"Damn," I said. "Now what do we do?"

"Looks like a job for the Centurion, kid. Stand back." Payne reached into his pocket and retrieved a spare key. "Told you we were close."

Outside, our unmarked tails watched across the street from their car.

"You got an ID on this address, yet?" Malone radioed back to Gill in police headquarters.

A few moments later, a desk clerk handed him a computer printout.

"Says here the occupant is Mitchell Gerber," Gill replied.

"Know anything about him?" Malone asked.

Gill flipped through his notepad. "Name sounds familiar. I think he works at Excelsior."

"Co-conspirators?" Malone radioed back.

"Not sure," Gill said. "Let me check with our weasel and I'll get back to you."

Gerber's apartment wasn't much to look at. In fact, the only light in the place came from a bulb above the kitchen stove. A warm coffee pot was still simmering on a back burner and the sink was piled high with dirty dishes.

We snooped around a bit but it wasn't until we searched Gerber's drawing room that we hit pay dirt. What we found confirmed our worst fears—photo cutouts of three of the murder victims—Vicki, Mike and Sanborn—all pinned up around his drawing table. In his bedroom next door we found all four issues of the Centurion murder mysteries, including the final installment that was missing from Excelsior's collection. In fact, the book was still open on his bed.

I picked up the comic book. "Listen to this," I said. "And then the two combatants—the evil sorcerer of terror and the gallant Sentinel of Light—engaged in a titanic struggle to the death on the roof of the Coliseum."

Payne shook his head in disbelief. "My God! He's plotting his next move. The only question is where."

Payne studied the book and wandered back into Gerber's drawing room. The setup was pretty basic—just an old drawing table, a rotary dial phone, an answering machine and a cup of warm coffee on a small stand.

"Looks like he left here in a hurry," Payne said.

He pressed the replay button on Gerber's answering machine.

"You have no new messages."

Then he eyed the pad on the drawing table. There wasn't a mark on it. But Payne noticed a tiny corner of the front page was missing, as if it had been torn off the page.

"Hand me a lead pencil," he said.

I fished through a mug on Gerber's desk and picked out one with a sharp point. Payne placed the pencil point on its side and started sketching over the section.

"What are you doing?" I asked.

"Playing a hunch, kid. Mitch likes to make little notes to himself. If he got a call and jotted down a number, it might have left an imprint underneath."

It was hard to read at first, but Payne continued penciling over it until three lines eventually appeared.

C
Columbus Circle
Midnight.

"Columbus Circle?" I scratched my head. "What's there?"

Payne looked at his watch. "Don't know, kid. But we've got forty-five minutes to find out."

At police headquarters, Matthews found himself back on the grill.

"Whaddya know about a Mitch Gerber?"

"Depends," Matthews asked. "Why are you asking?"

Gill ran his hands through his hair. "Because, wise guy, as we speak, your murder suspect with the over-active imagination is at Gerber's apartment with Matt Payne."

Matthews tried not to act surprised. "MacAllister is at Gerber's apartment? At this hour?"

Gill nodded.

Matthews shook his head. "Not good."

"Care to elaborate?"

"Mitch was helping me gather evidence," Matthews said. "He had a special talent for covert surveillance—"

"You mean he was doing all your dirty work."

Matthews frowned. "In a manner of speaking—"

"Keep talkin'," Gill said.

"I can only assume that Mister MacAllister has uncovered our little intelligence gathering operation and is enlisting the aid of his predecessor in exacting revenge."

"You think they've gone to Gerber's apartment to kill him?"

"That's a possibility I hadn't thought of," Matthews replied.

Gill headed for the door to alert Malone.

"Wait," Matthews said. "There's always the chance that Gerber's joined forces with them."

"Now why would he do that?" Gill asked.

"The most obvious reason would be to kill me, I suppose."

"And why would Gerber want to kill you?"

"I, uh, might have made him a few well-intentioned promises that I can't fulfill due to current circumstances beyond my control."

"What you really mean is you made him a few promises that you had no intention of keeping."

Matthews shrugged. "That's your interpretation, detective."

Gill shook his head. "You're slick, Matthews. Straddle the fence, string people along, manipulate them for your own personal gain. I can see you're a real paragon of corporate virtue."

Matthews scowled. "Regardless of what you may think of me, detective, I was trying to resolve this situation. For all my efforts, I now find myself directly in the line of fire, through no fault of my own."

"We're going to see about that," Gill said.

"W-w-what do you mean?"

"It means we're going fishin' and you're the bait."

The color started to fade from Matthews face. "You're going to let them come after me here?

"Nah," Gill replied. "Inspector Henderson doesn't take kindly to murder on the premises."

Matthews heaved a sigh of relief. "Oh, thank God—"

"Once we figure out where they're all going, we're gonna take you there ourselves and lay a little trap for your friends," Gill said.

This time, Matthews' face went completely white.

Gill lit another cigarette and headed for the door. "Just remember, Slick. In this business, location is everything."

Payne and I made it to Columbus Circle shortly before midnight. Even late at night, it was an incredibly busy part of town. What's worse, there were a million places where Gerber could be hiding.

"Any idea what we do now?" I asked.

"Look for Gerber, kid."

"I know that, but where?"

Payne scratched his head. "I got an idea, kid. We did this once in an old Centurion comic book. We stand back to back. You take one side of the street and I take the other. We keep looking until something catches our eye."

It struck me as a long shot, but at this point we had nothing to lose. So we lined up together—me facing east and Payne facing west—and slowly started canvassing the neighborhood.

"Call out whatever you see, kid," Payne said.

"OK," I said, "here goes. I see a dry cleaners…a print shop…a palm reader…an Indian restaurant…a subway station…three apartment buildings…and the Gulf & Western Building…"

"Why'd you stop, kid?"

"That's it," I said.

"That's everything?"

"That's everything," I said.

"Well start up where you left off and go back," Payne said. "Call it all out again."

"What about you?" I asked. "Aren't you going to do your side of the street?"

"Not yet," Payne said, rather sheepishly.

"Why not?"

"I can't see that far, damn it!"

So I went back to where I stopped and started all over again.

"There's a bakery…another apartment building…a deli…the subway station again…another high rise…and the Coliseum…"

As soon as I said the word, I stopped.

"Say that again, kid."

"The Coliseum."

"As in the New York Coliseum?" Payne asked.

Spotlights danced around the old building, which was being completely refurbished, inside and out, and crisscrossed each other in the sky.

"The name certainly fits," I said.

"That must be what the 'C' stood for in Mitch's note," Payne said.

Payne and I headed across the street—weaving quickly in and around the traffic circle—and up to the main entrance of the Coliseum. The building was surrounded by scaffolding, as it was being completely refurbished by Donald Trump.

"This is where we'll find him," Payne said.

"How can you be so sure?"

Payne pointed to the marquee above the front doors.

"CLASSIC COMIC BOOK COLLECTOR'S CONVENTION STARTS SATURDAY."

"I'll be damned."

A line had already formed outside the main door—mostly young kids and groupies—who were camping out overnight to beat the morning rush.

"He's inside," Payne said.

I looked around. The place appeared to be locked tight.

"Maybe, but how we gonna get in there?" I asked.

Payne winked. "Leave it to me, kid."

We casually walked up to a young security guard who was standing at the main entrance.

"Any chance we might be able to get inside?" Payne asked.

"Building's closed, guys. Big show starts tomorrow morning."

"Yeah, we know all about it," Payne said. "We're exhibitors. We were in there setting up earlier and I left my jacket inside."

"You got any ID?"

"It's in my jacket," Payne said. "So are the keys to my apartment. I can't do anything without it."

The guard picked up his clipboard, which contained a list of exhibitor's names. *Now we're sunk*, I thought.

"What outfit you with?" he asked.

"Comic Cave," Payne responded. "I'm with the Montanas."

The guard quickly looked up. "Why didn't you say so in the first place? The Montana family owns this place."

Payne smiled, and the guard opened the lobby door. "Take the escalator to the second floor. Exhibition hall is on your right."

"Thanks," Payne said. "OK kid, keep your eyes peeled."

Neither one of us realized it at the time, but our presence on the front steps of the Coliseum had created a stir among some of the fans waiting in line. Ordinarily that wouldn't have been a problem. But one of the fans was no ordinary kid.

"Did you see what I just saw?"

Larry Plunkett turned to his friend and nodded. "I saw them, Eddie. But are you sure it was them?"

"Positive," Eddie replied. "I've seen their pictures before."

"But what would Payne and MacAllister be doing here?"

"They're probably going to make a surprise appearance at the show."

"At midnight?"

"You just don't walk in during the middle of a show like this if you're a big star," Eddie replied. "They'd get mobbed."

Larry thought for a second. "My dad might be interested in this. Hold my place. I'm gonna make a phone call."

Across the street, Detectives Malone and Szymanski were also speculating about why we were poking around the Coliseum.

"There's got to be more to it than this," Malone said, as he watched from his car.

"Look at the sign," Szymanski said. "Don't you know anything about comic books?"

Malone smirked. "Sorry, I stopped readin' 'em when I discovered girls," he said. "You oughta try 'em sometime."

Szymanski frowned. "I betcha Payne and MacAllister are probably gonna show up here tomorrow. You know, surprise the fans, give a speech, sign a few autographs."

Malone looked at his watch. It was after midnight. "Aren't they just a tad early?"

"These guys are like gods at these conventions," Szymanski replied. "They'll get mobbed if they walk in during the show. They're probably looking for a back entrance while it's still quiet."

Malone rubbed his chin. "You sure?"

Szymanski nodded. "You saw the guard let them in without a hassle. Gill shows up with the cavalry and our cover is blown."

Malone radioed into headquarters. "Hey, chief, we've tracked 'em into the Coliseum."

"The Coliseum?" Gill asked. "At this hour?"

"Turns out there's a big comic book show opening tomorrow morning. Captain America here thinks they're just checking the place out for a back entrance."

Szymanski grabbed the mike. "We can keep an eye on things here, Chief. Why don't you hold off on the reinforcements for a while."

Gill thought about it for a moment. "You've got forty-five minutes. Then we're coming in."

Malone placed the microphone back in its holder and opened the door. "All right, genius. Let's go check this out."

"Wait a minute," Szymanski said.

"What is it now?"

"You gotta pen?" he asked.

"Yeah, I think so. Why?"

"This might be a great chance to get their autographs."

Chapter 31

New York Coliseum

The Exhibit Hall was huge, dark and very quiet—exactly the kind of place you'd expect to find the largest comic book show in New York. It was packed with tables and cardboard displays of muscular superheroes—including a giant Centurion cutout—tons of memorabilia, and thousands of comic books.

Payne was an old pro at these conventions. Just being there seemed to revitalize him. And he was turning out to be quite the detective. "You take the back of the room and I'll work my way up toward the stage," he said. "Keep a low profile. Mitch will come to you."

I made my way through the dark, snaking along the narrow aisles between tables. After a while, every row started to look alike. It wasn't until I had started making my way back to the center of the room that a shadow behind one of the exhibitor's tables caught my eye.

I quickly ducked behind a life-sized superhero display and waited. A minute or two later the shadow reappeared. I poked my head out from behind the display, just long enough to recognize Gerber's face. He didn't see me, but he was heading straight toward me. I didn't know what to do. A little voice inside me said go after him before he makes the first move. I've never been the type to initiate a fight, but this time I listened. I grabbed the cardboard display in my hands, thinking it was heavy enough that I could throw it at him and maybe gain the upper hand. But the display was too heavy. Before I could do anything with it, it slipped out of my hands and toppled over onto the floor with a thud.

The sudden noise was enough to startle Gerber. So much, in fact, that he lost his balance, stumbled over the display, and landed face down on the floor at my feet.

At first, he didn't move and I held my breath. Then he looked up at me and our eyes connected in the dark.

"Mitch?" I said. "Is that you?"

He quickly rolled across the floor—almost as if he was afraid of me—and hid under a table.

"Mitch!" I yelled loud enough so that Payne could hear me on the other side of the hall. "I know it's you, Mitch! And I know what this is all about."

He didn't respond, so I walked over to the front of the table.

"This doesn't have to turn out like all the others. No one is going to hurt the Centurion. I can promise you that. Let's talk this out."

Then I waited. And I waited some more. Finally, when nothing happened, I figured it was time to do something dramatic. So I grabbed the edge of the table and flung it on its side. It crashed to the floor with an enormous thud.

When the dust cleared, Gerber emerged from under a pile of comic books and trinkets, all hunched up in a ball clutching an envelope in his hands.

"Stop," he pleaded. "I got your message. I read the comic books, just like you said. I brought more sketches. And I came here. Don't hurt me."

I grabbed Gerber by the arm, and pulled him out from under the pile. He was shaking like a mouse.

"I'm not going to hurt you," I said.

"But you said you were going to kill me like the others ..." He started talking, faster and faster and faster.

"I never said I was going to hurt you, Mitch."

"Oh yes you did—"

He began sobbing uncontrollably, just as Payne reappeared.

"Mitch!" Payne put his arms around him. "What's going on here?"

"I got the phone call," he said. "He told me to come here. To help protect the Centurion."

"Who told you to come here?" Payne asked.

Gerber pointed at me. "Who do you think? I know what he's doing. He's trying to kill off the Centurion and take over the company—him and Lockwood. And he's getting rid of everyone who stands in his way—"

Payne grabbed Gerber by the shoulders. "Mitch, listen to me. You're talking nonsense. Rick's not trying to take over the company. And he's not going to kill the Centurion."

Gerber shook his head. "Like hell, he's not."

"He's trying to stop the killer," Payne said.

"But he called me an hour ago," Gerber said. "He told me to come here tonight otherwise he'd—"

"Rick's been with me all evening. He didn't call you."

Gerber looked directly at me. "You're really not going to kill me?"

"No," I said.

"And you're not going to bump off the Centurion?"

I shook my head. "I thought you were trying to kill me."

"Me?" Gerber asked. "I'm not trying to kill you."
"You didn't kill Vicki Connors?" Payne asked him.
"No," Gerber insisted. "I didn't lay a hand on her."
"You didn't kill Mike Billington?"
"Nope."
"And you didn't kill Sanborn or Montana or Lederer?"
Gerber stood up. "It wasn't me," he replied. "I swear to God."
I wasn't sure whether to believe him. I don't think Gerber believed me either.
"You're the one who's talking about killing people, MacAllister," he said.
"What are you talking about?" I asked.
"Your girlfriend," Gerber replied.
"What about her?"
"You said on the phone that if I didn't bring the sketches of the Centurion the girl was going to die."
My heart nearly stopped. "What?"
"You heard me," Gerber said. "That's what you said. Be here at midnight or the girl will die."
My mind started racing. "But we left her with—"
Payne gasped. "Oh my God. We never called them. If the killer has Julie then Alix must be with them."
Payne hadn't even finished the sentence when a loud noise—like firecrackers going off one right after the other—started erupting around the perimeter of the room.
"It's the exits," Payne shouted, "They have automatic locks."
Gerber ran to the closest door and tried to push it open. But it wouldn't budge.
"It's no use," he said. "We're trapped."
Then a voice rang out from the darkness.
"How ironic. And here you thought YOU were setting a trap for me."
Payne grabbed my arm. "Who are you and what have you done with Alix and Julie?"
"Who am I?" the voice replied. A bright spotlight suddenly illuminated the stage at the front of the exhibit hall. Standing alone at center stage was a slender figure, wearing a black ski mask and olive green fatigues.
"That's right," Payne said, indignantly. "Who are you?"
"If you have to ask—"
Payne pounded his fist on one of the exhibit tables.

"I have to ask damn it! Who are you?"

The Mask walked to edge of the stage. "Just your friendly neighborhood comic book serial killer."

"And what have you done with the others?"

"Don't worry your shiny little head off. They're safe."

"Not good enough!" I yelled up to the stage. "Where are they?"

The Mask laughed.

From behind the curtain I could hear a muffled cry.

"You're going to have to do better than that, my dear," the Mask said. "Little Ricky can't hear you."

The cries grew louder. "Rick! Rick! I'm here!" It was Julie's voice, no question about it. "Help me!"

"Where is she?" I demanded.

The Mask chuckled. "Just hanging around."

Slowly the stage curtain rose and I could hear the sounds of pulleys grinding and squeaking from above. A moment later Julie appeared high above the stage, tethered to a harness and cables like Peter Pan.

I immediately started to run toward her.

"Not so fast, flyboy," the Mask shouted. "One more step and Mary Poppins crashes and burns."

I stopped dead in my tracks. "What do you want from us?"

"Ahhhh," the Mask said. "What do I want? Now there's the magic question. Haven't you figured it out by now? God knows, I've dropped enough hints."

"Hints?" I asked. "What hints?"

"You should have seen the heads-up I gave Sanborn."

"Enough of this nonsense," Payne said.

"Now, now, now. Temper, temper big boy." Then the Mask looked up at Julie. "Why don't you tell them what I want, my dear."

Julie hated heights. She was hanging forty feet above the stage, as white as a ghost.

"R-R-R-R-Rick, you have to stop the Centurion project," she screamed. "T-T-T-The C-C-C-Centurion must live."

"Very good, my dear," the figure said.

"But I'm sure she told you," I said. "The Centurion is not going to die."

The Mask raised a hand. "Mister MacAllister, your nose is growing longer."

Payne stepped forward. "Listen to him. He's telling the truth."

This time the figure laughed. "I can't believe you bought that sorry story."

"But it's true," Payne insisted.

"Where is the truth in killing him off and bringing him back from the dead?"

"It's brilliant," Payne said.

"Brilliant my ass! It's blasphemous. You can't treat the world's mightiest superhero like a soft drink! I won't let it happen."

"And who are you to act like God?" Payne asked. "You don't own the character."

"The hell I don't! You created him. But I gave him life. I was there for him over the years—with millions of others—buying every issue. No one—not even you—can take him away."

I could see this was going nowhere so I decided to try another approach. "The project is dead," I yelled. "It died with Sanborn. None of it will ever be published."

"And you don't think your new boss won't pick up where he left off with all those pretty sketches you left for him?" the Mask asked.

"Not if you kill him off like everyone else," I said.

"That's the idea, Mister MacAllister," the figure said. "And that is why you're here."

"What do you mean?"

"You're the bait, my boy. You're all bait. Mister Gerber brought you here. Miss McKinney is going to keep you here. And you will now bring Norbert Matthews here."

"Is that what this is all about?" I asked. "Killing Matthews?"

The Mask howled. "No, no, no. Give me more credit than that. I'm not only going to kill Matthews, I'm going to kill all of you. In fact, I'm going to kill everyone who's had anything to do with this whole terrible episode all in one shot."

As the figure was talking, Payne whispered into my ear. "We need a diversion. Keep the conversation going."

I tried to inch closer to the stage. "Stay back, Mister MacAllister!"

The Mask reached behind the curtain and grabbed a lever. Julie immediately plunged several feet from her perch, stopping just inches off the stage floor.

"No tricks or next time she dies!"

I quickly backed away. Julie was hysterical. It wasn't what I wanted to happen, but it was enough of a distraction for Payne to slip into the shadows undetected.

Meanwhile, as I tried to keep the conversation going, Malone and Szymanski were outside the Coliseum working over the security guard who had let us in.

"Whaddya mean you just let them in?" Malone asked.

"The old guy said he left his jacket in there—"

"How do you know he wasn't a terrorist?"

"C'mon," the guard said. "The old guy told me he was with the Montana organization. That's all I needed to hear."

Montana? Malone's ears started ringing.

"Jez-us Christ."

Szymanski grabbed his partner by the arm. "What's the matter, Joe?"

"Organized Crime Unit said there might be a big pow-pow going on in the wake of Montana's death," Malone whispered back. "We may have just found it. This whole place could be crawlin' with goons."

"I dunno," Szymanski said, looking around. "Seems pretty desolate to me."

"You call Gill and tell him to bring reinforcements while I snoop around inside. This could be bigger than Appalachia in fifty-seven."

Malone drew his gun, raced into the building and headed for the exhibition hall. Inside, the Mask and I were still talking. But the conversation wasn't going anywhere.

"It's not too late to stop this," I said. "Let her go and we all walk away from this."

"No one's going anywhere," the Mask said. "Especially you, Mister MacAllister."

Payne's search for a diversion paid off, for at that very moment a fire alarm and strobe light went off inside the exhibit hall.

The Mask wasn't amused. "You're going to need more than the fire department to save you now, Mister MacAllister."

Then the assailant flipped the lever once more and Julie dropped to the stage with a thud.

"You're with me, sister."

The Mask quickly yanked off Julie's harness and cables, and then dragged her up a steep flight of stairs behind the stage.

I charged up the stage in hot pursuit, but I wasn't fast enough. As soon as I reached the top of the stairs, the Mask slammed an old metal door in my face and barred it from behind. I pounded on the door several times, but it didn't budge. The more I pounded, the more frantic I was becoming.

"Save your strength, kid," Payne yelled up to me.

"I have to go after her," I said.

"We will. But not from here."

I scrambled back down the stairs, where both Payne and Gerber were waiting.

"First order of business is to get wherever the killer is going," Payne said.

I looked around. "This place is huge. How are we going to know where they are?"

"Only one place they could be," Gerber piped in. "These stairs lead directly to a big ball room on the upper level. It covers the entire floor."

"How do you know?" I asked.

Payne smiled. "We've worked comic book conventions here before."

"But the exits—they're all locked."

"Follow me," Gerber said.

Gerber led us to the back of the exhibition hall to a well-concealed freight elevator. "This goes directly upstairs to a storage area off the ballroom."

As soon as the doors opened, I started to make my way onto the elevator.

"Not so fast kid," Payne said. "We're coming with you."

"You don't have to do this."

"Yes I do. Alix may be up there, too."

"But I'm sure the killer's armed," I said.

Payne held up his hand. "Should be a good match. We still have our brains."

So all three of us marched into the elevator, as unlikely a trio of combatants as you could image. But despite Payne's bravado, when the doors closed behind us I couldn't help wondering if any one of us would come back alive.

Chapter 32

Even as a little kid, Joe Malone had a nose for trouble. If it was out there—and he wasn't the cause of it—he knew how to find it. And sometimes, it would even find him. This was one of those times. Malone had followed his nose to the escalator, just as the security guard outside the Coliseum had told him. Halfway up the stairway a fire alarm went off inside the exhibit hall. Malone quickly grabbed his gun and ran up the remaining stairs, arriving at exactly the same moment as one of the Coliseum's security guards.

"Hey, Sherlock. What's going on in there?" he asked.

Bill Warren, a twenty-something rent-a-cop who was moonlighting from his real job as a speechwriter, just shrugged. "Probably another false alarm, Pop."

"Let's take a look and see," Malone said.

Warren shook the door handle several times. "That's strange. The doors are all locked. We can't get in."

"Why are the doors locked?"

"Beats me, Pop. There's an automatic locking mechanism that's controlled by the central security desk. But it's supposed to open during fire drills."

"It's a signal isn't it, Sherlock?"

Warren looked at him funny. "Signal?"

Malone grabbed Warren by his throat and slammed him up against the wall. "Don't play dumb, Junior. There's no fire in there. It's a warning signal to the families that the cops are on the way. Isn't it?"

"Families?" Warren gagged. "What families?"

Malone shoved the barrel of his revolver into his mouth and pulled the trigger back.

"Don't give me that crap, Sherlock," he yelled. "You know who I'm talking about. The Montanas. The LaDucas. The Rescignos. The Girardos. Any of those names ring a bell?"

Warren could barely nod his head.

"I thought so," Malone responded. "And they're all inside plotting the next big mob war. Right, Sherlock?"

Beads of sweat poured down Warren's forehead. At this point, he figured it was better to tell Malone what he wanted to hear. So he bobbed his head up and down once more.

"Damn!" Malone couldn't believe it. The biggest collar in the history of organized crime was his for the taking, but he couldn't get inside.

"Hey, wait a minute," he said. "We can't get to them, but they can't get out either. They're all trapped inside like rats."

Somehow Warren managed a smile.

Malone slowly pulled the gun out of Warren's mouth and patted him on the cheek. "Relax, Sherlock," he said. "All we gotta do now is wait right here until the cavalry arrives."

Across the river in Ft. Lee, New Jersey, Phil Plunkett climbed aboard Chopper Seven, which had been waiting for him on the helipad atop Scout's headquarters.

"You sure you want to do this at this hour?" the pilot shouted to him over the roar of the helicopter's rotors.

"Are you kidding?" Plunkett asked. "This might be good enough to break into programming with a live report."

Arty Crenshaw, Plunkett's cameraman, climbed on board and donned his headset. "What've we got, Phil?"

"I'm not sure what to make of it," Plunkett said. "My top source spotted Payne and MacAllister at the New York Coliseum about twenty minutes ago. We've also got reports off the police radio of a possible mob pow-wow going on there right now—"

"Je-zus Christ," Arty said.

"Plus," Plunkett continued, "fire alarms went off there just a few minutes ago and half the Fire Department is racing to the scene."

"Visuals are gonna be awesome," Arty said.

A moment later, the chopper lifted off the helipad and made a beeline for Columbus Circle.

The old ballroom above the Coliseum's exhibit hall hadn't been used in years. A musty odor hung over the room like a cloud. In its day, it must have been pretty wild. Even now, the ballroom looked like a set from an old Fred Astaire/Ginger Rogers movie. Marble columns lined the walls. A giant band shell hugged the stage. Potted palm trees filled every corner. At the center of the room, an enormous revolving dance floor sat directly under a domed skylight that sparkled under the stars. Add a few waiters and some people, and it was almost identical to the nightclub in *Murder in the Coliseum*.

"Maybe we should spread out," I whispered to Payne as soon as the elevator doors opened.

Payne shook his head from side to side. "You've been watching too many old movies, kid. It's better if we all stick together."

So the three of us slowly started inching around the room, braced for the worst.

"This isn't how it happened in the comic book," I said.

"Yeah, it is," Gerber replied. "The Centurion waited for Doctor Terror to make his grand entrance."

"I don't remember the scene," I whispered. "How did he get in?"

Payne and Gerber looked at each other, and then up toward the skylight. Chopper Seven had just arrived and was hovering directly over the building.

"Hey, Artie, do you see what I see down there on the roof?" Plunkett asked.

Artie peered down through his camera lens at a hooded figure perched on the rim of the skylight. "Holy shit," he said. "It looks like the Feds are about to storm the building."

Plunkett turned to the pilot. "Move in closer and get some light on the roof."

The pilot angled the chopper directly over the skylight and switched on the high beams. A powerful beacon of light cascaded down through the skylight into the center of the room. From where we were standing it looked like a UFO was about to land on top of us.

"I got it," Artie said. "Hold it right there."

Plunkett could feel his blood pumping. "Let's go to the video tape!"

Almost on cue, the masked figure plunged feet first through the dome, shattering the glass, and sailing to the ground in a perfect three-point landing just a few feet from where we were standing.

The Mask laughed. "Now get ready to meet your maker."

We each dove for cover. Payne ducked under an old table, Gerber scampered behind a potted palm tree, and I jumped in between some boxes that were piled up in neat columns on the floor.

"Come out, come out wherever you are, Mister MacAllister!" the Mask said. "You're the one I want. And there's no use hiding. I have what you want, lover boy."

Chopper Seven's high beams circled the room from above, stopping just above the center of the dance floor. In the light, I could see Julie sitting in an old chair, bound and gagged, struggling to get free.

"I still have your pretty young lady, Mister MacAllister. And if you expect to see her alive, you'd better show your face."

No one moved or said a word.

"No more games, gentlemen," the Mask continued. "I've read all your books. I know all your tricks. I've come here for a reason and I'm not leaving until my job is done."

Of the three of us, I was the closest to the dance floor—maybe twenty feet away from where Julie was being held. Ahead of me was a path lined with boxes and old chairs, just enough to cover me from the Mask's sights. So I crawled out from behind my perch and actually made it halfway across the dance floor. But that's as far as I got. My knee broke through a weak floorboard, and before I knew it my entire leg fell through a hole and I was trapped between floors.

The next thing I knew Payne was yelling frantically toward me. "Rick! Behind you!!"

THUMP!

A sharp pain tore through my shoulder, followed by a hot gush of blood. I couldn't move. A short, stubby arrow—just like the kind we'd practiced with in gym as a kid—ripped through me like paper. The pain was excruciating.

When I finally looked up a few moments later, all I could see was a black mask hovering over my head.

"Do you feel my pain? Do you feel the cold, empty loneliness that I feel when the one you love is in danger and you can't do a damned thing about it?"

I struggled to remain conscious. "Don't do this," I said. "You're wrong."

Before the Mask could say a word, a loud bang echoed throughout the room. A SWAT unit, under Gill's direction, was hammering away at the main door of the ballroom with a battering ram.

"This is the New York Police!" Gill shouted into a megaphone. "Throw down your weapons and come out with your hands up!"

"No!" the figure shot back in a rage.

"We've got the place surrounded," Gill yelled back. "There's no escape."

The Mask hesitated. "Tell your men to stop what they're doing or everyone in here dies right now."

Gill ordered the SWAT team to back away from the door.

"That doesn't sound like a mob kingpin," he said to Malone. "What the hell's going on in there?"

"Probably just a deception, chief," Malone replied. "They're cornered like rats. They'll say anything."

Szymanski wasn't certain. "That could be our comic book killer," he said.

"What makes you say that?" Gill asked.

"Bar next door has the TV on. I caught it on the way up. Channel Seven is flying their chopper overhead and they're showing pictures of some creep with a hood and hostages inside."

Gill glared at Malone. He felt like kicking himself for believing his mob fairytales. "Great. Half the goddamned city knows what we're up against. But we're here playing the Untouchables."

Indeed, anyone and everyone who was awake and watching Plunkett's report on Channel Seven at that hour had a bird's eye view of exactly what was happening.

"If you've just joined us, we're watching a dramatic hostage situation unfolding in the New York Coliseum," Plunkett reported, as the camera zeroed in on the killer.

"We believe the figure in the mask is the comic book serial killer. Just moments ago we saw the assailant shoot and injure one of the hostages—the man lying there on the floor—with a cross bow. Another hostage—it appears to be a young woman—is bound and gagged in the center of the room."

Artie's camera lens zeroed in on me, sandwiched between floorboards, and nudged Plunkett. "Isn't that MacAllister?"

Plunkett studied the picture carefully. "Wait a minute," he said. "The injured hostage appears to be Richard MacAllister, the comic book writer who has been at the center of the Centurion controversy."

Inside, Gill quickly grabbed a uniformed cop. "Get a television monitor in here on the double. I want to know what's going on in there."

Then he gave a thumbs-up to the SWAT unit, which resumed hammering away at the door.

"Knock it off and bring me Norbert Matthews or I'll finish everyone off now," the Mask shouted back over the noise.

The pounding stopped.

Gill rubbed his chin. "Szymanski, you and Don Corleone go get Matthews out of the car and bring him up here."

Inside the ballroom, Payne kept the pressure on.

"You'll never get away with this," he said.

"Shut up!" the Mask snapped.

"You think you're so smart. But you've really been lucky. The cops are all over this place."

The assailant paced up and down the dance floor. "Don't make me hurt you, old man!"

"That's not the issue," Payne said. "The real issue is where are you going to hide?"

The Mask looked frantically around the room for a way out. There was only one way to go—straight up—back through the shattered skylight and out onto the roof.

The figure tugged on the cable wire that was dangling from the skylight—it was still taut—and laughed. "Up, up and away, old man."

"That's not going to do you much good," Payne said. "The cops will be crawling out there before you know it."

"Save your breath, Payne. You know what I'm going to do next."

The Mask walked over to Julie, pulled the duct tape off her mouth, and began untying her hands.

"Time to move out, dearie. We're going for a little climb. And you're first."

Julie took one look at the cable, which was swaying back and forth from the top of the skylight and freaked.

"I'm not going up there."

The Mask grabbed her by her neck and shoved her toward the cable. "Oh yes you are, my sweetie, unless you want me to use your boyfriend for target practice."

Julie grabbed hold of the cable. "I hate this," she sobbed.

"The things we do for love," the figure grinned, and gently caressed the crossbow. "Now climb up to the roof and wait for me by the skylight. One wrong move—"

It took a while, but eventually Julie made it through the shattered skylight, and pulled herself onto the roof.

Then the Mask aimed the crossbow at me with one hand, and grabbed hold of the cable with the other.

"No tricks Payne, or little Ricky bites the big one. Understand?"

Payne stood up from behind the table. "Got it," he said.

Against a brilliant backdrop of light from Chopper Seven, the Mask quickly scurried up the cable and disappeared from view.

Chapter 33

"Kid, kid? You okay?"

When I came to I was flat on my back on a stretcher in an ambulance outside the Coliseum, and Payne was hovering over me like a nervous mother hen. My head was killing me. My shoulder felt even worse.

"Where's Julie?" I asked.

Payne shook his head slowly. "She's still up there, kid. Police are handling it from here."

"They're not going to resolve it—"

I tried to sit up, but the paramedic who was working on my shoulder held me down.

"Please, Mister MacAllister," she said. "We're still treating your wound."

"How is he, doc?" Payne asked.

"He's not going to be playing any tennis for a while," the paramedic replied. "But it looks worse than it is. I think he'll live until we get him to the hospital."

"I can't go to the hospital," I said, "not as long as Julie is up there with—"

Before I could finish, a plainclothes cop stepped up into the ambulance.

"Can I talk to him for a minute?"

The paramedic nodded and moved out of the way.

"My name's Szymanski," the cop said. "Jim Szymanski."

I recognized the face. "You followed us here from Connecticut."

"That's right," he said. "But we've got a pretty tense situation up there right now. And we could use your help. What can you tell us about the assailant?"

"Whoever it is," I said through the pain, "really knows how to use a knife and cross bow."

I don't know why, but I just had this sense that I could level with Szymanski.

"It's playing out just like in the comic book," I said, grabbing his arm. "The whole thing—the Coliseum, the trap, the hostage, the roof top confrontation—"

"I know," he replied. "I've got the book in my collection. Any idea who the assailant is?"

"Gotta be a fan," I said. "A fan who's convinced we're gonna kill the Centurion and wants to make everyone pay."

"Our latest intelligence indicated Mitch Gerber might be a likely suspect," Szymanski said.

Payne shook his head. "We thought at first that might be the case too. But he was lured here just like us. This is all a very elaborate trap."

It was at that point that Malone poked his head into the ambulance and pulled Szymanski aside. The two conferred outside for several minutes. When Szymanski returned he looked grim.

"It's Julie, isn't it?" I asked.

"Chief thinks you oughta be up there with us," Szymanski said. "Can you make it upstairs? We'll cover you."

I sat up and saw stars. The painkillers hadn't kicked in. But I could still walk and that was enough.

"Let's go."

Police Command Post in the Old Ballroom

Gill watched the spectacle unfolding on the roof of the Coliseum from a television monitor that had been rolled in from one of the conference rooms downstairs.

"Turn up the volume," he told one of the uniformed cops standing nearby. Phil Plunkett's urgent sounding voice resonated throughout the room.

"Since re-emerging on the roof of the Coliseum, the comic book killer has tied the hostage to the back of one of the giant search lights you see in the lower corner of your screen that hug the perimeter of the building."

"What the Christ is this lunatic up to?" Gill wondered aloud.

One of the uniforms immediately reached into his pocket and retrieved a money clip. "Fifty bucks says he's gonna turn on all the search lights and sizzle her right there, chief."

One by one, the Mask turned on all the searchlights—more than a dozen in all. Every one, that is, except the light to which Julie was strapped. From street level, it looked like a scene from London during the war. Beacons of light danced across the night sky and frantically crisscrossed the clouds, including one that had been rigged up with a Centurion logo for the upcoming comic book convention. The silhouette of the logo showed up directly above the Coliseum, smack in the middle of a churning storm cloud.

"Whaddya make of this?" Gill asked.

The uniform scratched his head. "Isn't this the place in the movies where somebody says, 'This is a job for the Centurion!'?"

Gill frowned. "You tell that to our hostage. She's gonna get fried if that high beam goes on."

Up in Chopper Seven, Plunkett watched in amazement. "This is absolutely incredible. The Coliseum is lit up like a giant birthday cake, and the hostage—who we now believe to be Excelsior artist Julie McKinney—is strapped to the side of the only search light that's not working."

It was at this point that Manny Schaffi's patience finally got the best of him.

"Flip the switch," he told an assistant producer.

"Without clearance from the network?"

"Screw the goddamned network!" Schaffi yelled. "This is big, it's dramatic, it's live and it's ours exclusively. Cut into the network feed with a bulletin."

A few minutes later, the entire world got a front row seat to the drama and just in time to see the Mask ramble into the center of the roof and start gesturing to the helicopter.

"The assailant appears to be waving at us," Plunkett reported. "Almost as if he wants us to set the helicopter down."

Inside the ballroom, Gill's nostrils flared.

"Get me a line into that chopper," he told one of the uniforms. "If they set down on the roof we're going to have three more hostages on our hands."

A few minutes later, Gill was talking directly to the pilot.

"Who's breaking in on this line?" the pilot asked. "It's a secure channel."

"New York Police," Gill replied. "Put the talkin' head on now."

The pilot patched the call into Plunkett's headphone.

"Plunkett here. Who's this?"

"Detective Charles Gill, NYPD."

"Hang on a second." Plunkett picked up his regular microphone and whispered to his cameraman. "Can you tap the audio on this call into the network feed?"

Artie nodded his head and rearranged a couple of the wires feeding into the video console in the chopper. "You're on, boss."

Plunkett cleared his throat. "We're talking live with New York Police Detective Charles Gill from the police command center inside the Coliseum below us."

A picture insert of Gill flashed up in the corner of the television screen.

Gill stared at the monitor—at the image of his own face smiling right back at him—and fumed.

"Goddamnit, Plunkett, this isn't a fucking interview," he shouted.

An assistant producer in the studio immediately lunged for the control panel in a desperate attempt to cut the transmission off the air.

"Don't touch that dial," Schaffi said. "It's after midnight. Let him swear as much as he fucking wants."

"Detective can you tell us what you're doing to diffuse this crisis?" Plunkett asked.

"In exactly one minute I'm going to send my sharpshooters up there with orders to bring down anything in the air. Comprende?"

Plunkett shook his head. "Thank you detective for that update. You heard it first on Eyewitness News. New York Police are preparing to use a massive display of force if this crisis doesn't end soon. More on this breaking story after these messages."

As soon as he was off the air, Plunkett immediately turned to his cameraman.

"Do we have a boom mike with an extension that we can lower down to the roof?"

Artie shook his head. "Yeah, I brought one along. But are you sure you want to do this? Gill sounds pretty serious."

"He said we couldn't land. He didn't say we couldn't interview the killer," Plunkett replied.

Artie peered out the side of the helicopter. "We could do it, but we're gonna have to move closer for the mike to reach down there."

Plunkett motioned to the pilot. "Get us close enough to drop a mike down there," he said. "And do it slowly so the cops don't think we're landing."

The Mask watched from below as the helicopter moved in closer. "Lower the boom!" Plunkett shouted.

Artie handed the camera to Plunkett and gently dropped the mike down through the helicopter's door like a cigar on a stick. The Mask quickly spotted it bobbing against the wind and approached the mike.

Plunkett, in his most serious news voice, immediately interrupted the commercial break.

"We're back live in New York where just moments ago we lowered a microphone to the masked figure on the roof of the Coliseum who we believe is the comic book serial killer. Let's see if the killer makes a statement."

Schaffi bumped up the sound from the mike—it crackled from the wind and the hum of the chopper's engines. A few seconds later, the Mask's haunting voice reached out to the world.

"The Centurion must live. There will be no peace until you bring me MacAllister and Matthews. Do you understand? Bring them both to me or the girl dies. Now."

Gill turned to Malone. "Where's Slick?"

"In the can."

"He's taking a dump now?" Gill asked.

"Nah, he caught some of this on the scanner when were coming in. He's puking his brains out in there."

"Clean him up fast and get him in here. Where's MacAllister?"

Szymanski and I had just walked into the room, with Payne and Gerber following closely behind.

"I've got him, chief," he said.

Gill gave me the once over. "What about you?"

I looked like hell. My pants were torn and my arm was in a sling.

"You can't send him up there alone," Payne replied before I could say a word. "Not in his condition. Let us go with him."

"I don't think so old man," Gill said. "We don't need two others in the line of fire up there."

"But we know how this is going to play out," Payne said. "The killer's gonna do it by the book and we can—"

Gill raised his hand. "Here we go again. Let me guess, the killer is gonna jump into a phone booth and emerge in a cape and tights."

"Chief," Szymanski said, "listen to them. They know exactly what's going on. It's straight out of the comic book."

Gill lit a cigarette and sneered. "I'm listening."

"The search lights are the key," Payne said. "It's a trap. The metal plate in front of the searchlights is charged with thousands of volts of electricity. Touch it and you're history."

Gill rolled his eyes and looked at the TV monitor. "What metal plate? I don't see no metal plate."

Szymanski studied the screen. "It's there all right. It's a sewer grating right in front of the main bank of lights."

"And how does this sewer grate mysteriously get electrified?" Gill asked.

"Circuit box is right underneath the grating," Gerber replied. "Shorts out whenever it rains. Maintenance man actually got killed there before I wrote the story."

Malone held his hand up under the shattered skylight. "It don't feel like it's raining to me."

Gill thought for a second and then turned to me.

"This is what we're gonna do. We found a stairway that leads up to the roof on the far side of the building. You and Slick go out there. Szymanski and a SWAT unit will be right behind you. They'll stay in the stairway, and as soon as there's trouble they'll jump in."

"What do we do once we're there?" I asked.

"We've got sharpshooters in position in all the high rises around the Coliseum. Talk to the killer long enough so we can get a clear line of sight."

Gerber shook his head. "You can't shoot as long as the killer's near the searchlight with the girl," he said. "If that light goes on she's got a minute. Maybe two, tops, before she fries. Your men won't be anywhere near enough to free her."

"Gentlemen," Payne interrupted. "Let me go up there and talk to the killer. I know I can help—"

"Save it, Payne," Gill said. "This is real life. People get hurt. We're not adding any more casualties to the list."

"Casualties?" Matthews emerged from the men's room, pale as a ghost, just in time to catch the end of the conversation. "What casualties?"

Gill patted him on the back. "Don't worry your pretty little head off, Slick. If you play your cards right you might even get a real charge out of all this."

Chapter 34

Matthews, Szymanski and I climbed the long flight of stairs leading to the roof of the Coliseum and waited anxiously behind the door in the stairwell for the all-clear sign to go out on the roof.

"Now I know how the troops felt at D-Day," I said.

Szymanski peered out of the tiny window in the door. "Good triumphed over evil in the end, right?"

I looked at Matthews who was hanging over the railing with the dry heaves. "Yeah, but I'd hardly call the two of us an invading force."

"I'm talking about in the comic book," he said. "Death at the Coliseum. It was Doctor Terror who died. Not the Centurion."

"That's true," I replied.

"If you're facing a foe who does everything by the book, maybe the way to defeat him is to use the comic book to your advantage. Whatever worked on Doctor Terror in the original should work for you here."

It made sense. But there was no time to think it out, to reconstruct the story frame by frame. Matthews was beginning to cave.

"I-I-I-I don't want to do this," he whined.

"You have to go," Szymanski said. "You have to buy us some time to get our people into position. There's a life at stake here."

Matthews wiped his brow. His stomach was erupting like never before, and this time it was bringing him to his knees.

"Can't I just pay you to go in my place?" he asked.

Szymanski's face grew red. Desperate times required desperate measures. So he borrowed a page from his partner's handbook, pulled out his revolver, and shoved it into Matthews' mouth.

"Listen up, Slick," he said. "You've got two choices. You can go out there and take your chances or you can stay in here and take your chances."

Szymanski drew back the hammer slowly and deliberately. "I'm not so sure I like your chances right now."

Five minutes later, the stairwell door opened and Matthews and I made our way onto the roof. At that exact moment—as luck would have it—a giant clap of thunder shook the city. Lightning arced across the night sky and rain started coming down in buckets.

"I hope you're happy now," Matthews said. "You and your spies are on the verge of complete victory. Excelsior will soon belong to the Scout Entertainment Network."

"You know that's not true," I said. "You brought this all on yourself. You fanned the flames with those sketches. You stirred up a lot of animosity among the staff. And now it's all coming back to haunt you."

Up above, Chopper Seven was broadcasting our every move around the world.

"Two figures have emerged from the stairwell," Plunkett said, as he peered through a set of high-powered binoculars. "The first one is definitely Rick MacAllister. The one behind him is Norbert Matthews, Excelsior's new publisher."

Slowly, we made our way across the roof, fighting the rain, the lights, and the wind gusts from Chopper Seven.

"Shut up and keep your eyes peeled," I told Matthews. "What's done is done—"

I never finished the sentence. A third voice finished it for me. "What's done is done and now there's no turning back."

Both Matthews and I jumped. Our stalker was behind us, crouching like a gargoyle on top of the unlit search light where Julie was being held.

"So we meet again, Mister MacAllister. And I see this time you've brought along some real scum."

"We came just like you wanted," I said. "Now what?"

"I have unfinished business to attend to."

"And what might that be?"

"You're still alive, aren't you? You must pay the price for your sins, just like your colleagues in crime. But first you must both see the light."

Matthews stepped forward. "If this is a matter of money, I'm sure we can come to some sort of suitable arrangement."

"Money?" the Mask shouted. "This isn't about money!! This is about truth, justice—"

"Yes, yes, yes," Matthews shook his head. "Truth, justice and the American way. I know the line. You can have as much of that as you want when you're rich—"

"SILENCE!"

Matthews quickly cowered behind me.

"No amount of money can undo the damage you've done."

"We haven't done a thing," I said. "The Centurion isn't going anywhere. I keep telling you no one has been harmed."

"Ah, but that's where you're wrong little Ricky. I keep trying to tell you that you've hurt me. You've tampered with the one thing in the world I could always count on—the Centurion."

Lightning lit up the entire neighborhood just long enough to blow the cover of every police sharpshooter in the vicinity. And then,

BOOOOMMMM!! An enormous clap of thunder shook the old building from top to bottom.

"I see you brought company," the Mask laughed. "Now they must see the light, too!"

The figure jumped down onto the platform that served as a base for the searchlights and began working a control panel. Three of the giant beacons immediately slipped out of their upright positions and locked onto the high-rise buildings surrounding the Coliseum.

"We can't see a thing, Chief," one of the SWAT commanders radioed into Gill. "It's like a wall of lights just went up around the entire building."

"What about Szymanski?" Gill asked.

Szymanski peered out of the tiny window in the stairwell door just as another searchlight fixed onto his position. "I'm out of commission too, Chief," he radioed back. "Goddamned light is aimed right at the stairwell."

Now the only thing linking us to the outside world was the camera aboard Chopper Seven. But that didn't last long either.

"One of those lights is coming right for us, Phil," the pilot said. "I can't get blindsided by that thing. We've got to move."

"This is incredible," Plunkett reported, as the helicopter pulled away from the building. "The masked figure is effectively holding the entire city at bay—including hundreds of well armed cops—as this hostage crisis continues to take one dramatic turn after another."

In the police command center, Gill was fuming. "Get a hold of Con Ed," he told one of his uniforms. "Tell them to cut the power to this building right now."

Then he adjusted his headset and ordered his police commandos to reposition themselves.

"It doesn't matter where we go," one of the SWAT commanders reported back. "We can't see through it."

Gill shook his head. "Let's hope MacAllister can buy us enough time to cut the power so we can storm the building."

Nearby, Payne and Gerber watched the spectacle unfolding in disbelief.

"I tried this scenario in the book," Gerber whispered into Payne's ear. "It's going to end in disaster."

"We've got to do something," Payne said. "Follow me."

The pair quietly slipped out of the room—unnoticed in the growing chaos—and made their way up the stairwell where Szymanski was stationed.

"What are you doing here?" he asked.

"Gill wants us to go up there and talk," Payne said.

"He didn't say anything to me, Mister Payne."

"There's no time to debate this, kid. The situation is desperate. It's just like in the comic books. Our hero is in trouble. And we're here to save the day."

Szymanski shook his head. "You're not invincible like the Centurion. And you're not going out there until I clear this with Gill."

Szymanski grabbed his remote mike, but before he could utter a word, Gerber started jumping up and down.

"Look," he said, pointing out the window. "Up in the sky—"

Szymanski pushed Gerber aside and looked for himself. "Where?"

"It's a bird—"

"No," Payne interrupted, "It's a plane—"

THUD. Szymanski felt the wood of a billy club strike the back of his head and he immediately slumped to the floor.

"It's one unconscious cop," Gerber said.

Payne shook his head. "Where'd you get that?"

"His partner asked me to hold it for him when we were downstairs."

The pair quietly slipped out on the roof and locked the door behind them.

Meanwhile, Matthews and I had taken cover behind a giant air conditioning compressor on the roof.

"I'm getting out of here," Matthews yelled over the compressor's roar.

"As soon as you run out there you're a target," I said.

"You stay here and be a martyr," Matthews said. "Not me."

Before I could react, Matthews shoved me to the ground and made a mad dash for the stairwell. But he didn't get very far. The roof was slick from the rain, and he tumbled to his knees. It took a few moments before he recovered, and when he finally stood up he knew that he wasn't alone. A giant shadow hovered over him like an ominous storm cloud.

"Who knows what evil lurks in your heart, Mister Matthews?"

Matthews' heart stopped and his stomach turned over. The masked figure was standing on a ledge just a few feet behind him.

"Only the shadow knows how your devious little mind works," the figure laughed. "You'll stop at nothing to enhance your stature in life."

Matthews slowly started walking away from the figure.

"STOP!" the Mask shouted.

Matthews dropped to his knees. "No," he said, "don't do this. I beg you."

"How did you react when we begged you to stop what you were doing?"

Matthews swallowed hard.

"All the letters and all the phone calls and you just ignored them. Then one by one, people died all around you. But still you didn't listen. And you didn't stop."

Matthews backed away from the figure once more, not realizing that every step he took brought him closer to building's edge. Lightning and thunder danced all around him, and he started sobbing.

Suddenly the shadow disappeared from view. All he could see was a bright blinding light.

"Do you see the light, Matthews? Do you feel the glow of the Sentinel of Light?"

Matthews nodded frantically and said the only thing he could think of that would save his hide.

"Yes," he said, "I-I-I-I see the light. I-I-I can't help but see it."

"Do you see the error of your ways?"

"I do, I do. Forgive me. I was out of my mind—temporarily insane. That's it. The Centurion will live. Now and forever. I promise you."

"Good," the Mask responded. "That's what I like to hear."

Matthews suddenly felt relieved, as if a giant weight had been lifted from his shoulders.

"Then it's okay to go?"

"Yes," the figure replied. "It's okay to go."

Matthews couldn't believe it. "This is all over? It's really over?"

"Yes," the Mask replied. "For you it's really all over."

Matthews never saw it coming. First it was an icy cold hand that grabbed him by the neck. Then came a powerful thrust that lifted him off his feet and over the side of the Coliseum in a dizzying death spiral. He died ten seconds later when his body hit the pavement several stories below with the force of a speeding locomotive.

The Mask peered over the ledge, at the cacophony of flashing squad cars and fire trucks below, and began laughing uncontrollably.

"Now THAT was good to the last drop."

But the thrill was short-lived. There was more work to do. It was time to focus on the one person who was going to make the Centurion's death a reality—me.

I have no doubt that the Mask would have come right after me, had it not been for some unexpected company.

"Your reign of terror is over, oh masked one."

The assailant turned around with a start.

"Payne! How did you get up here?"

"It doesn't matter how I got here. All that matters now is that you are stopped."

The Mask chuckled. "Men half your age couldn't stop me, Payne. What makes you think you can?"

Payne looked at the figure with eyes of steel.

"I know why you're doing this and I know what makes you tick," he replied. "You are the evil that lurks in mankind's soul. You can not defeat me, no more than Doctor Terror could have ever defeated the Centurion."

For the first time, the masked figure appeared shaken. There were no icy threats or laughter. Just hesitation and silence. It was an awkward scene, broken only by an enormous clap of thunder. Then the attacker struck, lunging at Payne from the ledge of the building.

But the attacker assumed Payne was alone, and never saw Gerber poke his adopted nightstick out from behind a nearby air vent directly into the attacker's path. The Mask tripped and sprawled face first into an enormous pool of water that was growing bigger by the minute, and didn't move.

"That was too easy," Gerber said.

Payne cautiously knelt down and rolled the figure over. "I know. This isn't the way the book ends. Stay here. I'm going to help MacAllister. Use the club if you have to."

Gerber tapped the stick in his hand, and Payne trudged off into the rain knowing full well that the final battle was yet to be fought.

Chapter 35

"Having saved Linda Lang from danger, the Centurion sets a trap of his own for the evil Doctor Terror. He reaches up toward the heavens with his sword, drawing forth a bolt of lighting that shakes the building.

"When the smoke clears, the Centurion lies motionless on the ground. Dr. Terror immediately pounces on the Sentinel of Light to finish him off. "I finally have you where I want you.' " But all is not what it seems. Little does Doctor Terror know that lightning is a source of the Centurion's great strength. His mighty powers have been restored. 'Your reign of terror is about to end.' Now it is the Centurion's turn to strike..."

The rain and the wind were relentless, lashing against the Coliseum with a vengeance, forcing Chopper Seven and a very frustrated Phil Plunkett to land on the helipad of a nearby high rise. Ordinarily, that wouldn't have been the worst thing in the world. But the skyscraper towered over the Coliseum, and the view from the helipad on the seventy-fourth floor was far too distant to capture any of the action where we were. Maria Vasquez Mitchell had picked up the story from the ground, with complete and extremely graphic coverage of Matthews' crash landing at street level. But Plunkett knew the real story was still unfolding on the rooftop of the Coliseum and he was determined to regain his bird's eye view.

"We just can't sit here," he complained in the cockpit. "The story of the year is right under our noses and we can't get close enough."

"Sorry, Phil," his pilot said. "We go up in this and we might become the main story."

Plunkett closed his eyes and prayed for a break—anything that would get him within camera range of the Coliseum. And sure enough, the answer came to him.

"Isn't this building being renovated?" he asked Artie.

Artie thought about it for a moment. "Donald Trump is refurbishing the whole thing."

"So there must be a construction elevator running up and down the side of the building."

In fact, there was. An open-air elevator tall enough to launch a rocket scaled the entire length of the building, all the way up to the helipad.

"Grab your camera, Artie," Plunkett said. "Next stop—the Coliseum."

Five minutes later, as Payne and I were frantically trying to untie Julie from the searchlight, a drenched and dripping Plunkett was piloting the elevator down the side of the building.

"Artie, get ready," he shouted. "We're almost there."

A minute later, the elevator came to a quiet standstill directly across from the roof of the Coliseum, and right behind Gerber, who never saw the elevator behind him. But the camera definitely liked what it saw: Gerber standing guard over a lifeless attacker in a barren, storm swept setting.

"Hit your lights, Artie," Plunkett yelled. "We're going live."

The camera's strobe immediately popped on.

Plunkett stretched out over the edge of the elevator with his microphone and yelled across the building: "Is that the comic book killer?"

Gerber jumped out of his skin. It was just a momentary distraction, but enough of a diversion for the masked figure to blindside him with a shot to the head from behind.

"My God," Plunkett reported. "We've got our answer. The masked figure is attacking Mitch Gerber…what savagery…"

Gerber put up a good fight, but in the end he was no match for the Mask. Within a few minutes, he was completely disabled and out cold.

"I have bigger fish to fry than you, little man." The Mask tossed Gerber's billy club over the side of the building and propped Gerber up against an old exhaust pipe. "Next time, pick your friends more carefully."

In an instant, the figure disappeared.

"This is incredible," Plunkett reported. "The attacker has just finished off Mitch Gerber and now appears to be heading after the others. With the police being held at bay, the question now is where are Rick MacAllister and Matt Payne?"

Both of us were out of camera range, trying frantically to untie Julie from the side of the searchlight. It seemed to take forever. The heavy rope was tight and soaked from the rain, and all we had to work with was a small Swiss Army knife that Payne had with him in his pocket.

Julie was still hysterical. As soon as I peeled the duct tape off her mouth, she began screaming about the attacker. I couldn't make out what she was saying but the Mask sure heard her voice and quickly honed in on our position. A moment later the Mask appeared out of nowhere and both Payne and I jumped.

"Perhaps I can shed some light on this matter?"

Then we heard a loud buzzing noise. The searchlight that Julie was strapped to started coming to life—thousands of candle lights firing up in a blinding beacon—right before our very eyes.

"You've got two minutes tops," the Mask laughed, "before the surface temperature of the lamp becomes hotter than a blast furnace. Then she's toast."

"Keep working," Payne said to me. Then he jumped off the platform—with all the bravado of one of his own comic book characters—and confronted the killer.

"You can't do this," he said.

"Who's going to stop me, old man?" the figure asked.

"I am," Payne replied.

The Mask laughed. "You? What makes you think you can stop me, Payne?"

"You can't kill me," he replied. "I am the light of the Centurion. Without me and without them, the Sentinel of Light will be extinguished forever."

The outer shell of the searchlight was getting hotter by the second, and I was nowhere near cutting through Julie's bonds.

"Rick," Julie said. "I smell something burning."

I could smell it too. It was the rope. The heat from the light started burning through the rope along the edge of the lamp. I tugged at it with all my strength and it started to fray. "Hang on," I told Julie. "It's coming loose." And none too soon. Payne was pulling out all the stops in a desperate effort to buy more time. He positioned himself like a football tackle in front of the searchlight.

"If you want to kill them," he shouted, "you're going to have to go through me first."

The Mask laughed. "Suit yourself, Payne." Then the figure ripped a pointy old exhaust vent from its moorings on the roof, and flung it directly at Payne.

Payne tried to dodge it, but he wasn't quick enough. He went down under a pile of rusted metal and never got up.

But it bought me just enough time to pull Julie off the lamp. Another ten seconds and she would have been history—the outer shell of the searchlight was hot enough to fry an egg. I grabbed Julie's hand and we quickly ducked for cover in between two other search lamps. She was free at last. But now we were very much on our own—cold, wet and exhausted—and trapped on a rooftop in a torrential downpour with someone who wanted us more dead than alive, as millions around the world watched our every move.

"Payne said out-think him," I whispered. "Just like the Centurion did with Doctor Terror."

"But you can't go by the book," Julie said. "The killer knows how the story ends."

I thought for a moment. "Then we have to come up with a new ending."

"Oh, Mister MacAllister," the Mask finally called out. "You whoooo. Come out, come out wherever you are."

"Think fast," Julie said. "We don't have much time."

In the original comic book, the trap that the Centurion had set for Doctor Terror was a common plot device—the old "dupe and dump" scenario where the hero fakes an injury and traps the villain.

As it played out in my mind, an idea came to me. Maybe we didn't have to change the ending at all, I thought, just the setup.

"I've got it. I'm the bait, and you're the line. Listen carefully."

A moment later, Julie broke our uneasy silence.

"Get away from me," she yelled. "I never wanted to kill the Centurion in the first place. This was all your idea and you forced me to do it."

Julie bolted out from behind the searchlights and darted across the roof.

"Don't do this!" I shouted. I waited a few seconds—long enough for her to put some distance between us—and then I ran out after her.

"You deserve to die!" Julie screamed back at me. "I'm not taking the fall for you."

The Mask watched all this from a distance with great interest.

"Listen to me, Julie," I yelled. When I caught up with her, I grabbed her by the shoulders and shook her from side to side. "Don't do this. You could be killed."

Julie broke away from me, and ran behind the shattered skylight. I ran after her.

"Stop!" she yelled. "Don't come any closer, or I'll jump."

I froze in my tracks, half way between the skylight and an old sewer drain embedded in the roof—the one that I had been warned about earlier.

Julie climbed atop the frame of the skylight, as if she was about to jump.

But then, just as I expected, the Mask appeared on a raised portion of the roof right behind the skylight, larger and more ominous than ever before.

"You're time has come MacAllister," the Mask said. "You must atone for your sins."

"You talk tough from up there," I shouted back defiantly. "But let's see how tough you are down here."

That did it. The Mask lost all semblance of rationality, forgot about Julie, and lunged directly at me. My game plan was to deftly step aside at the very last possible moment and let the Mask land directly on top of the electrically charged sewer grate behind me.

And that's exactly what I did. As soon as the assailant moved, I stepped back and shouted: "It's time for you to see the light." The Mask sailed by me, aimed directly for the grating. And then BOOM! A split second before impact the search lights fizzled, and the entire building plunged into complete darkness. The Mask landed feet first on a sewer grate that had lost its charge.

Inside, Gill shook his fist. "Thank you, ConEd." Then he immediately grabbed his hand mike and radioed his commandos. "Go," he said, "take out the assailant."

Once the word went out, sharpshooters all around our position grabbed their guns and locked onto the rooftop. But now, instead of too much light, there wasn't enough of it.

"Chief, we can't make out a thing," one of the unit commanders radioed back from a nearby high-rise. "It's too dark. The only light we can see is coming from a television camera across the street."

Gill couldn't believe it. "Goddamn it! I wanted Con Ed to cut the building, not the whole neighborhood."

"It wasn't Con Ed," one of the uniforms replied from a remote command station. "Lightning knocked out a transformer. The whole area's out. And it ain't coming back anytime soon."

The police weren't the only ones in the dark. We were all blind as bats. On the rooftop, the Mask and I stumbled around just a few feet from each other, waiting for our eyes to adjust.

Julie was the first to regain her sight, and from the top of the skylight she quickly spotted us.

"Rick, behind you!" she screamed.

I hit the ground for cover, and braced for the worst.

But the worst never came. In all the chaos, we forgot about Plunkett, who continued to cover the confrontation—blow by blow like a boxing match—from his perch in the construction elevator next door.

Julie spotted the camera's light out of the corner of her eye and started waving frantically in Plunkett's direction.

"Over here! Over here!" she yelled.

"Do you see the girl?" Plunkett asked.

"I've got her," Artie replied. "She's pointing at something."

Plunkett eyed the rooftop carefully. "To the left, ninety degrees. I think I see something moving."

Artie swung the camera around, until the Mask's shadowy figure came into the light.

"I've got a fix on him," Artie shouted. "It's the killer."

"Don't lose it," Plunkett shouted.

Julie kept at it too, screaming as loud as she could from the skylight.

"I think the girl is trying to tell us something," Plunkett said. "She keeps pointing to her face."

"Maybe she wants us to aim the light in the killer's eyes," Artie said.

"That's it. Do it."

A second or two later, just as I was beginning to feel my way around in the dark, the Mask got a blinding dose of Channel Seven's camera light right between the eyes. "AAAAAHHHHHH."

It was the break I needed. I quickly flung myself at the killer from behind. The impact sent the Mask head first into a nearby retaining wall, like a hockey player getting slammed to the boards at full speed. The killer was down for the count. But I couldn't be certain the fight was really over.

So I looked around for a weapon—something that would finish the Mask off quickly while I still had the advantage. I finally spotted an old cinder block sitting in a dark corner. As the adrenaline coursed through my veins, I grabbed the block with both hands, lifted it high above my head, and stormed back toward the assailant. All it would take was one final heave to finish off our attacker, but just as I was about to let go, I heard a cry for help. It wasn't Julie. It wasn't the Mask. It was Payne, reaching out from under the rubble of a shattered exhaust vent.

I looked at the killer, all bloodied and crumpled against the wall. Blood was seeping through the front of the mask. And then I looked at Payne. The old man's situation was desperate. A pool of water had formed all around him from the rain and it was getting deeper by the second.

"Rick," Julie yelled over from the skylight. "He needs help." I had to go to him. So I dropped the cinder block and rushed back to his side.

I pulled some of the debris off of him and gently lifted his head out of the water. His face was cut and he was having trouble breathing. "Don't move," I said.

"The k-k-killer," he gasped. "Where's the killer?"

"I don't think he's going to bother us anymore."

It was a pretty dramatic scene—not unlike something you'd see on the front cover of a comic book. And Plunkett was loving every minute of it.

"You've just witnessed an incredible confrontation and rescue atop the Coliseum," he reported, as the wind rattled his elevator cage from side to side. "It appears the comic book serial killer has been stopped by Rick MacAllister—with an assist from Eyewitness News—and comic book legend Matt Payne has been rescued from almost certain death."

As soon as he finished talking, Artie tugged on his sleeve. A warning light started flashing on his camera.

"We've got a problem," he whispered.

"Whattsa matter?"

"Batteries are running low. We're gonna lose our lights any second now."

"Now?" Plunkett gasped. "We can't run out of juice now."

"Sorry, Phil. I didn't think we were gonna be on the air this long with lights."

"Didn't you bring any other batteries?"

Artie shook his head from side to side. "We ran out so fast—"

A few seconds later, the camera's light fizzled and we were thrown into complete darkness once more. Julie and I continued to pull Payne from the ruble. He was still pretty shaky, but his breathing was starting to return to normal.

"The killer," he finally said. "What about—"

"Take it easy," I replied, "the killer's out. We're safe now."

"Kid, how did you do it?"

"We changed the ending a bit," I said, "and I got my big break on TV at the right time."

"The sewer grate worked?"

I shook my head. "No, we lost power. The killer ran into a brick wall."

Payne grabbed me by the shoulders. His knuckles were white with fear. "Is the killer dead?"

"I don't think so," I said.

"But that's not how the story ends," he said.

"I know that—"

Payne tried to stand up but stumbled. "Don't you see? This is a battle to the death. The killer won't quit until the ending from the book plays out."

Julie and I looked at each other at the exact same moment and realized what he was trying to say. The crisis wasn't over.

A moment later we turned around. Towering over us—and poised to attack with the cinder block that I had left behind—was the Mask.

We all froze. There was no time to react, and there was nothing we could do to prevent the Mask from finishing us off.

"Your time has come MacAllister. Now you will see the light."

I grabbed Julie, closed my eyes and said a silent prayer. Everything after that happened so fast, it's a blur. First came this humming sound, like the kind you hear when you get too close to high tension wires or a transformer. It was followed by the crackle of electricity dancing through the air. And finally a scream—a haunting, blood-curdling scream—that I'll remember as long as I live. When I opened my eyes sparks were flying everywhere and the killer was standing up straight as an arrow—on top of the sewer grate—glowing from head to toe.

The Coliseum's emergency generator had kicked in, a little late perhaps, but just in time to send a deadly surge of electricity through the drenched sewer grate.

The Mask shook violently in place for what seemed like an eternity, and eventually collapsed right in front of us in a heap of smoldering flesh.

We were all so stunned that we just stared at the body. After several moments, Payne reached out to the killer.

"Be careful," he said, checking for a pulse. "He's still alive."

Julie and I quickly backed away. But Payne stayed right there, unfazed and unmoved.

Eventually, his curiosity finally got the best of him. When he was certain there was no danger, he threw caution to the wind and yanked off the mask. A long flowing mane of silver hair spilled forth and Payne gasped.

"No! No! No! How could it be you?"

My heart nearly stopped. The face beneath the mask belonged to Payne's wife, Alix. Julie buried her head in my shoulder and cried.

"My God," I said, "we left you there in the house with her all alone."

"It was horrible," she said.

Payne cradled his wife's head in his arms and started sobbing. "Tell me this isn't happening."

Alix opened her eyes and tried to speak. But at first the words weren't there.

"H-H-How's our boy?" she eventually said.

Payne swallowed hard. "Saving the world from the evil that lurks within mankind, thanks to you."

Alix smiled.

"I-I-I did this for you," she said. Her voice was so weak that I could barely make out the words. "I couldn't let them kill our little boy."

Julie squeezed my hand tightly and whispered into my ear. "She was the brains behind the Centurion. She wrote the stories. He was the son they never had."

Alix winced. The pain was too much—every fiber of her body was on fire.

"He'll live now, won't he?" she asked.

Payne gently stroked her hair. "Forever, my darling," he sobbed. "The Centurion will live forever."

A moment later she closed her eyes and died. Our comic nightmare was finally over.

Chapter 36: Postscript

Present Day

A little piece of us all died that night at the Coliseum.
Alix Payne's brilliant Olympic career became the first casualty, as the tabloids and TV news magazines jumped all over the story and promptly beat it to death. Even now, all these years later, her name is synonymous with the "Comic Book Serial Killer," and her tortured story is among the most highly rated features on A&E's Murder Mysteries program.

Matt Payne recovered from his injuries but he never really got over Alix's death. He lived the remaining years of his life in seclusion, refusing all interviews, tributes and offers to speak at comic book conventions. In a strange way, this only added to his stature as the industry's founding father among comic book devotees. Every year, on the anniversary of his death, devoted fans make pilgrimages to his grave in Martha's Vineyard.

Mitch Gerber recovered too, but he left the comic book business to start a new life as a corporate security consultant in Sunnyvale, California.

Excelsior disappeared. Sydney Lockwood acquired Trieste in bankruptcy court and sold it off piecemeal, just as Sanborn had threatened to do with Scout. Excelsior's operations were folded into Renegade, more than half the staff lost their jobs, and most of the firm's characters were discontinued.

The Centurion, however, lived to fly another day. Lockwood made good on Sanborn's promise to Hollywood, and sold the movie rights to Pinnacle Pictures in a deal that was worth millions. The Centurion became a huge box office draw, with lavish special effects and big name villains. Each sequel proved to be bigger than its predecessor.

Lockwood rewarded Phil Plunkett for his ground breaking reporting work by naming him Channel Seven's new general manager, complete with a fat new contract and stock options. He promptly fired Manny Schaffi and became a frequent guest host on *Saturday Night Live*. Plunkett later wrote a book about the Centurion story called, "Graphic Novel," which became a national best seller and went on to win the Pulitzer Prize.

His son, Larry, to no one's surprise, became a venture capitalist in Silicon Valley.

His first deal—a leveraged buyout of Montana's Comic Cave franchise—made him a millionaire by the time he was twenty-two.

Plunkett's ex-wife, Maxine, eventually became the new Mrs. Donald Trump and, a year later, she became the Donald's newest ex.

Police Detective Charles Gill was publicly credited with exercising restraint during the Coliseum crisis, and was named New York's police commissioner by the new administration in City Hall. Szymanski became his second in command, the youngest deputy commissioner in the city's history. Joe Malone was drummed out of the police force. But he wasn't out of work for long. A Hollywood talent scout spotted him on videotapes from the Coliseum crisis and liked his rugged New York looks. He subsequently went on to become one of Hollywood's most successful criminal comic actors and a mainstay on the Sopranos.

Julie and I got married and moved to Brooklyn, leaving the comic book business behind. Julie worked for a while in advertising—as she had hoped to do when she finished her graduate work—and then left Madison Avenue to start a family. To this day, she hates bright lights.

I became an English teacher at Pratt, and occasionally have nightmares about the Centurion.

We have two young boys—James and Michael—both of whom love comic books. They ask about the Centurion all the time; questions you'd expect from healthy, inquisitive boys, like—"What was the Centurion like, Daddy?" "How old were you when you started working on the Centurion, Daddy?" And, "Why is the Centurion so powerful, Daddy?"

Neither one has dropped the big one yet: "Daddy, what really happened when you were working on the Centurion?"

I've spent a lot of time—and many sleepless nights—thinking about the answer. But I must confess, even after all these years, I still don't know where to begin.

Author Bio

Mark Misercola has a dual career. By day he is a mild-mannered public relations executive in New York. On weekends, he ducks into his favorite comic book store and reads comic books. (He is a comic book traditionalist, and prefers that his characters be served up over easy with plenty of super powers.)

During his career, Mr. Misercola has written speeches for senior executives at some of the world's largest companies, including IBM, PepsiCo, Avon Products, NYNEX, Union Carbide, Pricewaterhouse-Coopers and Deloitte. He began his career as a business reporter with the former Buffalo (N.Y.) Courier-Express.

He has also ghostwritten two books for management consultant Bill Morin: Silent Sabotage, Amacom, 1995, and Total Career Fitness, 2000, Wiley.

Mr. Misercola serves as an adjunct professor teaching advertising copywriting at Western Connecticut State University College in Danbury, CT., and marketing communications at Manhattanville College in Purchase, N.Y.

He is a graduate of the State University of New York at Buffalo, and currently resides with his wife, Nancy, and two children—James and Regina—in Norwalk, CT.

Visit Mark's web site:
http://www.markmisercola.com

Don't miss any of these other
exciting mainstream novels

➤ Jerome and the Seraph
(1-931201-54-4, $15.50 US)

➤ Unraveled
(1-931201-11-0, $15.50 US)

➤ WolfPointe
(1-931201-08-0, $15.50 US)

Twilight Times Books
Kingsport, Tennessee

Mail Order Form

If not available from your local bookstore or favorite online bookstore, send this coupon and a check or money order for the retail price plus $3.50 s&h to Twilight Times Books, Dept. FD504 POB 3340 Kingsport TN 37664. Delivery may take up to four weeks.

Name: _____

Address: _____

_____

Email: _____

I have enclosed a check or money order in the amount of $_____
for _____ .

If you enjoyed this book, please post a review
at your favorite online bookstore.

Twilight Times Books
P O Box 3340
Kingsport, TN 37664
Phone/Fax: 423-323-0183
www.twilighttimesbooks.com/